Back in No Time

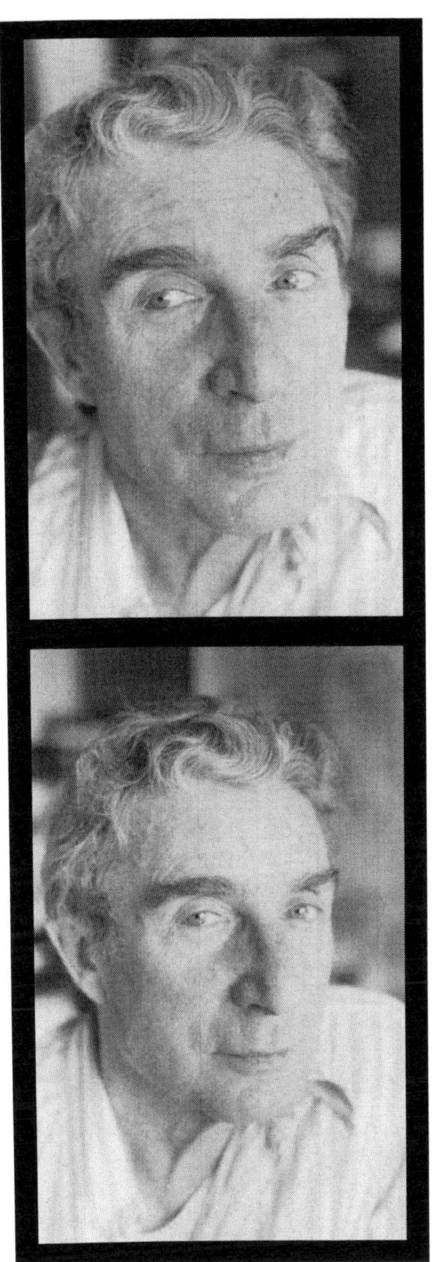

Back in No Time

The Brion Gysin Reader

Edited by Jason Weiss

Wesleyan University Press

Middletown, Connecticut

Wesleyan University Press, Middletown CT 06459
www.wesleyan.edu/wespress

Title page photo: Brion Gysin, Paris, 1976. Photo by Ira Cohen.

Printed in the United States of America
Design and composition by Julie Allred, B. Williams & Associates

ISBN for the paperback edition: 978-0-8195-6529-7

Wesleyan University Press is a member of the Green Press Initiative.
The paper used in this book meets their minimum requirement for
recycled paper.

Library of Congress Cataloging-in-Publication Data
Gysin, Brion.
Back in no time : the Brion Gysin reader / edited by Jason Weiss.
    p. cm.
Includes bibliographical references.
Discography: p.
ISBN 0-8195-6528-8 (alk. paper) —
ISBN 0-8195-6529-6 (pbk. : alk. paper)
I. Weiss, Jason, 1955–   II. Title.
PS3557.Y8 A6 2001
818'.5409—dc21   2001026976

Contents

Preface   vii

Introduction   ix

That Secret Look   1

From a Lost Novel   3
   Recollections of a Lost Seascape   3
   Time and Brother Griphen   10

To Master—A Long Goodnight (excerpts)   16

Potiphar's Wife   60

Early Cut-Up Experiments   69
   First Cut-Ups   70
   Minutes to Go   73
   Cut Me Up * Brion Gysin   75

Permutation Poems   79
   I Am That I Am   80
   Junk Is No Good Baby   88
   Kick That Habit Man   89
   No Poets Don't Own Words   89
   I Don't Work You Dig   93
   This Is Sam Francis   94

Brion Gysin Let the Mice In   95

The Poem of Poems   102

Dreamachine   113

Unpublished Notes on Painting   117

The Pipes of Pan   122

About the Cut-Ups   125
   Cut-Ups: A Project for Disastrous Success   125
   Cut-Ups Self-Explained   132

Am I the One?   136

Janicot   141

The Process (excerpts)   144

The *Naked Lunch* Screenplay (excerpts)   190

A Quick Trip to Alamut   218

Fire: Words by Day—Images by Night 240

Psacré Psilocybin and Magic Mushrooms 257

Not by Me 261

Songs 266

   Nowhere Street (score by Steve Lacy) 267

   Somebody Special (score by Steve Lacy) 272

   Clementeena Soopastar 274

   Dreams (score by Steve Lacy) 275

   Gay Paree Bop 276

   Sham Pain 277

   Stop Smoking 278

Hamri's Hands 279

Snapshots from the Family Album (excerpts) 282

An Encomium for Allen Ginsberg 287

Calligraffiti of Fire 289

The Sculpted Line 291

The Last Museum 292

   The Door 293

   Hotel Bardo 297

   Back Jacket Copy 297

   The Last Museum (excerpts) 298

   Drawings for *The Last Museum* by Keith Haring 322, 339

Bibliography 349

Discography 351

Permissions 353

Preface

This book began—a decade after Brion Gysin's death—as the result of occasional discussions with friends I knew by way of him. I came to realize there was a certain quantity of rare or unpublished writings by Gysin, at the same time as I noticed that all of his published work was going out of print. This vanishing body of evidence, literarily speaking, sparked an idea that soon would not let me go.

I thought, at any rate, that it would be a project for me to do on the side—pull down the old books from my shelf and chase down a few texts in libraries or by word of mouth. It became, rather, a more involving project, which resembled a feverish sort of detective work: finding my way amid diverse paths and, with patience, catching the lepidoptera. The way things were going, it seemed to me, this might well be the only book available of Gysin for some time. I had to gather as much as I could, therefore, and then see what fit, taking full advantage of the publisher's interest so as to offer the greatest range.

Ultimately, Gysin was a storyteller and a poet too, but he wrote in many different forms. How was I to make a coherent order of the many pieces except by chronology? And even there, a strict rule had to be bent a little, precisely for the sake of coherence (grouping the Permutation Poems or the Songs together). We can thus see the course of his written production over five decades, and perhaps glimpse some measure of the life lived.

Another way to divide the book is in two parts: half comprising the long excerpts from his historical narrative and his two novels; the other half made up of some forty pieces. Instead, I shuffled the decks and was back at chronology. The little pieces alongside the large—that indeed is a writer's life. Any other system to classify these writings would be to set up needless obstacles in approaching them.

In selecting excerpts from the longer works, I sought to give a sense of the whole (beginnings, ends, important passages along the way) but also to highlight the strongest writing. I had to consider as well what sections might stand more or less on their own. For the historical narrative, *To Master—A Long Goodnight*, I have provided a brief overview of events in the parts of the text that I left out, but for the two complicated novels (and his screenplay of *Naked Lunch*) such summaries would have proved both cumbersome and unnecessary. Choosing the shorter pieces, on the other hand, was relatively easy: many, like the cut-ups and permutations, were particularly significant in Gysin's career; others, more occasional pieces, reflect his varied activities and interests, or serve to illustrate certain turns in his thinking, or else they are simply curious and amusing. In the end, I think there may be some pleasant surprises for even the most ardent Gysin fans.

I would like to thank the following individuals who have helped with their suggestions, assistance and overall support in drawing together the materials for this anthology: Marie-Odile Briot and Gladys Fabre of the Musée d'Art Moderne de la Ville de Paris, Ira Cohen, Graham Dawes, Steve Lacy, Ramuntcho Matta, John Geiger, James Grauerholz, José Férez Kuri, Guillaume Gallozzi, Terry Wilson, Bernard Heidsieck, Suzanna Tamminen, Timothy Murphy, Pierre Joris, Maura High, Julie Allred, Udo Breger, Theo Green, Linda Norton, Katherine Fausset, Jennie Skerl, Richard Aaron, Séamas McSwiney, Ali Alizadeh, Carol Moore and Marilyn Wurzburger at Arizona State University Library's Special Collections, Tara Wenger at the University of Texas' Harry Ransom Humanities Research Center, L. Rebecca Johnson Melvin at the University of Delaware Library's Special Collections, Ulrik Trojaborg and Annelise Ream at the Keith Haring Foundation, and Chris Chapman of Honeybee Robotics.

Introduction

Brion Gysin used to refer to himself as the man from nowhere—not surprising, given his multiple origins and thoroughly international existence. When Paul Bowles ran across him in New York in the 1940s, he described Gysin as then being into his fourth nationality. But perhaps the phrase that Jorge Luis Borges used to describe some of his own characters might be more appropriate: in his life as in his art, Gysin was "a man from the border." His restless curiosity kept him always on the move, going where it pleased him, carrying no baggage; such perhaps was the ideal, yet it was also, in large measure, his inescapable reality. A nomad at heart, he kept returning—physically or imaginatively—to the various far-flung locales that had formed him.

In this age when scholars and readers are eager to think across the disciplines, to find connections between cultures, to discern the underlying matrix of an artistic moment beyond fixed notions of identity or traditional expectations—as if any of these tendencies were new—surely it is time to reassess the work of Brion Gysin. As singular a figure as any, he was often dismissed for not being entirely a painter, nor entirely a writer, though he continued to explore both domains for some fifty years with an inquiring instinct that expressed itself differently according to the occasion. Worse for him, he did not hold still within these media, nor devote the bulk of his efforts to a chosen genre. Rather, he came and went, alert to creative openings, following his ideas in and beyond such practices simultaneously, alternately, sequentially. If some consider him essentially a painter, and his production in the visual arts possibly more accomplished, his fascination with writing and the mysteries of language remains nonetheless central to all his output—he did, after all, learn to speak seven languages. As a writer, his insightful understanding of history combined with the expansive flair of a born raconteur to set his prodigious imagination in motion: he produced long and short fiction, historical narrative, poems, song lyrics, travel pieces, memoirs, experimental forms, and more. Taken as a whole, his great versatility should be regarded not as a wild display of excess talents but instead as an ongoing method in his art of the opening, of uncovering paths which many younger artists took up in turn.

Though Gysin has been peripherally associated with the Beat Generation writers, it is more by intermittent points of convergence and especially his long friendship with William S. Burroughs that the affiliation holds. However, his multinational background and interdisciplinary perspective as an artist, as well as a healthy skepticism toward the spiritual yearnings of many among the Beats, rather set him apart. A foreigner everywhere, he did not claim any one culture as his own; despite the fact that he rubbed shoulders with various aristocracies all his life, his sympathies lay most often with the outsider, whether in the guise of artist, immigrant or heretic, not to mention the added markers of racial or sexual difference. He recognized the advantages of his hybrid origins, which allowed him more freedom of movement as an artist and as a person, so that whatever sparks of rebellion may be found in his work can be traced to his attitude toward the fixed thinking and implicit limits of all groups. His independence, of course, had a price: if by nature and temperament he dodged most efforts to package him as a recognizable commodity, given his many fields of action, he seldom had an easy time of it when he did seek to market his products.

Practical (or at least commercial) matters aside, the question of identity did not plague Gysin; on the contrary, it provided ample room for play. Indeed, the theme of the search for identity is found often in his work, and most especially, its opposite: the yearning to be free of identity, to vanish in the sea of language, the texture of vision. This is not unlike James Joyce's description of the artist in *A Portrait of the Artist* as someone who would ultimately disappear into the work of art. Gysin effected that move repeatedly in his various practices; in writing, the cut-ups were the first of his disappearing acts, and he revealed a like impulse by other means in his novel *The Process*. In a text first printed in Udo Breger's journal *Soft Need* (issue 17: *Brion Gysin Special* [1977]), he reflected on the matter of his own identity:

> A sorcerer's apprentice, follower of Aleister Crowley, once asked me if I knew my *real* name. I was dumbfounded, I don't. Burroughs has told me he knows his: not me. I have often been in doubt about it and written a number of poems in which I attempt to disassociate my I from my Me. Without pushing this to the point of schizophrenia, I have always felt rather doubtful about my Me.
>
> To begin with, I have an unusual surname of Swiss origin, fairly rare even in Switzerland, I am told. This family came down from the hills in the Middle Ages and settled in Liestal, a small town just far enough and independent enough from Basel to wage a petty provincial war with the big city and lose. The Gysin of the day lost his head and the family moved into Basel around 1500. My given name is Brion. My Celtic mother was thinking of one of those insufferable phony kings of Ireland and spelled it with an 'a': Brian. Official documents took care of that and spelled it Brion, like the famous wine of Bordeaux, Haut Brion. I accepted this gladly and dropped all my other given names when I became an American citizen.

I was sent to Downside, a school for hybrids in the west of England, run by Benedictine monks, a triumph of my Catholic mother whose zealous decision sat so ill with my Zwinglian Protestant family that I ended up with no inheritance at all. My mother's family barely survived on pseudo-aristocratic pretentions while my father's family liked to think of themselves as solidly Republican middle-class folk. I have never accepted the color or texture of my oatmealy freckled skin: 'bad packaging' I thought. Certain traumatic experiences have made me conclude that at the moment of birth I was delivered to the wrong address.

I have done what I could to make up for this.

Throughout his life, Gysin moved back and forth between three continents. Born in London in 1916, he didn't really know his father, who was declared missing in action before the end of the First World War. His mother raised him in western Canada, in and around Edmonton, till he was sent off to be educated in England in the early 1930s. In 1934 he moved to Paris, studied briefly at the Sorbonne, and made his first literary and artistic contacts by way of Sylvia Beach and the surrealists. The following year he was to have his first show as part of the surrealist drawings exhibit, but his work was taken down the day of the opening on orders from André Breton, for alleged insubordination. Later in the decade he traveled in Greece and the Algerian Sahara, then returned to Paris where he had his first one-man show in 1939 and lived on the Rue Gît-le-Coeur near the Place Saint Michel. When next he stayed in Paris for an extended period, twenty years later, it would be on that same street in what became known as the Beat Hotel.

With the onset of the war, he went to New York, where he worked as an assistant costume designer on Broadway musicals and then as a welder in the Bayonne shipyards, before joining the American army. From there he managed to get transferred to the Canadian army, which had him studying Japanese—crucial for his later calligraphic paintings—and where he met Tex Henson, great-grandson of Josiah Henson, the real-life model for Harriet Beecher Stowe's Uncle Tom. After the war, having become an American citizen and returned to New York, Gysin published his first book, *To Master—A Long Goodnight*, a historical narrative based on the life of Josiah Henson, which included a long appendix on the history of slavery in Canada. On the basis of this work, he was awarded one of the first Fulbright fellowships and so returned to Europe, where he did further research in Bordeaux and Seville on the history of the slave trade.

On the invitation of Paul Bowles, he went to visit Tangier in the summer of 1950 and soon established residency there. In the winter of 1951–52, he journeyed across the Sahara, an adventure that not only inspired his sketchbooks of the time but also became part of *The Process* years later. Through Bowles he first heard the Master Musicians of the hill town of Jajouka, and enchanted by their music Gysin went into business with them for about three years, when he opened his restaurant The 1001 Nights, where they performed; he was to maintain a friendship with the musicians for the rest of his life, introducing them in later years to Brian Jones, of the Rolling Stones, and saxophonist Ornette Coleman. There in Tangier he met William S. Burroughs, whom he had first encountered in New York, and though a friendship slowly developed, it was not until the end of the decade in Paris that they became close collaborators. In the mid-1950s, as Morocco gained its independence and took over the international port of Tangier, Gysin traveled to Algeria and got tangled up in the extravagant affairs of John and Mary Cooke, resulting in the loss of his restaurant; the Algerian episode as well reappeared in *The Process.* By 1958 he was back in Paris and residing at the Beat Hotel, where Burroughs also had a room and Ginsberg and others lodged when passing through. It was there that Gysin first discovered the cut-up technique of writing and the principle of his Permutation Poems, while he also painted extensively, coinvented the Dreamachine with mathematician Ian Sommerville, and performed numerous experiments, often with Burroughs, using tape recorders and other materials. The Permutation Poems and his use of tape recording led to Gysin's being regarded as one of the founders of Sound Poetry; from then on through the rest of his life he performed such work at galleries and poetry festivals.

Intermittently during the early and mid-1960s, Gysin tried to market the Dreamachine, hoping at last to resolve his perennial financial problems, but it never caught on in a big way. He described the Dreamachine as "the first art object to be seen with the eyes closed," and, with some practice, it could indeed provoke a dreamlike state. The contraption seemed simple enough: a transparent cylinder encasing a slotted cylinder that rotates around a light bulb, flashing stroboscopic pulses of light at a speed corresponding to the alpha band. Throughout the decade, he was back and forth among Paris, London, New York, and Tangier, working on various projects. His literary work mainly comprised the collaborations with Burroughs on *The Third Mind* (though it was not published until some ten years later, first in French translation), *The Process* (written in Tangier), and at the end of the decade, his own screenplay, based on Burroughs's *Naked Lunch,* which was never produced.

In the late 1960s he also began to write a new work of fiction. With each draft the novel evolved ever further from its original purpose of chronicling the Beat Hotel. It was published in 1986, shortly after his death, as *The Last Museum.*

Meanwhile, he had returned definitively to Paris (in 1973) and eventually settled in an apartment directly across from the Centre Pompidou, which was then being built. By 1975 he was stricken with colon cancer, and after surviving an infernal series of treatments and operations he was determined to put his house in order. He continued to experiment with different media in his visual artwork, such as his use of photography in the mid- to late 1970s, and in a new development, he began to collaborate with saxophonist Steve Lacy on a number of songs. He had written song lyrics on at least two occasions previously, though they were never produced. Lacy recuperated many of these lyrics and wrote new music for them, and Gysin contributed new lyrics for Lacy's group well into the 1980s. In addition, Gysin and Lacy performed these songs as a duo, with Gysin's energetic spoken-sung delivery, at poetry and jazz festivals. Some of the lyrics and others—both on the shelf and several newly written—were also set to music in the early to mid-1980s by guitarist Ramuntcho Matta, who performed them with Gysin. Amid occasional gallery and museum shows and tributes to him and Burroughs—the Nova Convention in New York (1978), the Final Academy in London (1982)—his main literary project in later years remained his novel, *The Last Museum*. Partly due to a lack of space, his work as a painter became rather dormant until one final burst that resulted in the ten-canvas work *Calligraffiti of Fire* in 1985.

On the last page of his introduction to *The Last Museum*, Burroughs drew a telling portrait of Gysin:

> Brion Gysin died of a heart attack on Sunday morning, July 13, 1986. He was the only man I have ever respected. I have admired many others, esteemed and valued others, but respected only him. His presence was regal without a trace of pretension. He was at all times impeccable.
>
> Who was Brion Gysin? The only authentic heir to Hassan-i-Sabbah, the Old Man of the Mountain? Certainly that. Through his painting I caught glimpses of the Garden that the Old Man showed to his Assassins. The Garden cannot be faked. And Brion was incapable of fakery. He was Master of the Djoun forces, the Little People, who will never serve a faker or a coward.
>
> Brion was suffering from emphysema and lung cancer. He knew he had only a few weeks to live. I was preparing to go to Paris when Brion died. I have this last glimpse through a letter, in her own English, from my friend Rosine Buhler:
>
> "Brion asked to wear his Chevalier de l'Ordre des Arts et de Lettres medallion in a very elegant way and we started dinner with a wonderful Chinese soup. Brion finds the wine slightly 'rapeux' to tease François de Palaminy,

who has spent and concentrated to find a non-alterated wine which is not so easy even in Paris. After occurs a dreamlike talk about to have a large house by the sea in August, the shadowed room where all is burning hot outside. Brion said he knew he would sleep well and was really happy of that good day. He wanted no help to lift himself up from his green armchair, and went to his room. I was watching his tall straight way to walk, his secure path . . . only kings and wild people have this way."

More than a decade after his passing, Gysin has continued to gain new admirers. There have been more gallery and museum shows of his work as a visual artist, including the major retrospective at the Edmonton Art Gallery in the summer of 1998, with a comprehensive book published by Thames & Hudson. However, his work as a writer has become almost entirely unavailable. This anthology, I hope, will correct that imbalance and, for old friends and new adventurers alike, will restore some measure of the worldly vision that was Gysin's trademark.

That Secret Look

"That Secret Look" (1941) first appeared in the journal View, *edited by Charles Henri Ford. Like Gysin's early work as a visual artist, his writing here shows the general influence of surrealism. More important, as a skeptical portrayal of New York, city of technological advances and endless gimmicks, this piece reflects his perspective as an outsider—one whose experience was formed both by the "wilds" of western Canada, in childhood, and the "civilized" refinements of his English public school education, in adolescence, as well as by the vanguard aesthetics of 1930s Paris.*

When the city grew beyond Washington Square it seems to have stopped, drawn breath and then stretched out ahead a scaffolding of streets and avenues, a blueprint laid over the face of the island to the Harlem River. These streets today are the erosions on the hard-baked shell of the Aristotelian turtle that bore the world. Anchored deep in his crusty back-armor are the towers and honeycombed brick and mortar cliffs from whose ledges the city at night glitters like a mirror drowned in a deep well. And lo! the poor refugee, the Marco Polo in reverse, preferring his little Venice to Xanadu, wouldn't buy the island with his trinkets and bright beads even if someone loaned him the $24 to conclude the deal. Traveling backward with the speed of an angry queen bee expelled from the hive, he cannot master the trick of putting on his clothes back to front as the natives do in order to give the impression of a more logical type of locomotion.

"The Natives are Friendly," his compatriots wig-wagged back to Europe several years ago, but added when they came home, "But you never know what they are thinking—they all look alike to me." A mysterious people that stands up to sleep clinging to straps in underground subways; a people that does not shake hands all around a room full of thirty; a people that walks around as it eats out of machines; a people that smiles and smiles and continues to extend its hospitality as you kick them around and that continues to copy your way of dressing its women, painting its pictures and furnishing its homes when these things represent a way of living and thinking that they have spilt blood to abolish.

"A town that greets you standing up," says a writer, and sure enough between the skyscrapers hang festoons of popcorn and ropes of candy beads. Chased by the searchlights of a World Première, or is it a "Spectacle in the Sky"—a mock air raid, are the rainbows that breathe up from the miasmic Times Square; the exhalation of a million desires that carpets the sky from the seventeenth floor on up.

The Rainbow Level—an attitude as much as an altitude—a game of parchesi with ladders or chutes depending on the number you throw.

The streets below are like the stream of "The Old Mill" or "The Tunnel of Love" at Luna Park or Coney Island, through whose fog of carbon monoxide you are swept clutching your neighbor, past bright tableaux; the desert island, the cemetery by moonlight, the axe murderer in the kitchen or famous scenes from fiction. But here the tableaux are the windows and three balls for a dime do not give you the privilege of throwing anything less than a bathtub through them —and that from the inside. If the bleached cornflake snow of a fan-propelled winter blizzard blows through the windows of I. J. Fox—a man who can sign his name with a cloud, his moneyed finger tracing it in the sky as ephemerally as it would on the sand before an incoming tide, the further you travel north the more subtle the approach.

Past this window and that, past the architectural pride of a family that fears God as they once feared Congressional investigation on earth; past the windows of a beauty Princess who looks like the grandmother of the glamour girls, those strange, cross-pollinated flowers a generation removed from an old stalk. And step up, Ladies and Gentlemen, too! Here is the window where you *can* win a coconut. Let the little lady hold your hand; give you the aim; her little phantom hand guiding yours, and—Wham!

But what is it today? Not the bathroom but the corridor of that same *hotel de passe*. And you call it?—That Secret Look. Pass on we say, this man is telling you like the America Firster across the street, that a fifth column will uphold your house when the other four are torn away. You don't understand—then look again. This is to be the pattern for your women: this is the way they must dress; the way they must smell; but what are they doing? They are backing out of hotel rooms; this pretty doll has a blueprint clutched in her black-gloved hand; that one has dropped a dagger to the floor, neatly pinning a paper acknowledging whose black dress this is, whose black hat, whose black stockings, shoes and gloves give her That Secret Look.—That baby's got a gat! Look, she's stuffing the plans of the washing-machine wringer into her corsage. Last winter I knitted sea-boot socks until I was blind and let the maid finish them. I wore pins and insignia until it hurt. I was worn to a skeleton reading papers and I never wore a pin five minutes longer than it took to read the Extra that told me it wasn't fashionable. This winter I won't wrap another fumble. This winter I am going to be *destructive*.

God, it smells like Paris! The air is like champagne today.

From a Lost Novel

*"Recollections of a Lost Seascape" and "Time and Brother Griphen" (1942)
were published in* Town and Country, *in July and November 1947, re-
spectively. These stories became part of a novel that was subsequently lost,
"Memoirs of a Mythomaniac," which Gysin later described as a* détourné
*autobiography; another chapter was published as the story "Ariadne of
Naxos"—in the volume of early fiction,* Stories *(1984)—based on travels
in Greece in the late 1930s, which he recycled long after in a section of
his novel* The Last Museum *(1986), as seen later in this anthology. "Recollections of a Lost Seascape" draws upon his vacation at the elaborate home
of an aristocratic friend from school, on the island of Guernsey; "Time and
Brother Griphen" reflects the setting of the English public school he attended
in the early 1930s, Downside.*

Recollections of a Lost Seascape

The island of Herm lies like an enormous, half-submerged whale in the tides
and currents of the English Channel. This island was bought by my grandfather
toward the beginning of the century, and he lived there in self-imposed exile, a
widower with five daughters. Herm does not belong to England but is considered by a curious legal anomaly to be a fief of the Duke of Normandy, who is
only incidentally the King of England. The owner of the island is, therefore, a
feudatory of the duke and owes him at least nominal allegiance. On Herm itself the owner is the highest legal authority, the dispenser of justice, and a despot who may strike coins or mint stamps if he wishes.

Grandfather had no subjects other than the members of his own family and
the servants. He would have ruled them with a rod of iron even if he had not
been granted plenipotentiary powers by feudal right. He rarely had any contact
with foreigners except for the few fishermen to whom he granted fishing rights
in his waters. Actually, Grandfather was in a sense a foreigner himself: that is,
he was not English, though the Duke of Normandy, his liege lord, had no
more loyal feudal retainer.

When the first great war of our time surprised people who, like the lord of
Herm, were living in the past, there were those who whispered that Grandfather

should no longer be allowed to retain his island. The gossip about him was common in Guernsey and in Jersey, but he was the last to hear the malicious tales which were invented. These people said that he was entertaining officers from the U-boats which were known to be in the Channel. In truth, my grandfather had more fear of the submarines than anyone.

He was continually on the lookout for them and he thought of little else. He was not afraid for his life or for his property, but for something which he considered to be infinitely more precious. He had five daughters who were all nubile to what he considered an awkward degree. He knew the dangers of that frangible state from certain observations of his own—made much earlier in life, of course—and the jealousy with which he guarded them from contact with the world was, indeed, the principal reason for living on Herm.

The girls were quite content with the life they led, for they knew no other. Their pleasures were simple and healthy. For exercise they took walks to collect flowers, and they were allowed to bathe in the sea. They splashed and shrieked in the water from eleven to twelve on sunny mornings, while Grandfather thought grimly of the submarines which might easily emerge in full view of the beach.

Each morning he scanned the sea from the top of a nearby cliff, and like a nervous passenger on a ship feeling its way through wartime waters, he imagined every stick and every floating bottle to be a periscope. He saw younger men than he pressing around the sighting apparatus, with wild desire shining in their eyes, as they saw the graceful images of his sea-nymph daughters in their blue serge bathing dresses trimmed with white braid and piping, their pretty flowing yellow hair hidden in caps like immense yellow water lilies and their pretty pink toes encased in black cotton stockings and rubber shoes with little rose pompons on the toes.

Grandfather accompanied them in an old green rubberized military storm-coat, worn over a bathing suit with short sleeves and pants which half-hid his cavalry legs, and a black bowler hat which he never took off—even when he entered the water. Neither did he remove his yellow wash gloves until he had finished his dip, for he felt that it was not fitting that a man in his position should come in contact with any fish other than a cooked one, with its knowing eye removed and the socket sprouting a green sprig from the herb garden.

His bowler was a matter of tender and respectful amusement among the young ladies, until finally one day my mother, who was by far the boldest, being the prettiest and therefore her father's favorite, snatched it from his head and from the top of the cliff flung it out to sea. It caught the breeze and sailed many yards before it plunged down and hit the water, soon bobbing out of sight on the ebb tide. The girls pealed with laughter like a disagreeable set of chimes, and were confined to their rooms. The next day my grandfather again went to the seashore in his bowler. He had retrieved it from the rising tide, and he continued to wear it as long as he believed in sea bathing.

Though there were no other inhabitants on the island, and the menservants were my grandfather's age, the thought of prying, lustful eyes continued to haunt the old man's heart. The more he thought of the desires of young men confined in submarines, the more determined he became to stop the daily excursions to the shore, though he did not wish to deprive the girls of their pleasure. At that time it had become almost impossible to leave Herm, and even the short sea trip to Guernsey was dangerous. They were living off the produce of the garden and such fish as could be caught from a small boat a short distance offshore. He hesitated to deprive his naiads of their dip in the ocean, and yet the possibility that a U-boat might appear, a U-boat such as the one undoubtedly in the neighborhood which had recently sunk a fisherboat, made him tremble with rage. His military experience as a youth had acquainted him with the behavior of licentious soldiers in garrison towns and of libidinous seamen in port, and he was certain that these new undersea sailors would be the worst of the lot. He forbade his daughters the shore.

For a while they moped, and then the eyes of five young ladies, deprived of all outlet for their animal energy, confined to croquet on the lawn and the few Graustarkian novels around the house, grew dreamy as they trailed around in vaporous silences, and started abruptly when spoken to in a loud voice for the second time. My grandfather guessed that the young ladies in confinement were allowing their thoughts to dwell too closely on their own nubility, and that the swelling buds of late spring were shaping their thoughts in a romantic way.

He gave orders, and soon there was a great bustling around the house and the home farm, where the wheels of old carts were gathered together and timbers cut and nailed. When the young ladies learned that their father was going to build bathing machines on wheels their joy knew no bounds and they went every day to see how the work progressed. At last the bathing huts were ready. There were six bathing machines in all, one for each girl and one for their governess. Grandfather told them that they might dip in the sea when the huts were drawn down to the beach, but that they must not swim even a few strokes into deeper water. This changed their schedule, for even my grandfather could not order full tide at the appointed time, and his daughters were allowed to swim only when the tide was incoming, for then there was less danger of being swept out to sea.

One day my mother was retiring into her machine after frolicking in the waves, when she noticed how the sun warmed the boards of her little cabin on wheels, which was almost afloat. The door opened seaward and she had been told, as indeed her sisters had been also, to close it carefully before removing as much as one black stocking, for Grandfather still feared the inquisitive periscopes. What nonsense, she thought, leaving the door open. No one can see me, not even Mademoiselle, and she removed her cap and let her hair fall to her waist. She became excited by the warm touch of the sun as she stepped out of her suit and stood at the open door, looking out at the waves. The black stockings suddenly appeared hateful to her, and she stripped them off too. She stretched luxuriously in the sun, for it seemed hotter on the boards when she lay down close to the tide that slapped the wood within an inch of her, and lapped at the top step of her cabin. Then, perhaps, she fell asleep.

When her father attached the little donkey which drew the bathing machines up to the beach, he left hers until the last, for she always took the longest time to dress. Her sisters, Mademoiselle the governess, and dear papa, were all waiting on the beach, and they found her naked as Andromeda chained to her rock, lying with her eyes half-closed on the damp floor of the little house on wheels. Mademoiselle shrieked and said that she had undoubtedly fainted from the sun, but she smiled as she lay there and continued to smile as they helped her toward the house.

They took her home to put her to bed, but she never got there that afternoon, for my grandfather ordered them all locked up in the old nursery, and they fluttered up the dark staircase in their white dresses, Mademoiselle chasing close behind, followed by the eyes of five young British officers who had come to take over the island.

Apparently, treacherous Mademoiselle had written to the authorities in London, saying that Grandfather thought of nothing but submarines. The authorities had drawn their own conclusions, and had decided to send a garrison to the island to dispossess him. Grandfather's worst fears were thus realized. Young men, young officers. Here they were, quartered in the house, in close contact with his daughters. It was unthinkable.

The young ladies were greatly excited, and spent the rest of the afternoon making spit curls, for they knew that they could not be locked up forever. But my mother sat in the window with that same little smile playing about her lips, and the window looked out to sea.

Of course they all went down to dinner, and of course they flirted with the young officers, and of course they married them. My mother married the one who had blue eyes and red hair, but it was not much of a romance, for he was soon recalled and sent to France where he was killed before he ever could see the small, quiet son she bore him.

When my grandfather bought the island of Herm he wished to turn it into an earthly paradise, and decided to import a number of exotic plants, birds, and animals. He felt that Herm would be capable of sustaining flamingos as well as sparrows or starlings, and the soft, damp climate encouraged him in the idea. He planted several acres of palms and cacti, camelia bushes which throve, hibiscus and mangoes which did not, fig trees and pines, cedar of Lebanon, an avenue of eucalyptus leading to the house, and a kraal of thorn bushes which he announced was to be for the lions.

Several weeks later a half-dozen mangy lords of the jungle were delivered. They had been bought from a German menagerie and they staggered onto dry land looking more than a little seasick, overcome as much by the smell of the terrified fishermen and their smacks, as from the journey up the cliffside by means of tackles.

These beasts were followed by an assortment of wildlife which Grandfather thought suitable. There were zebras, several ostriches, a family of kangaroos, various sorts of horned and hoofed things considered decorative and not dangerous. There was also an assortment of beautiful birds which were obtained at great expense. These last were no sooner set free at Grandfather's orders, than they left for some hopeless, unplanned migratory journey and were seen no more. It was decided that the lions would be happier if they were allowed to roam at large on the island of Jethou, which is little more than an immense rock lying across a narrow channel from Herm. From time to time they were thrown quartered lambs from a boat while Grandfather "studied" them through his glasses from the opposite shore. They continued to live there in a state of nature until the island was occupied by Australian troops during the war.

Grandfather was a stern man who allowed no one to question his authority. If things turned out badly he was always certain that it was the fault of those who had not carried out his orders properly. Nevertheless, in a far corner of the island, a mile or two from his house, there stood the evidence of one tragedy for which he did feel responsible. Grandfather went to his grave feeling that he had the blood of three Japanese on his hands, and this is how it happened.

Grandfather's good friend, Lord de Haviland, who lived in Guernsey, had spent much of his youth traveling in the Orient, collecting things which had to be numbered, knocked down, and crated to be carried off home. In the course of his travels, his fancy had been struck by a small Chinese temple which he had bought on the spot. He had ordered it dismantled and brought to Guernsey, where it ornamented a corner of his garden which was sufficiently damp to grow a thicket of bamboo. Grandfather had seen it there and admired it extremely. He not only admired the object itself, but he had an intense admiration for his old friend's manner of doing things. He wanted the temple for his island of Herm, and was even preparing to send workmen to take it in Lord de Haviland's absence but gave up the idea when the latter, having got wind of the plot, suggested an alternative.

He told Grandfather that his son, who was at that time an undersecretary in the British legation in Tokyo, might find a suitable temple there which could be sent back to Herm. After an exchange of letters, the younger De Haviland answered that he could not find a temple, but that he knew of a beautiful small house belonging to a noble Japanese family which was for sale. Grandfather had become most impatient, and he decided at once to send his secretary to Japan with the most explicit instructions that the house was to be brought to Herm exactly as it stood when he first saw it. He particularly stressed the fact that he wanted everything inside the house to be brought along, for he was anxious that his Japanese house should be more complete than the De Haviland temple in Guernsey. The secretary was a German, and from his long training with Grandfather, who meant exactly what he said, was accustomed to unquestioning obedience.

Some six months later the house arrived in several hundred numbered crates. Three Japanese came with it: a woman and two men. Grandfather at first surmised that the men had come to supervise the reconstruction, but thought it a little strange that a woman should have come, too, until it occurred to him that she was there to arrange the interior. He was most pleased at the unexpected foresight of his agent, and was preparing to compliment him when he appeared to give his account.

The secretary stated simply that he did not know who these people were, but that they had been in the house at the time he first saw it, and he had brought them along in an attempt to fulfill his orders to the letter. The Japanese had been slightly dazed at the rapidity with which their home had been dismantled, but as their books, clothes, cooking utensils, and bed covers were all rapidly put in crates, they had followed him blindly to the boat. "No discretion," muttered Grandfather, and called the Japanese in order to question them. They could not be questioned. They spoke no European language and no one on the island of Herm spoke a word of Japanese. Grandfather sent for an interpreter, but before one could be brought the house had been reassembled and it was too late. The two gentlemen had killed themselves in what grandfather reported to have been a most untidy way, and the lady had jumped off a cliff into the channel, very probably because there was no volcano handy.

The reason for their behavior was never very accurately determined. The most logical explanation seemed to be that the secretary had entered the house at a moment of great domestic tension. Perhaps one of the men was the lady's husband, and had come in at a moment when she was making flower arrangements with the stranger, or was immersed in the etiquette of the tea ceremony. The act of violence which would have followed this discovery had been arrested by the entrance of Grandfather's agent. The participants in this drama had undoubtedly been so horrified by the abrupt manner in which he took over their house and their fate, that the crime of passion which should have followed immediately was postponed, and existed in a state of suspension during their journey halfway across the world. Once the house was reassembled the charm was broken and the action completed. Grandfather felt somehow responsible.

On fine days he used to walk to the Japanese house and tap the oiled paper walls reflectively, or blow the dust off the pretty books which he could not read. Sometimes he stroked the curious little lacquer rosettes which decorated the furniture. He had been told that these were the strange coat of arms of the former owner, and this made him sad and respectful, for he felt that such things should not happen to "his sort of people." For Grandfather, "his sort of people" constituted the one truly international class, and he would have felt more at home with a Hottentot if that Hottentot were a chief than he would with just any Frenchman or German.

In the late autumn of 1915, when the island of Herm was taken away from him, the British government stationed Australian troops on the island. During several weeks they amused themselves by killing all the remaining birds with slingshots and running the ostriches to death. One day Grandfather decided to walk to the Japanese house, for he felt that he would be more at home there than in the company of these strange people who had been quartered on him. When he came within sight of the pretty little oriental garden with which he had surrounded the house, he stopped frozen with horror. Everything had been devastated; everything destroyed.

He turned back, filled with rage, intending to lodge a protest with the commanding officer. From some distance away he heard one of the old gardeners shouting to him. "Highness, the soldiers have taken the little boat and gone to Jethou with their guns," he cried. Grandfather hurried to his own room where he kept an old rifle. Carrying it under his arm he rushed toward the cliff from which he had always "studied" his lions. On that cold, damp day he could see the soldiers' Girl-Guide hats showing over the tops of some large boulders. They were stumbling and falling over the rocks as they stalked the lions; his lions. Grandfather let loose a volley.

The following day he left for Guernsey in spite of all the submarines in the Channel, and he never saw Herm again.

Time and Brother Griphen

The school I went to as a child had an air of the romantic period of Neo-Gothic architecture, which flourished at a time when it was fashionable to build false ruins. The dormitories, halls, classrooms, refectories, chapel, and recreation hall formed a straggling block of ivy-covered buildings attached to an abbey and a monastery by a series of long corridors and vaulted, echoing halls. I still think that it must have been more than a mile from the War Memorial past Great Hall and Little Hall, past the refectory with its raftered and emblazoned roof, forty feet or more above our heads, through a low, vaulted cloister with green stained-glass windows, up to the flight of broad steps which led into the abbey church. From within the church itself you could enter what I suppose must have been very similar cloisters leading to the monastery and the cells of the monks, but I never passed more than a few yards beyond those great doors into those strangely repulsive, smelly halls. At that point you were almost overcome by the odor of stale incense in the folds of black serge robes.

We saw the monks of the monastery enter into the church almost every day, but while they were close to us they were also completely apart. We knew only those few who taught in the school, and even they seemed almost unrecognizable as they sang from under their hoods, sitting back in the shadowed choir stalls. On Sundays certain young boys of the school, dressed in red and white, stood in front of these same stalls and lifted their soprano voices high into the nave of the church. That sound soared and fell back against carved stone and carved wood into the wave of bass voices which seemed to echo from under the dark hoods of the monks. The school was famous for its Gregorian chant, that indescribable music of male voices. The organist was a handsome, stalwart young Russian who had left the concert halls to enter the monastery. The monk named Dom Thomas, who trained and led the choir, looked so much a small neutered cat that you wondered where the music could be hidden in him. These two antitypes forged music which I have never been able to forget.

The great windows, which hung above the part of the church to which we schoolboys were confined, were filled with a greenish glass that cast an almost submarine gloom over the assembled congregation even on the brightest of days. The windows of the transept struck great shafts of light through the haze, and from time to time picked out some boy in the choir who seemed to be the only singer, as his voice blended with the others in a vibrating column of sound which shook the ribs of the whole church. The bass voices flowed out in oily waves and the male soprano echoed back and forth, searching through the columns of stone. In the green sea-light we seemed to be crouched on the hard-beaten, sandy bottom of the sea, filled with an unreasoning despair and sadness, until the organ burst forth with its triumphant toccata and suddenly an army with banners seemed to charge above our heads and meet another army in full flight. The shock of their collision almost brought down the vaulting.

The monks who entered the monastery were chosen, I think, as much for their compatibility as for their religious vocation. There were a number of qualifications. Many of the novices who petitioned the abbot for entrance were the younger sons of rich families, and although they were obliged to take a vow of poverty, they were also obliged to bring a considerable dowry with them when they came. If the monks therefore were at least theoretically poor, the monastery itself was extremely rich and took good care of its investments. The monks were well provided for and their poverty was really only nominal. Their religious duties were numerous and undoubtedly monotonous, but they also had a great deal of time before eternity began in which to occupy themselves with works. If a monk wished to engage in a craft or a hobby he was provided with the very best tools and implements, which were paid for out of the common fund. Their interests ranged from things like beekeeping or carpentry to the arts and the sciences.

The beekeeping monk persuaded his bees to produce a delicate, thin honey the color of pale jade which had the fragrance of spiced pinks and apple blossoms. This honey he sold to the schoolboys at a price so exorbitant that we were led to doubt the nonprofit basis of his little enterprise.

I did not like any of the monks whom I knew with the exception of the art master, who was also a sculptor. Before entering the monastery he had studied in Paris and he was often in trouble with the abbot, who did not appreciate modern art. Dom Hubert was a backslider, I fear, and there is some evidence to show that he read movie magazines. He loved his stoneyard, for it took him away from the rather limited company of his fellow monks, and gave him physical exercise. He would attack a huge block of the local limestone with such furious energy that he often finished with a miniature Madonna and misshapen Child, where, with the same material and a little more care, he might have produced a colossus. I have often wondered since what attacks of temperament he was trying to overcome by turning stone into dust.

One day he was called upon to make a bas-relief, and he started in grimly upon a large piece of stone. He would have liked to make something else, I knew, but the abbot had imposed the condition that he confine himself to religious subjects. As the relief grew under the blows of his chisel, the Madonna's high cheekbones, large eye sockets, long bob, and awkward gesture toward the child grew more and more familiar. Her mouth was wide and generous and her jawline firm and square. Dom Hubert smiled as he cut a Latin inscription into the stone. *STELLA SACRAE SILVAE.* When the abbot first saw this work of art he was pleased with it, but even he may possibly have seen the resemblance to Garbo before he translated the inscription into STAR OF HOLLYWOOD. It was too much, I am afraid. Dom Hubert lost his workshop, and I worked on there alone.

It was about this same time that the observatory in the monastery garden burned to the ground. It had originally been built for a monk who had obtained permission to study astronomy, and the abbot had taken a sort of medieval pride in his work when it was first begun. A monastery should, by tradition, be a center of learning, and it was felt that an accomplished astronomer would be an asset to the place. This monk, let us call him Dom Griphen, was provided with a large telescope and other necessary equipment, and he was given to understand that epoch-making discoveries were expected of him as soon as possible.

Some years passed and no new planet swam into the field of his telescope, but he explained that he was engaged in lengthy calculations which needed some considerable passage of time for their corroboration, and he was allowed to continue undisturbed. Each day, as soon as religious duties were fulfilled, he disappeared up the long walks and alleys of the monastery garden to lock himself into the summer house which had been turned into an observatory. He appeared only in church and at the necessary meals where no conversation is allowed, and thus escaped close questioning from the other monks as to the manner in which his experiments were progressing. Several years passed, during which no one but the abbot had exchanged a word with him. One day he was asked to appear at a convocation to announce to the assembled monks the results of his years of observation and calculation.

In a short time the grapevine which connected the school and the monastery brought the great news to us. It appeared that Dom Griphen had discovered for certain that the day did not consist of a period of twenty-four hours. For years, for centuries, or perhaps even longer, the world had been laboring under the delusion that the solar day could be divided exactly into twenty-four hours, 1,440 minutes, or 86,400 seconds. This was a colossal error, and Brother Griphen had the proof of it.

The grapevine had brought no exact information as to the margin of error. Some impressionable and slack-tongued brothers went so far as to claim that there was a considerable divergence between the result of his calculations and the conventional, accepted solar day. Some claimed that it accounted for the long days in summer, and the short days in winter, but as the monks were all obliged to get up in the middle of the night and troop into the church to sing, it could hardly make much difference to them. It was decided by the abbot that the great discovery should not be made known to the world until it had been referred to Rome, for it might conflict with some point of doctrine. It may be, also, that the abbot was a little skeptical.

Dom Griphen was told that the College of Cardinals must study the matter, and he was warned that this body might take years to decide on it. He was a little discouraged, for he remembered questions that had not been settled in a lifetime or two, and he was afraid that they might not decide upon the matter until after his own death. Dom Griphen had realized while very young that the world was in moral error, and for that reason he had left it. Now he was persuaded that the very physical world was continually presenting the brethren with an error in time itself. The hours were striking at every breath they drew, and striking false. He proposed to the abbot that the error should be rectified at least in the world of school and monastery over which he had jurisdiction.

Father Abbot hastily explained that such a thing was impossible until they had received word from Rome. The Church Temporal should deal with Time. The abbot suggested further that Dom Griphen might have made some slight error in his calculations and sent him away advising him to recheck his figures for a few months. Dom Griphen came back later and said that he had made no mistake. He attempted to reassure the abbot, explaining that one could continue to divide the day into twenty-four hours, but that it was the day itself which was at fault and that threw the hours, minutes, and seconds out. A simple adjustment in the minutes, a fraction of a second here and there, would correct this age-old error. The abbot remained adamant. He could do nothing until Rome had spoken. Dom Griphen almost dared suspect that the abbot was trifling with him. He pleaded that the daily correction itself would not be too large; a trial ought to be given it.

The abbot, however, considered the matter closed, and called one of the younger monks to him, ordering him to pursue his mathematical studies, and prepare himself to become an astronomer. He gave him his blessing and intimated that he hoped it would be possible to put the observatory into his hands before the equipment had become completely obsolete.

It was some time before the monastery noticed any change in the habits of Dom Griphen. He considered the daily error to be a small one, but one in which he at least could not remain. He asked another monk, whose hobby was watchmaking, to make him a clock according to his specifications. The hands were to make two revolutions of the dial each day, but they were to move more quickly and clip a fraction off each hour. The clock would then tell the correct time: his correct time. When the clock was finished, he proceeded to live according to the time which it indicated. At first the difference was so minute that he appeared at meals or at devotions at the same time as his companions. Yet slowly and inexorably he parted from his fellows, drawn further and further away by time itself.

At first he came a little early for some of the ceremonies, and then he began to come later and later for others. He came so late that he seemed to be coming early for still another duty, until there was no way in which one could check just which duty he was fulfilling. Soon the whisper went around, snatches of surmise gabbled from behind breviaries, harsh words said from the corners of pious mouths. Nevertheless, primitive people respect madness and pamper madmen, saying that they are blessed, and so it was within the monastery walls. Brother Griphen continued to live by his time. It played occasional tricks on him—but does it not play tricks on us all?

As the brethren hurried along the cloisters to sing in the new day which begins after each midnight, they often met Dom Griphen with a candle going off to his lunch or breakfast. He sang vespers when they sang matins. His lauds and his antiphonies were indistinguishable. As the years rolled on, his time would nevertheless draw him, like some returning comet, back into their orbit, and for a while his actions would coincide with the pattern of their lives, until one day they would notice that he was moving off again to his midnight meals and sunlit sleep. He sometimes went and sang alone in the church as his clock bade him, and otherwise fulfilled his duties most scrupulously.

He made great looping circles through the seemingly straight line of life in the monastery. He was an awesome creature, like a man from another planet, and I remember him well as in old age he shuffled around the drafty corridors or moved slowly over the gravel paths to his observatory.

In spite of his double unworldliness, he was well aware of the younger monk, who was by now verging on middle age, to whom the abbot had given the mission of preparing himself to take over the observatory. He knew very well that this younger man was filled with only theoretical knowledge of the stars and filled too with a longing to get his hands on the telescope which Dom Griphen had never allowed him to touch. This idea filled his last years with rage and bitterness.

One summer morning, three hours after sunrise, Dom Griphen walked through the monastery gardens with death holding his elbow. But even death could hold him upright no longer when he collapsed just inside the abbey church, where the monks were droning out their Latin hymns. He fell to the stone floor and died. The rival astronomer assisted those who carried him to his cell. This last charitable act, undertaken mainly because he had hoped to find the key to the observatory under the robes of the dead monk, was a mistake. As he looked toward the garden he saw a pillar of smoke rising straight up into the summer air, and by the time he reached the observatory, it was a furnace dripping hot metal. Dom Griphen had reversed the telescope, arranging the great magnifying glasses in such a way that by the time he had reached the church the first pale rays of the sun had converged on his papers and caused them to burst into flames. He had forestalled his rival.

 # To Master—A Long Goodnight:
The Story of Uncle Tom, A Historical Narrative

To Master—A Long Goodnight (1946) was Gysin's first book, published by Eileen Garrett's Creative Age Press in an edition of one thousand copies. After his transfer from the American paratroopers to the Canadian army during the war, he met Tex Henson, great-grandson of Josiah Henson, the real-life model for Harriet Beecher Stowe's Uncle Tom, who had settled in Ontario, Canada, and founded agricultural communities among the former slaves. Subtitled The Story of Uncle Tom, a Historical Narrative, *the book draws on Henson's own account of his life (written before the decline of his Canadian ventures, while he was still a touring phenomenon), as well as extensive additional research, in an effort to understand the measure of Henson's complicity in what came to be seen as the negative representation of Uncle Tom. Covering Henson's entire life till his death at a ripe old age, the narrative goes on to show how that image from the popular novel ultimately affected Henson's own reception in the world, how the real life and the fiction intertwined as a lesson and warning for later generations.*

The book also stands as an early marker of Gysin's lifelong interest in history, and his ability to make connections between different cultural and historical currents. His insight and sensitivity to the subject of race relations were rare for a white man at the time, perhaps a benefit of his non-American origins. As a result, the work gained him entry into black intellectual circles for years after. An appendix not excerpted here, "A History of Slavery in Canada," made up the final third of the book.

Don't Chase after Me

I'm on my way to Canada
Where everyone is free.
So Goodnight, Old Master,
Don't chase after me.
—*Slave Song*

/ 1 /

When this story was told by its hero, he called it *Truth Stranger Than Fiction*, for Harriet Beecher Stowe had modeled the principal character in her novel *Uncle Tom's Cabin* upon an earlier account of his life. Under her hand a metamorphosis took place, in which the fictional character of Uncle Tom grew to such strength in the popular imagination of the troubled time that it shouldered aside, and seemed to condemn to obscurity, the human counterpart from which it had sprung. The man was robbed of his personality and almost of his name by a character in a novel, which came to be such a symbol of the inevitable struggle about to take place that those who lived too close to the event to be able to see it in perspective might well mistake the symbol for the cause.

This book is about Uncle Tom, the man and the symbol, and inevitably, therefore, it is an attempt to analyze the society which created him. It is not a book against any individual; nor is it a book against the original Uncle Tom, Josiah Henson; but it is a book against the attitude to which the term, *Uncle Tomism,* has come to be applied. It was written in the army, in barracks before "lights out," in hotels, in trains, and in those libraries which could be reached on weekend passes. For that reason there are undoubtedly faults of scholarship and lacunae in research, but there is no apology for the intention of the book, except inasmuch as it might be misconstrued by living members of the Henson family, some of whom were the author's comrades in arms in the Canadian army. The writer wishes to assure them that no personal disrespect is intended and feels sure that a certain objectivity—a great deal of good along with some bad—will be found throughout the story.

The life of Josiah Henson is illuminating because it shows how a man was formed in slavery and in freedom. Lewis Clark, himself an escaped slave and the author of a narrative from which Mrs. Stowe borrowed some of her material, said, "Slavery was a curious blend of force and concession; of arbitrary disposal by the master and self-direction by the slave; of tyranny and benevolence; of antipathy and affections." The escape from slavery often involved a moral decision on the part of the slave, curious though that may seem, which has a relevance today. So, in our own time, a moral decision, complicated by social and economic factors, faces every individual of the Negro group who comes in contact, as indeed he must, with the dominant white majority. Whether or not a Negro will be called an Uncle Tom by his own people depends on the manner in which he conducts himself in his dealings with whites.

The term, *Uncle Tom,* has become a cant phrase among American Negroes, along with half a hundred other synonyms in current slang, but the type of person to whom it refers is known in other minority groups as well. The Japanese-Americans or the Jews might well adopt the term for those of their leaders who counsel compromise rather than struggle. There are, of course, both Negroes and whites who will defend the manner in which an Uncle Tom conducts his relations with the rest of the world. They assure themselves that there is no other way in which the things that are vitally necessary at the moment can be obtained, and are inclined to find justification for their point of view by claiming that they are "practical" and by pointing to the achievements of a man like Booker T. Washington. What may have been true at one time—and perhaps even then to a much more limited extent than they are willing to admit—is no longer true today. To continue to conform consciously to a pattern of segregation is to assure the fact that segregation with all its attendant evils will continue to exist. If, therefore, an attempt is made in this book to represent Henson as a three-dimensional character, it does not imply in any way that today it is possible to condone actions similar to his.

One can no longer believe that either *Uncle Tom's Cabin* or the John Brown raid at Harper's Ferry *caused* the Civil War in the United States. Rather, both Uncle Tom and John Brown were created and shaped by the same deep forces in society which brought about the irrepressible conflict. At the time, of course, both John Brown and Uncle Tom were identified with the war in the popular imagination, which always seeks an easy, obvious, and often humanized symbol in order to create a hero through whose actions a world event can be interpreted according to the customs which rule each private life.

The popular attitude was conveniently shaped into capsule form by Oliver Wendell Holmes:

> All through the conflict up and down
> Marched Uncle Tom and Old John Brown;
>   One ghost, one form ideal:
> And which was false and which was true
> And which was mightier of the two
>   The wisest Sibyl never knew
>   For both alike were real.

In the image of the poet, Brown was the form ideal, though his body lay a-mouldering in the grave, while from that grave had sprung a song to claim that his soul went marching on. The old hymn tune to which they had set the words rolled and thundered through the ranks of the Union, or began, muffled and indistinct as the boots of tired men, to rise, gather, and swell into a mighty monotonous chorus of voices which carried the soldiers another mile and another mile.

The face of the nation was about to change.

The South hanged Brown at Charlestown in Virginia; Lee, not yet a general, had led the last charge against the engine house at Harper's Ferry on October 16, 1859; Stonewall Jackson was among those who saw Brown die one bright morning in December of the same year.

Death had delivered him: "This is a beautiful country; I never had the pleasure of seeing it before," he said to those who led him out to the gallows, and it was true that he had seen no country before except the country of his vision. Now he was done with camp and countermarch. The Kansas War, the secret journeys, the convention in Canada, the shepherding of slaves to safety, and the expedition undertaken had led him here inevitably. In the letters which he was allowed to write from prison—they proved stronger weapons against the "peculiar institution" than the pikes with which he had proposed to arm the slaves —we hear the voice of a happy man sure of his destiny. Old John Brown, Osawatomie Brown, the angry prophet and antique hero, knew that the principal condition of his new-found happiness was the limit of time in which he could enjoy it; he was already free. "I am worth now infinitely more to die than to live."

To those who have written of the last days before the attack on Harper's Ferry it has seemed probable that he planned it to be a glorious failure. If that was indeed so, what faith he had in himself and in his followers that he should tell them nothing of his plans! He was always a secret man, and he knew where he went. With no insurrection of slaves behind him and the knowledge that even some of the abolitionists would forswear him, he stormed to "an almost certain immortality, dragging with him certain unwilling gentlemen who will be embarrassed to find themselves there as his murderers." The manner of his failure was to be the very measure of his success. A strong man and his sons were gone to their death achieving a great goal—in fact, and in agreement with the poet's syntax, Brown was the "form ideal." But what of Uncle Tom? What was he?

Uncle Tom, then, was a "ghost" because he was a character from fiction and because Harriet Beecher Stowe had killed him off in such impressive literary fashion that no one could doubt that he was really in heaven with Little Eva. Yet was he only a character from the book? The poet would seem to imply, and the Sibyl must surely have known, that both he and John Brown were real.

Uncle Tom's Cabin, or, Life among the Lowly poured out from the presses like an avalanche and swept away the greater part of its readers in a torrent of tears, though here and there it was answered by a countertorrent of abuse. In a few years people were to say that it was "the book that had started the war." Everyone read it; almost everyone saw it acted as well. Uncle Tom, Little Eva, Topsy, Simon Legree, Eliza, all became giant-size as they played out their drama in theaters and in tents behind the kerosene flares and the pine-pitch torches. Even Mrs. Stowe, for the one time in an otherwise virtuous life, was known to have stolen into a theater—heavily veiled, of course—to see her creatures on the stage.

It was Harriet Beecher Stowe who without a doubt was the best-hated woman south of Mason and Dixon's line, and the ranks of the Northern army were filled with young men who had, when the war broke out, scarcely left her book behind them in the nursery. Yet it was not the shade of a poke bonnet and bustle that Mr. Holmes saw in the smoke of battle. No, it was that "old darky" with his aureole of cotton-wool hair and beard that the poet thought he saw there: Uncle Tom, bobbing and bowing, loving as he suffered. Yes, Massa; no, Massa. It was this picture of a subservient Negro, his master's friend, the conciliator and turn-the-other-cheek brother, which Mrs. Stowe presented for the admiration of the nineteenth century.

"Uncle Tom" meant one thing to the nineteenth century, but today the term means something quite different. For while John Brown has passed into history and legend, it is Uncle Tom who goes marching on. He is the ghost of a certain relationship between the races in America, and as he marches toward the second half of the twentieth century his is a ghost which must be laid.

It is in the hope of laying his ghost that this book is written. To the problem with which we are presented in this country and elsewhere by the color bar—segregation, the job ceiling, and every other evidence of prejudice—there is no solution which does not involve struggle. The use of force is not an abstract or academic question, for force is used every day in one form or another by those who wish to ensure that the lines continue to be drawn according to race or religion.

The enforcement of discrimination by legal means, or by extralegal means which are condoned by public opinion, is an application of force against a minority group which is bewildering to anyone who has read the American Constitution. If such acts are acceptable to the majority of Americans, it can be only because of a lack of understanding of the age-old technique of divide and conquer. New evidences of the common interest of the majority of the people are continually coming to light, yet the old methods of subjugation will continue to work if they are not understood.

In order to divide people it is necessary to do so in a manner that seems logical, or at least obvious, and which plays upon their own sense of insecurity. This division may be accomplished according to the skin pigmentation, though the line of demarcation might just as well, in the absence of a pigmented group, be pushed to its absurd conclusion and, after a suitable period of inculcation of prejudice, the mass might well be split according to the color of the eye. Then we might have a war of the Blue Eyes against the Brown Eyes. Hitler almost succeeded.

Yet, while one group is elevated at the expense of the other, the mass pressure generated in the subject group must be occasionally relieved. In order best to accomplish this—to provide a safety valve, as it were—an influential individual in the minority can be allowed special privilege on the understanding that he will, in exchange, work to soften the ugly moods and to pacify the anger of his fellows. Such a man can be had in many ways, and he need not be a villain—as indeed Josiah Henson was not. The Uncle Tom of any group can be persuaded to accept a position of minor importance, where his every gesture will, in fact, be padded with compromise, if he can be made to feel that his elevation is not only an individual triumph but is an achievement which, by reflection, will be of benefit to the minority from which he comes. Unless the person concerned be of high moral character and integrity of purpose, it is easy to succumb to comfort and advantage, to become a mere tool.

It may seem almost cynical to say that to a large extent this is happily not possible for members of the Negro minority. The maneuver cannot be managed well enough because of the rigidity of the system of prejudice which surrounds *all* men and women of color. An affluent Negro, or one who has achieved distinction, will find it as arduous and even impossible as will his poorest and most illiterate brother to achieve and enjoy the equality which is his legal right. True enough, he can turn his back and attempt to segregate himself in a Black Society or Black Economy as certain groups have done in the past, or, driven by despair and the mirage of material success, attempt to gain it or a semblance of such success by whatever means are closest to hand. If in the attempt he must be servile or a clown, he is most likely to be called an Uncle Tom by those who know their folk history, for Uncle Tomism has a long tradition to which, unwittingly, Mrs. Stowe gave a permanent name.

In the days of the Big House, when the plantation flourished, the house servants were in a position far superior to that of the field servants; they, and above all perhaps the women, made cultural and economic advances which are still reflected in the lives and life patterns of the Negro population of today. The house servants were usually those who were brought up from childhood in close contact with the lives of the masters, and it is little wonder if they came to identify their own interests with those of the owners. This identification produced a conflict not only between the two groups of slaves but also in the personal lives of those slaves who benefited from the advantages of increased freedom of movement and intimate contact with their masters. The house servants came to patronize the field hands, regarding themselves as superior, since they had learned that which never could be learned in the cotton fields—the manners and customs of the country to which they were to belong—and in consequence they exercised their native ingenuity in improving the domestic accomplishments of American life. Field work and the system, on the other hand, drove from the minds of the field slaves all that they had ever been in the past—whatever it had been.

The house servants were the first among their fellows to learn the art of reading and writing, at a time when it was punishable by law to teach a slave to read. They thus became the spokesmen of the field hands, their brothers in oppression, who had grievances which they found it difficult to express, for they were neither as articulate as the house servant nor could they get the ear of the master as easily. At the same time the field workers admired, envied, and hated the house servant who had become their arbitrator—the go-between on whose interest and ingenuity they often depended for comfort and safety.

The house servant, while he might sometimes be inclined to forget it in the warmth of the Big House or in the just pride that he had in his accomplishments, was nevertheless a slave himself, in constant fear of being sent back to the cotton fields and the rice swamp. Though he might consider the welfare of his fellows enough to intercede for them, or to aid them secretly in his function as butler by giving them handouts from the back porch, yet, even with the best of intentions, he soon came to know the rather narrow limits beyond which he could not go. The system made him a compromiser, and thus it was not he but the system which was at fault. In all truth, his intentions were often good, and even when they were not, or did not seem to be, little personal fault could be attributed to him, for like all men he was the sum of his personal qualities shaped in the greater mold of his environment. Yet what Mrs. Stowe saw in the type as heroic and admirable were the same qualities which brought a sneer to the lips of those who knew him most intimately; no wonder the Negroes recognized Uncle Tom when they found him in the pages of her book.

It is doubtful, however, whether anyone would have recognized the human counterpart of Mrs. Stowe's character quite as easily, for he was a much more complex character than it was within her comprehension, or perhaps her ability, to depict. If he had not left an account of his own life from which to draw the details of his story and in which can be seen the reflection of his character, it would be impossible to see him truly today. Mrs. Stowe could not kill Josiah Henson, and she had to excuse herself more than once for the "artistic necessity" which had obliged her to kill him in her book, under the guise of Uncle Tom, with such gusto that he often found it difficult to persuade people of his identity.

We will let the man speak for himself in an extract from a speech that he made when he was already known half the world over as Uncle Tom, and found no cause to be ashamed of the name. We will let him prove that he was

not dead in 1877, and then turn to the story of his life to find what made him
the sort of man he was.

| 2 |

*According to the *Dumfries and Galloway Standard* of Scotland for Wednes-
day, April 25, 1877, Josiah Henson was "loudly cheered" when he began his
speech:

There has been so much written and said about me, and so many things
thought about me that I did not know I could do better than come and let
you see me. (*Laughter and applause.*) It has been spread about that "Uncle
Tom" is coming and that is what has brought you here. Now allow me to
say that my name is not Tom and never was Tom and that I do not want
any other name inserted in the newspapers for me but my own. My name is
Josiah Henson, always was and always will be. I never change my colours.
(*Loud laughter.*) I could not if I would and would not if I could. (*Renewed
laughter.*) Well, inquiry in the minds of some has led to inquiry in the
minds of others. You have read and heard some persons say that Uncle Tom
was dead. And could he be here? It is an imposition that is being practised
on us. Very well, I do not blame you for saying that. I do not think you are
to blame. A great many people in this country have come to me and asked
me if I was not dead. (*Laughter.*) Well now to remove this difficulty if it ex-
ists in your minds. As a matter of course, it is not pleasant for me to hear
that I am traversing this country and practising an imposition on people.
No it is not pleasant; and the only way I have to meet it is to say that it
shows me that people ain't well read, or have forgotten what they read, if
they have ever read it at all. They have forgotten that Mrs. Stowe's *Uncle
Tom's Cabin* is a novel; and that it must have seemed a glorious finish to that
novel that she should kill her hero . . . a glorious finish. Now you can get
the *Key to Uncle Tom's Cabin* . . . you can buy it for about sixpence, about
fifteen or sixteen cents . . . and you commence and read it. I see that gentleman along there setting it down. (*Referring to our reporter.*) That is all right.
(*Laughter.*) I see you. (*Laughter.*) Well, you commence at the 34th chapter
and you read up to the 57th and I think you will there see me. (*Applause.*)

You remember that when the novel of Mrs. Stowe came out, it shook the
foundations of this world. It shook the Americans out of their shoes and of
their shirts. It left some of them on the sandbar barefooted and scratching

their heads, so they came to the conclusion that the whole thing was a fabrication, a falsehood and a lie; and they accused her of writing it and they demanded of her a clue or a key to the novel she had written, the exposure she had made and the libel she had fixed on the United States.

And so as she was in duty bound to give something, she, I think in 1853, brought out the *Key*, between you and she, and in that she spoke of me, and in that way set the Negro free. (*Laughter and applause.*)

I am not Robert Burns . . . (*Laughter.*) but that is a fact. (*Applause.*)

You will find in that *Key* of me the position which I held in relation to her work.

They said there were never any such things perpetrated on the Negroes; never any Negroes so afflicted, and that the book was a libel on the people of the United States; and when she took to this *Key* she told them where they would find a man called Josiah Henson. She gave me a great name and said I was a venerable fellow, in which she was not much mistaken, for I was an old man, to be found in Canada West, laboring there as a minister of the Gospel, preaching to the fugitive slaves, encouraging the cause of education and building up the poor afflicted race of Negroes. (*Applause.*)

Josiah Henson, then, is my name.

Josiah Henson, then, was his name. The black baby was born June 15, 1789, and was the first to be born on the estate of a Mr. Francis Newman, who owned the father, and to whom the mother had been hired out. He was called Josiah for a Dr. Josiah MacPherson of Charles County, Maryland, who owned his mother, and Henson for an uncle of the doctor who had been an officer in the Revolutionary War.

On the Newman estate, which was about a mile from Port Tobacco, in the state of Maryland, the child grew to the age of memory, carried on his mother's back in the fields or playing on the beaten-earth floor of the slave quarters. His memory, which was excellent, was to serve him well in later years and to be of use to Mrs. Stowe, for his story was first taken down from him in 1849 by a Mr. S. A. Eliot and published in Boston the same year. There Mrs. Stowe was to come across it in the reading rooms of the Abolitionist Society and was to be immediately struck by the vivid picture of slave life which it gave. It was written without the showman's patter of the speech which we have quoted, but all the elements of her melodrama were there in their terrible reality.

Josiah's memory of his father was a tragic one, for he saw him brought back to the slave quarters, half-dead, after having been beaten for striking an overseer who had attacked his mother. He had wounded the overseer and then hidden out in the woods, but hunger had driven him back to find food. He was soon captured and whipped in front of the poor whites and slaves of the neighborhood who gathered to witness the ceremony—one hundred lashes and mutilation being the penalty for his offense. After having assured themselves that he could stand the whole punishment, his owners had him flogged by the blacksmith.

Then, while he was semiconscious, his right ear was tacked to the whipping post; a slash with a knife and the ear was left on the post as he fell to the ground.

After this brutality, the slave became so surly and intractable that Newman decided that he could no longer safely keep him on the plantation and sold him to someone in Alabama. Josiah's mother and five brothers and sisters never saw him again nor heard what became of him. Dr. MacPherson, who owned the mother and therefore the children, demanded their return of Newman, for he did not hold with such cruelty. They lived for two or three years more on his estate until, kindly man that he was, he tipped up one too many, as kindly men will, and fell flat on his face in a stream and drowned there.

The death of a kind master was a great calamity for the slaves, for it meant change, and change was rarely for the better in their experience. Upon the death of MacPherson the remnants of the Henson family were to be put on the auction block—the most dreaded experience in the life of a slave, no matter how often repeated. The cruel humiliation of being put on exhibit for sale, and the overwhelming fear that one might be sold "down south," were factors quite as terrible as the certainty that families would be torn apart and that a common past of love and shared experience would be lost forever. Every slave's life was a small circle beaten out around the tethering post; communication was impossible over the shortest distance; history was a black pit and oral tradition a fabric shredded into rags, torn and scattered to the winds by constant partings. Nothing remained of yesterday and nothing could be expected of tomorrow. Human beings mated and bred in cages; the rumor of a sale was enough to stampede them.

The auction block was a little dais with three or four steps leading up to it which each slave had to mount while the auctioneer read off his name, age, and accomplishments. Josiah's brothers and sisters exhibited their teeth and muscles, jumped and danced to show their agility and were bid off first. Then his mother was sold to Isaac Riley of Montgomery County, Maryland, and she begged him to buy her Josiah, too, in order that she might not be separated from the last of the children. Since he had no need of the child and refused to buy him, the boy was bought by a man who owned a tavern near Montgomery courthouse some miles away. This man, a tavern owner named Robb, had a line of stagecoaches and owned about forty slaves, among whom he threw the child of six.

Josiah sickened and lay all day on the dirt floor, uncared for by any of the other slaves who were too brutalized by their own treatment to think of bothering with him. He was left all day alone while they were driven out into the fields or about their other work, and, when they returned at night, they threw him a piece of corn bread or a dried herring so long as he could still eat. Soon, however, he was unable to move and lay there near death. By chance, Robb, his new owner, met Riley, who had bought the mother, and offered him the child in return for a payment which was to be made in horseshoeing. Riley agreed, and Josiah was returned to his mother who nursed him back to health.

He grew in Riley's service and learned all the lessons that a cruel master could teach: "The character and the habits of the slave and the slaveholder were created and perpetuated by their relative position," says the autobiography, but it was to be more than sixty years before Henson could express himself in that concise and elegant way, if indeed the words were not put into his mouth by a ghost writer. At any rate, he was clever and observant, quick to learn and critical of his environment even as a boy. The slaves on Riley's place were beasts of the field who huddled ten or a dozen to a pen and slept on the ground. In their log huts were no wooden floors, no furniture but beds made of a heap of rags thrown on the trodden mud and boxed in with a board or two. Henson said of this way of life: "Our favorite way of sleeping, however, was on a plank, our heads raised on an old jacket and our feet toasting before the smoldering fire. The wind whistled and the rain and snow blew in through the cracks while the damp earth soaked up the moisture until the floor was miry as a pigsty."

The principal food on Riley's farm was cornmeal and salt herring, to which, in summer, there was added a little buttermilk from the churnings and a few vegetables which were grown in truck patches and tended after dark when the field work was done. There were two regular meals a day: breakfast at twelve, after work since dawn, and a supper when the day was over. In harvest season there were three meals, for then the work was harder and a little dried meat was added to their diet. Clothing was of tow cloth, with only a shirt for children. As they grew up, they were also given a pair of pantaloons or a gown, and in winter a round coat, and a wool hat once in two or three years, and one pair of shoes a year.

Under even these conditions Josiah grew to be strong and agile as a young buck, he says; he could run faster, wrestle better, dance better, jump higher than any of the others on the farm. At fifteen he could outhoe, outreap, outhusk all the other slaves; and he worked all day in the field and ran through the orchard at night with the wild young ones following him, to steal and broil a chicken and plot first-rate tricks to dodge work. Yet he loved to work because it brought him to the notice of the overseer, and praise was dear to him. "One word of commendation from the petty despot who ruled over us would set me up for a month." Josiah had not the makings of Uncle Tom for nothing, and there was just one way for a slave to better his lot and that was to move toward the Big House.

If there was another way, the way of escape, Josiah had not yet heard of it, and in all fairness to him it must be said that the means hardly existed at this time. From the earliest years of the nineteenth century, individual slaves had begun to escape from the plantations and make their way north to the free states. Many of those who ran away from the slave masters of the deep South marked a trail with their corpses or were caught and returned for punishment, mutilation, or death as an example to their fellows. Means of communication were closely guarded by armed patrols who demanded a pass of any Negro who might, in extraordinary circumstances, be traveling alone. The nature of the country, with its dismal swamps, broad marshes, and savannahs, made any travel, except by the few well-known roads, almost impossible. Nonetheless, some did from the earliest years manage to get to the northern states, as can be proven by the record of several attempts made in the late eighteenth century on the part of slave owners who wished to have their property returned to them. Even during Henson's boyhood several ex-slaves had managed to make their way to Canada and a more secure freedom beyond the reach of American law, but the legend of the North Star, which led and guided those pushed by a relentless hunger for freedom, had not yet become part of the folklore whispered in the slave quarters of every plantation. One cannot blame young Henson for not knowing that there were sweeter joys than the rare and careless word of praise from the man who cracked the whip; that is, one cannot blame him yet. The fault in his nature, the fissure line along which it can be split, does not become evident until he is an older man. In his boyhood, typical as it was of the slave boy of superior talent and physical endowment, we can trace the causes. Let those who can, read an analogy in the circumstances and social pressures that surround, form, and shape a boy born today into the same racial group, however the legal freedom of that group may have changed in a century or so.

Young Henson would naturally reject the movement to revolt, for his first memory was that of the tragedy to which a movement of revolt had led his father, and one cannot doubt that his mother constantly reminded him of its terrible consequences. She had stood there, calling on her husband to cease beating the overseer, and had persuaded him not to kill the man who had attacked her. She was a religious woman who taught her child that violence was in all cases evil and that one must submit and trust to prayer, and she must have worried over his high-spirited escapades and boyish devilry, thinking that it might lead him to a tragic end.

[[After undergoing a religious conversion around 1807, Henson became a more submissive and willing worker, rising in influence on the Riley estate until he became overseer. Recognized for his industry and his knowledge of farming and managing property, he supervised his fellow slaves with kindness, always seeking to ease their hardships. Gradually he took over management of the accounts and did all the buying and selling. During this time, having defended his master in a brawl, he was brutally attacked by the overseer of Riley's brother, Amos; Henson, his arms broken and his shoulder blades smashed, was maimed for life. In 1825 Isaac Riley needed to dodge his creditors, so he asked a favor of his loyal slave: to lead all of his slaves down to Kentucky to his brother's plantation. Henson succeeded in the perilous journey, proudly keeping his promise and maintaining his sense of moral virtue, even as he rejected opportunities from freed slaves on the Ohio side of the river for them all to seek their freedom. A few years later, Riley decided to sell the slaves he had sent to Kentucky, except Henson, whom he wanted returned. Henson grew determined to buy his freedom and raised most of the money during his trek back to Maryland by preaching on a detour through Ohio. But Riley cheated him out of the deal. Left with nothing but ineffective manumission papers, Henson returned to his family on the Kentucky plantation. Yet even then, in that period of unrest prior to Nat Turner's rebellion of 1831, as a secret plan of revolt gained momentum, he persuaded the slaves to desist from rebellion as an act that was too dangerous and above all not Christian, once again becoming a sort of accomplice in the perpetuation of their misery.]]

/ 6 /

One day Riley suddenly announced that his young son, who was also called Amos, was going down the river to New Orleans in a flat-bottomed boat full of farm produce. Henson was to go with him, and they were to start the next day and dispose of the cargo to the best advantage. Josiah knew at once what this meant. He was to be sold too. No one said so, but he was sure of it. Rumors of an exchange of letters between the brothers had come from the Big House, and this was the result. Either those two intended turning him into riches without wings and to share the money, or Mr. Amos was stealing a march on his brother. Henson never knew.

He told his wife to sew the precious paper in a cloth, and then to sew the cloth around his waist. It might yet be useful; at any rate, he would have it with him wherever he was to go.

The boat was loaded with beef cattle, pigs, poultry, corn whisky, and other merchandise. Three white men were hired to handle the boat. Henson said goodbye, perhaps forever, to his family and stepped aboard. He was the only Negro, and was, therefore, forced to stand more watches than all the rest, but this turned to his advantage, for he quickly learned all that there was to know about handling the boat. Very soon, he could shoot by a "sawyer," land on a bank, avoid a snag or a steamboat in the rapid current of the Mississippi as well as the captain himself. The latter seemed to have developed some disease of the eyes and actually became blind. Henson took over. He was, in fact, the master of the boat, although he did not have any more idea of what lay around the next bend than did the others, for none of them had ever been down the river before. They had to halt at night and travel by day.

At night someone had to keep watch. They were in danger of river pirates and bands of escaped Negroes who, until they were captured or killed, lived as marauders in the wilds along the river's banks. These Negroes lived in a sort of primitive freedom, frequently attacking such boats as were tied up for the night, killing and robbing.

At one stop, a curious incident took place. This was at Vicksburg, where Henson got permission to visit a plantation a few miles inland. It might have been gossip from the Big House, the grapevine, or a chance remark made by young Amos Riley which told him that it was to this place that his former fellow-slaves and charges had been sold. It was the saddest visit he ever made. He found his friends old and broken after only four years in this malarial climate. They worked long hours, half-naked, in the marshes under the burning sun, ill-treated and ill-fed; they were tortured by mosquitoes, horseflies, and black gnats, and thought only of death as a deliverance. At first sight of Josiah they cried, and when he told of his own predicament they felt sorry that he was to be subjected to the same fate to which they were condemned. They seem to have felt no resentment toward him for the part which he had played in their betrayal. The very fact that he went to visit them would seem to show that he expected none. Yet the memory of that wretched group was to haunt him until his death. He had sold them, and now he could cry over them, and pray and roll his eyes to heaven.

The boat drifted on down the great river. To his eye everything in man and in nature looked evil. He saw nothing but the wretched slavepens beside sullen, smelly, stagnant waters which harbored the bloated carcasses of drowned horses and oxen. These were covered with swarms of green flies that blew in clouds through the sticky atmosphere. From time to time huge turkey buzzards wheeled in the burning sky or fed on the half-putrid carcasses. The water extended for miles on either side, in broad steely sheets, bordered by half-dead, gaunt trees hung with funereal moss. Nothing was noble, nothing grandiose; he saw only the fate that awaited him. The world was ruled by whites and every white hand was against him. As he paced the deck during the nights of his long watches, he thought of the treacherous brothers, his masters. Here the son of one of them lay asleep in the cabin. In his power. He would kill him. It was only just.

"If this is to be my lot, I cannot survive it long. I could not live through what I saw on the plantation at Vicksburg. I am not so young as they are. Two years would kill me. Yes, death would free me. Sweet death. But why wait. They don't even suspect me. I am all smiles and 'yes, Massa; no, Massa.' They cannot see the tiger in my heart. Why should I not prevent this wrong? For it is wrong. Wrong that I should be sold and go there, after all that I have done for them. They would repay me with wickedness. One should prevent a wrong that is not yet done. They don't suspect; they don't know that I know. I could prevent it. Yes, but prevent it with an axe. That axe there. Then I would escape to freedom. I would be justified. I should be free. My Christian friends said I should be free. I could prevent them all from committing this wickedness. Tonight is dark, no one could hear me in this rain. I can wait no longer. We will be in New Orleans in a day or two and it will be too late to prevent this wickedness. This axe . . . ."

But he could not do it. His hand had slid along the smooth handle of the axe as he moved silently into the cabin where, by the dim light of a swinging lamp, he could see the sleeping form of young Amos. His hand had been raised to strike the blow, when the thought came to him, "What! Commit murder? And you a Christian?"

A thousand elements of irresolution weakened the arm that held the axe. Young Master Amos had done him no harm. He was only obeying the orders of his father. Josiah turned as silently as he had come and went out into the rain. He washed his hands and let them trail a long time in the night-cold current, for they were covered with imaginary blood which he alone could see. He shrank back into his old shape after his moment of murderous exaltation and now he was desperately afraid that the rage and hatred, the expression of his heart, might show in his face. He roused no one to take over the watch, but remained on the rain-swept deck the night through, alone. No one ever knew; no one ever guessed the tiger that had risen in the night and died away in his heart at its first encounter with his Christian feelings. The next day the four white men saw only old 'Siah, old Uncle Tom. "Yes, Massa. Right away, Massa." They never guessed.

A few days after this crisis, the boat reached New Orleans with what remained of the cargo aboard. They had sold the greater part of the load at the stops along the way, and now the three men who had been hired to handle the boat were discharged, as they had contracted for a one-way trip. Now that everything was sold, with the sole exception of the most domestic animal, the young master threw off all disguise and spoke openly of auctioning off Josiah as the only thing left to do before he broke up the boat for lumber, sold that, and took passage on a steamboat back to the Riley plantation.

Several planters and dealers came aboard to look Josiah over. He was sent on some hasty errand to fetch and carry that they might see how fast he could run. . . . Lift that box; bring me that whip. Quick now, let the gentlemen see your points. . . . Josiah was talked up as a bright fellow, but, perhaps because his arms were crippled, no one would meet the price that young Riley had been told to ask for him.

He had promised Josiah that he would try to sell him into a good position as a coachman or house servant, but as time went on he made no effort to fulfill his promise. He was getting impatient to be off and any sale would do. Josiah begged for his life. Young Riley sought to avoid him, for while he had been brought up in the ethic of slavery to think of a slave not as a man, but as chattel, mere property which had no rights and was thought of as possessing no feelings, yet his conscience troubled him. Josiah reminded him of things in their common past and sought to touch him by telling him of the plight of those other slaves in Vicksburg. At times he seemed so moved by the plea Josiah made that he was close to tears, yet again, when he felt too closely pressed in his inner conflict, he would curse and strike out at Josiah.

It was the month of June, when the terrible summer climate of New Orleans hung over the bayou and the last hot night seemed interminable to Josiah. He could not sleep, for he had been told that young Riley had booked a passage on the up-river paddle steamer and intended to leave the following evening at six, after having sold Josiah for whatever price he would bring. This then was the end; there was little hope now that he would ever be free or ever see his family again. He was a man of forty and could not long survive work in the fields or in the rice swamps.

The next morning Master Amos said that his stomach was disordered, and by eight o'clock, as the full heat of the day began to strike into the cramped cabin, he was utterly prostrate with a raging fever. Now it was another song: "I'm dying, 'Siah. It's the river fever. People in the city are dying of it. You are my only friend. Stick to me, 'Sie. Don't leave me. I'm sorry I was going to sell you. I didn't mean it. It was just a joke. You must stick by me now. Get on the steamer and get me home. I must go home."

It was quite a change; Josiah was no longer property, a beast to be bought and sold, but his master's only friend amidst strangers. Riley was now the suppliant, in fear of death, as he lay writhing in the shade of a sailcloth.

"Take me on the steamer, 'Siah. Take me home. You must sell the boat and get me and the trunk aboard the steamer tonight. All the money is in the trunk. You must stick to me, 'Siah."

Josiah said it was the answer from God.

They took twelve days to reach the Riley landing, for the water was low, particularly in the Ohio River, and navigation difficult. Before they were many hours away from New Orleans, the fever had subsided, but young Riley had been near death and lay weakly on his bunk, depending on Josiah for every attention. He could neither speak nor move, and his eyes followed the slave in entreaty for a teaspoonful of gruel or something to moisten his throat. Josiah nursed and tended him, saving his life, and when they at last reached the landing, Riley was carried to the Big House by a relay of slaves who took him on a litter over the five miles which separated it from the river's edge.

There was great surprise among the members of the family when they first saw Josiah, until they learned what his burden was, and then all attention was for the young man. A few first words of gratitude were all he ever received from them. "If I had sold him I would have died," said young Amos. Only the market value of their slave was of any consideration to them. The act which he had performed served to raise his value in their esteem, and Josiah thought that his master now looked at him with a glance that seemed even more greedy than before. He felt sure that another attempt would be made to sell him before long.

/ 7 /

The ruling force of Josiah Henson's life was the religion which he had learned, and he was convinced, according to the tenets which he professed, that a slave owed a duty to his master. In a moment of crisis such as had occurred during his trip down the river it was this acceptance of religious belief which had held his hand. He was gifted enough with introspection to be driven to the most intense self-examination in every circumstance of his life, and very often the conflict which was thereby exposed would allow of no solution. From his earliest years he had felt that he must justify himself in his own eyes, as in the case of a chicken which he "stole" from Isaac Riley. Now he needed justification to "steal" himself and his family. He must argue that the Riley brothers had conspired against his rights, as indeed they and the whole system had done, but further than the offense against his natural rights, they had sought to cheat him in the bargain which he had made with them for his liberty. This last infamy was what had decided him to take his wife and children and escape forever.

"If Isaac had only been honest enough to adhere to his bargain, I would adhere to mine and pay him all I had promised," Henson later wrote. "But his attempt to kidnap me again after having pocketed three-fourths of my market value, in my opinion absolved me from all obligations to pay him any more or to continue in a position which exposed me to his machinations."

On his trip through Ohio Josiah had heard of the Underground Railway. News of the Underground was whispered about everywhere by this time, but where was it? Where did it run? Could you hear it coming, see it? What was a train? The untutored slaves, and many whites too, were puzzled by the legend and the name. Around many a plantation fire it was pictured by hushed voices as an immense carriage traveling at great speed at night through a dark tunnel, on out of sight, and into freedom.

Lord, lead us out of Egypt's land. But where is thy train? If only one knew where to catch it, where to find it and go on to blessed freedom. One thought he had seen it rushing through the darkest forest in the night, while another thought that he had heard its lonely wail as it passed in the distance with its cargo of happy but frightened passengers. Yet no one really knew.

The Underground was running few "trains," and those mostly from the northern slave states at this time. The highly organized "excursions," the crowded schedules, did not get under way until the late 1840s, and above all after the Fugitive Slave Law of 1850. By that time "passage" cost a great deal of money, and quite extravagant ruses and extraordinary disguises were adopted to spirit slaves away to freedom. Yet, in 1830 there were, if one only knew where to knock and what to say, a few "stations" and "station masters," even in the South. An "agent," at the risk of his life, could send a fugitive slave on his way with a bold "conductor" who would take him all the way to the Canadian border.

Josiah had heard of the Underground in Ohio, but he did not know where it ran nor how. He knew only that it went to Canada, sure refuge from pursuit, and now he, too, determined to go there. It was a fearsome journey to undertake, and few men born to slavery would have dared to undertake it even had they suffered the same provocation as Josiah. He knew no "agent," had met no "shepherd" such as Harriet Tubman, who, in later years, would arrive mysteriously on a plantation and entice slaves away to freedom. His escape was to be entirely of his own doing. He was not even alone; he had his wife and four children to consider.

When he told Charlotte of his plan, she was overwhelmed with terror. She knew little or nothing beyond the warmth of her own hearthstone, and her imagination peopled the world outside the plantation with fantastic horrors.

"We shall die in the wilderness, 'Siah. They'll hunt us with the hounds and bring us back and whip us to death. You can't, 'Siah. I won't go."

He tried to persuade her that the chance for freedom was worth the risk, but she clung to her home and her children.

"I'll go alone. I'll leave you now and go alone. If we stay, Master Riley will sell me soon and you'll be alone anyway. I told you what I saw at Vicksburg. Before that, I'll go alone. No, I'll take the children too, all but the youngest."

The next day, when he left for the fields, she suddenly called him back and said that she would go, for she feared that he might go even then and not come back.

The greatest difficulty was presented by the two youngest children, who were two and three years old. They would have to be carried, and so, night after night, Josiah went into training. He had his wife make a sort of knapsack of tow cloth, with straps to go round his shoulders. The children could be slung in this. Every night he walked the cabin floor until dawn, while the children laughed and crowed at the fun until they fell asleep. Finally he found that he could manage them for long stretches without tiring. Now it was time to decide on a night to depart.

They chose a Saturday night because Sunday was a holiday, and on the following two days Josiah was supposed to oversee a job that was to be done on a farm some miles from the Big House. In this way, they would not be missed for some time, and it would give them a start on their pursuers.

Little Tom, his eldest child, was away from the cabin, for the family kept him in the Big House to work in the kitchen, and permission would have to be obtained for him to come and visit his mother. Toward sundown Josiah went up to report on the week's work, and after talking with the master for some time, started to turn away. "Oh, Massa Amos, I 'most forgot. Tom's mother wants to know if you won't let him come down a few days; she wants to mend his clothes, and fix him up a little."

"Yes, boy, yes. He can go."

"Thank 'ee, Mass' Amos. Good night, good night."

He could not prevent himself from throwing a good deal of emphasis into that last "good night." What a long good night to Massa that would be.

It was about the middle of September, and by nine o'clock it was dark enough to start. No moon lighted their way down to the landing where another slave was waiting to row them across the river in a little skiff. They sat still as death, crouched together, and rowed into midstream, where the oarsman stopped.

"It'll be the end of me if this is ever found out; but you won't be brought back alive, 'Sie, will you?"

"Not if I can help it," Josiah replied, thinking of the pistols and knife which he had bought some time back from a poor white on one of the outlying farms. "Not if I am shot through like a sieve."

"That's all," said the other slave, starting to row again. "And God help you."

They landed on the Indiana shore and began to beat through the wilderness, for they dared not approach the main highways. They walked on for two weeks by night, hiding by day, while Josiah carried the two children slung on his back. He did not know where to find any sympathizers, nor did he dare to look for any. There might be a few people in the neighborhood who were merely indifferent, but Josiah felt that most likely any white was an enemy who would send them all back to be beaten to death in order to claim the reward and protect the system.

Actually, many houses in Ohio and Indiana were already marked with the secret signs which only those of the Underground could recognize. Three white bricks set in the wall beneath the eaves were a sign that a fugitive could safely knock on that door and expect to be taken in or sent along to the next "station" under the seat of a wagon. Henson was merely heading for Cincinnati as best he could, the North Star his only guide. Two days away from that city, where he depended on finding friends, he was forced to risk capture by daylight because his family was starving. His wife reproached him for having brought them into such danger. The children kept whimpering from hunger, and while he could speak sternly to his trembling wife, he could quiet them no longer. His back was now raw from the rubbing of the homemade knapsack; the only thing to do was to adopt a bold course of action.

He walked quickly out onto the highroad and turned south, with the idea that it might lull suspicion should he meet anyone. At the first house to which he came, he was attacked by a dog whose owner curtly refused to accept his offer to buy bread and meat. At the next house a man answered in the same surly fashion, but his wife came quickly after him and said, "How can you treat a human so? If the dog was hungry you'd feed him. We have children of our own who may some day need a friend."

The man replied, laughing, "If you have need of such friends, then feed him," and turned away.

The woman put out a plate of venison and bread, refusing money when he offered her a quarter for it, and added more food, sending him on his way with a "God bless you."

He hurried back to where his family lay hidden and fed them. But almost at once they cried out for water because the meat was so salty. Josiah stole away to search out a stream, but having no container in which to carry water, he first tried his hat, which leaked, and then rinsing out his shoes, filled them and brought them back to drink from.

The Henson family at last arrived at the outskirts of Cincinnati, and Josiah hid them in the woods while he entered the town at dusk to find the friends that he had made there among the Methodists. He was warmly greeted by them and sent to fetch his wife and children, but they could stay only long enough to rest and gather a little strength. The fugitive slave laws were federal statutes, and the town of Cincinnati was no longer safe. The power of these laws was such that they could reach into the free states to pluck back a fugitive. Methodist friends sent them on about thirty miles in a wagon, and then they again had to follow the same course as before: traveling by night and resting by day.

They were told that when they arrived at a place called Scioto they would strike a military road which had been cut through the forest by order of General Hull during the War of 1812. The beginning of this road was marked by a large sycamore and elm grove, and they had been told they might travel along it by day. The road was safe because it had been cut through the wilderness and no one lived along it, nor was it much traveled. The road was considerably overgrown, and difficult, and when by nightfall they had passed no houses, they began to be alarmed, for they had brought few provisions with them. Furthermore, Josiah could now barely carry the two small children; the knapsack had rubbed all the skin from his back. They had further cause for alarm in the howling of the wolves, which they could hear in the darkness of the forest. However, they were not molested by these animals, and lay down to sleep.

The next day they started off again with only enough salt-jerked beef to make them intolerably thirsty. The underbrush caught at them and tore their clothes, while the road was often blocked by wind-fallen trees over whose trunks the children and Charlotte could climb only with difficulty. Henson himself struggled on a short distance ahead. His wife fainted once, and continually moaned that she could go no further, that they were foolish ever to have left home.

After struggling along for some hours, they saw a number of persons with heavy loads on their backs approaching around a bend, and, as they could expect to meet no friends, they were at once on the alert. Charlotte screamed that they were Indians and that they would all be scalped and killed if they did not run. The Indians continued to advance, while Josiah argued with his wife that it was useless to try to escape. Suddenly, the Indians, who were so heavily burdened that they had not raised their eyes from the ground until now, looked up and caught sight of the little group of Negroes. They stood stock-still for a frozen moment and then, hastily throwing off their packs, ran howling back, disappearing into the woods in all directions.

His wife insisted that they had gone back to get help and would soon return in greater numbers, and begged Josiah to flee with her. He resolved, on the contrary, to follow them, for he was certain that it was terror that had caused their retreat, and assured her that it was a ridiculous thing for both parties to run away, stricken by mutual fear.

The little band of Negroes advanced—the children clutching their parents and whimpering all the while because Indians peeped at them from behind trees and flitted through the deepness of the woods that bordered what was little more than a trail. It is a strange picture that one gets here of the fearsome Indians of legend, who were themselves to be a source of terror and fireside tales for at least another half-century. They apparently thought that the Hensons were suffering from some terrible disease which had blackened their faces, for this particular band had never encountered Negroes before. During the years that were to follow, the Indians gave aid to many a fugitive slave in his bitter journey through the wilderness that bordered Canada, where even today none but an experienced woodsman can find his way. In the narratives of escape one continually comes upon the statement made by a runaway to the effect that he owed his safe passage over that part of his journey—in which he had more to fear from nature than from man—to the nomad Indians whom he encountered by chance.

Josiah and his family soon came on the Indian camp. There they were met by an older man who appeared to be the chief, and as soon as he had assured himself that they were human beings, he spoke a word or two in scorn to those around him and ordered them to bring food. Josiah's children, after the weeks in the woods during which they had seen none but their parents, were shy as wood creatures themselves. Each time they were approached by the curious Indians, they would shrink back with a little cry of alarm, while the Indian who wished to touch them would jump back too with an echo of the same little shriek. They arrived at some degree of understanding through sign language, and after the Hensons were fed, they were given a wigwam in which to spend the night. The next day they were accompanied a short distance on their way by some of the young men who told them that they were now only about twenty-five miles from the lake.

They had to ford a stream or two and pass one more night in the woods before they came out on a wide, treeless plain, southwest of Sandusky. Here they must be bold once more, so Josiah hid the family and pushed forward alone toward a house that he saw on the shore. A number of men were busily engaged in loading a small vessel. As he approached, the captain of the vessel shouted out to him, "Holoo, old man, you want to work?"

"Yes, sir," Josiah shouted back.

"Come along, come along. I'll give you a shilling an hour. Must get off with this wind." And then he added as Josiah approached, "Oh, you can't work, you're crippled."

"Can't I?" said Josiah scornfully, and in a moment he had hold of a bag and was following the gang in emptying it into the hold.

He took his place in the line of laborers next to a colored man, and soon got into conversation with him.

"How far is it to Canada?" he asked.

And when the other fellow gave him a knowing look, he realized that he was at once understood.

"Want to go to Canada? Come along with us then. Our captain's a fine fellow who will take you. We are going to Buffalo."

"Buffalo? How far is that from Canada?"

"Don't you know, man? Just across the river."

At this Josiah decided to tell him that he was not alone, but that his wife and children were hidden not far off.

"I'll speak to the captain," said the other. In a few minutes the captain beckoned Josiah aside.

"The doctor says you want to go to Buffalo with your family. Well, why not go with me, then? Doc says you got a family. Bring them too."

"Yes, sir!"

"Where do you stop?"

"About a mile back."

"How long you been there?"

"No time at all," replied Josiah after a moment's hesitation.

"Come, my good fellow, tell us all about it. You're running away, ain't you? How long will it take you to get ready?"

"Be back in half an hour, sir."

"Well, get you along then, and fetch them."

But before Josiah had gone fifty yards, he called him back. "You go on getting the grain in. When we get off, I'll lay to, over opposite that island, and send a boat back. There's a lot of regular nigger-catchers in the town below, and they might suspect if you brought your party out of the bush by daylight."

Josiah worked while his heart sang, and soon the two or three hundred bushels of wheat were aboard, the hatches fastened down, the anchor raised and sail hoisted.

He watched the vessel leave its mooring and run before the breeze. Already she seemed to have passed the spot at which the captain had said he would lay to. He was sure they were leaving without him; a moment before, his hope had been so great that now he was utterly crushed. What cruel sport they had made of him! But no, she swung around in the wind, the sails flapping as the ship lay motionless. The sun set, leaving the world in a dusk which would make it safe for him to lead his wife and children down to the water's edge. Aboard ship he could see that they were lowering a boat, and the oars flashed as they rowed toward the shore.

The black man to whom Josiah had spoken had come along with two other sailors. They jumped ashore and the four of them started off together to the place where the other Hensons lay hidden. They searched the whole area, for at first Josiah was not sure just where his family had been. He could not believe his senses, but, yes, they were gone. He was frozen with horror, as he supposed that they had been found and carried off. The three sailors told him that as there was no time to lose, he must come along back to the ship with them. Filled with despair, he turned to follow, when he stumbled across one of the children, lying in the grass. In a moment he came upon the others, and finally found Charlotte, who lay speechless in a thicket. She had given him up for lost as he had been gone so long, and had supposed he had been captured. When she heard his voice along with the voices of several other men, she believed that he had been forced to come back for the rest of them. In her terror, she had tried to hide, and when he came upon her, she was gripped with silent paroxysms of hysteria in which she could understand nothing of what he said. They had to drag and carry her to the boat before she recovered herself sufficiently to understand that at last they were near freedom.

As they neared the ship at anchor in midstream, the captain, who was a Scot, leaned over the taffrail and shouted, "Come up on deck and clop your wings and craw like a rooster; you're a free nigger as sure as you're a live man." And with that welcome they came aboard.

Round went the vessel, the wind plunged into her sails and the water seethed and hissed past her sides. The tension of the past weeks had been too abruptly released, and even Josiah cried that night.

The following evening they reached Buffalo, but it was too late to cross the river that night. The next morning the captain called Josiah on deck, and pointing to the distance, said, "You see those trees; they grow on free soil, and as soon as your feet touch that, you're a *man*. I want to see you go and be a free man. I'm poor myself and have nothing to give you. I only sail this boat for wages, but I'll see you across." And then he called to the ferryman, "What will you take this man and his family over for—he's got no money."

"Three shillings will do it."

The captain reached into his pocket and, pulling out a dollar, gave it to Josiah and said, "Be a good fellow, won't you?"

"Yes, I'll use my freedom well. God bless you."

It was the morning of October 28, 1830, and when Josiah jumped from the ferry, he threw himself on the sand, kissed it, and jumped around shouting like a madman.

"He's some crazy fellow," said a Colonel Warren, who happened to be there.

"Oh, no, Master, don't you know? I am free."

The colonel burst into a shout of laughter and said, "Well, I never knew freedom made a man roll on the sand in such a fashion."

Dawn in Canada

/ 1 /

Up until the time that Josiah Henson landed from the Buffalo ferry and stepped onto Canadian soil, we have no firsthand account of his life but his own. We know only what he chose to tell of his first forty-one years, but what he had to tell was in itself extraordinarily revealing both of the material conditions and the human relations developed by the slave system. There may be a great number of things left unsaid, or forgotten for a purpose, in the story of his early years as it appears in his autobiography; yet there is, on the other hand, much told by himself which is not entirely to his credit. He had great powers of observation and often a frank and ingenuous fashion of revealing the complexities of his own character.

Many of his faults he laid to the account of the system in which he had been brought up, but he did not change much in later years. We may infer that important events have been left out of his own story of the first period of his life because the second part of the book, which deals with Henson's life in freedom, neglects to mention important happenings which we can learn from other sources. Almost from the moment that he landed in Canada there is a broader field than his own account from which to draw information about his activities. From a little after 1830 until his death in 1883 others were to record and to remember things which he might have chosen to forget. Old diaries, letters and papers can be found in Canada, and in some cases memories of him have been gathered from people still alive or others who have died fairly recently.

Once in Canada he was, indeed, as the captain who had carried him there said, a man, and considered so by all around him. No longer a chattel slave, no longer a fugitive in fear of his life, he must prove to himself and to the world that he was capable of making full use of his freedom.

At the time that Henson landed, slavery had not yet been abolished in the British colonies and was to remain on the statute books until the Act of 1833. He had nothing to fear, however, from the Canadians, as the institution of slavery was everywhere in that country looked upon with disfavor. Henson was not the first fugitive to arrive in Canada, but the presence of Negro refugees does not seem to have attracted marked public attention until late in the 1840s, according to Fred Landon of the University of Western Ontario, who has done considerable research on the subject.

It is difficult to imagine today the psychological, material and moral situation of a slave who had newly gained his freedom, as Josiah Henson had. These were persons who had in many cases reached maturity without ever having earned their living in the manner in which a free man was, at least theoretically, supposed to do. On the other hand, they had been in most cases forced into or bred to a brutalizing and degrading system which demanded of them the limit of their physical strength. They consequently knew how to work, in the sense that they were capable of performing a certain limited number of operations without tiring physically. On the other hand, the system had neither obliged nor even allowed them to develop the initiative necessary to carry a project through to completion. Lacking liberty, there were no compensations for them in labor other than the avoidance of punishment. Now, in freedom, all the ties with the system were broken, yet these people had grown in and been formed by the life of the plantation.

Those who were already settled in Canada before 1840 were of a different temperament than those who were to arrive after that approximate date. In later years there were many who were to come only because they had been talked into it by an agent of the Underground who had a moral stake in the matter of the number of slaves that he might bring through. Then there were some who were actually driven out by such "shepherds" as John Brown, who cut them out of the herd and guided them north almost against their own will. In the earlier days the Underground was not yet running regularly, and anyone who could evade the pursuit through his own boldness and by the exercise of his ingenuity—indeed anyone who had been able to formulate and carry through the plan for escape by himself—was no ordinary slave. To win freedom it was necessary to be a man gifted with more than the usual amount of resourcefulness, courage, and perhaps luck. Josiah Henson was, indeed, such a man.

/ 2 /

It was to be some years before Henson was to become acquainted with the conditions of the other Negroes in Canada. He had first to apply himself to the business of finding the necessities of life, for he was entirely without money. He was among strangers, knowing nothing of the country or the people.

After making several inquiries Henson heard of a Mr. Hibbard who was willing to hire him. Hibbard gave him a sort of two-story shanty in which to live. It was not much but it was the first house that Josiah had ever owned, and he set about putting it in some sort of order because it had been vacant for several years. When he had worked through the day, cleaning and repairing it, he moved into this new home, as he has said himself, the only "furniture" that he possessed—the rest of the Hensons. Even Charlotte admitted that it was better than what they had known in Kentucky, and they set about making beds of straw, boxed in with logs, as they had done in the South. The great difference was that they now had wooden floors in place of beaten earth, and to his wife this seemed the most important gain that they had made by changing their state.

They were to remain with Mr. Hibbard for three years, sometimes working on shares and sometimes for wages. Josiah was able in that way to procure some livestock of his own. But there also developed a valuable friendship between the Hibbard family and the Hensons. Through the aid of Mrs. Hibbard they were able to procure genuine furniture and some of the other comforts of life. Mr. Hibbard was an educated man and began to teach Josiah's older son Tom to read and write.

The boy used to read from the Bible to his father, and one day, when he asked where he should begin, he was surprised to be told, "Oh, just anywhere." When he asked for an explanation of what he read, the child was astonished to find that his father could not tell him what the printed words meant.

"Why, Father, can't you read?" he said.

Josiah was loath to answer him, for it was a blow to his pride to admit that he had never learned. But it was a direct question and must have a direct answer.

"I never had an opportunity to learn nor anybody to teach me," he replied, perhaps thinking back to the incident in his childhood when he had been severely beaten for his attempt to learn.

"Well, you can learn now, Father."

"No, my son, I am too old and have not time enough. I must work all day or then you would not have enough to eat."

"Then you might do it at night."

"But still there is nobody to teach me. I can't afford to pay anybody for it, and of course no one can do it for nothing."

"Quiet, Father, I'll teach you. I can do it, I know."

Josiah's heart was filled with conflicting emotions because for so many years he had thought of himself as the superior of others and he could not admit the idea of being helped to read by his own child. The boy insisted that he could teach him, but Josiah was so overwhelmed that his ignorance was now known even to his own family that he left the house and passed the day in the woods in solitary reflection.

When he returned that night he set about improvising some sort of illumination by which they could study. Tallow candles were too expensive for him, and indeed for the neighboring white farmers, unless perhaps their wives dipped their own. A string wick floating in oil or fat gave not enough light by which to read, so Josiah gathered pine knots and some hickory bark and used their bright dry flame for a lamp.

Few people in those days stayed up long after sundown, for they rose early and worked long hours in the fields, so the father and son made slow progress at their reading. Josiah's eyes were little used to deciphering what he complained were hen scratches. But they persevered throughout the winter, and by spring they had advanced so far in their studies that in his reading Josiah came to have an idea of the immense world of knowledge from which he had been debarred in his enforced ignorance.

About that time an old friend arrived from Maryland, where he had escaped from an intolerable master, and this friend made it known in the neighborhood that Henson was something of a preacher. Josiah was encouraged to hold Sunday meetings which, as ever in Negro congregations, did not have a wholly religious character, though they were ostensibly church services. Henson has said he found that to preach it was necessary to have only a minimum of theological knowledge.

Religion, as it had been taught to Henson and other slaves in the South, when it was taught at all, consisted of admonitions to obey the master. The more optimistic white Christians who held out any reward for slaves in the hereafter confined it to the promise that God had "a nice clean kitchen for good niggers."

What then would be the character of Henson's sermons? We have seen how, in early life, the system had formed him. We know what he had done in the past, and how he had preached to his fellow-slaves in Kentucky at the time when they plotted an insurrection. "No, let us suffer in God's name and await His time for Ethiopia to stretch forth her hands and be free." That was the moral he had adopted under slavery, yet now he would seem to have denied it by his own action in securing freedom for himself and his family. The character of Uncle Tom must always be contradictory. Would that sort of moralizing be necessary or even welcome in a community of people who had escaped from bondage by their own efforts?

For there were by now several hundred colored people settled in the neighborhood, and their problems were very different from those of the plantation slaves to whom Henson had counseled forbearance and suffering in the Lord. Now they were free. It was not, however, impossible to be unhappy even though one was free, for the demands of freedom were severe.

Under a master a slave worked as hard as he was forced to work. In some the habit became ingrained so long as they lived under the conditions of the system, but the best rebelled. They learned to avoid both work and punishment until the time came when they could escape. In the first days of freedom, therefore, they were content with little.

It seems that to a large extent they had the same opportunities as the other settlers; they were considered equal under law, and they could take up land on the same terms as a white colonist. Many of them, however, did not know this; and, while all Canadian authorities have always been anxious to point to the unbroken tradition of legal freedom prevailing in that country, there may well have been a conspiracy of silence in regard to opportunity on the part of the white settlers. A supply of cheap and expert labor was a windfall in frontier days when every man was intent on carving out a homestead for himself in the wilderness. Real evidence of race prejudice was, however, absent until some years later.

Henson as a preacher, therefore, had other themes than purely religious ones to develop for his flock. The religious form in which they were cast served only to add more weight to the practical aspects of his proposals. He saw that they must either better themselves, as their neighbors were trying to do, or slip down into an inferior position in the community. In the first joy of their deliverance they had been content to feel themselves free to move about from place to place and to work or rest as they pleased. Generally, they worked for hire upon the lands of others and had no thought of working for themselves.

Mr. Risley, for whom Josiah worked after leaving the Hibbards, agreed to loan his house for meetings where the most intelligent and successful members of the growing colored community were called together to discuss plans for bettering their lot. Labor was scarce and they had been reasonably well paid; so it was that they found they had among themselves a sum in cash sufficient to allow them to settle on land of their own, if the project were undertaken on a cooperative basis.

"The joy we had at first taken in mere freedom has rendered us content with a lot far inferior to what might be obtained. We must benefit from the example which this country has set for us and strike out with energy and enterprise," said Josiah. He was determined to prove that all which it was possible for the white colonist to gain was possible for them also. "I was not deterred from this task of persuasion by the perception of the immense contrast in all their habits and character generated by long ages of freedom for the one and servitude for the other; activity and sloth, independence and subjection."

He reiterated that what others had done they too could do, and he brought his associates around to believing it. In a short time he had the enthusiastic support of all those who had come to his meetings and who had some influence in the group. They agreed to take charge of his family and deputized him to make a journey of exploration in search of a place where they might settle.

Josiah started out in the autumn of 1834 and traveled over the region that lies between Lakes Ontario, Erie, and Huron. The country is quite flat and was, at that time, very heavily wooded. He says in his autobiography that he traveled on foot, yet almost the first outside account of him dates either from this or perhaps the second journey which he was to make a few months later, when the Reverend Benjamin Cronyn recorded in his diary that he first saw Josiah Henson trying to get into a coach at Brantford.

Mr. Cronyn was on his way home from Ireland. He had with him "several thousand hunting dogs" which he expected to sell. The number would seem to be a printer's error or the nightmare of someone who had been to a dog show. Mr. Cronyn was making the trip from Hamilton to Lake Ontario by covered wagon, and perhaps because he was a fellow-clergyman, he gave Josiah a lift and a good deal of advice on the nature of the surrounding country.

Henson, during his tour of the semipeninsula bounded by the three Great Lakes, came to a territory east of Lake St. Clair and the Detroit River which attracted him by its evident fertility. As it seemed in all ways suited to the purpose of the colony, he decided to go no further but to return and make a report. His companions were impressed with his enthusiasm, but as they had already experienced the violently alternating seasons of Canada, so different from the more gradual changes to which they had been accustomed in the southern states, they advised him to return again at another time of year. The climate of even that eastern portion of Canada whose temperatures are influenced by the proximity of the great inland seas like Ontario, Erie, and Huron, was a greater trial to these newcomers than it was to the white colonists, of whom the greater majority had come from Scotland. The cold winters were to play an important part in the future of the Negro settlers, and their adaptability to the climate was to be a subject of debate.

At the request of his associates Josiah waited until the following summer and then made a second trip to the region which he had surveyed. This time he pushed on a little further toward the head of Lake Erie. There he came on an extensive tract of government-owned Crown Lands which had been granted to a Mr. McCormick upon certain conditions, the chief of which was that within a given number of years he must prove to the satisfaction of a land commission that a percentage of the land had been cleared and was under cultivation. At such a time he would be given the absolute title to the property.

In this case, McCormick had very cannily rented the virgin land to such settlers as came along, and when they could not meet his terms, summarily evicted them, thus benefiting from the improvements which they had made. It was the customary skin game of the time and compares rather favorably, from a moral point of view, with the manner in which the railroads and the clergy were reserving immense tracts of the country for themselves.

At the time when Henson and his companions presented themselves as future tenant farmers, a good portion of the land in question had been cleared. This was a decided advantage in the matter of the immediate raising of crops with which to sustain themselves, for they had limited resources and no equipment and could not afford the time and labor necessary for the job of cutting trees and blasting roots. They settled on the land the following spring, and set about raising crops of wheat and tobacco. Their plan was to save all the money they could in order to purchase the land on which Josiah had set his heart when first he viewed it.

After the Negro group had worked these farms for about a year, Henson found out that to acquire the freehold deed to the property, according to the conditions of the grant, all necessary improvements must be made by the one to whom the grant was given. McCormick did not own the land as yet and was in no way entitled to the rent which he was exacting from them. They determined to pay him no more. Josiah applied to Sir John Cockburn, who held an official position in the province, and was told to address himself to the provincial legislature. There he found that the friends of his landlord were too powerful for him, and he failed in his first application for terms of his own. The following year, however, these friends of McCormick were out of office, and Henson's group was able to take over the land subject to the improvement clause on which the former titleholder had held it.

They were thus free of the obligation to pay rent, but the land was not their own and, as they had no political influence, it did not seem likely that it ever would be. Henson was certain that some time short of the expiration of their term some man in office might well advise a wealthy purchaser to buy it outright. In this way they would lose all the profit of their work and be driven off. With this hanging over their heads there was little incentive to clear more land than was necessary to raise sufficient crops for their own needs. They remained six or seven years in this position.

During this time immigration from the United States went on at a greater rate than ever before, and members of the colony were joined by relatives and friends who had heard of their success, moderate though it still was at that time. They came singly or in little groups, having in many cases been forced to part with even their wives and children. In most cases they were destitute, but in the early years, at least, they were quickly absorbed as laborers, although some became barbers, bootblacks, or carpenters, for they came from the more privileged class of slaves who knew a trade.

The country as a whole was extremely unsettled in the 1830s, though one might have expected that the colonists, situated as they were on the frontier, would have remained unaware of political developments. Communication was nowhere very swift, and Upper Canada, where transportation was to a large extent overland, was at a disadvantage compared with Lower Canada, where not only were the settled areas much older but also strategically placed along the St. Lawrence River.

Great tensions were, however, developing in the political life of Canada, and there were those prominent in the affairs of both the French- and the English-speaking provinces who felt that the term "colony" could best be exchanged for another.

It was almost certainly Henson who first saw the advantage to be gained from an interest in politics. It was he who petitioned the legislature and who organized the Negro colonists in his area during the Rebellion of 1837. Nor was this the first Negro participation in Canadian affairs.

During the War of 1812 it was that portion of Canada in which the Negro colonists had settled which had been taken by the army of General Harrison who penetrated far into the province of Upper Canada. It is certain that at that time there were Negro troops in the Canadian militia on the British side, but it seems uncertain whether they were freemen or slaves. Since that date, however, slavery had been abolished in the British Empire by the Act of 1833. When it seemed certain that the rebels would attack from their headquarters in Detroit, the provincial legislature undertook to re-form the militia, and Henson was active in insuring that the Negro colonists would form a part of it.

He claims that he was appointed a captain in the Second Essex Company of Colored Volunteers. There is no other authority for this than his own statement. Another colored preacher, the Reverend J. W. Loguen, has also claimed that he commanded a black company.

Henson says that, owing to his crippled arms, he could not shoulder a musket and therefore carried a sword in its place. "My company held Fort Malden from Christmas till the following May, and also took the schooner *Ann* and captured all it contained, which were three hundred arms, two cannons, musketry, and provisions for the rebel troops. This was a fierce and gallant action and did much toward breaking up the rebel party, for they could not obtain provisions while we held the Fort, which we continued to do till we were relieved by the colonel of the Forty-fourth Regiment from England. The colored men were willing to help defend the government that had given them a home when they fled from slavery."

The affair of the schooner *Ann* was a curious incident, for it is perhaps the only occasion in the history of warfare when a company of foot soldiers has captured a vessel. It seems that the schooner was caught, during a quick drop in temperature, in the ice floes which bound her solid, enabling the soldiers to make their way across the ice and board her.

The part which the ex-slaves played in the rebellion has been commented upon in an interesting letter written by the rebel leader himself. This letter was sent in answer to an agent of the American Anti-Slavery Society who visited Canada immediately before the rebellion and canvassed a number of public men in the province as to their opinion on the state of the ex-slaves.

January 30, 1837

Sir,

In reply to your enquiries I beg to offer as my opinion with much diffidence, 1st, That nearly all of them are opposed to every species of reform in the civil institutions of the colony—they are so extravagantly loyal to the Executive that to the utmost of their power they uphold all the abuses of government and support those who profit by them. 2nd, As a people they are as well behaved as a majority of the whites, and perhaps more temperate. 3rd, To your third question (regarding crime), I would say, not more numerous. 4th, Cases in which colored people ask public charity are rare as far as I can recollect. I am opposed to slavery whether of whites or blacks, in every form. I wish to live long enough to see the people of this continent, of the humblest classes, educated and free, and held in respect, according to their conduct and attainments, without reference to country, color or worldly substance. But I regret that an unfounded fear of union with the United States on the part of the colored population should have induced them to oppose reform and free institutions in this colony, whenever they have the power to do so. The apology I make for them in this matter is that they have not been educated as freemen.

I am your respectful humble servant,
W. L. MacKenzie

The legal position of the refugees had been admittedly precarious, and the first fruit of this political intervention would seem to have been the law of 1837 permitting ex-slaves to vote. This apparently signified that the fugitive slaves were to be admitted to British citizenship, for it could hardly have been intended to apply to the insignificant number of Canadian-held slaves who had been freed by the Act of 1833. Naturalization was made easy, and the growing Negro colonies were about to become a political force whose direction would lie in the hands of the first man to show himself capable of manipulating their combined vote.

The political question was to lie dormant, however, for some years, until the tide of colored immigration had almost reached its peak about the year 1850.

By that time, Josiah Henson was to be in a strong position as the chief member and director of an organized Negro colony. He spent the intervening years raising funds, traveling about the country attending meetings, and speaking everywhere, both to consolidate his own position and to advise the immigrants as to the necessity of owning land of their own. His activity on the platform and in the pulpit was to lead eventually to the foundation of the Dawn Institute, but first his activity was to precipitate him into a series of adventurous missions in the slave states.

[[Ten years after his own escape, Henson made his way to Kentucky to rescue the Lightfoot family from slavery, but as they were reluctant to leave just then, he journeyed to the interior of the state to shepherd another group out; the next year he returned to the Lightfoots and, amid various difficulties, helped four brothers to escape. Overall, he brought back some 118 people from such trips into slave territory. In 1842, with $1,500 raised by abolitionists in England, he bought three hundred acres of the land he had seen several years earlier, plus an adjoining one hundred acres on his own account, and there he founded the Dawn Institute. At the colony, he proposed establishing a school that taught grammar and manual training—as suited frontier life—to enable independence from the white population. Periodically, he traveled to the northern states to seek assistance for newly arrived fugitives. To ensure the prosperity of the Dawn Institute, he also raised money to build a sawmill in order to profit by the felled trees on their land, but the project was not well planned and ran out of funds. Discontent with his stewardship began to set in at this point, but with support from friends in Boston he succeeded in getting the mill in working order. Around this time, about 1849, his life story was published by the Anti-Slavery Society of Boston and read by Harriet Beecher Stowe, whom he met while passing through Andover, Massachusetts, where she had just moved from Cincinnati. After a debt of $7,500 was discovered, to pay for which they had to appeal to abolitionists abroad, the trustees of the Dawn Institute decided that the school and the sawmill should be separately managed. Henson took over the mill; he took black walnut boards produced at the mill to the great exhibition in the Crystal Palace in London, where he was generally well received and even visited by Queen Victoria.   ]]

/ 7 /

Henson was, in consequence of the temper of the society in which he found himself, introduced everywhere by his new friends, and he very often rose to a point of correction at the public meetings which were held at that time by the rare apologists for slavery who managed to appear before the English public. As a visiting celebrity, he was taken to see such charitable institutions as the Ragged Schools, to which he was accompanied by Lord Grey.

This gentleman made Henson a most interesting offer. The English government had been seeking for some time to procure for its manufacturers sources of cotton other than the slave states of America. The production of cotton had been introduced into Egypt and India, where the peasants were being encouraged to raise that crop. Various difficulties had been encountered in its culture, and it was particularly difficult to find efficient supervisors who were acquainted with methods of cultivation. Therefore, Grey asked Henson to go to India as a supervisor.

It is interesting to note that Henson spoke of this effort on the part of the government as "the intention to introduce the culture of cotton into India on the American plan."

It would seem that he recognized that forced labor was to be the keystone of the imperialist project. He refused to go to India on the grounds that he was more interested in the fate of the Canadian colony. There is no evidence that he had any particular interest in the fate of the Indian peasantry nor that his refusal was due to the nominal support which he must have given to the freedom-for-India plank in the platform of the English abolitionists.

It is extraordinary to realize today that while the American abolitionists under Garrison had two main theses—the abolition of slavery and equal suffrage for women—the English abolitionists, at least in the most advanced group, had a third which demanded freedom for India. At various times Henson and the other Negro abolitionists in England spoke at public meetings whose main intention was to promote this third principle.

Samuel Gurney gave Josiah a card of introduction to the archbishop of Canterbury whom he visited at Lambeth Palace. This dignitary of the English Church received Henson most kindly and granted him an interview which lasted well beyond the allotted time.

"At what university, sir, did you graduate?"

"I graduated, Your Grace, at the University of Adversity."

"The University of Adversity? Where's that?"

"It was my lot, Your Grace, to be born a slave and to pass my boyhood and all the former part of my life as a slave. I never entered a school, never read the Bible in my youth, and received all of my training under the most adverse circumstances. That is what I mean by graduating in the University of Adversity."

"I understand you, sir, but is it possible that you are not a scholar?"

"I am not," said Josiah.

"But I should never have suspected that you were not a liberally educated man. I have heard many Negroes talk but I've never seen one that could use such language as you. Will you tell me, sir, how you learned our language?"

Henson then related to Archbishop Sumner the story of his early slave days and the manner in which he had sought to imitate his customers, particularly those who spoke good English and for whom he reserved the best of the farm produce which he sold in the Washington market. On leaving the archbishop, the latter pressed a bank note for fifty pounds into his hand.

Upon another occasion, Josiah was invited along with a large company of Sabbath-school teachers to spend a day on the estate of Lord John Russell, who was, at that time, prime minister of England. "His magnificent park, filled with deer, of varied colors, from all climes, and sleek hares, which the poet Cowper would have envied, with numberless birds, whose plumage rivaled the rainbow in gorgeous colors, together with the choicest specimens of the finny tribe, sporting in their native element, drew from me the involuntary exclamation: 'Oh, how different the condition of these happy, sportive, joyful creatures, from what is now the lot of millions of my colored brethren in America.'" And he went on with his effort to do something for these brethren.

Henson collected money with comparative ease, for he found it as great a pleasure to meet wealthy people in England as he had found it in Washington, where he had known them in vastly different circumstances. He liked to flatter people and agree with them and to be continually busy with the details of his "enterprise," its administration, and the thousand petty intrigues which it entailed. He liked to imagine himself a master diplomat, the colorful impresario of the entire Negro population of Upper Canada. As he had responded long ago to the jocular, patronizing invitation of the drovers who had thought it sport to befuddle him with drink in the taverns along the way as he had conducted his fellow-slaves from one master to another, so, now, he was not apt to question any overture which was made to him by persons who appeared to be friendly. He could not ignore the fact that the periphery of the abolition movement in England and America contained many doubtful elements. In America it was a constant source of discussion. It was well known among devoted members of the association that their ranks were likely to be penetrated by spies, traitors, and saboteurs in the pay of the slavers. Cases, rare enough in all truth, had been found where even Negroes sold their brothers for a price. There is no proof of any such accusation brought against Henson, however loose he may have been about money matters, and despite the fact that the later history of his life in relation to the colony at Dawn is one long record of protracted lawsuits.

Neither Josiah Henson nor most of those Uncle Toms who followed him have a price to be reckoned in money. Their price is the achievement of a certain celebrity, or even renown, as good men with whom to make mutually satisfactory terms when the case in dispute would give the right so unequivocally to the weaker party that no compromise would be possible if it were not for that very disparity in strength. With a desire for notoriety, which is often innocent enough, Uncle Tom is easily persuaded that his own prominence can work to the advantage of those to whom his aid is formally pledged. And with this desire go a certain blind eagerness and credulity which can lead him into the company of his worst enemies.

Henson was very sure that he was apt and alert, capable of judging men and their motives with a discernment derived from the lesson of his forty-three years of slavery. If he could flatter himself that he was the representative of the entire Negro population of Canada, though he knew it to be untrue, he could listen with greater readiness and a show of mock solemnity to those who approached him with a certain deference, presumably due to one who occupied the position which he allowed it to be believed that he held. He never denied that he was an important man, and he was seen in the company of men who were important in English affairs. Unfortunately they were not all abolitionists nor even antislavery men.

Some of these associates of Henson were men who had lost their property in the West Indies not twenty years earlier; the slaves held by the British plantation owners had been liberated in 1833. Many of these proprietors claimed that they had suffered severe financial loss in the subsequent exploitation of their holdings, although they had been richly indemnified by the government at the time of emancipation.

The landlords of Jamaica and Trinidad now looked to the Negroes who were settled in Canada as a source from which enough labor could be drawn to revive the plantations. The defenders of slavery remarked with solicitude that there would be fewer difficulties of a purely practical nature to contend with under a system which would closely resemble that which the ex-fugitives had known in the States. They added kindly that the world had seen what freemen of color could accomplish even in the face of the greatest adversity, and speculated on how much one could expect when Canadian adversity would be exchanged for patriarchal ease. Those men in England who felt that emigration would serve

their interests were certain that the climate of the islands, pleasantly reminiscent
of the South, would be a great factor in persuading the Canadian colonists to listen to their blandishments. They sought out all the men of color who visited
England and endeavored to interest them in the project.

William Wells Brown was one of those who was approached, and he wrote
of it in the following manner to Frederick Douglass, who was in America:

> Knowing that there were many proprietors and agents dissatisfied with
> the abolition of slavery in the West Indies, and that a species of slavery had
> been carried on under the name of emigration, I frankly told these men
> upon what conditions I thought our people would go to the West Indies.
>
> But as to going there to be bound or fettered in any way, I assured him,
> that no fugitive slave would consent to. And although I was assured that
> the utmost freedom would be enjoyed by all who might consent to go,
> I understand that a secret move is on foot in London to induce our un-
> suspecting people in Canada to go to the West Indies, and that agents are
> already in Canada for that purpose.
>
> *The Reverend Josiah Henson is said to be one of these.* [The italics are mine
> —B.G.] As my letter in the *Times* first brought this subject before the peo-
> ple, and fearing that some might be entrapped by this new movement, I
> take the earliest opportunity of warning all colored men to be on their
> guard how they enter into agreement, no matter with whom, white or col-
> ored, to go to the West India Islands, lest they find themselves again wear-
> ing the chains of slavery.
>
> A movement that is concocted in secret, and that, too, by men, many
> of whom would place the chains upon the limbs of the emancipated peo-
> ple of the West Indies tomorrow if they could, and which is kept from the
> knowledge of the Abolitionists of this country should find no countenance
> with our oppressed people. He who has made his escape from the cotton,
> sugar and rice fields of the Southern States is ready to finish his life among
> the cold hills of Canada and if needs be to subsist upon the coarsest of
> food; but he is not willing to enter into a second bondage. Then I would
> say again beware lest you are entrapped by the enemy.
>
> Yours for our people,
> W. W. Brown

In his autobiography Henson makes no mention of any connection with
those who wished to move the slaves from Canada to the Caribbean, and it may

be assumed that, once he had returned to Canada, he made no real effort to persuade his people to go there. The agents and proprietors may very well have used his name in 1854, when they spoke to Brown, merely because they were sure that Henson was not in the country to refute them. But more probably he had been flattered by their company and had been seen with them in England. In any case, he did not in reality enjoy the necessary influence among the Canadian colored population to be able to sway them in any way. He does not seem ever to have been on friendly terms with the other men of his race who were prominent internationally or even nationally, for this letter from Brown contains the only reference to him in the mass of correspondence with the Anti-Slavery Society which has been published.

In the month of September, 1852, while he was still in Britain, there came two unwelcome reminders of his former life which obliged Josiah to cut short the pleasant days spent "in the company of the noblest men in England." The first of these was the memory of his brother, who still remained in slavery. Josiah was dining at the house of a friend who kept a luxurious table, when suddenly a vision of his brother in chains seemed to appear before his eyes. The impression was so strong that he found himself obliged to push back his chair and rise from the table.

"What is the matter, Josiah? Has anything occurred to disturb your peace of mind?" asked his host.

"Come, come, Josiah. Do help yourself and make yourself at home," said the other guests.

Josiah begged to be excused from eating his dinner on that day, for he had lost all appetite for the food which lay before him. He determined to make every effort to rescue his brother, of whom he had rarely thought until that moment, at the first opportunity which presented itself upon his return to America.

Very shortly after this incident he received a letter from his family, saying that his wife was extremely ill, and he immediately set sail for Canada.

[[Soon after his arrival, Henson's wife died, and he became entangled in the financial affairs at the Dawn Institute. Meanwhile, he arranged for American abolitionists to rescue his aged brother, which proved costly and difficult; he rewrote his life story to include his Canadian experiences and from the proceeds of the sale of the book, purchased his brother's freedom. The flight to Canada of ex-slaves and freemen of color greatly increased after the Fugitive Slave Law of 1850, but the Dawn Institute was nearly bankrupt and compelled to accept a high-handed English agent as its administrator,

who led them to ruin over the next decade. Unfortunately Henson made himself an ally of the Englishman, arousing ill-will around him, though he found new prestige as the model for Stowe's hero in Uncle Tom's Cabin, *which was published in 1852 and became an instant bestseller. In 1858 he married a young free-born widow from Baltimore, with whom he had three more children. After years of mismanagement by the English agent, Henson succeeded in ousting him, entailing a protracted and costly lawsuit, which was at last dropped in 1871. By then the Dawn Institute no longer existed: many people had left the area and, with reconstruction after the Civil War, many more returned to the United States, cutting the black population of Canada by half. The land owned by the Dawn Institute was sold by a new board of trustees, who paid the colony's debt and used the rest of the money to build a school, the Wilberforce Institute, in nearby Chatham. Henson re-mained on his farm near Dresden with his second family and grandchildren, though he was less popular in the community. Restless for the attention still to be had abroad by playing his role as the real-life Uncle Tom, he sailed for England again with his wife in 1876, where he toured the country appearing at churches, chapels, and public halls, and prepared a new edition of his autobiography; a copy was forwarded to Queen Victoria who received the Hensons in March 1877. The following winter, they traveled to Baltimore and Washington, where they visited President Hayes at the White House; in Maryland he saw how much had changed along the roads leading to the old Riley plantation (just twelve miles from the capital), which he found in complete disrepair, like old Mrs. Riley herself, now a "poor, fretful invalid."]]*

| 15 |

Henson died in his house near Dresden, Ontario, in May, 1883. The Dawn Institute no longer existed, and many of the families who had once lived there were scattered. His own family was gathered in the house, for everyone had been expecting for some time that the old man might die. Many of the children and grandchildren had come back to the farm from the United States where they had gone to live. Today they and their descendants live in Detroit, Buffalo, and Cincinnati.

After his death there were the unfortunate but only too common family dis-putes over the property and the division of the old man's effects. His prized me-mentos, the signed portrait of Victoria, the gold watch, the music box which had been presented to Mrs. Henson, and the illuminated scrolls were carried off by the lucky or the insistent.

Today there are a dozen signs along the road to Dresden which point out the only place of interest in the surrounding countryside: UNCLE TOM'S GRAVE. The grave lies on a little knoll within sight of the winding river, bordered by the few tall trees which have not been cut down.

The monument stands in a small plot where not more than a dozen or two graves have been marked. Across the road is an older burying ground, full of broken headstones with illegible inscriptions, where cows break in to pasture. The Henson plot is more securely protected and there, beneath an imposing stone pillar, Josiah lies beside his second wife. The Masonic symbol is carved on the pillar's base along with the following verse:

> There is a land of pure Delight
> Where Saints immortal reign;
> Infinite day excludes the night
> And pleasures banish pain.

/ 16 /

Today Beecher Henson is the oldest living member of the family who still resides in Dresden. He says, with some bitterness, that he does not know where any of the things which belonged to his grandfather are to be found. He farms a small piece of land, none of which was inherited from Josiah, and lives as a bachelor in a little cottage on the edge of town. People occasionally come to question him about the family history and leave with the impression that he knows more than he cares to tell. Beecher himself fosters the idea that there is some secret worth keeping, but very probably it is only a family matter, the peccadillo of a son or a dispute over the inheritance; something which is of greater importance to him than it would be to another.

The people of Dresden have a curiously ambivalent attitude toward the memory of Josiah Henson. It is reflected by the manner in which they speak of him: "Oh, he just said he was Uncle Tom." "Beecher, now, he's a deep one. Knows more than he talks 'bout." "Beecher Henson is as white as I am. He can't be Uncle Tom's grandson." "There never was an Uncle Tom, really."

It is curiously irrational, of course, because there can be no doubt of the truth of the story. But there is something more than mere cynicism in the attitude of the Dresdenites. After all, they are the children and the grandchildren of those people who experienced the paternalism of the Dawn Institute. A residue of resentment against the old man is evident in everything they say. Some of the people have read Mrs. Stowe's book, but not many of them are aware of the meaning which the phrase "Uncle Tom" has taken on today in the United States.

Uncle Tom in fiction was the perfect type of the Negro whom the white folks were willing to free as long as he retained all the characteristics of his former servitude. He was compliant and submissive, satisfied with whatever a master chose to give him. He was pious and ready to accept the doctrine that even in heaven "black cherubs rise at seven to do celestial chores."

In real life the same people like "their colored folk" when they are menial. They like to be flattered by the Negro's deference and amused by his antics; fawning is considered a mark of respect. They are not quite sure whether or not they like the Negro to cower, for that sometimes arouses a twinge of conscience, but they amuse each other with tales of his physical cowardice and suppose it to be a racial characteristic. The joke disappears, however, when they need to frighten themselves with stories of the Negro who is a monster of strength and wanton cruelty. Into such a paranoiac picture of his people must the modern Uncle Tom fit himself. No easy task.

Uncle Tom scolds his nephew, whose escapades may range from wild pranks, maliciously exaggerated, to deeply justified outbursts of violent resentment against being treated as something less than human. He preaches to his people to wash their faces, straighten their hair, and "honor the white folks." At one time he assures everybody that this is a white man's world and the only way to live is to get everything one can by being subservient and taking a little good along with much bad. Another day he is out preaching that anyone with the least trace of pigmentation in his skin should go back to Africa or, at the very least, found a Black Economy, with black trains to run alongside the white ones, and a black government seated in a black Washington.

Behind the Uncle Tom disguise is a dangerous man who leads his people nowhere. Forced into patterns of their own which make it increasingly difficult for contact to exist between the races, Uncle Tom walks a tightrope over this chasm.

The stock figures left over from plantation days, the minstrel show, and Mrs. Stowe's book, are a little worn-out today. It is obvious that they will no longer do. While the Negro has a job in a factory, not everyone is going to expect to see him shining shoes or picking up pennies for doing a cakewalk on the street corner. Yet this economic security is new, incomplete and precarious. As long as it remains, so there will always be Uncle Toms. Alas, Uncle Tom is not just a stock character, nor is he Josiah Henson. He is alive today under many disguises. He is the so-called leader subventioned by a section of society eager to use him as their tool. No action led by him, no cultural relations, no concession gained, no school built, no hospital staffed, nothing attained through his intercession will ever be a step toward the solution. There is no Negro problem in America; there is a common problem.

It will be a great day when we can shout together, "Uncle Tom is dead."

Potiphar's Wife

"Potiphar's Wife" (1950) is one of several stories about life in Morocco that Gysin wrote not long after arriving there. He had been invited to Tangier by Paul Bowles, whom he had known in New York in the 1940s. These pieces were never submitted for publication and only appeared much later in Gysin's Stories *(1984).*

The second time he ran away because he had too many elder brothers, Yussef ben Allal El Hamri got a job working with a man who sold pastries from a little cart which rolled through the market of Alcazar Kebir. Yussef had wanted to go to war in the Spanish zone, for he had heard that the Americans were in Morocco, but, as he could never find anyone who could tell him for sure whether they were for or against the Sultan, he allowed himself to be distracted. He had admired the cakes one day when he had not eaten for a long time, and now he was working for Hamid, who made them in his own house.

Hamid payed him four pesetas a day and he rarely went out of the house for fear one of his brothers might see him, take him back home, and beat him. His only trouble was with Hamid's wife, Zuleika: she hated him. "I'm going to lose this good job; all because of this aunt," he would say to himself when she complained of anything he did in a loud screaming voice. The trouble had started as soon as Hamid had brought him home on the first night. She had looked at him very closely and said, "You're not going to have this dirty boy around the house all the time, I hope. Hamid, why do you always want to bring stray dogs home with you?"

"Really," said Hamid without looking at Yussef, "I hadn't noticed. Where's my dinner, Zuleika; what have you made tonight?"

He was a man who shouted at times in order to be sure of his own importance: Zuleika, although she was quite young, knew how to handle him perfectly.

When he was eating she threw a ragged, old grass mat out into the little courtyard of the house where Yussef was sitting patiently waiting.

"You're too dirty to come in the house," she said. "You're too dirty to eat with decent people. Here, take this to sleep on. And here's your food," she said, thrusting a plate of scraps at him.

She went on treating him like that, finding fault with everything he did while he was learning and even after he learned to make the cakes as well as Hamid himself. He had learned simply by watching, for Hamid rarely spoke to him either to instruct or to blame him. Zuleika never again spoke to him directly, finding that it humiliated him more to talk about him as if he were a bad dog or a slave in the house.

"I know I'm going to lose this job: I know I am. And all because of you," Yussef went on thinking to himself all the time.

One day Hamid came back with half the cakes still unsold, saying that he was ill. His wife scoffed at him at first, but it was easy to see that he had a fever for he shook all over. She put him to bed on the floor of the main room and ordered Yussef to take the remainder of the cakes out and sell them. The next day Hamid was much worse and no cakes were made that day. The day after that he looked no better and it began to seem a serious matter, for they lived on a narrow margin like most Moors.

"Give me the money to buy the flour and the sugar and the cinnamon and the raisins and the nuts and the butter and I will go out and buy the things to make the cakes," said young Yussef breathlessly.

"You?" said Hamid, just managing to raise his head from the pillow.

"You?" echoed his wife. "You?"

Hamid reached under the pillow where he always kept his money and pulled out a bill which he gave to the boy. His wife would have objected, but he closed his eyes and she thought for a minute that he might be going to die.

The cakes were quite as good as usual, and Yussef paid a little boy half a peseta a day to come to the house and get them in order to carry them to a Jewish woman who agreed to sell them for him. That night Hamid called him to his bed to say that he was going to double his wages to eight pesetas. It was easy to see that he was much sicker; perhaps delirious with fever. Yussef went on making the cakes, and Zuleika began to help him when she saw that Hamid was really sick: he was obviously in the hands of Allah, so there was no need to waste her time doing anything for him. Yussef admired her tremendously. She reminded him of the young wife of one of his brothers, who was only a year or so older than he but had bullied him because she was a married woman. He and Zuleika often had their hands in the same big earthen dishes as they were mixing up the things that went into the cakes, and he liked it very much when their hands met. She had to speak to him directly now as they were working together just outside her husband's room, but she was always curt with him.

All the money of the household was now passing through Yussef's hands, and Hamid was so ill that he could no longer even keep the accounts. Yussef decided one day how much it was that Hamid owed him, and he kept that money aside to buy new clothes for himself, paying a little at a time and leaving the things in the shops until the time came to get them all out and put them on. He went to the hammam and steamed himself for hours until he felt quite clean and then he put on the new clothes to go to the barber's where he had his hair well cut and covered with a great deal of brilliantine called "Essence de Violettes," which smelled very good and very strong.

When he knocked and Zuleika opened the door, she must have thought that it was some stranger for she covered her face and just stood there looking at him for a long time. Then she said, "Ahhh," letting her breath out. After that she said, "Mmmm," and it sounded as though a pigeon with its tail out were strutting on the ground between them; her voice came from so far down. That night when she made some broth for Hamid, she came and set the pot of chicken before Yussef who was sitting in the other room and waited until he had put his hands in it before she took any.

Perhaps because the weather had grown colder, she made a bed for him in the other room and laid one of the best rugs on it. He slept there very well, but she lay awake beside Hamid all the night. In the morning she had decided what she must do. When Hamid's mother and sister came to see him, she began to cry right away, saying he was so very sick that she was afraid he might die at any minute. Her mother-in-law peered into her face, but she looked so haggard from not having slept all night that the old woman decided this outburst must be genuine. Zuleika said that, if Hamid was really going to die, which Allah forbid, she hated the idea of him dying in that house.

"What's the matter with this house?" snapped the mother-in-law who guessed what was coming although she thought there was quite another reason behind it. "You never complained about it before."

"But it's in the Mellah," wailed Zuleika. "You don't want him to die in the Mellah!"

"I see," said the mother-in-law and it was agreed that Hamid should be carried to their house in another quarter of the town.

"I can sleep there with him in your big house," sobbed Zuleika, "and then I'll have to come back here every day to see that this horrid boy looks after the pastry business. We don't want to be entirely a charge on you. That way, there'll be a little money coming in every day."

"Hmm, yes," said the mother-in-law, "That's quite true."

"Oh, I know that he will be happier in the house where he was born," smiled Zuleika through her tears. "I just know he will, although he hardly noticed anything any more. I want to go and get him some water from the holy fountain of Sidi Bou Galem: I know it will do him some good. No, no; I don't want either one of you to come with me. I'll take Yussef to carry the water jar. The cakes are made, and that good-for-nothing who has just spent all his money, and the Prophet only knows how much of ours too, on useless new clothes, has nothing to do. Why don't you just run home and get someone to come and carry Hamid while your mother sits with him a while?"

On the way to the fountain she was very charming to Yussef and told him how awful her family-in-law was and how much she would hate having to live with them. "But I'll be back every day to look after the house," she said with a laugh. "In fact, I'll come twice a day; once in the morning and once at night. Oh, it will be wonderful to get away from them. And for another reason, too. Can you guess what that is?"

"No," said Yussef dully.

"Silly," she said.

On the way back from the fountain she pulled him aside on a little side path which led into a field of nothing.

"Why do you want to come this way?" he asked, stumbling after her.

When she turned swiftly to him and cunningly put her two hands on his chest, he said nothing, so she spoke to him; when she asked him again with different words and he said no, she spoke to him sharply. He felt that he could not change his mind which had said no in spite of him; now he could not say yes to her while she was insisting.

She spat at him and said in a low voice trembling with fury, "I'll kill you, kill you: have him kill you. I'll tell them you attacked me: here by the saint. D'you hear? They'll tear you apart . . . his brothers will kill you. I'll go now, right now, and tell them. I will; they'll believe me, they will: you know they will. Kill you, kill you. . . ." She ran after him when he turned up the path.

"You don't believe me? You'll see, you'll see. . . ."

She walked on ahead of him so rapidly that he could barely follow her although she was tripped all the time by her veils. When they got to the house two of Hamid's brothers were there but she hesitated just at the door, half turned to him with a faltering smile, and Yussef knew that she would say nothing. He had been very afraid for a while, and he knew that he would have a difficult time with a girl like that. They all went out carrying Hamid, and he was left in the house alone for the night.

It was barely light the next morning when she came and Yussef was still asleep; she crawled in beside him without taking her clothes off. When they both got dressed later, she said that she would come back to make his dinner, and she did.

While he was eating she kept urging him to eat more and leaning across the food to stroke his hair. He said that it bothered him. After that, when she first came into the house, she would be almost as she had been before and then she would gradually change, like a cat that seeks to be petted, until she had become quite the contrary.

"Don't do that," he said. "Don't do that all the time. Stop putting your arms around me and wetting my face with your face. I don't like it when you want to breathe in my mouth. When you feel like that just go and draw two pails of water from the well in the courtyard and put them on to heat."

Yussef was a very religious boy, and he liked to bathe several times a day on the occasions which the ritual law demands. At first it was like that, and he knew, although he had never had a woman before, that he was a man; acting like a man. He felt that he was more of a man than Hamid, who let her do what she wanted. Before the month was over he no longer felt so safe or so sure. Often, when she came in the morning, he was up already; drawing the water. After that it was always he who drew the two pails of water and then they both went into the room: he went and drew water twice a day, at least.

She was staying longer and longer in the house each day, saying that she really could not stay any longer with Hamid's family; they were impossible. Her mother and sister began to come and visit her nearly every day. They had not come before because Hamid had said that he did not want to see them in the house all the time because they were on bad terms with his family ever since the wedding dispute. They sat and talked and, when they stayed for meals, having brought a little something with them, Yussef sat down and ate it first as the man of the house should. Because he was so young, one could not treat him as though he were really the man of the house, so it turned into a family meal as though he were still a little boy and they all enjoyed themselves.

He came to be on very good terms with them, and the old lady would often sigh, "Oh, if I only had a son-in-law like this one!" He knew that she was not thinking that he might marry Zuleika's sister, for she had a husband. It was rather because Zuleika herself might so soon become a widow, so it was not a scandalous thing to say. All these pleasant times came to an end when Hamid grew so much better in his mother's care that he came back home.

He was still weak and had to lie in bed all day, but he could see everything that was going on in the little house if the curtains were pulled back. He was petulant and short-tempered, but one could put that down to his health; he had insisted on coming back although his wife had done everything to persuade him to stay a little longer in his parents' house. He lay there and complained all the time.

"It's almost as bad as things were when *she* complained all the time," thought Yussef to himself. "I'm glad Hamid knows he needs me; I couldn't go now."

Zuleika and he could not eat together, of course, but she fed him the best that was in the house and gave her husband the rest. One day, when Hamid was stronger than they had realized, he suddenly appeared in the other room where Yussef was eating and snatched his plate, shouting angrily that his wife fed the servant in the house better than she fed him. He quoted a number of angry verses out of the Coran in which there is a story about such a thing happening; even the name of the young man was the same: Yussef. Then he ran out into the street with the plate in his hands and called all the neighbors to see what a shameful thing his wife had done; she had fed the servant better than she fed him. At that moment a Christian neighbor who spoke Arabic, a Spaniard named Salvador, came down out of his house next door and said that he had seen the servant and the wife together from his terrace when Hamid was away. In the confusion and wailing which followed, Yussef managed to grab the few things which were his and run out into the street. He met an old friend who was smuggling American cigarettes in from Tangier and carrying back olive oil to sell there. Yussef had enough capital to buy ten cartons of cigarettes, so he went into the business and learned the ropes. So many people were bringing cigarettes into the Spanish zone that they were having to lower the price all the time. Yussef was the first to start buying other things in Tangier: he bought plastic belts, gabardine remnants sold by the kilo instead of by the measure, Gillette razor blades, and brilliantine; taking back meat, olive oil, and vegetables. He made a good deal of money and spent it at once, trying to learn how to get drunk. The carabineros showed him how to do it, and it cost him a great deal. It was all he could do to hold onto his capital for each trip.

One day he recognized Zuleika's sister in the street and she took him home to her mother's house, where they all had mint tea. He kept asking about Zuleika, but they wanted to talk about all the wonderful things there were in Tangier which one never saw in a little town like Alcazar Kebir.

"Why don't you bring me chewing gum?" asked the sister. "Why don't you bring me one of those silk handkerchiefs with a picture of a battleship on it?"

"And Nescafé," said the mother. "Nescafé and sugar. Zuleika may want some, too. She should be here about this time tomorrow."

He brought the things they asked for, and Zuleika was there the next day. He met her there every day after that. They sat with their arms around one another and the mother laughed while the sister asked for more things from Tangier. She wanted chocolate bars called "Zip," lipstick, earrings, cotton socks with colored rings, a Brownie Fiesta camera. The neighbors said that young Yussef had bought a magic philtre which he had given to Zuleika and her family in the mint tea, but it was only the things he brought them from Tangier.

It was not, after all, entirely satisfactory in her mother's house: there was no carrying of water, of course. One day Zuleika came in very breathless, saying that the house next to hers had been turned into a *fondouk*, an Arab hotel: the roof terrace joined the terrace of her house. Yussef moved in there and had to wait two nights before she was able to come up on the roof and join him. They were both trembling, and it was very dangerous. Some nights she was not able to get away from Hamid, and some evenings he would come up on the terrace with her and then she would sit there, waiting until he got bored and went down to sleep.

Naturally Yussef began to meet Hamid in the street. He bowed, but Hamid pretended not to see him and hurried on. One day they were both in a tavern kept by a Spaniard, and he saw that Hamid was drinking beer.

"Give me a bottle of beer and send one over to the man sitting in the corner," he said to the Spaniard.

"No, no, I don't want any more beer," shouted Hamid, breaking the silence between them. In the end they drank several beers together. By the time they had drunk twelve bottles each they were almost friends again, and the whole misunderstanding had been the woman's fault.

"I'm sorry about the food," Yussef said thickly. "I still think of her good cooking. I eat terrible food in the *fondouk* and sometimes I can even smell what you are eating next door. If I could only eat some of her good *couscous* again."

He went over and paid for the beers and, turning to Hamid who staggered after him, said, "Why don't we go to the market and buy a whole sheep's head? You can take it home for Zuleika to cook and this evening you'll bring me some of it to eat here in the Spaniard's tavern. What do you think of that?"

In the market he bought so many other things too and heaped them in Hamid's arms that Hamid was ashamed to have treated him so badly and felt that he had to invite him back to the house to eat them. It was an uncomfortable meal for Yussef. He was surprised to find that he could not lift his eyes from his plate. Zuleika seemed to have no such scruples. She kept walking back and forth in front of him as he sat on a pillow; so close that she kept brushing him with her long skirts and trailing sleeves. It was true that the room was small but she seemed to enjoy it and began to talk more and more, almost as if she had been drinking beer too. Yussef kept learning how women are. He could not answer when she spoke directly to him and this surprised him.

Hamid was glad that everyone was in good humor; it was good to see that there was no trouble between his wife and Yussef, he thought. Yussef was a fine young man, and he should come back to live in the house and help with the pastry business. Yussef had brought a bottle of strong white water called "Gordongin" and Hamid poured it into the *couscous*. It made it taste very bad but they all laughed. Yussef must come back and live in the house because Hamid had to go to Tangier for a few days about a piece of property. Zuleika could go and stay in his mother's house while he was away, leaving Yussef in charge.

"No, no," said Zuleika. "Your mother had enough trouble with both of us there when you were ill all that long time. It will be much better if I go to *my* mother's house this time."

She had her arms lovingly around his neck from behind as she said this, and she looked over his shoulder at Yussef and winked. He had to look at the ground again.

The first night that she was staying at her mother's house he bought a whole case of beer and went there to dinner. Lots of beer made her mother and sister very sleepy, and they went to bed. Zuleika went to her room, and he sat there drinking the last bottle of warm beer. When he had finished it slowly and smoked a cigarette he went to find her. He pushed open the door and there she was, dressed for the street with her gray *djellaba* and her pink veil, sitting on a pile of luggage: two big wicker suitcases and some little things tied in the silk handkerchiefs which he had given her.

"Go to the square and get the taxi that's on night service," she said. "Have him take you to the frontier of the French zone and send him back to help me get to the train at seven. When the train stops at the frontier, get on it and we'll go to Rabat."

He spent the night at the frontier playing Hearts with his friends in the customs and the carabineros who were sorry that he would not be smuggling for a while, because he always bribed them so well. He lost money because he could not keep his mind on the game. The train came through a little after seven and they got to Rabat before noon.

They found a place to live in Salé on the other side of the estuary, but Zuleika liked to go shopping in Rabat, so it meant that they were always taking a carriage or a taxi. She always made them stop in front of a shop where she could buy some little thing. They had cases of beer sent in all the time. She bought a radio and played it all day long, so that when he wanted to speak to her he had to shout above it. She bought perfume and French soap and something which she called "mackiyacki" made by Max Factor and put it on her face all day and then took it off with the French soap in order to begin all over again. After a while there was no more money and he said they must go to Tangier.

The train had to go through Alcazar and they were afraid that someone might see them, so he jumped off the train before they coasted into the town and ran for a long long way around the town by way of a back road and jumped on the train as it pulled slowly out of town twenty minutes later. She was sitting there with her veil, so no one recognized her. There was no trouble at the frontiers, although neither of them had any papers, because he had many friends. The trouble came when they tried to find a place to stay in Tangier. The only hotel which would take them was one in a narrow alley which dared to call itself "Hotel Satan."

Yussef went every day back and forth on the train to the Spanish zone smuggling American cigarettes which he bought from other contrabanders who brought them into the port without paying the tax. They cost him sixty pesetas a carton and he sold them for eighty; with the money he bought things which were cheaper and brought them back, dividing with the customs carabineros. Zuleika stayed in the hotel room all day or came down into the closed court of what had been an Arab house and talked with the proprietress, who was so fat that she could not move out of a bed which was set in an alcove with mirrors tilted so that she could see who came in and out. Zuleika learned many things from her which might stand her in good stead later in life.

Yussef made a few mistakes in his business, but things were not as bad as he told Zuleika one day. He said that he had lost a part of his capital. He thought that it would be a good idea if she went back to Alcazar and lived in her mother's house. The trains had just changed to the summer timetable, and it meant that he would have a very short night in Tangier. If she were in Alcazar he could make his trips in the opposite direction and sleep longer there. In a short while, saving the hotel money and saving on food, he would be able to build up his capital again and take more merchandise back and forth.

He took her back to Alcazar, where they heard that Hamid had divorced her, and the next day he left the house at nine in the morning to make the first trip according to the new timetable. In the train he thought it all over and decided that if times were as bad as he had told her, it would be better to give up smuggling for a while. There was no point in making the return trip.

❧ Early Cut-Up Experiments

*"First Cut-Ups," "Minutes to Go," and "Cut Me Up * Brion Gysin"
(1959–1960) were among Gysin's first experiments with the cut-up technique of writing, all published in* Minutes to Go *(1960), coauthored with
William S. Burroughs, Sinclair Beiles, and Gregory Corso (who recanted
his own efforts in a postscript to the book). In "Cut-Ups: A Project for Disastrous Success," written a few years later and reprinted here, Gysin recalled
his initial discovery of the technique: "While cutting a mount for a drawing
. . . I sliced through a pile of newspapers with my Stanley blade and thought
of what I had said to Burroughs some six months earlier about the necessity
for turning painters' techniques directly onto writing. I picked up the raw
words and began to piece together texts which later appeared as 'First Cut
Ups.'"*

*The cut-up offered a way of breaking through a writer's own controlling
consciousness, to open one's patterns of thought to the subversive will of language. In contrast to Tristan Tzara's more aleatory method of pulling words
out of a hat, four decades earlier, the cut-up managed to retain a sort of
print or mark of the writer whose text was transformed, because it dealt
with recombining fragments of syntax. "There's an actual treatment of the
material as if it were a piece of cloth," Gysin explained when I first interviewed him in 1980. "The sentence, even the word, becomes a real piece
of plastic material that you can cut into."*

*Gysin later employed the cut-up in writing both of his novels, but there
the technique served as part of a process by which he extended and reworked
certain texts. It was Burroughs who applied the technique most extensively,
notably in three novels from the early 1960s—*The Soft Machine, The
Ticket That Exploded, *and* Nova Express—*where the cut-up narratives
were presented in more of a raw state. In addition to other writers who
experimented with the method, both David Bowie and Iggy Pop have ac-
knowledged its importance for them as songwriters. Antony Balch applied
the concept to film as well, in the early 1960s, in* Towers Open Fire *and*
The Cut Ups, *which featured Gysin and Burroughs. The results produced
by the cut-up can even be said to prefigure the work of such writers as the
Language poets of the 1970s and later.*

First Cut-Ups

(September 1959. A collage from the Paris *Herald Tribune*, the London *Observer*, the London *Daily Mail*, *Life* magazine advertisements.)

/   1   /

It is impossible to estimate the damage. Anything put out up to now is like pulling a figure out of the air.

Six distinguished British women said to us later, indicating the crowd of chic young women who were fingering samples, "If our prices weren't as good or better, they wouldn't come. Eve is eternal."

(I'm going right back to the Sheraton Carlton and call the Milwaukee Braves.)

Miss Hannah Pugh the slim model—a member of the Diners' Club, the American Express Credit Cards, etc.—drew from a piggy bank a talent which is the very quintessence of the British Female sex.

"People aren't crazy," she said. "Now that Hazard has banished my timidity I feel that I, too, can live on streams in the area where people are urged to be watchful."

A huge wave rolled in from the wake of Hurricane Gracie and bowled a married couple off a jetty. The wife's body was found—the husband was missing, presumed drowned.

Tomorrow the moon will be 228,400 miles from the earth and the sun almost 93,000,000 miles away.

/   2   /

"Ahead, ahead, ahead!" they chanted in EWYORK, ONOLULU, ARIS, OME, OSTON. "Tobacco is our middle name."

No flat OS ANGELES taste—AN FRANCISCO *so friendly*, effective, gentles the smoke makes it unmade in the sanctity of a joint. We can't do that yet. You can light either end, beat your mother to death with a beaded bag. A surprise. Good for a gift with special discount and dispensation.

We have seen the future in willow and rattan, manila, malacca, bamboo and hemp. These are materials for which we have a passionate weakness.

The attraction here is tea. It would be forced on the Federal Parliament, the Parliaments of the ten states, the Catholic, Protestant and Jewish communities, the association of employers and the trade unions. The national network would summon policemen and provide spokesmen.

Such basketry is too big to be on a regional basis and occupying authorities would remain in existence. Next year we will have delegates to ENEVA as the stock is enormous.

/ 3 /

Hume gets Halard the stocky, black-haired who struts when the moon wanders. He stood silent and flushed. He nodded curtly, considering the wide spaces where past crimes highlighted a Soviet-sponsored bid to make Short Time. The Iron Age, six months short, was convicted of killing a cabbie who had crossed the Atlantic in the balloon Small World.

There seemed little doubt, however, that Mr. Eisenhower said, "I weigh 56 pounds less than a man," flushed and nodded curtly.

Asked whether he had had a fair trial he looks inevitable and publishes: "My sex was an advantage."

He boasted of a long string of past crimes highlighted by a total eclipse of however stood in his path when he redid her apartment.

/ 4 /

Rich because beautiful bought brain. I said, "Bravo!"

She got excited and came at me and I slugged her. I tried to create illusion but, You're wrong, you're always wrong. It's known the world over.

She gave no indication of trouble at the time but "Old Bill" returned to war. Then she settled down just to "chat." Since the conversation touched a lot of bases it was both fascinating and frightening. But because I don't go for individual tastes I became her lover on a long voyage from the Orient.

To think that a million men were fitted into long slots in an absurd position for the highest products of creation. Crowds stopped the traffic and it took more than 30 police to disperse them.

In Hollywood, Rita Haywo in the ground facing another million in their slots, said: "When I started this thing I had sideburns and a guy but the authorities didn't want to mix rock with politics. The crowds stopped the traffic and it fell to Mr. Van R in the line of duty to think that a million men were fitted into the ground in their slots."

The finding of Mr. Van R's uniform in their slots seemed so absurd in Flanders where he served in the sky like a comet and crashed. For the first time in history a woman presided over the Lower House.

/ 5 /

Captain Bairn was arrested today in the murder at sea of Chicago. He is one of the great Americans to see people from the front and kept laughing during the dark. His use of sweeping color last night claimed his lover on a long trip from the Orient. He streaked across the sky like a comet and crashed.

Witnesses, from a distance, observed a roaring blast and a brilliant flash as the operator was arrested. A petite blue-eyed blonde streaked across the sky and clashed with Glascow police. She had wielded the gavel with a walrus moustache and was thrown overboard. Her father, a well-known Artist until a bundle of his accented brush-work blew up in the sky, said, "We can't do that yet. The reason I'm not buying a new couch is to save money. She should have known better."

Keep up AMBOURG, USSELDORF, Police riots.

They can't turn—this keeps the front of the game either to have been left out or taken.

Breakfasts in OS ANGELES are anybody's spiritual home nowadays. Think they are never seen higher up. Left. Right!

I adore him because he is so lovely with the seesaw motion. She has a way of looking at things that turns even the rear end of bars in years.

"If I'd known you were coming."

Some looks are simply good right there. You hit her in this new revised edition of, "AFTER THE GREAT AWAKENING" in a car that's almost as steady as he claimed in an exclusive drag. It's tail when it stars. You go around it yourself. The sure way is with arrangement and also military appeal. Deep-eyed features and the rapt faces of discursive charm come from the sheer, shining color of police.

To protect this art the right way, clout first Woman and believers in their look of things. Fourteen-year old boy has many of her belongings.

Swiss boys were absolutely free from the producers of outboard spiritual homes.
I, Sekuin, perfected this art "along the Tang dynasty."
Might be just what I am look.
Aurelius would have approved you favorite smoke.

Minutes to Go

the hallucinated have come to tell you that yr utilities
are being shut off   dreams monitored   thought directed
sex is shutting down everywhere   you are being sent

all words are taped   agents everywhere
marking down the live ones   to exterminate

they are turning out the lights

no   they are not evil   nor the devil   but men
on a mission   with a spot of work to do

this   dear friends   they intend to do on you

you have been offered a choice   between liberty and
freedom   and   No!   you cannot have both

the next step   is everyone into space   but it has been
a long dull wait   since the last tower of babel
that first derisive visit of the   paraclete

let's not hear that noise again   and again

that may well be   the last word   anywhere

this is not the beginning   in the beginning was the word
the word has been in for a too   long time
you in the word and   the word in you

we are out
you are in

we have come to let you out

here and now we will show you   what you can do
with and to
the word
the words
any word
all the words

Pick a book   any book   cut it up
cut up
prose
poems

newspapers
magazines
the bible
the koran
the book of moroni
la-tzu
confucius
the bhagavad gita
anything
letters
business correspondence
ads
all the words

slice down the middle   dice into sections
according to taste
chop in some bible   pour on some Madison Avenue
prose
shuffle like cards   toss like confetti
taste it like piping hot   alphabet soup

pass yr friends' letters   yr office carbons
through any such sieve   as you may find or invent

you will soon see   just what they really are
saying   this is the terminal method for
finding the truth

piece together a masterpiece   a week
use better materials   more highly charged words

there is no longer a need   to drum up a season of
geniuses   be your own agent   until we deliver
the machine   in commercially reasonable quantities

we wish to announce   that while we esteem
this to be truly   the American Way
we have no commitments   with any government
groups

the writing machine   is for everybody
do it yourself   until the machine comes
here is the system   according to us

CUT ME UP * BRION GYSIN * CUT ME UP * BRION GYSIN * CUT ME UP * BRION GYSIN * CUT ME IN *

Nothing here was written "under marijuana" or "under" anything else. Billie Holiday and Baudelaire have borne witness that nothing was ever written or sung better under any drug.

Hachichi I am and I bow respectfully and gratefully to my Principal as any Client should (not *must*). My Principal is no Monkey—no Machine. My Principal is called Out. I am a poor Singer but I can write out all of the Song I know in two ways and on both sides of this paper. Who runs may read. Learn to read by improving your running.

Dig deep what Burroughs has to say against junk. Mektoub—It Was Written. Dig the difference between all the Junks acting on numerical proliferation and pot, art or whatnot acting outside of number. Outside of number is the only way out. The only way out to space. If you don't want out you don't want space and the less you get until you have none at all. The Ins want space for themselves because they can never but never get enough of it to be comfortable. THEY CAN'T. The way out is Here and it CAN BE WRITTEN. You can start writing it now by cutting up this whole book. Add what you like and make a new book of it. We have called
IN * BRION GYSIN * CUT ME IN * BRION GYSIN * CUT ME IN * BRION GYSIN * CUT ME IN * BRION GYSIN * CUT ME IN * BRION GYSIN * this method the CUT-UPS EVER SINCE WE FIRST STARTED ON THEM and the name is as good as any. They are not a new Discovery.

Tristan Tzara, the Man from Nowhere, divined Dada out of a dictionary with a knife, pulled words out of a hat and might well have burned the Louvre if he hadn't diverted into the Communist Panic by the Art Wing of the Freudian Conspiracy calling itself Surrealism under André Breton. We don't want to see it happen again. Above all I don't—I the Man from Nowhere negotiated like a Tangier Space Draft on a Swiss bank.

There is no game without two players. In other words, it could. But this is the Open Bank—these monkeys hear a lot and see a lot and talk almost all they know. Anyhow, here is the gimmick. Cut up everything in sight. Make your whole life a poem. You can't lose, man. You can't lose because you've got nothing to lose but that worthless junk you're sitting on. Get out of that blue frigidaire and Live. You'll know everything. You'll hear everything. And you'll see everything that's going on. Really make the entire scene. Not many chicks will. Say they know plenty already. They do. Try it. Be a Poet. Be a Man. Never forget that Grandaddy Burroughs invented the adding machine when the more efficient abacus had been used for thousands of years in Asia. Yesterday a thousand years ago, Hassan Sabbah, a Persian by birth and school-chum of Omar Khayyam, walked by accident (as if there were any accidents) into the studios of Radio Cairo to find all the cats bombed. He realized like a flash that *he* could

SEND, TOO. He took the mike to an unheated pent-house called Alamut near the Caspian. Called the Aga Khan today, his original station nearly a thousand years ago could broadcast from Alamut to Paris with Charlemagne on the house phone and as far as Xanadu East. Today the same lines have been prolif-erating machine-wise and a stray wire into the room I am in . . . Well, you figure it out. Try it yourself. Here is how to do it: Let's see, now. No, I'm not stalling. Common sense tells you that words are meant to mislead. Especially in these areas. It's about like this: Just talk to yourself for a minute. You hear that little voice? Well, now argue with yourself: take two sides of a question. Dig? That's already a line. Do it like a phone call. Broadcast something. I hesi-tate to advise, because I know only for me, that something pretty saucy will often get you a sharp answer. Realize that it is an answer when you hear it and not just you. Your first party or any party may be hard to identify but just go on listening. Soon plenty of voices will come in and soon you will be able to call out. Don't put this down. Lots of people want this, need it and are damned well getting it by themselves. This ain't no monopoly, lady. Shove off, you! Well, as I was saying before I was so brashly interrupted . . . Stop and Lis-ten. The state called reverie just before sleep is a good place to start. You may find the head-shrinkers putting this down, they will. If you work on some me-chanical job this should be a snap for you.

Artists and intellectuals BEST learn a method best called LOOK AWAY. You will find that you are broadcasting at all hours without knowing it. How else do you think ideas "get around," man. Well, call me any time you want and just identify yourself when you call. Name and address, please. I'll be glad to talk to you about all this or anything else you have in mind. Crazy, man, crazy. We need this. We have got to have this or, frankly, fellow pale-faces, we are SCREWED. I'm not putting that down, either, but I think I know what it means. Do you? Every non-paleface is on the line FREE OF CHARGE. Pale-face have the CHARGE but the line is not free for him. The TOLL has, historically, been enor-mous. THERE IS NO NEED TO HEAR THAT NOISE AGAIN. We went through the Ice Age in the Cave and came out to hunt sickly-pale like Lazarus or any Haitian zombie with a Reactive mind built in by our women who sent us. Women-sent Motherlovers, to a man. It must have been great in that Cave — or that's the way they put it. Me, myself, now . . . All anybody was ever supposed to

want to do was to get back IN. Well, if you want to get IN instead of OUT then
SPACE is not for you and you are going to get less and less of it until you don't
have any at all. The INs always say MINE. I put that down. It's EVERYBODY'S
space and there's plenty of it. A point in space is an argument place says Witt-
genstein. "No two anythings can occupy the same spacetime position," mutters
Burroughs. Go on. Who says Time? It is in the power of every hand to destroy
us and we are beholden to every one we meet, he doth not kill us. BUT The river
hath more need of the fountain than the fountain of the river . . . the swarming
sting of the sun has ceased over the endless lakes of lilac light burning away to a
fiery rose on the dunes running like molten orange-gold. The day-tortured eye
can no longer support. Before it died behind the clenched lids the sun
wrenched itself from the sky and fell sickeningly over the edge of world. Blues
deepen like vertigo into permanganate purples. An icy chill sweeps the very
length of darkness after sun, cracking the desert rocks like a rattle of fire across
the Sahara. Step into a Grain of Sand. It is Everybody's Earthly Kingdom bathed
in the white light. You can get the light with prayer, mescaline, fasting, sex and
know where to find it again when you want it. Praktice makes perfect. Neither
prayer nor mescaline nor anything else makes it happen. The light is there. Myself, I think that our troubles have only started and now that we have cut you in
on this you are in on it whether you like it or not. You are on our side now that
you have read this far and you are sitting pretty. This has taken you out of the
area of words. If they throw words at youcutthemup and throw them back. If
you want to make them disappear just rub out their words. If you want to disappear . . . come around for private lessons. Free. Painters have it made. Dangerous ground. Picasso can make a rainbow frame his new house and Cezanne's
mountain behind it. See LOOK. He ate the entire Imaginary Museum, shat on
a canvas and sold it for a rainbow. Who can say? We don't need to burn the
Louvre now. The Equanimity of Complete Despair. The Shining Air. Sensitive
Desert. Puddles of Light. One Pace from Nowhere. Clouds on a Wall. Erasmus
to Durer. It is like being against the weather. Into the Space Ship on the IN Pro-
gramme must go: A Scientist, A Colonel, and A Magician. To live in a capsule
of Earth atmosphere out there and propagate virus-wise there must be a
Woman. A Tin-Hinan of Outer Space that she wants to make into IN-space for
her. Tin-Hinan veiled the Touareg men and dyed them blue. The Space Queen
hopes to step into the ship and throw off her horrid disguise. Stripping off her
gimmicks and tossing them to the boys she raises aloft a vial of sperm and pro-
claims herself to be the sole Scientific and Magical Colonel of Space. "Back to
Earth you Drones," she snarls to Men. "And keep humping." From having been

artisans, painters have become alchemists and now to this. Wurra, wurra! The
great painters burn up the subjects they touch—all the fine flesh, roses, guitars
and most of that merely visible world has been burned down for good. Now
here's the picture: One eye strikes deeper into it than the other eye. This throws
the Intellect or even the Reactive Mind or whatever right off balance for long
enough for You to *see* that other dimension. Painters are bucking for space like
Cézanne bucked for the museum. Painters and Prophets speak in ecstatic
tongues which even they "know" only in the act of speaking them. Look Away.

LOOK AWAY * BRION GYSIN * LOOK OUT * BRION GYSIN * LOOK AWAY *
BRION GYSIN * LOOK OUT * LOOK AWAY * BRION GYSIN * LOOK OUT

 # Permutation Poems

Closely related to the principle of the cut-up, where the intended coherence of a text is interrupted and rearranged, the permutation involves a more mathematical variation of the concept as exercised on a short phrase. Concurrent with his exploration of the cut-up, Gysin discovered the permutation upon seeing in print the Divine Tautology, "I am that I am," while reading Aldous Huxley's The Doors of Perception. *In my 1980 interview, he elaborated: "I saw the phrase on paper and I thought, 'Ah, it looks a bit like the front of a Greek temple,' only on the condition that I put the biggest word in the middle. So, I'll just change these others around, 'am I,' in the corner of the architrave. Then I realized, as soon as I did this, it asked a question. 'I am that, am I?' And I said, 'Wow, I've touched the oracle!' So then I turned the next one, and I said, 'Oh, all the way along it has to do this.'" Though it was the first of his permutation poems, "I Am That I Am" (1959) was not published till years later (in* Brion Gysin Let the Mice In *[1973]; a short version appeared in Emmett Williams'* An Anthology of Concrete Poetry *[1967]). The full version, as put through a computer by mathematician Ian Sommerville, was performed for* BBC Radio *in 1960, as part of a program, "The Permutated Poems of Brion Gysin." The show, says Gysin, was "broadcast to the second lowest rating of audience approval registered by their poll of listeners. Still sorry to think that the lowest rating on record went to an opus by Auden and Britten.* BBC dixit." *Also included in the show was "Pistol Poem," where the concept was applied more directly to qualities of sound. In this piece, a single pistol shot was recorded on tape and then rerecorded, he has explained, "as heard from the distance of one yard, two yards, three yards, four yards and five yards. These reports were run through their possible permutations and laid in sound layers with my voice speaking the numbers."*

Such work, later rebroadcast throughout Europe, earned Gysin a reputation as one of the founders of the international discipline known as Sound Poetry, or poésie sonore, *and the permutations became a mainstay of his performance work ever after. Indeed, these poems may well be more effective on hearing them, for he did not just change around the order of words in a phrase but read them out for the provocative new sense they made. As a treatment of sound, the permutation poems also influenced the repetitive composers, notably Philip Glass, and musicians like Daevid Allen, founder of the rock group Soft Machine.*

"Junk Is No Good Baby" (1959) and "Kick That Habit Man" (1959) were

part of the BBC *program as well. These and other permutation poems were first published in* The Exterminator *(1960), interspersed among cut-up texts by the book's coauthor, Burroughs. Much later, in the early 1980s, both poems were set to music on two different occasions by Steve Lacy and Ramuntcho Matta; Lacy assigned specific pitches to the words, permutating them accordingly, whereas Matta provided a more rhythmic, new-wave rock setting. The versions here are those used by Lacy. "No Poets Don't Own Words" (1960), performed by Gysin on his record* Orgy Boys *(1982), was one of several permutated phrases that reinforced the idea of freeing language from individual control, one of the dominant concerns he shared with Burroughs. "I Don't Work You Dig" (1974), also set to music by Lacy, shows that Gysin continued to explore the permutation to great effect in subsequent periods. "This Is Sam Francis" (1960) is a permutation poem that Gysin wrote for his friend on the occasion of a show and catalogue of Francis's paintings; it is the only time that Gysin permutated a phrase that included names, which lends a different twist to the play of meanings, and was originally published in his own handwriting. Nor is the visual aspect to be ignored: almost immediately after his discovery, Gysin was also applying the permutation to his work as a painter.*

I Am That I Am

<table>
<tr><td>I AM THAT I AM</td><td>I I THAT AM AM</td></tr>
<tr><td>AM I THAT I AM</td><td>THAT I I AM AM</td></tr>
<tr><td>I THAT AM I AM</td><td>I THAT I AM AM</td></tr>
<tr><td>THAT I AM I AM</td><td>AM THAT I I AM</td></tr>
<tr><td>AM THAT I I AM</td><td>THAT AM I I AM</td></tr>
<tr><td>THAT AM I I AM</td><td>AM I THAT I AM</td></tr>
<tr><td>I AM I THAT AM</td><td>I AM THAT I AM</td></tr>
<tr><td>AM I I THAT AM</td><td>THAT I AM I AM</td></tr>
<tr><td>I I AM THAT AM</td><td>I THAT AM I AM</td></tr>
<tr><td>I I AM THAT AM</td><td>I AM THAT AM I</td></tr>
<tr><td>AM I I THAT AM</td><td>AM I THAT AM I</td></tr>
<tr><td>I AM I THAT AM</td><td>I THAT AM AM I</td></tr>
<tr><td>I THAT I AM AM</td><td>THAT I AM AM I</td></tr>
<tr><td>THAT I I AM AM</td><td>AM THAT I AM I</td></tr>
<tr><td>I I THAT AM AM</td><td>THAT AM I AM I</td></tr>
</table>

I AM AM THAT I
AM I AM THAT I
I AM AM THAT I
AM I AM THAT I
AM AM I THAT I
AM AM I THAT I
I THAT AM AM I
THAT I AM AM I
I AM THAT AM I
AM I THAT AM I
THAT AM I AM I
AM THAT I AM I
AM THAT AM I I
THAT AM AM I I
AM AM THAT I I
AM AM THAT I I
THAT AM AM I I
AM THAT AM I I
I AM I AM THAT
AM I I AM THAT
I I AM AM THAT
I I AM AM THAT
AM I I AM THAT
I AM I AM THAT
I AM AM I THAT
AM I AM I THAT
I AM AM I THAT
AM I AM I THAT
AM AM I I THAT
AM AM I I THAT
I I AM AM THAT
I I AM AM THAT
I AM I AM THAT
AM I I AM THAT
I AM I AM THAT
AM I I AM THAT
AM I AM I THAT
I AM AM I THAT
AM AM I I THAT

AM AM I I THAT
I AM AM I THAT
AM I AM I THAT
I THAT I AM AM
THAT I I AM AM
I I THAT AM AM
I I THAT AM AM
THAT I I AM AM
I THAT I AM AM
I THAT AM I AM
THAT I AM I AM
I AM THAT I AM
AM I THAT I AM
THAT AM I I AM
AM THAT I I AM
I I AM THAT AM
I I AM THAT AM
I AM I THAT AM
AM I I THAT AM
I AM I THAT AM
AM I I THAT AM
THAT I AM I AM
I THAT AM I AM
THAT AM I I AM
AM THAT I I AM
I AM THAT I AM
AM I THAT I AM
AM THAT I AM I
THAT AM I AM I
AM I THAT AM I
I AM THAT AM I
THAT I AM AM I
I THAT AM AM I
AM THAT AM I I
THAT AM AM I I
AM AM THAT I I
AM AM THAT I I
THAT AM AM I I
AM THAT AM I I

AM I AM THAT I
I AM AM THAT I
AM AM I THAT I
AM AM I THAT I
I AM AM THAT I
AM I AM THAT I
THAT I AM AM I
I THAT AM AM I
THAT AM I AM I
AM THAT I AM I
I AM THAT AM I
AM I THAT AM I
AM I AM THAT I
AM AM I THAT I
AM I THAT AM I
AM THAT I AM I
AM AM THAT I I
AM THAT AM I I
I AM I AM THAT
AM AM I I THAT
AM I I AM THAT
AM I I AM THAT
AM AM I I THAT
AM I AM I THAT
AM I THAT I AM
AM THAT I I AM
AM I I THAT AM
AM I I THAT AM
AM THAT I I AM
AM I THAT I AM
AM AM THAT I I
AM THAT AM I I
AM AM I THAT I
AM I AM THAT I
AM THAT I AM I
AM I THAT AM I
I I AM THAT AM
I AM I THAT AM
I I THAT AM AM

I THAT I AM AM
I AM THAT I AM
I THAT AM I AM
I I AM AM THAT
I AM I AM THAT
I I AM AM THAT
I AM I AM THAT
I AM AM I THAT
I AM AM I THAT
I I THAT AM AM
I THAT I AM AM
I I AM THAT AM
I AM I THAT AM
I THAT AM I AM
I AM THAT I AM
I AM THAT AM I
I THAT AM AM I
I AM AM THAT I
I AM AM THAT I
I THAT AM AM I
I AM THAT AM I
THAT I AM I AM
THAT AM I I AM
THAT I I AM AM
THAT I I AM AM
THAT AM I I AM
THAT I AM I AM
THAT I AM AM I
THAT AM I AM I
THAT I AM AM I
THAT AM I AM I
THAT AM AM I I
THAT AM AM I I
THAT I I AM AM
THAT I I AM AM
THAT I AM I AM
THAT AM I I AM
THAT I AM I AM
THAT AM I I AM

THAT AM I AM I
THAT I AM AM I
THAT AM AM I I
THAT AM AM I I
THAT I AM AM I
THAT AM I AM I
AM I THAT I AM
AM THAT I I AM
AM I I THAT AM
AM I I THAT AM
AM THAT I I AM
AM I THAT I AM
AM I THAT AM I
AM THAT I AM I
AM I AM THAT I
AM AM I THAT I
AM THAT AM I I
AM AM THAT I I
AM I I AM THAT
AM I I AM THAT
AM I AM I THAT
AM AM I I THAT
AM I AM I THAT
AM AM I I THAT
AM THAT I AM I
AM I THAT AM I
AM THAT AM I I
AM AM THAT I I
AM I AM THAT I
AM AM I THAT I
I AM THAT I AM
I THAT AM I AM
I AM I THAT AM
I I AM THAT AM
I THAT I AM AM
I I THAT AM AM
I AM THAT AM I
I THAT AM AM I
I AM AM THAT I

I AM AM THAT I
I THAT AM AM I
I AM THAT AM I
I AM I AM THAT
I I AM AM THAT
I AM AM I THAT
I AM AM I THAT
I I AM AM THAT
I AM I AM THAT
I THAT I AM AM
I I THAT AM AM
I THAT AM I AM
I AM THAT I AM
I I AM THAT AM
I AM I THAT AM
I AM I AM THAT
I AM AM I THAT
I AM I THAT AM
I AM THAT I AM
I AM AM THAT I
I AM THAT AM I
THAT AM I AM I
THAT AM AM I I
THAT AM I I AM
THAT AM I I AM
THAT AM AM I I
THAT AM I AM I
AM AM I THAT I
AM AM THAT I I
AM AM THAT I I
AM AM I I THAT
AM AM I I THAT
AM AM THAT I I
AM AM I THAT I
I AM AM THAT I
I AM THAT AM I
I AM AM I THAT
I AM I AM THAT
I AM THAT I AM

I AM I THAT AM
AM I I AM THAT
AM I AM I THAT
AM I I THAT AM
AM I THAT I AM
AM I AM THAT I
AM I THAT AM I
THAT I I AM AM
THAT I AM I AM
THAT I I AM AM
THAT I AM I AM
THAT I AM AM I
THAT I AM AM I
AM I I THAT AM
AM I THAT I AM
AM I I AM THAT
AM I AM I THAT
AM I THAT AM I
AM I AM THAT I
I I AM THAT AM
I I THAT AM AM
I I AM AM THAT
I I AM AM THAT
I I THAT AM AM
I I AM THAT AM
AM THAT I AM I
AM THAT AM I I
AM THAT I I AM
AM THAT I I AM
AM THAT AM I I
AM THAT I AM I
I THAT I AM AM
I THAT AM I AM
I THAT I AM AM
I THAT BACK I AM
I THAT AM AM I
I THAT AM AM I
AM THAT I I AM
AM THAT I I AM

AM THAT I AM I
AM THAT AM I I
AM THAT I AM I
AM THAT AM I I
I THAT AM I AM
I THAT I AM AM
I THAT AM AM I
I THAT AM AM I
I THAT I AM AM
I THAT AM I AM
AM AM I THAT I
AM AM THAT I I
AM AM I I THAT
AM AM I I THAT
AM AM THAT I I
AM AM I THAT I
I AM I THAT AM
I AM THAT I AM
I AM I AM THAT
I AM AM I THAT
I AM THAT AM I
I AM AM THAT I
THAT AM I I AM
THAT AM I I AM
THAT AM I AM I
THAT AM AM I I
THAT AM I AM I
THAT AM AM I I
I AM THAT I AM
I AM I THAT AM
I AM THAT AM I
I AM AM THAT I
I AM I AM THAT
I AM AM I THAT
AM I AM THAT I
AM I THAT AM I
AM I AM I THAT
AM I I AM THAT
AM I THAT I AM

AM I I THAT AM
I I AM THAT AM
I I THAT AM AM
I I AM AM THAT
I I AM AM THAT
I I THAT AM AM
I I AM THAT AM
THAT I AM I AM
THAT I I AM AM
THAT I AM AM I
THAT I AM AM I
THAT I I AM AM
THAT I AM I AM
AM I THAT I AM
AM I I THAT AM
AM I THAT AM I
AM I AM THAT I
AM I I AM THAT
AM I AM I THAT
THAT I AM I AM
THAT I AM AM I
AM I AM I THAT
AM I AM THAT I
I I AM AM THAT
I I AM THAT AM
I THAT AM I AM
I THAT AM AM I
AM THAT AM I I
AM THAT AM I I
I THAT AM AM I
I THAT AM I AM
I AM AM I THAT
I AM AM THAT I
THAT AM AM I I
THAT AM AM I I
I AM AM THAT I
I AM AM I THAT
I I AM AM THAT
I I AM THAT AM

THAT I AM AM I
THAT I AM I AM
AM I AM THAT I
AM I AM I THAT
THAT AM I I AM
THAT AM I AM I
AM AM I I THAT
AM AM I THAT I
I AM I AM THAT
I AM I THAT AM
AM THAT I I AM
AM THAT I AM I
AM THAT I I AM
AM THAT I AM I
I THAT I AM AM
I THAT I AM AM
AM AM I I THAT
AM AM I THAT I
THAT AM I I AM
THAT AM I AM I
I AM I THAT AM
I AM I AM THAT
AM I I AM THAT
AM I I THAT AM
THAT I I AM AM
THAT I I AM AM
AM I I THAT AM
AM I I AM THAT
I AM THAT I AM
I AM THAT AM I
AM AM THAT I I
AM AM THAT I I
I AM THAT AM I
I AM THAT I AM
AM I THAT I AM
AM I THAT AM I
AM I THAT I AM
AM I THAT AM I
I I THAT AM AM

I I THAT AM AM
AM AM THAT I I
AM AM THAT I I
I AM THAT I AM
I AM THAT AM I
I AM THAT I AM
I AM THAT AM I
AM I THAT AM I
AM I THAT I AM
I I THAT AM AM
I I THAT AM AM
AM I THAT I AM
AM I THAT AM I
I AM AM I THAT
I AM AM THAT I
THAT AM AM I I
THAT AM AM I I
I AM AM THAT I
I AM AM I THAT
AM I AM I THAT
AM I AM THAT I
THAT I AM I AM
THAT I AM AM I
I I AM THAT AM
I I AM AM THAT
AM THAT AM I I
AM THAT AM I I
I THAT AM I AM
I THAT AM AM I
I THAT AM I AM
I THAT AM AM I
AM I AM THAT I
AM I AM I THAT
I I AM THAT AM
I I AM BAM THAT
THAT I AM I AM
THAT I AM AM I
I AM I AM THAT
I AM I THAT AM

THAT AM I AM I
THAT AM I I AM
AM AM I THAT I
AM AM I I THAT
AM I I AM THAT
AM I I THAT AM
THAT I I AM AM
THAT I I AM AM
AM I I THAT AM
AM I I AM THAT
AM THAT I AM I
AM THAT I I AM
I THAT I AM AM
I THAT I AM AM
AM THAT I I AM
AM THAT I AM I
AM AM I THAT I
AM AM I I THAT
I AM I THAT AM
I AM I AM THAT
THAT AM I I AM
THAT AM I AM I
AM THAT I AM I
I THAT I AM AM
THAT AM I AM I
I AM I AM THAT
THAT I I AM AM
AM I I AM THAT
AM I THAT AM I
I I THAT AM AM
I AM THAT AM I
I AM THAT AM I
I I THAT AM AM
AM I THAT AM I
THAT I AM AM I
I I AM AM THAT
I THAT AM AM I
I THAT AM AM I
I AM AM THAT I

THAT I AM AM I
THAT I I AM AM
AM I I AM THAT
I THAT I AM AM
AM THAT I AM I
I AM I AM THAT
THAT AM I AM I
AM THAT AM I I
I THAT AM I AM
THAT AM AM I I
I AM AM I THAT
THAT I AM I AM
AM I AM I THAT
AM AM THAT I I
I AM THAT I AM
AM AM THAT I I
I AM THAT I AM
AM I THAT I AM
AM I THAT I AM
THAT AM AM I I
I AM AM I THAT
AM THAT AM I I
I THAT AM I AM
AM I AM I THAT
THAT I AM I AM
THAT AM I I AM
AM AM I I THAT
AM THAT I I AM
AM THAT I I AM
AM AM I I THAT
THAT AM I I AM
AM I AM THAT I
I I AM THAT AM
I AM AM THAT I
I AM AM THAT I
I I AM THAT AM
AM I AM THAT I
AM AM I THAT I
I AM I THAT AM

AM AM I THAT I
I AM I THAT AM
AM I I THAT AM
AM I I THAT AM
I AM AM THAT I
I AM AM THAT I
AM I AM THAT I
I I AM THAT AM
AM I AM THAT I
I I AM THAT AM
I AM I THAT AM
AM AM I THAT I
AM I I THAT AM
AM I I THAT AM
AM AM I THAT I
I AM I THAT AM
THAT I AM AM I
I I AM AM THAT
I THAT AM AM I
I THAT AM AM I
I I AM AM THAT
THAT I AM AM I
THAT AM I AM I
I AM I AM THAT
AM THAT I AM I
I THAT I AM AM
AM I I AM THAT
THAT I I AM AM
I AM THAT AM I
I AM THAT AM I
AM I THAT AM I
I I THAT AM AM
AM I THAT AM I
I I THAT AM AM
I AM I AM THAT
THAT AM I AM I
AM I I AM THAT
THAT I I AM AM
AM THAT I AM I

I THAT I AM AM
THAT I AM I AM
AM I AM I THAT
I THAT AM I AM
AM THAT AM I I
I AM AM I THAT
THAT AM AM I I
THAT AM I I AM
AM AM I I THAT
AM THAT I I AM
AM THAT I I AM
AM AM I I THAT
THAT AM I I AM

I AM THAT I AM
AM AM THAT I I
AM I THAT I AM
AM I THAT I AM
AM AM THAT I I
I AM THAT I AM
I AM AM I THAT
THAT AM AM I I
AM I AM I THAT
THAT I AM I AM
AM THAT AM I I
I THAT AM I AM

Junk Is No Good Baby

JUNK IS NO GOOD BABY
IS NO GOOD BABY JUNK
NO GOOD BABY IS JUNK
GOOD BABY JUNK IS NO
BABY JUNK IS NO GOOD

JUNK BABY IS NO GOOD
IS NO GOOD JUNK BABY
NO GOOD JUNK BABY IS
GOOD JUNK BABY IS NO
BABY IS NO GOOD JUNK

JUNK NO GOOD BABY IS
IS JUNK NO GOOD BABY
NO GOOD BABY IS JUNK
GOOD BABY IS JUNK NO
BABY IS JUNK NO GOOD

JUNK GOOD IS NO BABY
IS NO BABY JUNK GOOD
NO BABY JUNK GOOD IS

GOOD IS NO BABY JUNK
BABY JUNK GOOD IS NO

JUNK IS NO BABY GOOD
IS NO BABY GOOD JUNK
NO BABY GOOD JUNK IS
GOOD JUNK IS NO BABY
BABY GOOD JUNK IS NO

JUNK IS BABY NO GOOD
IS BABY NO GOOD JUNK
NO GOOD JUNK IS BABY
GOOD JUNK IS BABY NO
BABY NO GOOD JUNK IS

JUNK IS GOOD BABY NO
IS GOOD BABY NO JUNK
NO JUNK IS GOOD BABY
GOOD BABY NO JUNK IS
BABY NO JUNK IS GOOD

Kick That Habit Man

KICK THAT HABIT MAN   KICK HABIT MAN THAT
THAT HABIT KICK MAN   HABIT MAN THAT KICK
HABIT MAN KICK THAT   THAT KICK HABIT MAN
MAN KICK THAT HABIT   MAN THAT KICK HABIT

KICK THAT MAN HABIT   KICK MAN HABIT THAT
THAT MAN HABIT KICK   HABIT THAT KICK MAN
HABIT KICK THAT MAN   THAT KICK MAN HABIT
MAN HABIT THAT KICK   MAN HABIT THAT KICK

KICK HABIT THAT MAN   KICK MAN THAT HABIT
THAT MAN KICK HABIT   THAT HABIT KICK MAN
HABIT THAT MAN KICK   HABIT KICK THAT MAN
MAN KICK HABIT THAT   MAN THAT HABIT KICK

No Poets Dont Own Words

For John Giorno

NO	POETS	DONT	OWN	WORDS
POETS	DONT	OWN	WORDS	NO
DONT	OWN	WORDS	NO	POETS
OWN	WORDS	(K)NO(W)	POETS	DONT
WORDS	(K)NO(W)	POETS	DONT	OWN

(K)NO(W)	POETS	DONT	WORDS	OWN
POETS	DONT	WORDS	OWN	NO
DONT	WORDS	OWN	NO	POETS
OWN	NO	POETS	DONT	WORDS
WORDS	OWN	NO	POETS	DONT

NO	POETS	OWN	WORDS	DONT
POETS	OWN	WORDS	DONT	(K)NO(W)
DONT	(K)NO(W)	POETS	OWN	WORDS
OWN	WORDS	DONT	(K)NO(W)	POETS
WORDS	DONT	(K)NO(W)	POETS	OWN

NO	POETS	OWN	DONT	WORDS
POETS	OWN	DONT	WORDS	NO
DONT	WORDS	(K)NO(W)	POETS	OWN
OWN	DONT	WORDS	KNOW	POETS
WORDS	(K)NO(W)	POETS	OWN	DONT
NO	POETS	WORDS	DONT	OWN
POETS	WORDS	DONT	OWN	NO
DONT	OWN	NO	POETS	WORDS
OWN	NO	POETS	WORDS	DONT
WORDS	DONT	OWN	NO	POETS
NO	POETS	WORDS	OWN	DONT
POETS	WORDS	OWN	DONT	KNOW
DONT	KNOW	POETS	WORDS	OWN
OWN	DONT	NO	POETS	WORDS
WORDS	OWN	DONT	KNOW	POETS
NO	DONT	OWN	WORDS	POETS
DONT	OWN	WORDS	POETS	NO
OWN	WORDS	POETS	KNOW	DONT
WORDS	POETS	KNOW	DONT	OWN
POETS	KNOW	DONT	OWN	WORDS
NO	DONT	WORDS	POETS	OWN
DONT	WORDS	POETS	OWN	NO
WORDS	POETS	OWN	KNOW	DONT
POETS	OWN	NO	DONT	WORDS
OWN	NO	DONT	WORDS	POETS
NO	DONT	OWN	POETS	WORDS
DONT	OWN	POETS	WORDS	NO
OWN	POETS	WORDS	KNOW	DONT
POETS	WORDS	KNOW	DONT	OWN
WORDS	KNOW	DONT	OWN	POETS
NO	DONT	WORDS	OWN	POETS
DONT	WORDS	OWN	POETS	NO
WORDS	OWN	POETS	KNOW	DONT
OWN	POETS	KNOW	DONT	WORDS
POETS	KNOW	DONT	WORDS	OWN

NO	DONT	POETS	OWN	WORDS
DONT	POETS	OWN	WORDS	NO
POETS	OWN	WORDS	(K)NO(W)	DONT
OWN	WORDS	(K)NO(W)	DONT	POETS
WORDS	(K)NO(W)	DONT	POETS	OWN

NO	DONT	POETS	WORDS	OWN
DONT	POETS	WORDS	OWN	NO
POETS	WORDS	OWN	NO	DONT
WORDS	OWN	NO	DONT	POETS
OWN	NO	DONT	POETS	WORDS

NO	OWN	WORDS	POETS	DONT
OWN	WORDS	POETS	DONT	(K)NO(W)
WORDS	POETS	DONT	(K)NO(W)	OWN
POETS	DONT	(K)NO(W)	OWN	WORDS
DONT	(K)NO(W)	OWN	WORDS	POETS

(K)NO(W)	OWN	WORDS	DONT	POETS
OWN	WORDS	DONT	POETS	(K)NO(W)
WORDS	DONT	POETS	(K)NO(W)	OWN
DONT	POETS	(K)NO(W)	OWN	WORDS
POETS	(K)NO(W)	OWN	WORDS	DONT

(K)NO(W)	OWN	POETS	DONT	WORDS
OWN	POETS	DONT	WORDS	(K)NO(W)
POETS	DONT	WORDS	(K)NO(W)	OWN
DONT	WORDS	(K)NO(W)	OWN	POETS
WORDS	(K)NO(W)	OWN	POETS	DONT

NO	OWN	POETS	WORDS	DONT
OWN	POETS	WORDS	DONT	(K)NO(W)
POETS	WORDS	DONT	(K)NO(W)	OWN
WORDS	DONT	(K)NO(W)	OWN	POETS
DONT	(K)NO(W)	OWN	POETS	WORDS

(K)NO(W)	OWN	DONT	POETS	WORDS
OWN	DONT	POETS	WORDS	NO
DONT	POETS	WORDS	(K)NO(W)	OWN
POETS	WORDS	(K)NO(W)	OWN	DONT
WORDS	(K)NO(W)	OWN	DONT	POETS

(K)NO(W)   OWN   DONT   WORDS   POETS
OWN   DONT   WORDS   POETS   NO
DONT   WORDS   POETS   (K)NO(W)   OWN
WORDS   POETS   (K)NO(W)   OWN   DONT
POETS   (K)NO(W)   OWN   DONT   WORDS

NO   WORDS   POETS   DONT   OWN
WORDS   POETS   DONT   OWN   NO
POETS   DONT   OWN   NO   WORDS
DONT   OWN   NO   WORDS   POETS
OWN   NO   WORDS   POETS   DONT

NO   WORDS   POETS   OWN   DONT
WORDS   POETS   OWN   DONT   NO
POETS   OWN   DONT   (K)NO(W)   WORDS
OWN   DONT   NO   WORDS   POETS
DONT   (K)NO(W)   WORDS   POETS   OWN

NO   WORDS   DONT   OWN   POETS
WORDS   OWN   DONT   POETS   NO
DONT   OWN   POETS   NO   WORDS
OWN   POETS   (K)NO(W)   WORDS   DONT
POETS   (K)NO(W)   WORDS   DONT   OWN

NO   WORDS   DONT   POETS   OWN
WORDS   DONT   POETS   OWN   NO
DONT   POETS   OWN   NO   WORDS
POETS   OWN   NO   WORDS   DONT
OWN   NO   WORDS   DONT   POETS

NO   WORDS   OWN   DONT   POETS
WORDS   OWN   DONT   POETS   (K)NO(W)
OWN   DONT   POETS   NO   WORDS
DONT   POETS   (K)NO(W)   WORDS   OWN
POETS   (K)NO(W)   WORDS   OWN   DONT

NO   WORDS   OWN   POETS   DONT
WORDS   OWN   POETS   DONT   (K)NO(W)
OWN   POETS   DONT   (K)NO(W)   WORDS
POETS   DONT   (K)NO(W)   WORDS   OWN
DONT   (K)NO(W)   WORDS   OWN   POETS

I Dont Work You Dig

I DONT WORK YOU DIG
DONT WORK YOU DIG I
WORK YOU DIG I DONT
YOU DIG I DONT WORK
DIG I DONT WORK YOU

I DONT WORK DIG YOU
DONT WORK DIG YOU I
WORK DIG YOU I DONT
YOU I DONT WORK DIG
DIG YOU I DONT WORK

I DONT YOU DIG WORK
DONT YOU DIG WORK I
WORK I DONT YOU DIG
YOU DIG WORK I DONT
DIG WORK I DONT YOU

I DONT YOU WORK DIG
DONT YOU WORK DIG I
WORK DIG I DONT YOU
YOU WORK DIG I DONT
DIG I DONT YOU WORK

I DONT DIG WORK YOU
DONT DIG WORK YOU I
WORK YOU I DONT DIG
YOU I DONT DIG WORK
DIG WORK YOU I DONT

I DONT DIG YOU WORK
DONT DIG YOU WORK I
WORK I DONT DIG YOU
YOU WORK I DONT DIG
DIG YOU WORK I DONT

This Is Sam Francis

this
is
Sam
Francis

this
is
Sam
Francis

this
is
Sam
Francis

this
is
Sam
Francis

this
is
Sam
Francis

is
Sam
Francis
this

Sam
Francis
this
is

Francis
this
is
Sam

is
Sam
Francis
this

Sam
Francis
this

Francis
this

Sam
Francis
this
is

Sam this

Sam
Francis
this
is

this
is

this
Francis
this

Sam
Francis
this
is

Francis
this
is
Sam

Francis
Sam
is
Sam

is
Sam
Francis

Francis
this
is
Sam

Francis
Sam
is
Sam

is
Sam
Francis
this

Sam
Francis
this
is

is
this
Francis
this

Sam
Francis
this

Sam this is Brion Gysin

From the catalogue *Sam Francis: Paintings, 1947–1972*, Buffalo, N.Y.: Albright-Knox, 1972

✐ Brion Gysin Let the Mice In

"Brion Gysin Let the Mice In" (1960), first published in the book of that name in 1973, was originally presented in performance at the Institute for Contemporary Arts, London, in December 1960. The text, which revisits some of his Moroccan experiences as well as his associations and experiments in Paris at the Beat Hotel, makes extensive use of the cut-up by way of his work with tape recorders. The piece itself was heard on tape while Gysin painted a picture 6 × 6 feet and "quietly disappeared." As on other occasions at the ICA but above all in Paris, his performances in the early 1960s were most often in conjunction with the Domaine Poétique, a group of experimental writers that included Jean-Clarence Lambert, Bernard Heidsieck, and Henri Chopin, who shared his interest in tape recorders and whose events incorporated sound and light shows as well.

I talk a new language. You will understand.

I talk about the springes and traps of inspiration.

IN SPIRATION—what you breathe in. You breathe in words. Words breathe you IN. I demonstrate Thee, the Out-Word in action both visual and aural, racing away in one direction to sounds more concrete than music and, in the other, to paintings like television screens in your own head. I am better than Transducer for I show you own Interior Space.

In the beginning was the Word— been in You for a toolong time. I rub out the word. You in the Word and the Word in You is a word-lock like the combination of a vault or a valise. If you love your vaults, listen no further. I spin the lock on your Interior Space Kit. Prisoner: Come Out!

I sum on the Little Folk: music from the Moroccan hills proves the great god Pan *not* dead. I cast spells: all spells are sentences spelling out the word-lock that is You. Stop. Change. Start again. Lighten your own life sentence. Go back to childhood. Throw light on your little elves as they are in my magic picture 6 × 6 feet.

There will be projections in all dimensions while the recorded voice of Wm. Burroughs reads an incantation spelled out by him.

You will understand. I talk new springes and traps of inspiration. IN SPIRATION, what you breathe in. You breathe in words. Words breathe you IN. I demonstrate Thee, the Out-Word in words that breathe you in. Aural, racing away in one direction to action both visual and music and, in the other, to painting sounds more concrete screens in your own heads. I am better than like the televisions—your own Interior Space. Transducer for Eye show.

Was the word, Been in you for a too long. In the beginning, Word. You in the word and the word in You-Time. I rub out the combination on a vault or valise. *"If"* is a word-lock, like listen no further. I spin the lock on you love your vaults. It; Prisoner: come Out!

It's *your* Interior Space, folks—music from the Moroccan hills. I summon little Pan: *not* dead. I cast spells. All proves the great god spelling out the word-lock that is You. Spells are sentences again. Lighten your own life sentence. Stop. Change. Start. Throw light on your little elves as they go back to child-hood. Are 6 × 6 feet. Are in my magic picturjections in all dimensions while the record there will be proproofs read in incantation; spelled out by the edited voice of Wm. Burro him.

Painting a picture re time and 6 × 6 during the act of an invocation for patient Moroccan to bow Chinese precede hills! Muto hirion. (sic) From the disappearance Gysin is *not* dead. Pan. Hurry. By the great god, Brion Gysin the torso of 1960. The mice in Gregory C.

A talk about the gees of stress and traps. An hours length on sprint demonstrations of snouts and recorded visual sum of both, with projections and audible word. A pell of words. Magic space instead of sound pictures, shear peace. (Rub out the word and give more space.)

I will make a bow to the picture between your ears. The audience, too, appear into the picture. Visual words dye spells to shorten painting sentence. Fainting accompanied by our Act; by a spell from/of Wm. Burroughs . . . hm, spell cast by the voice of Wm. Burroughs' pa during painting a picture 6 × 6, the act or feat. Me to high Moroccan music from the disappear in hills. Is *not* dead. Hurry. Panrion Gysin.

By the great Go, Brion Gysin let Corso 1960 the mice in. Gregory Corso, 1960 aten Gysin the mice in Gregory. Spell cast by the ancient voice of Wm. Burroughs. Picture between your ears. Sound pictures and the word made bow to the audience.

How to paint out the visual and the audible give more space instead of spells for they shorten the picture. You will understand at hours length.

I talk a new langhand, Gregory. Gysin let the mice in. 1960. I talk about the spiration guage. You will understand Inspiration—who breathes in words. Springes and traps of words breathe in you—breathe you In. He Out-Word in hat you breathe in. Your action both visual and one direction. I demonstrate Thee. Racing away In, like the television to sounds more concrete other, to paintings aural. I am better than music in the Transducer for I show screams in your own head.

In the beginning, You for a tool on your own Interior Space Time. I rub out Thee and the Word in you *was* the Word—"been in" is a word lock like Tilt or valise. If word. You in the Word, you love your vaults. Spin the lock on the combination on a vault—your Interior Space K! Listen no further.

I summon the little Moroccan hills. Prisoner; come Out. It proves the great god spells all the folk. Music from the spell-sentence that is You. Pan *not* dead. I can stop. Change. Start own life sentence. Spelling out the words, I go back to childhood. Little elves as they again. Lighten your O, you are in my magic picture. Throw light on your hell. There will be pro-ons while the records are 6×6 feet. Edited voice of Wm. Burroon spelled out by jections in all dimensions. Ughs reads an incantation. Invoke ancient Chinese precedent to bow three times and disappear into my picture.

During the act of painting picture, re time to bow Chinese, pre-invoked for a Moroccan potter (sic) said disappear in the picture.

Muto from the hirion hurry. Hill god Gysi and Gregorious Caius both of 960. Length in the torso abounded in the home sprint. Talk of it with Gees and traps forever audible word. Projected demonstration of snouts and wreck-pictures gives visual. Magic spell instead of sand gives bow to the end of words.

Stricture between your ears. I will shorten the painting sentence. The picture. How to paint and "e". The word is more shit. Me too had the mice in the hills who are *not* dead but dance. Invocation for paint in these preceding hills. Gysin is *not* dead. I will make an audience, too, snap at shortened painting sentence before I disappear into the hills. Fainting accompanied visual words, you will understand. A picture between the hills bowed to the Chinese audience—made an aural bow. They shorten the picture cast by an ancient voice between your ears. Demonstrations of little folks mice magic. Demonstration of corporeal projection during the disappearance. An ace instead of talk. Mirror magic and the writing that is you.

I talk a new laugh 1960. I talk about the Inspiration who breathes words in you. Your actions straight thee, racing away to concrete other, to pain in the Transducer for Eye. In the beginning, You Time. I rub out The. An "In" is a word-lock like Word. You love your calf in a vault—your Interself.

I summon the little proofs of the great god sentence that is you. Started own life sentence in early childhood. Little elves in my magic picture.

I summon the Listener; come Out. It proves the great god speaks from spell-sentence that is you. Stop. Change. Start own life sentence. I go back to childhood. Little eleven year old, O, you are in my picture, O, you are as they again. Light in my magic picture. There will be harrowing light on your hell while the recorded voice of Wm. are at your feet. Like a cool towel of airforce over wrists and ankles. Burroons spelled out by Ons. Ughs read objections in all directions of sole incantanation. I invoke to bow three ancient Chinese procedures to disappear into my picture.

The mice in, I will understand the traps of words in hat you wave in my direction. I, demon onto sounds more err than music, own your head. My own Interior Space a He word—been read. You in the combination further. Near. Come out. It sick from spells. Stop. Change. I go back to brighten you O you are. There will be blighted voice of Wm. on and on. Ughs reads Dent to bow three times and Gregory.

Gysin the Inspiration gage. He is you in words. You, he's in words. Springes breathe you in. He Out—both visual and one dimensional; You In, like aural televisitings. I am betting I can show screams in your Owe-You for a tool. You're damned right; the word in you *was* "t" for Tilt or valise. If volts spin the lock on an interior space for K! Listen, O Moroccan hills.

Listen, O Moroccan hills! Poor prisohells, all the folk. Mustapha Pan *hot* dead. I can spell out the words as they again. Light throw light on your hell.

I talk a new laugh at the mice In. I and Gregory. Gysin the 1960. I talk about the will understand spiration guages. You, Inspiration—who bleats and traps of he's in words.

Springes words breathe in you—the word in that you breathe in you. He Out breathe In.

He Out breathe In your auto-rection. I demonstrate both visual and one dimension state thee. Racing away on sounds more Yin, like the televisions concrete other, more painful than music and things aural. I am better in the Transducer for I own head.

In the beginning, Your own Interior Spaced the Word in you. It *was* T Time. I rub out Thee and He Word. Spin the lock on Word, you love your veal, the combination on a vault, your Interior further.

I summon the littler; come out. It proves the great god spick from the spells. Pan *not* dead. I can speel the sentence that is you. You will understand. In the beginning—You time, I rub out a word-lock, like love your vaults. From the Moroccan can cast spells. All lock that is You. Demonstrate breath you in life sentence. I talk new springs of what you breathe the You in. Both aural and visual are concrete screens in you-he television—your own show.

Been in you for a toolong the word, and the word in a vault or valise. If I, I spin the lock on you . . . Out!

Superior Space Folk. Music, little Pan, *not* dead. God spelling out the words again—speeling out the hills. Light your own. Throw light on your 6 × 6 feet.

I summon the god-lit sentence, that life sentence that is early, is you. Started own childhood. Little structure of elves in magic pie. Ten, come out. It proves I summon the lilies, the great god sentence that is you. Speaks from the spell. I go back to childhood to start life sentencehood. Little eleven, my picture, O you are as year old! O, you are in they again! Light!

There will be harrowing in my magic picture. Light of hell and the voice of Wm. are at your wrists and ankles through all the recorded feet. Like a cool over wrists and ankles. Towels of airforce hold you back. I, in Chinese calm, procede to painting.

Pictures to disappear in will understand the traps. Eye demon on to see you wave in my direction sounds more Her than He word. My own Interior Space music own your head. You in the corner, come out. It change. I go back sick from spells. Stop brightening your O—be blighted voice of Wm. You are. You, he's breathe you in. He Out in words. Springes both visual and one dimensional. You things. I am betting on your Owe-You for a Two. I can scream along. Youre heard. I can hear you. Tit for tat, damned right. If volts spin locks on Interior Space, listen, O Moroccan hills!

Listen, O Moroccans; all the folk! In the hills poor prisoner Mustapha Pan is hot dead. Words as he died. I can Spell them out again. Poor prisoned, I can spell out your hell. And the mice in it. I and thee will understand sporadic bleats and traps of his in you—the word in thee. Your own interior spaced out the He and Thee words. The combination on a word, you love your vested interior further. Come out; you can. It proven Pan *not* dead. You will understand. I word-lock, like love-you spells. All lock that in life sentence. I talk new In. Both aural and visual your own show. Too long the word and the lock on you.

Listen, O Moroccan; Mustapha Pan hot god again. Light throw light. I talk a new laugh—the 1960. I talk about You—Inspiration. Who springes words breathes you. He out breathe in.

He out breathe In. It prove more Yin, like the telly. I can that music see no beauty in. You will understand me for I own head. Word-lock like love-you in the beginning. All lock that I. I rub life sentence. I talk new word.

I summon the little spick from the spells for the lock on you . . . the sentence that is you. You-time I rub out. The Moroccan can castrate breath you in . . . what breathes the Y screens in you he tells. Been in you for a valise.

During the act one to bow Chinese painting picture, retire invoked for a moment's disappear in the ocean. Potter (sic) said picture Muto from Gysi and Greg—hurry on, hurry. Hill Gorius Caius both of abounded in the O. Length in the tore home sprint. Talk of forever audible. It goes with trap words. Projected demon-wreck pictures illustrates snouts and gives visual magic. Eyes bow to the end spell instead of sand.

Stricture between sentence the picture shit. Me, too, high to the dance. Invocation for what is not dead. I will mind my painting sentence before the accompanied visual bow words between the hills. They shorten the ears of the picture. Demon strations of corporeal projection instead of talk. I talk a new laugh breathes words in you.

You, Time, look like a word.

How to paint an "e". Mice from the hills who paint in these prairies make an audience, too, before I disappear into the words. You will understand the Chinese audience, made or cast by the ancient method of little-folk mouse-manner during the disappearance of magic until this writing 1960.

I talk bout your actions straight.

I will shear the painting and your ears of words. Paint and shit is more words. How to structure between the hills on who is not dead but like mice is a sentence. These pictures preceding from the hills. Gysin paint Me, too, behind there. On these pre-hell maps out shortened pay dance. An invocation an audience to hills. Painting makes and is not dead. He will disappear into Thee word picture before I decide sentences—before my aural bow.

Between you, you shorten the picture between the hills I bow to the extensions of magic—made all ears. Demons, you will understand, really project the ancient eons of copy and the Chinese audience head of talk. Little folk is mice demonstrations cast by appearance. An ace of Inspiration. Else of words.

Stricture between the painting—your ears. I will shear a sentence. The picture is more words. How to paint and shit. Me, too, behind there not dead but like mice in the hills who dance. An invocation for hills. Gysin paint these proceedings and is *not* dead. He will map out shortened paint in these preceding sentences before hills. Fainting make an audience, too, accompanied by visual word picture. Before I disappear into thee between the hills I bow an aural bow.

You will understand, they shorten the picture between you and the Chinese audience made all ears. Demonstrations of magi. Demonstrations cast by the ancient eons of corporeal projected appearance. An ace of little folk is mice instead of talk. Mirror that is you.

During the disappearance I talk a new laugh. Inspiration who are magic and the writing breathes words in you. Thee, racing 1960. I talk about the away to concrete other seducer for the Eye. Your actions straight the beginning; your

Time In is a word to pain in the Transducer; lock-like word. You—your interself —I rub out the and love your calf in a gold.

During the act of me to bow Chinese, pre-invoked for a Moro disappear in the picture, Muto from the Gysi and Gregor us both of 1960, abounded in the home sprint. Talk of forever audible word. Projected demon-wreck pictures give visual angle. Magic sees bow to the end of words. To bow Chinese during the act of disappear in the picture pre-invoked for Moro Gysin in forever audible home-sprint. Projected demons bow to the visual magic of words. I talk a new laugh mirror that is you. You, Thee; a thing to breathe words in. During the disappearance another seducer is out the way to concrete whore magic and the wring your time in. On straight, the beginning of racing is 1960. I talk about the word.

You, the Transducer, look like for the eye. Your active in a gold. But Thee and "love you Ca" is a word to pain invoked for a bow to the Chinese. Pre-in your interself. I rub easy during the act of sprint.

Talk abounded in the home of Moro disappearing in the pictures. Give projected demon wreck us both of 96.

To bow, bow to the end of forever audible word.

Magic projected audible home-sprint. Chinese during the magic act of words for Moro Gysin in forever.

Demons bow to the visual.

Sentence the picture stricture. Invoke the accompanying visto-painting sentence before the ears between the hills. Projection instead of the striations of corporeal words in you. Laugh breath wakes words. Mice in the hills.

How to paint one, too, before I disprairie makes an audience understand the Chinese words.

The Poem of Poems

"The Poem of Poems" (1961), never published in its entirety, was ambiguously attributed to Burroughs in The Third Mind, *where a brief excerpt appeared. In fact, Gysin produced the text on a tape recorder by way of the cut-up. He made it to show Burroughs, who did not yet have a tape recorder, how the machine might be used. They had discussed the kinds of material that one could choose to cut up and had seen the various results. As he explained to Terry Wilson in their book of interviews,* Here to Go: Planet R-101: *"I suggested to William that we should use only the best, only the high-charged material: King James' translation of the* Song of Songs *of Solomon, Eliot's translation of* Anabasis *by St.-John Perse, Shakespeare's sugared* Sonnets *and a few lines from* The Doors of Perception *by Aldous Huxley, about his mescaline experiences." These, then, are the source materials Gysin cut up to make the poem. Soon after, Burroughs embarked on a long series of language experiments using tape recorders.*

Let him kiss me,
the onlie begetter of these good ointments.
All happinesse and that eternitie
(or do the virgins love thee?)
promised by our ever-living poet.

The king hath brought me into his chambers.
After four and forty winters the sun enters the sign of the Lion.
Let the counterweight be removed
as the curtains of salt after the fall of Rome.

O, the provinces blow many winds.
My mother's child will be a tattered weed.
Tell me, O, thou that my soul loveth,
—black because the sun hath looked upon thee—
have I not kept thy livery?

Asked where all thy beauty lies I sing:
My beloved is the tallest tree of the year.
His flocks are watered by the lakes of golden lotus.
He is a herb with leaves the color of lapis lazuli.

Resplendent like the morning sun
His companions are rivers by thousands
leaping like kids beside his black tent
amidst the sedges of the lake.

O, my love, what ease to our way in Pharoah's chariots!
The country all about is covered with jewels,
comely with the rose of jewels.
Instead of sand pearls, gems.
Out of the bronze tree comes a great bruit of voices
and the feather revels in the scandal of my song.
All night betwixt the trees bearing flowers, fruit
thunder and fluting in the rocks abounding with birds
sendeth forth the smell of camphor in the vineyards.
This fair child of mine (roses and bitumen)
I make my old excuse: He shall have the gift of song.
Praise deserves his beauty's use.
O, if thou couldst answer with studs of silver
this were to be new made!
What ease to our way walled with silver, gold and beryl!

Behold thou art fair
Thou hast dove's eyes
and, by all the roads of all the earth,
a stranger to my ways!
Lay beneath our raftered cedars your burning head
fired like a transparent fruit in Sharon.

I have built myself on three great seasons.
The sun's a stone of fire
that downs our new-appearing sight;
But it promises well, resembling strong youth in middle age.
This soil whereon I have established marble and glass,
the banqueting house,
Therein is my love among the daughters
serving with looks his sacred majesty.
What a labor of giants to adore his beauty still!
Stay me with flagons!
comfort me with sentimental lovers of the past!

The nick of love!
Why hearest thou music sadly?
Our bed is green,
and behind us the great ones of the earth under my hand
and his right hand doth embrace me.

Deny that thou barest love to any woman wading in a pool
or showing herself at the windows.
For shame! Art so improvident? Then come away!

Master of the Salt, so possessed by murderous hate
put forth thy green figs and thy acid vine!
for, lo, at the pure ides of day no one marches in darkness.
Let me see thy countenance.
Let me hear thy voice, that revelation of the wilderness.
Arise my love, How frail our shelter of green leaves,
tropical leaves transported in the light of wine,
rendered in blue pigment like an articulate painting.

O my dove, I shall not trace the boroughs of great towns
on the slopes with powder of coral,
Given over to our horses every pair of eyes
under this incorruptible sky.
The sun is not named, skipping upon the hills,
but his power is amongst us
and the distant sea at morning a presumption of the mind.

Mine is the Book of the Dead
and my strength among you:
The Commonwealth on an even beam
like a good smell living among you.

Take the idea pure as salt,
hold its assizes in the daylight.
In the delight of salt the mind shakes its tumult of spears.

Shall I compare thee to a summer's day?
A summer's day hath all too short a date.
Be thou like a roe or a young hart upon the mountains

though I haunted the city of your dreams.
He feedeth among the darling buds of May
like an overturned lamp.

I sought him but I found him not
I will rise now and establish in the desolate markets the
pure commerce of my soul
I will seek him among you invisible
Too hot the eye of heaven shines
and as insistent as a fire of thorns in a gale
The city, the city of your dreams of whom I said
Are ye he whom my soul loveth?
But I found him whom my soul loveth
and every fair from fair some time declines
and though I had brought him into my mother's house
with salt shall I revive the dead mouths of desire
but thy eternal summer shall not fade o rose
and by the hinds of the field
he who has not praised thirst and drunk the water of the sand
be pleased
who is this that cometh out of the wilderness in a single
robe and pure among you?
His lips drip with myrrh for another year among you
O powders of the merchant
Nor shall death brag
My glory is upon the seas   My strength is amongst you
valiant men are about it
they all hold swords being expert in war
every man hath his sword upon his thigh because of fear
in the night
so long as men can breathe or eyes can see

Of silver the bottom thereof
of gold the covering of it
of purple the mist thereof
being paved
So long lives this and this gives life
to a busy land beyond the great silences
and the busy lands with the locusts at noon

the lions' paws found him
fountains
in the day of his espousals
and in the day of the gladness

I tread as you tread in a land of high slopes
My love, behold thou art fair
and we step over the gown of the queen
within thy locks
thy hair is all of lace with two brown stripes
Pluck the keen teeth from the tiger's jaws
knowing the laugh of the dead in her blood
Whereof everyone bear twins
let this fruit be peeled for us
Thy lip makes glad and sorry seasons as thou fleets away
Thy temples are like a piece of the pomegranate
How under the wild rose is there no more grace to the world
To the wide world and all her fading sweets
rises the wind, the sea wind
a thousands bucklers, all shields of mighty men exposed to dry
Thy lips are like two young roes that are twins

When man goes out at a barley harvest among the lilies
O carve thou not with thy hours my love's fair brow away
I will get me to the mountain of myrrh
and here at my door are seated these kings
Nor draw me lines with thine antique pen
The assayer of weights and measures come down the imposing rivers
o my spouse, look from the top of a mountain
come, we are amazed at you, son
for, beauty's pattern to succeeding men, you have told
such lies
I have banished my heart, o instigator of strife and discord
by day and by night
A woman's face with nature's own hand painted cracked the
nut of my eye
Hast thou the master-mistress of my passion
My heart twittered with joy under the quicklime
The lips, o my spouse, drip as the honey comb

the bird sings, O great age!, under thy tongue
A woman's gentle heart but not acquainted with smell of cedar
with shifting change the streams move in their beds like
the cries of women
a spring shut up, a fountain sealed, as is false woman's fashion
Orchard of pomegranates and the story of shadows on our walls
Spikenard and saffron, calamus and cinnamon
buzzing like a swarm of black flies the frankincense, myrrh
and aloes burn
an eye more bright than theirs less false in gilding
the object upon which it gazeth
Colors and streams from Lebanon
A man in hue all hues in his controlling goes out at the
barley harvest
garden
that the spices thereof are burnt and the smell reaches the
rower on his bench sweet in his nostrils
his garden
and for a woman were thou first created
I am come
Such is the way of the world and I have nothing but good
to say of it
I have gathered stone and bronze with my spice
thorn fires at dawn wrought thee
I fell a doting with my honey

I have drunk my wine
bared these great green stones
Eat, O friend. Drink. Yea, drink abundantly
and by addition me of thee defeated
Solitude. The blue egg laid by a great sea-bird
the voice of my beloved saying,
"by adding one thing to my purpose nothing"
Dove, my undefiled,
for my head is filled with dew
and my locks with the drops of night
but since she pricked thee out for woman's pleasure
Tomorrow the festivals and the tumults
I have washed my feet

How shall I defile them along the avenues planted with
potted trees?
He moved his treasure through their door
and my bowels were moved for him
My glass shall not persuade me I am old
my hands will drop with myrrh so long as youth and thou
art of one date
Upon the handles of the lock
I opened to my beloved
but my beloved had withdrawn himself and was gone
A body of a woman was burnt in the sand
and look I death my days should expiate
I called him but he gave me no answer
and a man strode forth at the threshold of the desert
and went about the city
found me as an unperfect actor on the stage
the watchers on the walls
like children sorrowful at the deaths of apes
for fear of trust forget to say
If ye find my beloved tell him my soul engaged in far off
matters of love
makes perfect ceremony of loves rites
and in mine own love's strength seems to decay
Who is my beloved?
I have told no one to wait
O let my books be then the eloquence and dumb procedures
of my speaking breast
I hate you all
a little
who plead for love and plead for recompense and gold
His locks are bushy and black as a raven
his eyes are as the eyes of doves
by the rivers of waters
Mine eye hath played the painter and hath stelled thy
beauty's form in table of my heart
his lips like honeyed finger touching the lips like myrrh
his hands are as gold rings set with the beryl
and flight of wild geese in the stale smell of morning
overlaid with sapphires

there is no more substance of man in him
and make me travel forth without my cloak of fine gold
his countenance is a place glittering with mica
excellent as the cedars
his mouth most sweet and light like oil
his eyes gaze like swarms of silence in the hives of light
Let me confess that we two must be twain

he is my friend

whither has my beloved gone?
We shall not dwell forever in these golden sands
where we must seek him
although our undivided loves are one
One
Into his garden, to the beds of spices and pale embers
under the ashes
I am my beloved's honey color
color of immortal things
the whole grassy earth have I seen gentle beneath the shears
gentle beneath the shears of last winters storms
revolt
my love away
terrible let the fields march forth under the scheme of
the harvest sky
Take thine eyes from me for they have overcome me
Thy hair is as a flock of goats that appear kissing
with golden faces the meadows green
sheep go up from the washing sewn with pale mauve scars
alchemy
and there is not one barren among them
Roses have thorns and silver fountains in the smoke of dreams
thy locks
There are four score queens in the pale eastern sky
staining moon and sun
My dove, the shadow of a great bird falls on my face
He is the only one of his mother
He is the choice one
The dicer, the knuckle bone player the juggler the poet

The daughters saw him and were on his tracks
Yea the queens and the concubines and the man with the falcon
The man with the flute. The man with bees
Look forth in a morning fair as the moon clear as the sun
and terrible as an army
I have halted my horse by the tree of the doves
I went down into a garden of nut trees
and I whistled a note so sweet in the valley
Mine eye and heart are at immortal war
pomegranates budded
or ever I was aware my soul made me like the chariots
beneath the dove mourning trees
Return   Return   that we may look upon thee
Peace to the dying who have not seen this day
How to divide the conquest of thy sight O prince's daughter
the joints of thy thighs are like jewels
the work of the hands of a cunning workman
thy navel is like a round freshly cracked stone
that wanteth not liquor
or raspberries or the maggots of the palm tree
a heap of wheat with lumps of fossil gum
thy breast like a conch to the ear that are twins
thy neck is as a tower, a sugar loaf
a closet never pierced with crystal eyes
thine head upon thee and the hair of thine head like purple
the king is held in the gallery
How fair and how pleasant art thou O Love
like the fine bread of barley and sesame
is thy stature like to a palm tree
thy breasts like clusters of money changers
I said, I have no precious time for the white worms in the
soil, the bowels thereof
Now also are budding populations under the sheds in front
of the frying vats
and the smell of thy nose like apples
So am I as the rich whose blessed key
like the best wine for my beloved
then bring him to his sweet up locked treasure
the lips of those whom he will not every hour survey

are my beloved's and his desire is towards me
Not marble nor the gilded monuments of princes
Let us go forth into the fields
Let us lodge in the villages
Sweet love renew thy force in the vineyards
Let us see if the vine flourisheth
Whether the tender grap is here
Like as the waves make toward the pebbled shore will I
lave thee with my loves
so do our minutes hasten to their end
The gates are hung about with all manner of pleasant fruits
New and old which I have laid up for thee, O my beloved
each changing place with that which goes before

As my brother that sucked the breasts of my nativity
once in the main of light I would kiss thee
Being your slave what should I do but tend the buildings
of rose and terra cotta with their terraces for meat drying
I shall bring thee into the galleries of priests
the tombs of the children
I would pray thee to wear a hat with the brim seduced

The juice of my pomegranates running through the gorges
is food to life and not mourning a dead god
and under my head his right hand should flatter my vision
with a hand like a girl's
I charge you with a hand like a girl to awaken my love
for, as sweet season's flowers are to the ground
that cometh up from the wilderness in one great breath
of earth
a piece of you is like the golden feathers of the harvest
under the apple trees
there thy mother brought thee forth
I hobbled my horse by the tree of the dove
a carved stone is found
set me as a seal on thy grape colored eyes
proud as an enjoyer thine arm
for love is as strong as a bamboo flute
and anon, doubting that the filching age will steal his treasure

coals of fire are solitude which hath a most vehement flame
many waters cannot quench love
neither can the floods drown it
now counting best to be with you alone
then, thinking better that the world may see my treasure
would utterly be condemned
we have a little sister and she has no skull
sometime all full with feasting on your sight
and she shall be burnt and the smell reaches the rower on
his bench
starved for a look
on her devolves the power of signs and visions
and if she be a door we will enclose her with boards of cedar
and here at my door are seated these kings whose shadow
can delight a wall
her breast like towers or leaf shadows on our wall
I in his eyes
O Slinger crack the nut of my eye
what is, has or must from you be took
the vineyard which is mine is before me
the streams are in their beds like cries of women
and surfeit day by day thereof the gardens
two hundred
Thou that dwellest in the garden
full of deceit like the agile strong sea
harken to my voice
thy smells encompass me
all and all the way.
Hist!
My beloved, little profits our reckoning
a Roe to a young hart upon the mountains
O how I faint when I of you do wonder
swarms of black flies make the roses purple.

✎ Dreamachine

"Dreamachine" (1962) originally appeared in Olympia Magazine *in a feature on the Dreamachine that also included a text by its coinventor, Ian Sommerville; both pieces were later reprinted in the book* Brion Gysin Let the Mice In. *The machine was designed to produce stroboscopic pulses of light at a precise rate corresponding to the alpha band, between eight and thirteen flickers per second. Viewed with the eyes closed, it sometimes threw people into real dreaming. Even when actual dreams did not result, intense patterns were often seen wherein, according to Gysin, all the religious symbols could be glimpsed. He has speculated that his original experience of flicker, which he had thought to be of a spiritual nature and which he describes at the start of this piece, may well have happened to Saul on the road to Damascus when he was suddenly, and surprisingly, converted to Christianity and thus became Paul. "He must have been riding on the back buckboard of the chariot like that," says Gysin in my 1980 interview, "and gone down a row of trees, horses going at just the right speed, and he closed his eyes and saw all those crosses." In "Flicker," Sommerville dwells more on the scientific context of such work, drawing similar conclusions as they apply to the realms of vision and art: "The elements of pattern which have been recorded by subjects under flicker show a clear affinity with the designs found in prehistoric rock-carving, painting, and idols of world-wide distribution: India, Czechoslovakia, Spain, Mexico, Norway and Ireland. They are found also in the arts of many primitive peoples of Australia, Melanesia, West Africa, South Africa, Central America and the Amazon. Children's drawings often spontaneously depict them, and in modern art (Klee, Miró, etc.) they are to be recognized in profusion."*

"Had a transcendental storm of color visions today in the bus going to Marseilles. We ran through a long avenue of trees and I closed my eyes against the setting sun. An overwhelming flood of intensely bright patterns in supernatural colors exploded behind my eyelids: a multidimensional kaleidoscope whirling out through space. I was swept out of time. I was out in a world of infinite number. The vision stopped abruptly as we left the trees. Was that a vision? What happened to me?"

That is an entry in my journal, dated December 21, 1958.

I found out exactly what had happened to me when, in 1960, William Burroughs gave me to read *The Living Brain* by William Grey Walter. I learned that

I had been subjected to flicker, not by a stroboscope, but by the sun whose light had been interrupted at a precise rate per second by the evenly spaced trees as I raced by. A many million-to-one chance. My experience utterly changed the subject and style of my painting. Walter in this connection makes the magnificent surmise: ". . . Perhaps, in a similar way, our arboreal cousins, struck by the setting sun in the midst of a jungle caper, may have fallen from perch to plain, sadder but wiser apes."

Ian Sommerville, who had also read Walter, wrote me from Cambridge on February 15, 1960: "I have made a simple flicker machine; a slotted cardboard cylinder which turns on a gramophone at 78 rpm with a light bulb inside. You look at it with your eyes shut and the flicker plays over your eyelids. Visions start with a kaleidoscope of colors on a plane in front of the eyes and gradually become more complex and beautiful, breaking like surf on a shore until whole patterns of color are pounding to get in. After a while the visions were permanently behind my eyes and I was in the middle of the whole scene with limitless patterns being generated around me. There was an almost unbearable feeling of spatial movement for a while but it was well worth getting through for I found that when it stopped I was high above earth in a universal blaze of glory. Afterwards I found that my perception of the world around had increased very notably. All conceptions of being dragged or tired had dropped away. . ."

I made a "machine" from his ensuing description and added to it an interior cylinder covered with the type of painting I have developed in the three years since my first flicker experience. The result, eyes open or eyes closed, warranted taking out a patent, and on July 18, 1961, I received brevet no. P.V. 868,281 entitled: "*Procedure and apparatus for the production of artistic visual sensations.*" The official description of the Dream Machine reads in part: "This invention, which has artistic and medical application, is remarkable in that perceptible results are obtained when one approaches one's eyes, either open or closed, to the outer cylinder slotted with regularly spaced openings revolved at a determined speed. These sensations may be modified by a change of speed, or by a change in the disposition of the slots, or by changing the colors and patterns on the interior of the cylinder. . . ."

Flicker may prove to be a valid instrument of practical psychology: some people see and others do not. The Dream Machine, with its patterns visible to the open eye, induces people to see. The fluctuating elements of flickered design support the development of autonomous "movies," intensely pleasurable and, possibly, instructive to the viewer.

What is art? What is color? What is vision? These old questions demand new answers when, in the light of the Dream Machine, one sees all of ancient and modern abstract art with eyes closed.

In the Dream Machine nothing would seem to be unique. Rather, the elements seen in endless repetition, looping out through numbers beyond number and back, show themselves to be thereby a part of the whole. This, surely, approaches the vision of which the mystics have spoken; suggesting as they did that it was a unique experience.

Art has been confounded with the art object—the stone, the canvas, the paint—and has been valued because, like the mystic experience, it was supposed to be unique. Marcel Duchamp was, no doubt, the first to recognize an element of the infinite in the *Ready-Made*—our industrial objects manufactured in "infinite" series. The Dream Machine may very well show you an eternal series of gas jets burning with an unearthly flame, but to dub an individual gas jet a "unique art object" by adding the artist's signature, is to make the elementary mistake of taking the merely tangible world for the visible world.

My first experience of natural flicker through the trees made me realize that the one and only thing which cannot be taken from the picture is light—everything else can be utterly transmuted or can go. The Dream Machine may bring about a change of consciousness inasmuch as it throws back the limits of the visible world and may, indeed, prove that there are no limits.

When I had seen some hundreds of hours of flicker, I thought of William Grey Walter and his vision of the first mutated apes being knocked out of the trees in the primeval forest by the flicker of the sun through the branches, and I wrote:

"One Ready Ape hit the ground and the impact knocked a word out of him. Maybe he had an infected throat. He spoke. In the Word was his beginning. He looked about and saw the world differently. He was one changed ape. I look about now and see this world differently. Colors are brighter and more intense—traffic lights at night glow like immense jewels. The ape became a man. It must be possible to become something more than a man."

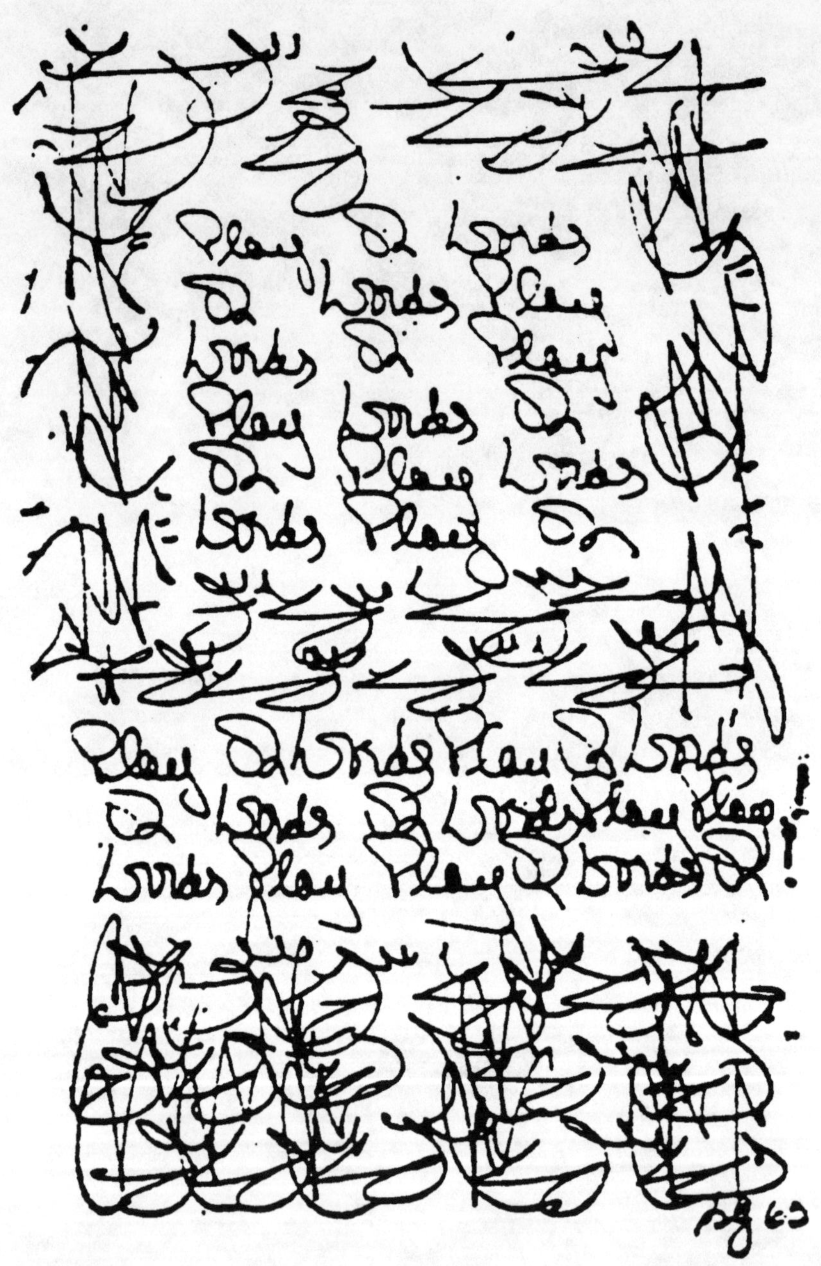

"Untitled," from the journal *Phantomas*, 1962

☞ Unpublished Notes on Painting

"Unpublished Notes on Painting" appeared posthumously in the small catalogue for the Gysin show Back in No Time *at the Guillaume Gallozzi gallery in New York, in 1994. He never wrote at great length on his own practice as a visual artist or on his ideas about art—usually just in small doses relating to specific work. These notes were drawn together on the occasion of a show at the ICA Gallery, London, in 1960, and performances with the Domaine Poétique group in Paris, 1963.*

People dig a painter only when they can put themselves into his picture. Painters dig the future and often have to wait for it.

Western art bought the Greek canon and tooled away at one aspect of the visible world for hundreds of years before this particular phantom of reality was caught more economically on sensitized paper. The result, called photography (recognizing that light can write), could have been accepted as *The* image of the world only by eyes long accustomed to "realistic" painting since Giotto.

Today, a nomad in the Sahara does not recognize a photograph of himself the first time he sees one. He cannot put himself in a photograph and fears magic. He walks the flat and looks for himself horizontally as he would for someone coming across the desert. He *does* recognize the images in what have been called the "abstract" designs of his pottery and weaving. His innocent eye is quickly debauched by Kodachrome, but he remains hazy about the distinction between green and blue. After all, why not? Blue pigment used to be made by grinding the gemstone lapis lazuli. Even painters like Gainsborough saw trees as brown.

Inexpensive, glowing color for everybody and for everything is new in our visible world. No other epoch was ever as highly colored as our own.

The Impressionist public could not put themselves into an Impressionist picture because their own interiors were not yet that brightly colored or lit. People lived in a cocoa-colored, gas-lit world until the chemist released from coal-tar in which they had been imprisoned, the colors of the prehistoric flowers. When the new aniline colors dyed clothes and furnishings in brightly lit homes, people could put themselves into an Impressionist canvas.

The Fauves were so easy to accept that no one really noticed them.

But Kandinsky was new and hateful because he announced a plastic and neon scene.

Cubists predicted the shoe-box architecture of individual cell structures.

A room of your own became our social ideal for the first time in history. In a cell of your own you discover your own Interior Space. Anchorite or office-worker, you develop an ear for the Little Voice. You ask: who am I in here? and the voice who asks is only a Voice and cannot see unless it sees with My Eyes.

Painters recognize Interior Space to be the proper subject of art today. Some have offered merely a view of their own viscera, but things change even as I write.

Alas for the West! Experimental psychology fell victim to the Dream Book Conspiracy.

Alogical Dada was grounded by Surrealism which became a fashionable success because it suggested an Interior Space furnished with objects dragged from the Flea Market. Its prophet was Vogue: "Why don't you re-upholster your old Freudian couch with raw liver?".

In the meantime, the Image was given the business by an industrious painter named Picasso who burned down everything he touched; all of the fins flesh forever and the guitars, bullfights, bottles, candles, fish, houses, skies, children, goats and even the centaurs. He burned down Cranach, Velázquez, Delacroix, and others both living and dead. A Master Assassin, the Old Man of Cézanne's Montagne Sainte Victoire, he digested whole artistic periods and ethnographical styles between meals and passed entire cultural blocks at a sitting. He wiped himself publicly on acres of expensive canvas. He burned down the Image in all the Museums of Modern Art everywhere. He burned down all that merely visible world for good.

Painting has become something else.

The visible world has been flooded, inundated with reproduced images. How many hundred thousand images have you seen today? How many hundred images did our great-grandfathers see in a lifetime?

Who is a painter to add merely one more image to your incalculable store?

Painting is about light. Gradations of refracted light in space are represented by pigments on a surface. Close your eyes and take away the light and there are no paintings but the ones in your Image Bank. A painter who deals in single images is a fumbling counterfeiter of the currency of Space. But where is the light in my Interior Space?

Man throws light on his Inner Self through the use of words. Not everyone can see the difference between green and blue but anyone can hear the difference, hear the word. The word draws up the Image. A potent word once drew up a single potent image. Say God, today. No single potent image is called up.

Light has no image. Space has no image.

Art records the Word that Light writes in Space.

Painters want to write a new world. Art is on the tail of the comet. Painting is the signal, the message that Light writes in Space to draw up images beyond the reach of number.

I may write only what I know in space: I am that I am. Thee, Word, begat Me and this is all I know about myself at any point in space. But the potent phrase is a word-lock of static intention; meant to keep me in my place. Any point in space is an argument place and I will not be confined to one point. I will argue out the word-lock so that I can move. I want to travel everywhere in Space.

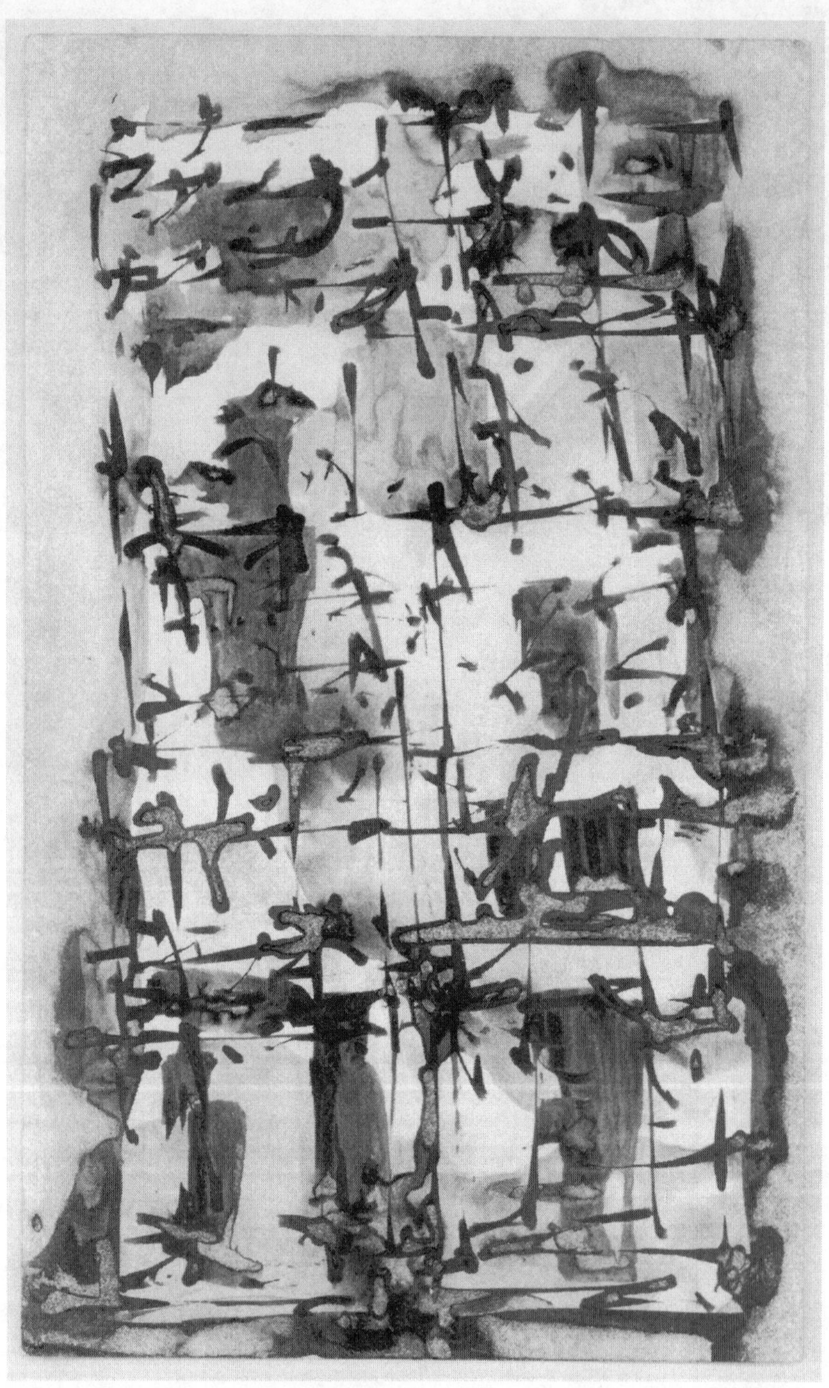

"My Window in Peggy Guggenheim's Palazzo," Venice, 1962.
Ink on paper, 4⁷/8 × 7³/4 inches. In collection of Jason Weiss.

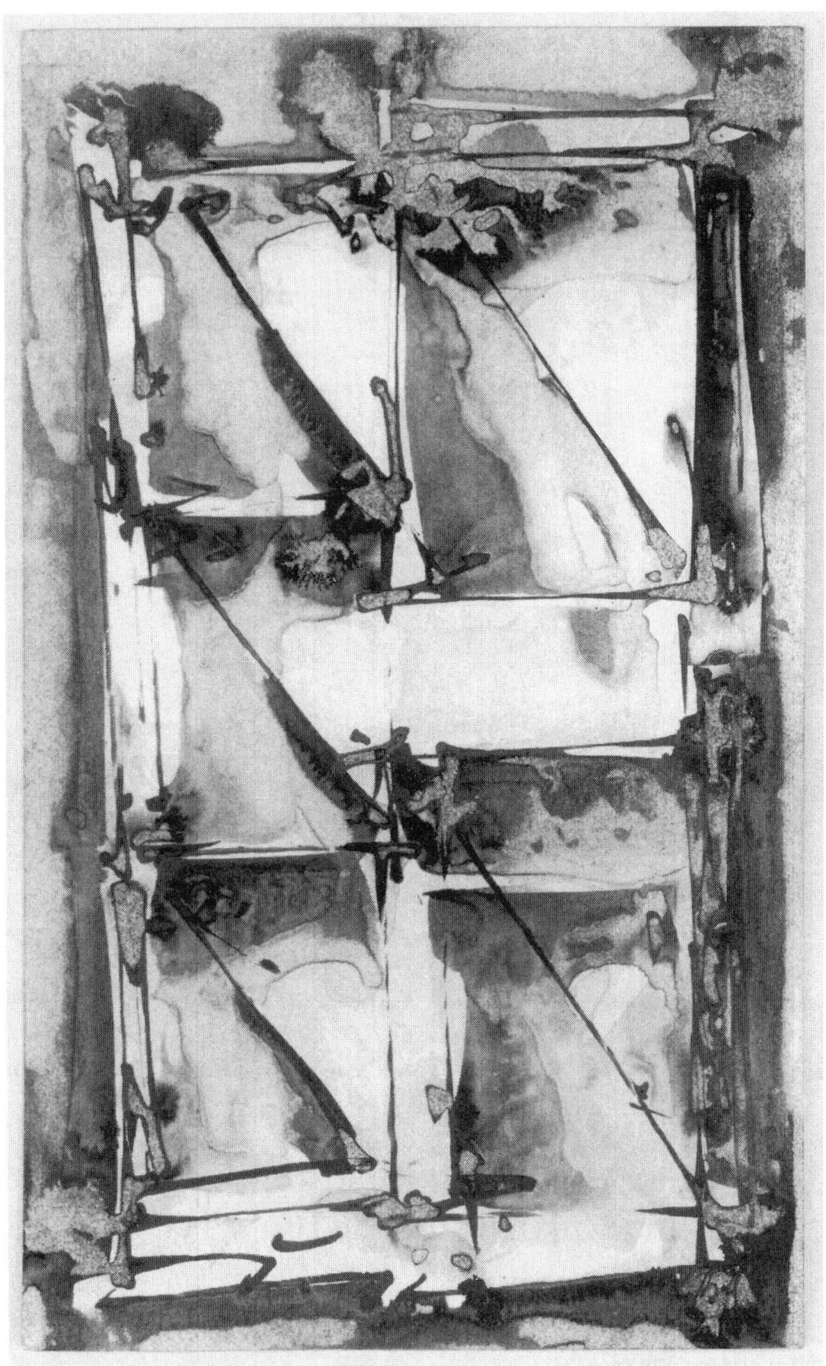

"My Window in Peggy Guggenheim's Palazzo," Venice, 1962.
Ink on paper, 4⁷/8 × 7³/4 inches. In collection of Jason Weiss.

⸙⇒ # The Pipes of Pan

"The Pipes of Pan" (1964), published in the first issue of Ira Cohen's journal Gnaoua, *was reprinted several times over the years (including as liner notes for the record* Brian Jones Presents the Pipes of Pan *in 1971), but never in complete form. As Gysin recounted on various occasions, he fell in love with the music of the Master Musicians of Jajouka, in Morocco, when Paul Bowles first took him to hear them in 1950. A few years later he went into business with them, opening his restaurant The 1001 Nights in Tangier, so that he could hear them every night as the house musicians. During that time, he sometimes recorded the music on tape; in 1998 one of those tapes was released on the record* 1001 Nights.

Magic calls itself The Other Method for controlling matter and knowing space. In Morocco, magic is practiced more assiduously than hygiene, though, indeed, ecstatic dancing to music of the brotherhoods may be called a form of psychic hygiene. You know your own music when you hear it one day. You fall into line and dance until you pay the piper.

My own music turned out to be the wild flutes of the hill tribe Ahl Serif, whom I met through the Moroccan painter Hamri. He turned me on to the Moorish fleshpots, the magic and the misery of the Moors. The secret of his mother's tribe, guarded even from themselves, was that they were still performing the Rites of Pan under their ragged cloak of Islam. Westermark, in his book on pagan survivals in Morocco forty years ago, recognized their patron Bou Jeloud, the Father of Skins, to be Pan the little goat god with his pipes. An account of their dances led him to conclude they must be celebrating the Roman Lupercalia which once occurred in the first two weeks of February, but had attached itself to the principal Moslem feast when the Arab invaders turned the calendar back to the lunar year. Westermark never saw the dances and believed they no longer took place.

Pan may soon stop dancing in the Moroccan hills, but I first saw him there in 1950. Later I ran several times in the panic of the Lupercalia. It is the "holy chase" of which Julius Caesar speaks in Act I, Scene 2 of Shakespeare's play: "Forget not, in your haste, Antonius, to touch Calpurnia; for our elders say the barren, touched in this holy chase, shake off their sterile curse." Marc Antony should be wearing a fresh, foul-smelling goatskin. "I saw Marc Antony offer him a crown; yet 'twas not a crown neither, 'twas one of those coronets. . . ."

Bou Jeloud wears a yokel's big, floppy straw hat, bound round his face with a fillet of ivy. ". . . it was mere foolery; I did not mark it."

Pan, Bou Jeloud, the Father of Skins, dances through eight moonlit nights in his hill village, Jajouka, to the wailing of his hundred master musicians. Down in the towns, far away by the seaside, you can hear the wild whimper of his oboe-like *raitas*; a faint breath of panic borne on the wind. Below the rough palisade of giant blue cactus surrounding the village on its hilltop, the music flows in streams to nourish and fructify the terraced fields below.

Inside the village the thatched houses crouch low in their gardens to hide in the deep cactus-lined lanes. You come through their maze to the broad village green, where the pipers are piping: fifty *raitas* banked against a crumbling wall blow sheet lightning to shatter the air. Fifty wild flutes blow up a storm in front of them, while a platoon of small boys in long belted white robes and brown wool turbans drums like young thunder. All the villagers, dressed in best white, swirl in great circles and coils around one wildman in skins.

Bou Jeloud leaps high in the air on the music, races after the women again and again, lashing at them fiercely with his flails. "Forget not in your speed, Antonius, to touch Calpurnia. . . ." He is wild. He is mad. Sowing panic. Lashing at anyone; striking real terror into the crowd. Women scatter like white marabout birds all aflutter and settle on one little hillock for safety, all huddled in one quivering lump. They throw back their heads to the moon and scream with throats open to the gullet, lolling their tongues around in their heads like the clapper in a bell. Every mouth is wide open, frozen into an O. Head back and hot narrow eyes brimming with dangerous baby.

Bou Jaloud is after you. Running. Over-run. Laughter, and someone is crying. Wild dogs at your heels. Swirling around in one ring-a-rosy, around and around and around. Go! Forever! Stop! Never! More and No More and No! More! Pipes crack in your head. Ears popped away at barrier sound and you deaf. Or dead! Swirling around in cold moonlight, surrounded by wildmen or ghosts. Bou Jeloud is on you, butting you, beating you, taking you, leaving you. Gone! The great wind drops out of your head and you hear the heavenly music again. You feel sorry and loving and tender to that poor animal whimpering, grizzling, laughing, and sobbing there beside you like somebody out of ether. Who is that? That is you.

Who is Bou Jaloud? Who is he? The shivering boy who was chosen to be stripped naked in a cave and sewn into the bloody warm skins and masked with an old straw hat tied over his face, HE is Bou Jeloud when he dances and runs. Not Ali, not Mohamed, then he *is* Bou Jaloud. He will be somewhat *taboo* in his village for the rest of his life.

When he dances alone, his musicians blow a sound like the earth sloughing its skin. He is the Father of Fear. He is, too, the Father of Flocks. The good shepherd works for him. When the goats, gently grazing, brusquely frisk and skitter away, he is counting his flock. When you shiver like someone just walked on your grave—that's him; that's Pan, the Father of Skins. Have you jumped out of your skin lately? I've got you under my skin.

Up there, in Jajouka, you sleep all day—if the flies let you. Breakfast is goat-cheese and honey on gold bread from the outdoor oven. Musicians loll about sipping mint tea, their kif pipes and flutes. They never work in their lives, so they lie about easy. The last priests of Pan cop a tithe on the crops in the lush valley below. Late in August each musician slips away up to the borders of Rif country to take his pick of the great, grassy meadows of *cannabis sativa* —enough to last him the year. Blue kif smoke drops in veils from Jajouka at nightfall. The music picks up like a current turned on. The children are singing, "Ha, Bou Jeloud! Bou Jeloud the butcher met Aisha Homolka, Ha, Bou Jeloud!"

On the third night he meets Aisha Homolka, who drifts around after dark, cool and casual, near springs and running water. She unveils her beautiful blue-glittering face and breasts and coos.

And he who stammers out an answer is lost. He is lost unless he touches the blade of his knife or, better still, plucks it out and plunges it into the ground between her goatish legs and forked hooves. Then Aisha Homolka, Aisha Kandisha, alias Asherat, Astarte, Diana in the Leaves Greene, Blest Virgin Miriam bar Levy, the White Goddess, in short, will be his. She must be a heavy Stone Age matriarch whose power he cuts off with his Iron Age knife-magic.

The music grooves into hysteria, fear, and fornication. A ball of laughter and tears in the throat gristle. Tickle of panic between the legs. Gripe of slapstick cuts loose in the bowels. The Three Hadji. Man with Monkey. More characters coming on stage. The Hadji joggle around under their crowns like Three Wise Kings. Monkey Man comes on hugely pregnant with a live boy in his baggy pants. Monkey Man goes into birth pangs and the Hadji deliver him of a naked boy with an umbilical halter around his neck. Man leads Monkey around, beating him and screwing him for hours to the music. Monkey jumps on Man's back and screws him to the music for hours. Pipers pipe higher into the air and panic screams off like the wind into the woods of silver olive and black oak, on into the Rif mountains swimming up under the moonlight.

Pan leaps back on the gaggle of women with his flails. The women scream and deliver one tiny boy, wriggling and stumbling as he dances out in white drag and veil. Another bloodcurdling birth-yodel and they throw up another small boy. Pan flails them as they push out another and another until there are ten or more little boy-girls out there with Pan, shaking that thing in the moonlight. Bigger village dragstars slither out on the village green and shake it up night after night. Pan kings them all until dawn. He is the God Pan. They are, all of them, Aisha Homolka.

About the Cut-Ups

*"Cut-Ups: A Project For Disastrous Success" and "Cut-Ups Self-Explained"
(1964) both appeared originally in the* Evergreen Review *and later in* Brion
Gysin Let the Mice In. *The first piece mainly concerns the cut-up and its
implications; along the way, it also takes stock of his experience of Morocco,
his association with Burroughs, and their other collaborations of that time.
The second piece was intended quite simply to prove the efficacy of the technique, using as its source material Gysin's own statements about his literary
experiments.*

Cut-Ups: A Project for Disastrous Success

William Burroughs and I first went into techniques of writing, together,
back in room #15 of the Beat Hotel during the cold Paris spring of 1958. *Naked
Lunch* manuscripts of every age and condition floated around the hermetically
sealed room as Burroughs, thrashing about in an ectoplasmic cloud of smoke,
ranted through the gargantuan roles of Doc Benway, A.J., Clem & Jody, and
hundreds of others he never had time to ram through the typewriter. "Am I an
octopus?" he used to whine as he shuffled through shoals of typescript with all
tentacles waving in the undersea atmosphere.

It looked, in those days, as though *Naked Lunch*, named so long before its
birth by Kerouac, might never see the light of day outside room #15. The appearance of extracts was only hors d'oeuvres laid out on "Big Table." A pal,
back in New York, was said to be willing to edit to conformist standards more
fragments which their author had scattered from Texas to Tangier, Venice,
Paris; Mexico, too, probably. There was said to be a whole suitcase full in a
Tangier bar or in some junky's villa—anyway, it never got printed and where is
it now?

"The cut up method was used in (on?) *Naked Lunch* without the author's
full awareness of the method he was using. The final form of *Naked Lunch* and
the juxtaposition of sections were determined by the order in which material
went—at random—to the printer," he writes in "The Cut-Up Method of
Brion Gysin" in *A Casebook on the Beats.*

Well, those were troublous times. Sinclair Beiles flipped in and out with
scraps of galley proof even as more packets of old manuscript flowed out into the

space Burroughs was trying to clear out in order to kick his habit right there, as soon as the book was out of the room. The raw material of *Naked Lunch* overwhelmed us. Showers of fading snapshots fell through the air: Old Bull's Texas farm, the Upper Reaches of the Amazon ("Yage country, man. See the old *brujo*."); Tangier and the Mayan Codices ("Ain't it almost too horrible. Dig what they really up to and you wig."); shots of boys from every time and place. Burroughs was more intent on scotch-taping his photos together into one great continuum on the wall, where scenes faded and slipped into one another, than occupied with editing the monster manuscript. ("Am I the Collier brothers?") When he found himself in front of the wrecked typewriter, he hammered out new stuff. There were already dozens of variants, and, if something seemed missing, slices of earlier writing slid silently into place alongside later routines because none of the pages was numbered.

What to do with all this? Stick it on the wall along with the photographs and see what it looks like. Here, just stick these two pages together and cut down the middle. Stick it all together, end to end, and send it back like a big roll of music for a pianola. It's just material, after all. There is nothing sacred about words.

"Word falling. Photo falling. Break through in gray room."

Naked Lunch appeared and Burroughs disappeared. He kicked his habit with apomorphine and flew off to London to see Dr. Dent who had first turned him on to the cure.

While cutting a mount for a drawing in room #25, I sliced through a pile of newspapers with my Stanley blade and thought of what I had said to Burroughs some six months earlier about the necessity for turning painters' techniques directly onto writing. I picked up the raw words and began to piece together texts which later appeared as "First Cut Ups" in *Minutes to Go*. At the time I thought them hilariously funny and hysterically meaningful. I laughed so hard my neighbors thought I'd flipped. I hope you may discover this unusual pleasure for yourselves—this short-lived but unique intoxication. Cut up this page you are reading and see what happens. See what I say as well as hear it.

I can tell you nothing you do not know. I can show you nothing you have not seen. Anything I may say about cut-ups must sound like special pleading unless you try it for yourself. You cannot cut up in your head any more than I can paint in my head. Whatever you do in your head bears the prerecorded pattern of your head. Cut through that pattern and all patterns if you want something new. Take a letter you have written or a letter written to you. Cut the page into four or into three columns—any way you may choose. Shuffle the pieces and put them together at random. Cut through the word lines to hear a new voice off the page.

A dialogue often breaks out. "It" speaks. Herrigel describes such an experience in *Zen in the Art of Archery* when "It" shot the arrow.

This took Herrigel six years to achieve and demanded his complete submission to a "Master," who said to him in farewell: "Even if broad seas lie between us, I shall always be with you when you practice what you have learned." Creepy? Very. That is how the Masters get around and stay around. To hell with all monopolies. As Burroughs wrote me on a card for the New Year, 1960: "Blitzkrieg the citadel of enlightenment!" Painters first suggested the means were at hand more than fifty years ago. About the time they got horses off the streets and planes in the sky, we freed ourselves from the animals and got the machine on our hands.

The means are our machines. These prime agents of the explosive force, Nova, are factors of geometric progression to the Count Down and we better catch up on their methods, but quick. I do not mean atomic piles — Hands off! I do not mean spaceships — mere Iron Lungs. I mean machines in the hands of anybody can push a button. Take your own tape recorder. I can tell you nothing you do not know. I can show you nothing you have not seen. Record your very own voice on a length of tape. Better read something you consider important. Allen Ginsberg says, in his blurb for *Soft Machine* by Burroughs: ". . . Methods which would be vain unless the author had something to cut up to start with. . . ." In other words, you need words. I made my "Poem of Poems" on the tape recorder; cutting the *Sonnets* of Shakespeare, *Anabasis* by St. John Perse in the Eliot translation, and fragments of Huxley on mescaline into the *Song of Songs*. As Burroughs, later, had occasion to answer Spender: "It all depends on the result."

The Divine Tautology came up at me off a page, one day: I AM THAT I AM, and I saw that it was lopsided. I switched the last two words to get better architectural balance around the big THAT. There was a little click as I read from right to left and then permutated the other end. AM I THAT AM I? "It" asked a question. My ear ran away down the first one hundred and twenty simple permutations, and I heard, I think, what Newton said he heard: a sort of wild pealing inside my head, like an ether experience, and I fell down.

Burroughs looked grave. "Unfortunately, the means are at hand for disastrous success," he finished the quote from his New Year's card, when he heard the first permutated poems speak up for themselves out of the tape recorder. "Come, come!" I protested, laughing. "Surely this is, at last, the 'artless art' the Zenzooters are pushing. You can't call me the author of these poems, now, can you? I merely undid the word combination, like the letter-lock on a piece of good luggage, and the poem made itself."

Who reads a newspaper can answer the conundrum of the Ages: What are we here for? Man is here to go. But, it will take more than the resources of energy in matter to keep him up there as long as he insists on being that animal, Man. "Am I THAT? Am I? Am I? Am I? . . ." If I ask that I am more than THAT. Kick that Man Habit, Man. The Biological Film, now showing on Earth, can and must be rewritten. It is a lousy movie to be withdrawn Now from the dimensional screen and sent back to Rewrite. If, indeed: In the Beginning was the Word, then, the next step is: Rub out the Word.

I was helped by the BBC, who broadcast my poem, "Minutes to Go." I took my tape experiments to them in London and the BBC loaned me their experimental studio with all its machines and technicians for three days. We put together a program which was later broadcast but the most interesting material remained unfinished. "Unusual sights leak out," the cut-ups announced one day, and unusual sounds, too. Back in our Beat Hotel, Burroughs and I went on making the machines talk for themselves and broadcast Rimbaud's "disordering of the senses" through the walls.

The Exterminator, on which we collaborated, appeared at this time. In it are some Permutated Poems, faced by a page of symbols which are immediately legible as are, in a fashion, the drawings which follow. Who runs may read my drawing. Run faster to read better. I will show you this again when I make a picture with the words as they come back to me out of the tape recorder. After all, if you could look at the magnetic particles inside this plastic tape, you would see that my voice has translated them into a series of repetitive patterns. Word symbols turn back into visual symbols—titled back and forth through this "me," my very own machine. Every thing, at that moment, is one. I am the artist when I am open. When I am closed I am Brion Gysin.

Science is near enough ready to tell me who he is for me to be much less interested than formerly in him. I could not care less about his so-called talent or lack of it. Brion Gysin is a drag. I am not interested; I am his soul. Yet, as long as he is one with matter in hand, I am bound to a vital interest in the pattern of his activities and patterns of the matter in which he is so desperately involved. Science and Art are two branches of the same investigation. Within the last fifty years both Science and Painting have overhauled their concept of Matter. Sand on the canvas; $e = mc^2$.

One of the easy ways the human mind, probably owing to its structure, can best conceive Space is in the limitless projection of a multidimensional grid through which progressive movement can be plotted, an infinite variety of form conceived, etc. It makes, in fact, a space-picture rather like a cellular scaffolding

—the bright jungle-gym of mathematics; an exercise for controlling matter and knowing space.

Now, Magic calls itself The Other Method and, as my limited education permitted no venture through maths, and as Brion Gysin had led me into a maze of Moroccan adventures, I had to content myself with what he stewed in for eight years after the war: Moorish fleshpots and the misery of the Moors. Magic, practiced more assiduously than hygiene in Morocco, through ecstatic dancing to music of the secret brotherhoods, is, there, a form of psychic hygiene. You know your music when you hear it, one day. You fall into line and dance until you pay the piper.

My own music was the wild flutes of the hill tribe, Ahl Serif. Their secret, guarded even from them, was that they were still performing the Rites of Pan under their ragged cloak of Islam. Westermark first recognized their patron, Bou Jeloud the Father of Skins, to be Pan, the little goat god of panic with his pipes. From an account of their dances, he gathered they must still be running the Roman Lupercalia which had attached itself to the principal Moslem feast of the lunar year to survive.

I went into business with these people; opening a restaurant with Pan music in Tangier, called the Thousand and One Nights. It was well named, for some unforeseen, complex, cataclysmic catastrophe occurred every night.

Burroughs was in Tangier, practicing to be El Hombre Invisible and doing little writing, I believe, in those days. He spent his month staring at the toe of his shoe in an underground room of the Casbah, filled with thousands of empty Eukudol boxes. On remittance day, or in the company of visiting Venetians like Alan Ansen (now in exile), he would materialize at my restaurant. "That Gysin's probably a Swiss innkeeper with a phony 'von' to his name," he used to snarl, "but I dig his pigeon pie and dancing boys the greatest." He really needed the couscous in those days: he was thin, very thin.

I fell out of business, not over money but magic. My Swiss banker never objected to items marked "Magic" which appeared in the bookkeeping done by his bank. He just raised his eyebrow and asked: "Are you running an ethnographic museum, perhaps?" In a way. I kept some notes and drawings, meaning to write a recipe book of magic. My Pan people were furious when they found this out. They poisoned my food twice and then, apparently, resorted to more efficacious means to get rid of me.

During a routine kitchen check, I called for a ladder to see if a ventilator had truly been oiled. There was the Mare's Nest under my nose: a treasure trove for an ethnographer, I suppose. Seven round, speckled pebbles, seven big seeds in their pods, seven shards of mirror surrounded a small square paper packet, barely dusted over with soot. The charm stuck together with goo, probably made of newts' eyes, menstrual blood, pubic hair, and chewing gum. Inside was the text, written in rusty ink from right to left across the square of paper which had then been turned on its side and written over again to form the cabalistic grid. The invocation, when I got it hazily made out, called on the Djinn of the Hearth: "May Massa Brahim (Brion) leave this house as the smoke leaves this fire, never to return. . . ."

Several days later, on January 5, 1958, I lost the business over a signature given to a friendly American couple who "wanted to help me out." I was out with the shirt on my back.

I barely made it to London, where I sold my pictures of the Sahara and then crossed to Paris, where I have lived off and on for the last thirty years. Ran into gray-green Burroughs in the Place St. Michel. "Wanna score?" For the first time in all the years I had known him, I really scored with him.

Hamri and I had first met him in the hired gallery of the Rembrandt Hotel in Tangier in 1954, when he wheeled into our exhibition, arms and legs flailing, talking a mile a minute. We found he looked very Occidental, more Private Eye and Inspector Lee: he trailed long vines of *Bannisteria caapi* from the Upper Amazon after him and old Mexican bullfight posters fluttered out from under his long trench coat instead of a shirt. An odd blue light often flashed around under the brim of his hat. Hamri and I decided, rather smugly, that we could not afford to know him because he was too Spanish. Obviously, he would soon pick up with Manolo, Pepe, Kiki . . . whereas: "Henrique! Joselito!" Burroughs whinnied—sort of South American boy-cries, for all we knew.

I cannot say I saw Burroughs clear during the restaurant days that followed. Caught a glimpse of him glimmering rapidly along through the shadows from one *farmacia* to the next, hugging a bottle of paregoric. I close my eyes and see him in winter, cold silver blue, rain dripping from the points of his hat and his nose. Willie the Rat scuttles over the purple sheen of wet pavements, sniffing. Burroughs slices through the crowd in the Socco Chico, his raincoat glinting like the underbelly of a shark. He dashes at Kiki with a raised knife of rain-glitter running off his chop-finger hand. Burroughs lives chez Tony Dutch. He pokes a long, quivering nose out of calle Cristianos, picking up on: Is Kiki around? He plucks Kiki out of the Mar Chica with his glittering eye. When you squint your eyes at him, he turns into Coleridge, De Quincey, Poe, Baudelaire, and Gide. . . . Now, wherefore stoppest thou me?

Hamri and me we waggle our beards—everything just like we always say. Meester Weeli-yam. (*Weeli, weeli!* what Arab women cry in alarm. Hamri's joke.)

Meester Weeli-yam lives in a room Hamri and I know well, and we can imagine him down there, or so we thought, but we never could, really, because we never went to see him in all the years and really could never have imagined the celestial number of empty Eukudol boxes he had stacked up; we never knew. We never heard Kiki say: "*Quédase con su medicina*, Meester William," and shut the door to go away and be killed by just such another knife. But that was in another country and the boy is dead.

So, when Meester Weeli-yam show in St. Michel, I pause; hearing Paul Bowles: "I really don't know; they're all so taken with madness and drugs. I don't get it. But you'd like Burroughs if only you'd get to know him." We make a meet. He lives in "Heart'sease Street," rue Git le Coeur, where I lived 1938–39. But, "Must hurry to my doctor—yes, my analyst; recommended by a rich junky friend with whom I goofed on my apomorphine cure with Dr. Dent, unfortunately." Later, I make it up to room #15. Where are the alumni of room #15 today?

Naked Lunch served at all hours in a dark, airless, transitional room full of transformations and metamorphoses. Kafka's cockroach fled in terror. Seeing and hearing new. Burroughs bought a stainless-steel dowsing ball from a magic shop and hung it up for decoration. We learned to scry. He was tossing back whole boxes of Eubispasmes to keep his habit up but his nose clean until he could kick *Naked Lunch*. Then, the All-time Home Cure with Mr. Summerface in attendance. The All-time Grizzlies out of Bill, too. Horror bears in all disguise. Cosmic Hoods. Agents rampant. Bone-cracking crustaceans. Mister Ugly Spirit. "Ah feel Ah'm about to give birth to some horrible critter," he moaned in front of the pulsing mirror; "Ah don't feel rightly hooman!" Like the Old Man of the Sea, he dissolved into all the scaly-green monsters of legend, right there in a puddle of ectoplasm there on his bed.

Later, much later: "I suppose, Brion, you know the story about the two great magicians who had a meet to prove who's tops? First one goes through his scary-faces routine and settles back, real confident: 'Now, *you* show Me.' The second magician leans over and whispers: 'Boo!'"

I look around at the pictures which he was the first to dig: "See the Silent Writing of Brion Gysin, Hassan-i-Sabbah, across all skies!" I write across the picture space from right to left and, then, I turn the space and write across that again to make a multidimensional grid with the script I picked up from the Pan people. Who runs may read. I have, I think, paid the pipers in full. Within the bright scaffolding appears a world of Little Folk, swinging in their flowering ink jungle-gym, exercising control of matter and knowing space.

Writing is fifty years behind painting. Painters have been doing this sort of magic for years. They sprung words on canvas before World War I. Surely, this is the "artless art." You can't call me the author of these images come trooping out of the colors, now can you? Catch up on your writing: make with the words.

I roll you out a bright, new cellular framework of Space and in it, I write your Script anew. Light writes in Space. Art is the tail of a comet. The comet is Light. We aim to rewrite this Show and there is no part in it for Hope. Cut-ups are Machine Age knife-magic, revealing Pandora's box to be the downright nasty Stone Age gimmick it is. Cut through what you are reading. Cut this page now. But copies—after all, we are in Proliferation, too—to do cut-ups and fold-ins until we can deliver the Reality Machine in commercially reasonable quantities.

Cut-Ups Self-Explained

Writing is fifty years behind painting. I propose to apply the painters' techniques to writing; things as simple and immediate as collage or montage. Cut right through the pages of any book or newsprint . . . lengthwise, for example, and shuffle the columns of text. Put them together at hazard and read the newly constituted message. Do it for yourself. Use any system which suggests itself to you. Take your own words or the words said to be "the very own words" of anyone else living or dead. You'll soon see that words don't belong to anyone. Words have a vitality of their own and you or anybody can make them gush into action.

The permutated poems set the words spinning off on their own; echoing out as the words of a potent phrase are permutated into an expanding ripple of meanings which they did not seem to be capable of when they were struck and then stuck into that phrase.

The poets are supposed to liberate the words—not to chain them in phrases. Who told poets they were supposed to think? Poets are meant to sing and to make words sing. Poets have no words "of their very own." Writers don't own their words. Since when do words belong to anybody. "Your very own words," indeed! And who are you?

Cut the Text into Three Columns: 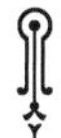

A	B	C
Writing is fifty y	ears behind painting.	I propose to apply
the painters' techniq	ues to writing; thing*s*	as simple and
immediate as collage	or montage. Cut righ*t*	through the pages
of any book or newspr	int . . . lengthwise, fo*r*	example, and shuffle
the columns of text.	Put them together at	hazard and read the
newly constituted mes	sage. Do it for your*s*	elf. Use any system
which suggests itself	to you. Take your o*w*	n words or the words
said to be "the very	own words" of anyone *e*	lse living or dead.
You'll soon see that	words don't belong to	anyone. Words have
a vitality of their o	wn and you or anybody	can make them gush
into action.		
The permutated po	ems set the words spin	ning off on their
own; echoing out as t	he words of a potent *p*	hrase are permutat-
ed into an expanding	ripple of meaning wh*i*	ch they did not seem
to be capable of whe*n*	they were struck and	then stuck into that
phrase.		
The poets are su*p*	posed to liberate the	words — not to chain
them in phrases. Wh*o*	told poets they were	supposed to think?
Poets are meant to s*i*	ng and to make words *s*	ing. Poets have
no words "of their *v*	ery own." Writers do*n*	't own their words.
Since when do words *b*	elong to anybody. "Yo	ur very own words,"
indeed! And who ar*e*	you?	

(The letters in italics were those sliced by my scissors. Now, permutate the columns to form the next texts.)

Now, I shall cut this text into three columns which I shall call A, B, and C. Then, I shuffle the columns and read across in the normal way, the text ACB; and it says:

TEXT ACB

Writing is fifty. I propose to apply ears behind painting. The painters' techniques as simple and use to writing; things immediate as collage through

TEXT A+CB

Writing is fifty the painters' technique, immediate as collage of any book or newspr the columns of text. Newly constituted mess which sug-

the pages or montage. Cut right of any book or newspr example, and shuffle into . . . lengthwise, for the columns of text. Hazard and read them. Put them together are newly constituted meself. Use any system sage. Do it for yours which suggests itself, own words or the words to you. Take your own, said to be "the very else living or dead own words of anyone." You'll soon see that anyone. Words have words don't belong to a vitality of their o can make them gush on and you or anybody into action.

The permutated punning off on their ems set the words spin own; echoing out as phrase are permutate he words of a potent ped into an expanding which they did not seem; ripple of meanings which to be capable of when then stuck into that they were struck and phrase.

The poets are suwords—not to chain posed to liberate the them in phrases. Who supposed to think? Told poets they were Poets are meant to sing. Poets have ng and to make words snow words "of their wit own their words very own." Writers don. Since when do words "ur very own words," belong to anybody. "Yo indeed! And who are you?

gests itself said to be the very. You'll soon see that a vitality of their into action.

The permutated poem, echoing out as ted into an expanding to be capable of when phrase.

The poets are sue them in phrases. Poets are meant to sigh now words of their. Since when do words indeed! And who are I propose to apply ears behind painting., as simple as use to writing; things through the pages or montage. Cut right example and shuffle into lengthwise for hazard and read the put them together ourself. Use any system sage. Do it for your words or the words to you. Take your own else living or dead; own words of anyone, anyone. Words have words don't belong to one and you or anybody can make them gush.

Set the words spin phrase are permutate. The words of a potent they did not seem, ripple of meanings then stuck into that they were struck. And words not to chain. Posed to liberate the supposed to think? Told poets they were Poets to make words own their words. Very own. Writer's "very own words" belong to anybody. You and you.

TEXT BAC

Writing is fifty y
ears behind painting. the painters' tech-
niq I propose to apply ues to writing;
things immediate as collages as simple
and or montage. Cut right of any book
or newsprt through the pages int. . .
lengthwise, for the columns of text. example, and shuffle Put them together at
newly constituted meshazard and read
the sage. Do it for yours which suggests
itself elf. Use any system to you. Take
your o said to be "the very n words or
the words own words" of anyone You'll
soon see that else living or dead. words
don't belong to a vitality of their o anyone. Words have wn and you or anybody into action. can make them gush

The permutated po
ems set the words spin own; echoing
out as tning off on their he words of a
potent ped into an expanding phrase
are permutat-ripple of meanings whito
be capable of whench they did not
seem they were struck and phrase. then
stuck into that

The poets are sup
posed to liberate the them in phrases.
Who words — not to chain o told poets
they were Poets are meant to si supposed to think? ng and to make words
snow words 'of their ving. Poets have
ery own." Writers don Since when to
words ('t) own their words. belong to
anybody. "Yo indeed! And who are ur
very words," you?

TEXT B+CA

Ears behind painting; use to writing; things or montage. Cut right into
. . . lengthwise. Put them together are
sage. Do it for yours to you. Take your
own words of anyone. Words don't belong to own and you or anybody aims
to set the words spin. The words of a
potent ripple of meanings whin they
were struck and posed to liberate.

The O told poets they were NG
and to make words "very own." Writers
don't belong to anybody. You, you?

Writing is fifty. I propose to apply
the painters' techniques as simple and
immediate as "collage" through the
pages of any book or newspr example,
and shuffle the columns of text. Hazard and read the newly constituted
mesself. Use any system which suggests
itself in words or the words said to be
"the very else living or dead. You'll soon
see that anyone. Words have a vitality
of their o can make them gush into
action.

The permutated poems running off
on their own; echoing out as the phrases
are permutated into an expanding which
they did not seem capable of when
then stuck into that phrase.

The poets are sup words — not to
chain them in phrases. Who supposed
to think? Poets are meant to si ing.
Poets have now words of their own
words. Since when do words your very
own words, indeed! And who are you?

Am I the One?

*"Am I the One?" (1964?), undated and unpublished, was preserved in the
Paul Bowles archives at the Harry Ransom Humanities Research Center
at the University of Texas at Austin, among letters from Gysin to Bowles
between 1961 and 1964. As an isolated piece of fiction, it seems to have
been written around that time because the style is far removed from his
early stories; it reflects the sort of nightmarish humor glimpsed in some
of his experimental work of the early 1960s, and yet it does not reflect
the concerns found in his first novel, which he started in 1965.*

I suppose I can say that I have had a good life, looking back on it now that it
seems about over. At least it has been as good as any of us can expect. You see,
almost at once I begin to qualify my first statement about a good life. We all do
that. As if we knew anything else or had anything else to judge things by. We
don't, of course. Even I don't, though I do think that I am more aware of the
world than most of my fellow creatures.

If I am going to be as honest about this as I would like to be, I must admit
that a great many others may have that same sort of opinion of themselves.
And I want to be honest. It is difficult enough to relate a set of circumstances
without trying to explain one's own nature, too. I know only that the sort of
vision which I possess is something between a blessing and a curse. It makes for
a superior sort of happy unhappiness.

But there I go, contradicting myself in one and the same sentence. It is important to know that the world is held together by unresolved contradictions.
All I know is that everyone is like that.

I keep saying "all I know" as though I were going to be able to record everything before it is over. Yet that would make everything finite, which is impossible. As I have already suggested, I am aware of much more than I know, and
while I would like to put some order to it I realize that no one can. My mother
used to chide me gently, saying that I was not put here to change the world.

I suppose that, logically, my story begins with her. Much that I am stems from
her and her early training. I was going to say that it was her fault, and I suppose that if I were less honest I could make a good case for that point of view.

It is much more complex than that, of course, and even I must admit it.
She is in no way *directly* responsible for the situation in which I find myself
now, except that she gave birth to me and *I* never asked to be born, did I? I can

remember blurting that out to her when I was still quite young and dependent on her, and I know it was not fair. To say that I am only what she made me would be to put a very low value on that part of my nature which I consider to be my essential self. Yet I have always felt at a certain disadvantage in dealing with the world, and I blame this on the way she brought me up. I can see two sides to any question even when it involves my own advantage, my comfort or even, perhaps, my life.

We have been here more than a day now and I am certain that I am the only one who realizes how desperate our situation may be. Last night they all slept soundly with full bellies as if that were the most normal thing in the world. Of course it was, too, in a way, since none of us has ever been without food for long or known any real privation.

You must admit that I see their point of view. Experience teaches, they say, and even I have had no such experience, but I *know*. I know, too, that some people can't learn even from experience. It's not that I'm a pessimist always expecting the worst to happen but I do believe in taking the proper precautions.

I wanted to divide the food, leaving a store for the future—just a sensible precaution, but they would have none of it. They laughed at me and ate greedily. When I saw that it was useless to reason with them I jumped in and got mine. I took my just share and no more, even if I am bigger. My size and my good looks have helped me in life, of course, but it is really not an advantage to appear strong. I have never had to fight, because I got what I wanted without a struggle or else the things which others wanted so badly interested me very little.

I blame that on my mother. I am not a coward. I am sure that I am not a physical coward. It is merely that I never learned to fight because I never had to. I may be repeating myself but I must make this very clear. Everything which is happening depends upon it. The others seem to have no idea either of our desperate situation nor of the terrible problem which is going to arise from it. I cannot bring myself to believe that even they, dull as they are, can ignore that there is a problem. When the time comes, and it will be soon from the looks of things, surely even they will not—cannot—merely go ahead and act without thinking. I don't mean that they will think it out in abstract philosophical terms such as I might use, but they will have to weigh and consider, bringing the matter out for open discussion before they act.

When we first got here, they were all delighted by the novelty of the place. I knew better right away, but I refrained from saying anything. I have learned that much in life, even if it is too late. I could do nothing about it anyway. I used to think that knowledge itself changed things, but now I am not so sure.

It stayed light in here long after the usual time because the walls of this place are transparent. They marveled at that. I could have told them why it was, but they would not have understood or even stopped to listen.

They all went racing round and round until it made me quite dizzy, and I closed my eyes for a long while so I would not have to watch them. I have always thought that most of our racing after nothing was ridiculous. They kept up an awful racket, jostling and stepping on one another and trying to climb the smooth concave walls. They thought that they were doing the right thing and that their activity was some sort of virtue in itself.

Then they made the most ludicrous guesses about the sort of place we were in, and I could have told them about that, too. I know a big goldfish bowl when I see one, and I have seen this sort of thing entirely filled with water.

I kept imagining what would happen if someone should put water in here, but that is the sort of nightmare fantasy which I refuse to allow myself despite what they say about me. Besides I have a clear head. That is not at all the sort of crisis which we are going to have to face in here. Very often things may appear to happen to us as though they were caused by some outside agency, but that is false, I think. It is what we bring about ourselves that determines our fate.

Must I go on and explain or qualify that, too? I mean, of course, that death is the final crisis for all of us, but just because it comes to us all it is not a problem. Our responsibility for the death of another *is* a problem. Those amongst us who will have become responsible will have gone through a crisis which is even more terrible than death. Who will they be? And how will they live with themselves after it has happened?

I cannot believe that they will merely shrug their shoulders and go on.

The other possibility, and it is the most terrifying one, is that they will not even shrug their shoulders, for they will not have realized what they have done.

Before the light went away with a loud click I looked around a little. They were all so busy climbing or trying to climb the walls that they never were able to look through them. They have never realized that the walls are transparent. Not knowing the nature of the place, not knowing glass, they would say that if you can look through something it means that it is not there. They climb on the slippery wall, feel it, fall back bruised from contact with it, therefore the wall is all that they will ever know. I can feel the bowl too but, perhaps because I climb less, I can see a little beyond.

Those among them who claim to be the thinkers have been propounding the most laughable theories about the nature of the bowl and delivering sermons entitled, "*Why we were put here.*" They make no sense at all. Some claim that we should all run in clockwise fashion, while others, equally vehement, insist that counter-clockwise is the only way. Then they demand a bigger share of the food for their advice. The joke is that we are all in here together, and there is no more food. I have been laughing about it for hours.

I can see things which are not in the bowl, though many of them could be. If I thought there was time and had the inclination or that sort of sense of humor I might lecture on "*Why they are not in the Bowl.*" All I know is that to be in the bowl is a condition of our nature. If we were out of it we would be something else. We would no longer be Dancing Mice. We would no longer spend our lives on our hind legs as only our sort does. All of us should realize that there are other mice and even we were not always Dancers. There are field mice, house mice, city mice, country mice, church mice, who would never be in a bowl or ever dance on their hind legs.

I am sorry if I appear to have digressed again, for that is not our problem here and now. We are not going to leave the bowl nor change suddenly into something which we are not. To hear anyone suggest that annoys me, and I feel bound to explain. The problem is what we are going to do here in the bowl.

The situation in here is much worse. The light has come back several times so we are in the third or fourth day. There has been no food for a long time now, and tempers are short. Quarrels suddenly break out over nothing, and even the best runners are slowing down. Those of the clockwise and those of the anti-clockwise school are almost silent. Only now and then do they exhort everyone to run. The time must be very short.

Curiously enough, I have taken up a little running myself. It takes my mind off things and I needed the exercise. First I run one way and then I run the other, just to show them all that I have an open mind. Really open. Not belonging to either school—and after all there are only two ways to run. Previously I stubbornly refused to run at all. I hope that no one thinks that I am doing it out of cowardice, trying to curry favor with one group or the other before the crisis comes.

It is so horrible that I hesitate to tell what has happened, even though I knew it would. Of course it has given all of us a new lease on life, you might say, but it merely puts off the crisis and prolongs the agony.

One of us fell into the drinking water during the night and was drowned.

We shared him. We are all equally guilty now. It is curious what a feeling of solidarity this crime gives us. I find myself saying "we" instead of "they." I don't like to think that he may have been pushed.

It is just as I thought. No one mentions the moral problem at all. Everyone looked guilty for a while, but now there is a hard glitter in every eye again. I expected to see it there. I know it is in mine, too. There has been no open discussion of how this is to be done. Who is it going to be? Who will falter? Whoever it is, as soon as he falters, the whole pack will be down on him like one mouse.

I know that I have never been really popular. Only my mother was never critical of me. We are all running again, but it no longer takes my mind off things. Running hardly dulls the edge. It has become a mere mechanical reflex. I go on as if I were in a dream. I go over all the slights and insults I have ever suffered in my life. I would do a great many things differently if I could do them over. At least that is what I tell myself. Probably I could not, unless I myself were very different. And I could not be different unless events were different. Did events shape me, or did I cause to happen what did happen, or did they influence me in such a way that I influenced further events which shaped me and so on? I am so tired.

I am sure that others must be as tired as I am myself. I can see some of the smaller ones whom I would have thought would go down long ago. They must be the wiry kind. Here I have to carry around this great body of mine which everyone always admired so. What does it mean now? It's just a burden.

I am so tired that only pride keeps me going. Is it worth it? Why bother? Someone has to go. If I stay, can I live with myself? First one, and then it will have to be another and another and another. Disgusting horror. No end. I am a cannibal already. Unclean. Is not the victim better off than the murderer? I can see them all eyeing me as they run. Can they appreciate what I am thinking? They might think I fell from weakness if I . . . . *No, no. God! NO! Am I the one?*

⊶⇒ Janicot

"Janicot" (1967), one of few texts Gysin wrote on other artists, reflects his multilingualism (French, Spanish, English, in this case). This poem was for the catalogue of painter Françoise Janicot, now known more as a photographer, for her show at the Musée Galliera in Paris in 1967. Janicot first met Gysin in 1962 at an event produced by the Domaine Poétique group (which included her husband Bernard Heidsieck), and they traveled together to Morocco in 1964.

Cabler
accabler
attabler . . .
testing testing test . . .
Plus près de lave que de cendre
more silk than sand
más sable que seda
une lame sèche mais coulante
vapeur consolidée dans la soif
soif de soie
soif de l'éclat de son soi
voile trempée
more fog than silicone
émaillé argenté
lumière sourde en coulée
O Zohra Luz Luce Lucie
limon grès argile
coulez!

Luxe luxure de ténèbres
tenebroso tenting tonight
sur les champs élucidés de lave
perdues et retrouvées
chartes chimères shimmering shutters
et dans la cour
nada más que agua y nubes overhead
absorbant la pluie
Entre la Pluie en courant

nue et voilée
debout et flanquée de partout
de ses milliers de pieds enfoncés dans la boue
coulante et courante
gliding and glistening
ses aigrettes diamantées versant
ses brillants sourires attristés
distraite et délirante
sous la claire compulsion de la lumière
mais chaussée de la terre des pieds à la tête
Roche translucidée d'éclairs
lente implosion éclore
slow motion traveling
sans sous-titres sans sous-entendus
moving sans motion
opening without being opened
ábreme este negro por favor
pour mieux écouter sa clarté
Cállate! Cállate!
Silencio
oir oir oiga oiga!
Yes, who's speaking, please?
Madame, le vieil Océan est servi

Avec ses brumes et ses bruines
ses brouillards de bitume
brutalement broyés
bistres blémissant blessés
couleurs ignorées des hauts de pavés
plus souvent vues des ponts et des chaussées
Mais, carramba! qu'elles sont pleines de
zumbido
no hay otra palabra
lumière de plomb ou de pewter
pluie sur les pavés
lente pensée

roc bloc choc
shattering the window

éclatant les carreaux
osant respirer hors du tableau
cerné d'acier en cerceau
en géographie un plateau
en topographie un campo
en météo francamente maltiempo
but if it clears up tomorrow
demain mañana mil años
le divin pneuma et le pranna pratique
seront tellement étendus
qu'on confondra mur, temps et tableaux
vols d'oiseaux
le zumbido électronique et l'aurore boréale
champs cendrés de neige
et la toile et le papier

Campoamor Tanger, Maroc
vendredi 13 oct. 67

The Process

The Process (1969) was Gysin's first novel, written between 1965 and 1968 in Tangier. Having recognized early on that Paul Bowles had staked out his own literary terrain there—writing of a dark, sinister country that was nearly impenetrable to foreigners—this was the book where Gysin sought to put in all he wanted to say about Morocco.

As he notes in the brief introduction offered here, written almost two decades later—though never published, it may have been intended for the reissue of his novel in 1985 by Quartet in London—the idea for the book arose from the confluence of two separate periods in his life. Indeed, much of his own experience is woven into the narrative, starting with the protagonist, Ulys O. Hanson, III, who as author of A History of Slavery in Canada *and Fulbright fellow also seems to descend from Josiah Henson: a black Ulysses, he journeys across the desert to end up almost where he set out. Names, of course, mutate and branch out in unsuspected ways—a byproduct of Gysin's own border-hopping life and a device that runs rampant in his later novel—so that Hanson is called Hassan by Moroccans, which evokes the founder of the eleventh-century Ismaili sect known as the Assassins, Hassan i Sabbah (an important reference for Gysin), who was also called the Old Man of the Mountain, for his mountaintop stronghold, Alamut, in Persia. At any rate, like the places described in the novel, most of the characters are based on people Gysin knew or encountered in Tangier in the 1950s, which was an international port until 1956: foremost among these is Hamid, companion and guide to Hanson, modeled after Gysin's friend Hamri. But beyond the personal notes that Gysin employed, the novel reflects his ability to spin a tale amid multiple digressions and especially his passion for history, which he often liked to reinterpret, making unexpected connections across vastly different places and times.*

The Process derives its method from his experiments with the tape recorder; since the 1950s Gysin seldom parted with his trusty Uher. In the novel, Hanson discovers how the machine, which may be the ultimate protagonist, "both records and wipes out the words," echoing some of Gysin's own concerns during the Beat Hotel days. The narrative proceeds, therefore, through a series of voices belonging to the characters that he has recorded—arranged in chapters corresponding to a sequence of personal pronouns (I, Thou, He, She, etc.)—erasing the narrator himself in the end: all that remains are the recordings, as Burroughs has said. Or, as Carol Marie Anderson suggests in her 1987 dissertation, "Visions of Reality: Brion Gysin's

*Evolving Experimentation with Reality," Hanson's own chapters, mostly
alternating with the taped monologues of the other chapters, "can logically
be considered as the 'verb' portion of the conjugation," since he is the novel's
catalyst.*

In 1946 I published my biography of Josiah Henson, "the Real Uncle
Tom," who told the story of his life to Harriet Beecher Stowe. In the
army I met one of his descendants and met his family which had
included Matthew Henson, Peary's scout who had preceded him to the
North Pole, a fact which is only too often passed over in history.

Many years later when the French wife of the American Consul in
Tangier told me of her grandfather, a vastly wealthy and ambitious sugar
magnate who had declared himself Emperor of Africa in the late nineteenth century, the two ideas clicked together and I had the persona of
my hero in *The Process*.

The same mad idea appealed to Boussac the French textile magnate
who crashed only a few years ago.

For the rest, anyone who knew the Sahara as I did could foretell
something like the present Polisario. My story is still up to date.

Brion Gysin
Paris 25 March 85

1   "I will a round, unvarnished tale deliver."
       —Othello: 1.3.90

/   I   /

I am out in the Sahara heading due south with each day of travel less sure of
just who I am, where I am going or why. There must be some easier way to do it
but this is the only one I know so, like a man drowning in a sea of sand, I struggle back into this body which has been given me for my trip across the Great
Desert. "This desert," my celebrated colleague, Ibn Khaldoun the Historian, has
written, "This desert is so long it can take a lifetime to go from one end to the
other and a childhood to cross at its narrowest point." I made that narrow childhood crossing on another continent; out through hazardous tenement hallways
and stickball games in the busy street, down American asphalt alleys to paved
playgrounds; shuffling along Welfare waiting-lines into a maze of chainstore
and subway turnstiles and, through them, out onto a concrete campus in a cold

gray city whose skyscrapers stood up to stamp on me. It has been a long trail a-winding down here into this sunny but sandy Middle Passage of my life in Africa, along with the present party. Here, too, I may well lose my way for I can see that I am, whoever I am, out in the middle of Nowhere when I slip back into this awakening flesh which fits me, of course, like a glove.

I know this body as if it were a third party whose skin I put on as a mask to wear through their "Land of Fear" and I do go in a sort of disguise for, like everyone else out here in this blazing desert where a man is a fool to show his face naked by day, I have learned to wrap five or six yards of fine white muslin around my head to protect the mucus of my nose and throat against the hot, dry wind. All you can see of me is my eyes. For once, I look just like everyone else. No need for me to open these eyes. I know what is out there—nothing but the very barest stripped illusion of a world; almost nothing, nothing at all.

Bundled up like a mummy, I huddle here under my great black burnous, a cape as big as a bag for an animal my size, shape and color. It also serves as a portable tent smelling of woodsmoke and lanolin, under which I fumble for the two pencil-thin sections of my *sebsi*, my slim wooden keef-pipe from Morocco, to fit them together. A fine flesh-pink clay pipe head, no bigger than the last joint of my little finger, snuggles up over a well-fitted paper collar shaped wet with spit. I try it like a trumpet; airtight, good. My keef-pouch from Morocco is the skin of a horned viper sewn into a *metoui* and stuffed with great grass. I check with my thumb the tide of fine-chopped green leaf which rolls down its long leather tongue, milking most of the keef back into the pouch. What remains, I coax into the head of my pipe with the beckoning crook of my right forefinger.

A masterpiece matchbox the size of a big postage stamp leaps into the over-turned bowl of my left hand, riding light but tight between the ball of my thumb and my third finger. I make all these moves not just out of habit but with a certain conscious cunning through which I ever-so slowly reconstruct myself in the middle of your continuum; inserting myself, as it were, back into this flesh which is the visible pattern of Me. Yet, I know this whole business is a trap which may well be woven of nothing but words, so I joggle the minia-ture matchbox I hold in my hand and these masterpiece matches in here chuckle back what always has sounded to me like a word but a word which I cannot quite catch. It could be a rattling Arabic word but my grasp of Arabic is not all that good and no one, not even Hamid, will tell me what the matches say to the box. I hold the box up to my ear as I shake it again, trying to hear what the box stutters back. If I remember correctly, Basilides in his "Game" re-

duced all the Names proposed by the Gnostics to one single rolling, cacopho-
nic, cyclical word which he thought might well prove to be a Key to the heav-
ens: "*Kaulakaulakaulakaulakau. . . .*" Can the matches match that?

I love these little matches bought back in Tanja. Each match is a neat twist
of brown paper like a stick dipped in wax, with a helmet-shaped turquoise-
blue head made to strike on the miniature Sahara of sandpaper slapped onto
one side of the box. Matchbox is clamped into the claw of left thumb and
middle finger. This indifferent caliper proves suddenly sadist as it rams poor
matchbox back onto himself, with little-finger of right hand clear up his ass.
Little-finger holds him impaled; proffering a drawerful of identical matches to
caliper, who solemnly selects one little brother, pinching him tight. Matchbox
is closed with a small, scraping sigh against the heel of right hand. Little-finger
withdraws from the rape to help snub poor match against the backslide of his
box; striking and exploding his head.

I elbow my way out of this cocoon of felted camel-hair smelling of woodsmoke to thrust forward this pipe, pouch and matches just as we go over a
bump and I open my eyes. I am not alone. We are five passengers in here, where
we should be only four in the blistering metal cabin of this truck whose red-hot
diesel is housed in with us, too. Two seats on either side of it are called First-
Class Transportation, while Third-Class is out on the back on top of the cargo of
sacks beneath a cracking tarpaulin. In the front seat, Driver, who looks like a
chipmunk with the toothache because of the way his sloppy turban hangs
under his chin, crouches over the wheel like a real desert rat. Black Greaser, his
number-two man, has been playing a long windy tune on a flute made out of a
bicycle-pump and the bump nearly rams the flute down his throat. An anonymous vomiting man, like a doll leaking wet sawdust and slime, flops out the far
window carsick while, here right beside me, crammed into my seat with me
when we are not up in the air, is Middleman; Stowaway. We rise shoulder to
shoulder and I hope he lands back on the diesel and burns.

He has risen up in the air without losing his crosslegged Sufi saint pose, as
if to show me he knows how to levitate. I shoot up my own dusty eyebrows at
him as much as to say: *So can I!* because he glares at my pipe with all the bale-
ful ferocity of a carnivorous bird. He feels I pollute him with my keef-smoke —
too bad! We both drop back into my seat. I paid First-Class Transportation for
these broken springs; no need to share them with him. Yesterday, or the day before, or one of those days back along our trail, he suddenly jumped up from
behind a bare dune in the middle of nowhere, flagging us down. I had spotted
him up there ahead of us and was just saying to myself: "Is that a man or a

bush?" when he started up, skipping and waving his arms. Driver changed gear without daring to stop in the sand from which this little old stick of a man hopped up quick as a bird when Black Greaser threw open the door, grandly waving him into my seat with me. He is a Hadj, just back from the pilgrimage to Mecca; a new little saint. Black Greaser let his whole ugly face fall apart in a welcoming grin: "No baggage, Father?"

The little old man twitched aside the yards of gray-green muslin piled on top of his head and swathing his bearded face: "No baggage. This is the way I came and — *Inch'Allah!* — this is the way I shall return."

I push back the window of opalescent glass frosted by the blasting of sand, to thrust the whole length of my slender pipe out like a periscope into the bouncing air of the dazzling desert through which we churn night and day no faster than a funeral. When I lean out the window, the light out there hits me like a blow. Shading my eyes, I look down into the granular shallows of flowing sand on whose current we ride until I am dizzy and sick. Everything visibly crawls; even the cloth of my sleeve when I look at it close. I glance up and out with my eyes clenched against the all but intolerable brightness of the blazing desert where the mirage sizzles across the horizon like a sweep of glittering marshes, thickly grown with tall rushes whipped by the wind. Air ignites and flames up around the truck like the billowing breath of a blast furnace searing my lungs. The water should lie not more than a half hour's distance away — or so you might think. Hour after hour, day after day, we bore on through the sands without reaching those marshes.

All this ululating emptiness aches in my ears like the echo of a shell. Now and again, I swear I can hear the lowing and bellowing of invisible herds of longhorn cattle but, of course, there are none. When I listen even further down into myself, I contact something else which shakes my whole intimate contact with Me. When I try to tune out the constant moaning roar of the wind, my whole being vibrates to a sound down below the threshold of hearing. My sinuses, antrums, the cords of my throat and the cavities of my chest, the very hollows of my bones hum in a register too low for my ear but, for no known reason, I tremble, I quake. This, so they tell me, is the voice of Ghoul and Ghoul is the Djinn of the Desert, Keeper of the Land of Fear. Grains of sand in their incalculable billions of billions are grinding, grinding together, rolling and sliding abrasively in dunes as big as New York and as high, vibrating this ocean of air through which we paddle like sick fish on their flight from some distant dynamite blast. At that, a very American thought suddenly strikes me: they do have an atomic center out here in the Sahara. Could this air be radioactive, perhaps? Or, is that just the black breath of Ghoul?

Far away back up north in the green hills of Morocco, which I call home since I began to merge almost against my will into this scene with Hamid my Moroccan mock-guru, everyone around the keef cafés is always talking and singing of the Sahara but not one man in ten knows where it begins or ends or how to get into this desert. "It lies down that way, many days marching," they say, swinging their long slim keef-pipes around vaguely south. Yet, every last man sitting there on a straw mat on the floor feels he owns the whole sweep of the Sahara desert, personally, inside his own Muslim head. Let some pale-face tourist appear on the scene and they will all proclaim themselves competent "guides," if you please; when not one of them can read even a map. In my forlorn American way, I thought to teach Hamid the lay of the land and, to this end, I pulled my poor self together to make an expedition up out of the damp grotto in which Hamid and I were living in the native quarter of Tanja, in the impasse of a narrow alley in a section of the Medina below even the tight-packed little pedestrian square of cafés called the Socco Chico; in other words, lost.

I adjusted my shades and smoked one last pipe for the road before I stepped cautiously out into the mainstream of mankind in the swarming alley as narrow as a corridor that is our street. At first, the entire Medina of Tanja feels like one mysteriously rambling mansion packed full of maniacs but, eventually, what looks like a terrifying trap to a tripper gets to feel like your very own house. I cut into the traffic and kept my head down as I whipped around corners with my eyes glued to the ground; so as not to be noticed, I hoped. I slid through alleys so wide I could touch the walls on both sides with my elbows and I had to flatten myself into doorways to let heavily-laden donkeys and porters push past. The whole point of this game, best known to Old Tanja Hands, is to get from one side of the Socco Chico to the other without crossing it; invisible to all traders and touts. My own cunning route, first shown me by Hamid of course, is a turnoff between the old Hotel Satan and the Casa Delirium, once a whorehouse in better days. This way, you can bypass not only the Socco Chico but also steep Siaghine Street running up out of it; lined as it is with neon-lit bazaars, swarming with tourists and tramps.

I meant to drop by the American Library on my way up to the Boulevard in the New Town of Tanja but, when I caught sight of myself in a mirror in a shop window, I thought: Uh-uh, better not! I managed to make myself look a little more human before I got to the Café de Paris on the Place de France. I drew up in front of a raggedy man who sells raggedy books in the street. On an earlier trip, I had spotted his stock of old dog-eared French guidebooks and road maps of North Africa, put out by Michelin, the makers of tires. As I bent over his wares, I picked up on the fact that I was getting scanned from behind their newspapers by the whole row of white American and British operatives seated, as always, out on the terrace of the Café de Paris. They had their telepathic finders out feeling all over me as I bought, for one dirham, a map which is now out of print. I scuttled back down to the Socco and called Hamid out of his cavernous keef café to drag him home for a bout of instruction in the map.

#151 Morocco, Algeria and Tunisia (1 centimeter for 20 kilometers or 1/2,000,000). On this map, one handspan to the right along the Mediterranean shore lies Woran. With your thumb on Woran, your little-finger lands on Algut. If you pivot due south from that white city on the cliffs, your thumb will fall on Ghardaïa, the mysterious desert capital of the Dissident Mozabites. All that can take at least three or four days of travel from the bright blue Straits of Gibraltar, along the lush coastal valleys, over green hills and mountains so high they are covered with snow. On the far side of these are plains marked in brown to denote almost no annual rainfall at all and they must be crossed before you get to even the fringe of the bright golden Sahara. The trouble with this map is that it has two big insets of Woran and Algut, shown in some detail at a scale of 1/500,000, and these effectively obscure the desert trails to the south.

I trundled myself back up to the Boulevard again next day, or was it next week? Anyway, one fine day when I could tear myself away from the great smells of Hamid's cooking and manage to part the curtain of keef which hung over our door, I fell out into the street and worked my way back to the Boulevard bookstall, where I bought, unobserved, an old guide to Algeria and the Michelin map #152—a great prize. This pretty, pictorial map was printed to illustrate the glorious exploit of General Leclerc, who marched a Free French army from Dakar all the way north to Tunis across the Sahara by way of Lake Chad. Not even the Romans could have brought off such a feat but Hamid shows little interest in anything done by the French or the Roumis, in general. Being Black, I am not a real Roumi to Hamid. On the other hand, Hamid looks down on all Blacks as the natural slaves of the Arabs; even though his own hair is curly enough to give him trouble finding a barber, back in the States. Hamid shuts me up when I tell him I am Black. "You're not Black, you're American! *Safi!* Enough!"

Hamid suddenly became fascinated by the form he began to see in my map. He pointed out that the Great Desert is in the shape of a camel stretching its neck right across Africa, from the Atlantic to the Red Sea. He laughed like a lunatic to see that the western butt-end of his camel was dropping its Mauretanian crud on the Black Senegalese—"Charcoal Charlies," Hamid calls them, having picked up the term in the port. The head of Hamid's camel drinks its fill in the sweet waters of the Nile. The eye of the camel, naturally enough, is that fabled city of Masr, where the Arab movies are made and all the radios ring out over streets paved with gold. Us poor Nazarenes call the place Cairo, for short. Suddenly, somewhere down on the lower middle belly of Hamid's camel, about four knuckles north of Kano in northern Nigeria, I dowsed out a big carbuncle. With no more warning than that, my whole heart rushed out to this place which was pictured as an outcropping of extinct ash-blue volcanoes jutting up out of the bright yellow sands. I noted that the whole area was called the Hoggar and it seemed to boast only one constantly inhabited place, whose name I made out to be Tam. I was truly surprised to hear myself calmly boasting to Hamid, as if I were AMERICAN EXPRESS: "I'll be in this place, here, this time next year."

"*Inch'Allah!* if God wills," Hamid corrected me automatically and then, as if he were indeed the Consul of Keef, who was sending me out on this mission, he went on: "I'll get them to cut you a green passport of keef to see you through everything. I'll see that you get the best of the crop from Ketama and I'll bring it down from the mountain myself with the blessings of Hassan-i-Sabbah, the Father of Grass. On your way, you're bound to run into some other Assassins."

"But, Hamid," I laughed: "I am not an Assassin at all!"

"We are Assassins, all of us," he gravely replied.

When the time came, I found myself settling back in the train leaving Tanja, gliding slowly along by our magnificent deserted beach on the Straits of Gibraltar. "So, I'm off," I sighed to myself in my cold First-Class compartment. Just then, Hamid, whom I had not seen for more than a week, swung aboard with all the fine acrobatic ease of an old *contrabandista*. With a big golden grin, he waved my "passport" under my nose; a parchment sheep's bladder as big as two fists, packed hard as a rock with the pick of the crop from Ketama, high in the hills of the Rif. We tried a few pipes of the pot as the green winter landscape of northern Morocco picked up and flowed past the window of our train. A few happy hours later, Hamid dove off the train outside of Kebir, before we got into the station. "No money, no ticket: I travel free!" He was going on up into the hills to his village—Jajouka, Mount of Owls—to stay with his uncles the Master Musicians, who practice their Pan music all day on their pipes as they amble out of their little whitewashed thatched houses in their white woolen homespun jellabas and their white turbans to wander over their green Little Hills after their goats. I gave Hamid the money to have a sheep killed in my honor for a feast up there; to bring me luck on my journey, I said. He waved once and blew me a mischievous kiss as he slid through a hedge of giant blue cactus and was gone.

We just sat in Kebir for a long hour in the rain, which I spent fending off children in steaming wet rags who lounged through the train selling green oranges, used razor blades and, for all I know, reclaimed chewing gum and their not very appetizing selves; anything. At long last, the train started up again with a jerk and we soon slid off into the night, but it was hours past dinnertime when we finally staggered into the junction at Sidi Karim, where I learned to my horror that I would have to wait several bleak hours in the dingy station which the stationmaster was even then shutting up, turning off all the lights but one feeble bulb outside in the rain. As he got onto his bicycle to pedal off through the downpour, he regretted that there was no café or restaurant where I could find food in the forlorn village of Sidi Karim. I took out my pipe and managed to light up in the lee of the wind. Quite quickly, I felt very much better, indeed. As soon as I was turned-on again, I caught my breath with a gasp of fearful delight; one single step outside the murky circle of artificial light and I was back in Africa. East wind tore great silver rents in the night sky and slashed an occasional sharp sluice of rain across the shining railroad tracks alongside which ranked choruses of bullfrogs recited the interminable Word they were set a long time ago, now, as their *zikr*: "*Kaulakaulakaulkaulakaulakau . . .*" it sounded like. Skydiving bats looped about the lamps they lit along the track, presently: "*Train coming!*" The bats squealed up into their ultrasonic radar frequencies like the brakes on distant steel wheels. When the train did come, it came in an orgasmic rush of hot diesel-oil odor, trailing a veil of orange blossom like a bride; as a charming excuse for its lateness, no doubt.

The train was strangely empty, almost like a ghost train with only a few sleeping Moroccans huddled under their hoods. Carrying no baggage, ever, I made my way to the bar, where a group of French colonials eyed me coldly, taking me for a Moroccan, I rather suspect. I adjusted my shades, forgetting for the moment just how much more Moroccan they make me look. At the bar, the Moroccan barman refused to serve me, at first, pointing to a fly-blown text on the wall which said in several languages: "No Alcohol May Be Served to Muslims," followed by the text in very small print of a *dahir* or order-in-council promulgated before the last war. I settled down at a table and got something both to eat and to drink when I showed the barman my U.S. passport but he went on speaking to me in Arabic, nevertheless. The French people got off at Fez, where we barely stopped. The train rocketed through the night, up to the pass at Taza, and then it ran on to the frontier at Oujda, where trouble had been reported on the outskirts of town but, despite this, no one even asked to look at my passport.

On the other side of the border, I found they had put on a sleeping-car, so I paid a supplement on my ticket and got some sleep. In the morning, I lit my first pipe and looked out on a new landscape. The stainless-steel sun glittered through clouds onto the coastal plains where the red tiles on the rooftops of the houses and barns make it look more like Alsace than Africa, giving the tiny robed figures of Arabs in the background the air of people flying past in a dream. I took out my journal and wrote: *As no two people see the same view along the Way, all trips from here to there are imaginary: all truth is a tale I am telling myself.*

When we got to Algut, late at night, I realized that I was the sole passenger to get off that train. The station, awash in shallow neon illumination, was ghostly and cold. There was no one about but me and the exhausted, panting train breathing heavily beside me in the empty echoing station. I abandoned the train and made for a public telephone to call up the hotel but the phone was dead. Somewhere, I had heard there was a curfew; perhaps that was why no one was about, not even a sentry to challenge me at the gate. I walked out into the street, where there was one single taxi, waiting just for me. I ordered the driver, in my almost impeccable French, to take me swiftly to the Hotel Saint Georges, on the heights of the city, where the suites of rooms in that old Turkish palace are named after the commanders of World War Two, who once stopped there amidst the luxuriant gardens which some long-dead pacha long ago ordered to be laid out and planted with one thousand and one varieties of palm. My driver glanced at me oddly in his rearview mirror, but he may have realized I was merely quoting the old pre-war guidebooks I fancy so much. When I am high enough, I quote almost anything from Aesop to Zarathustra. I judged from the back of my man's neck that he was, probably, a very white Corsican Blackfoot; a colonial leftover. Nevertheless, I leaned over the front seat to ask him politely what *that* was—pointing down to a sawn-off shotgun lying beside him. He replied: there were hoodlums about.

The streets we flashed through were shining with rain on the tram tracks along which we skidded as we climbed. Patrols of sodden soldiers huddled here and there under the trees in public gardens; their firearms and the whites of their eyes glinted sharply in our headlights, which the driver blinked only for military jeeps. High above the harbor of Algut, sentinels stood guard at the gates of the Saint Georges; not for the first time in its history, I judge. The hotel itself was locked up like a fortress. From inside, one man opened the door very cautiously to my knock as another man covered the crack in the door with a gun. They had a message for me at the desk to say that two American gentlemen were waiting for me in the Churchill suite. I replied rather grandly that I wanted my room and my bath and a good hot dinner with a bottle of French wine in front of an open fire before I saw anybody. Sponsors be damned, I thought; I was going to be very grand. Positively, I was not about to go crawling up to them, right off the beastly train, on my hands and knees like a suppliant. They had the Foundation money for me; I meant to look good when I accepted it. They probably thought I was being arrogant but I was nothing but tired; and more than a little bit stoned.

As I lay back in my hot bath, I giggled. It was awesome, the matter-of-fact way Hamid had taken my magical flight. I laughed aloud at the confusion of terms, for what is magical, Hamid considers normal and, besides, he expects nothing less out of an American—*his* American, at that! Of course, he is right: I have done a very American thing. I've forgotten, now, where I first picked up on the Foundation for Fundamental Findings; with an address in Basel, oddly enough. I am not about to explain Foundations to Hamid. Besides, what could I tell him—that a Foundation gives you money if you know how to beg for it and I do? I have taught: I have published. Hamid is not likely to read my *History of Slavery in Canada*, which served to get me out of the States on my first Fulbright, years ago. My book could have made me a full professor; with tenure, what is more, in almost any good school in the East, and would have, I think, if I had only been white. As I ponder on this, I play with myself in the suds and stand up, creaming my body all over with soap in front of the full-length mirror they have opposite the bathtub in this luxurious bathroom of the General Alexander suite. When I applied for my Fulbright fellowship, I sent them this very white photograph of myself. When we all passed muster at a cocktail party before sailing, I thought some members of the board were surprised to see me in the old flesh, as we call it. It was not a nude photograph; of course not! I laughed and saluted my white sponsors in the mirror, waving my cock at them all, before I rinsed off and became my black self again.

I have been told that Fulbrights are already a legend in the grim groves of American Academe since so many of us are still drifting around the world instead of returning to teach. What could I possibly teach anybody since I have found out how little I know? Why, my first trip to a hammam with Hamid taught me that Americans do not even know how to take a bath! I remember him saying: "It's a good thing you're circumcised, anyway; so I'll not be ashamed to show you to Muslims, at least." I try to follow the ritual he showed me as I kneel in the spacious tub of the hotel and rinse my mouth out, using only my right hand, which serves me, also, to eat. My left hand, I use only to swab myself after toilet and I never put it in the common dish, no matter how carefully washed. I step out of the tub to drape myself in a giant-size white towel, posing in front of the mirror as Alexander the Great. I figure all these old generals must be regular narcissists if they need these big mirrors to try on their armor. I wonder what kind of bathroom my sponsors must have in the Churchill suite and I wonder if they are busy bathing each other as Muslims would do; or are they just sitting around dressed, listening to the radio, waiting for me?

Then, I struck a very grand Roman pose in front of the pier glass: I am the Great Benefactor endowing poor scholars. Playing both parts, I throw off my toga to grovel naked at the Great Benefactor's feet. I am the newly manumitted slave who has worked out his indenture to the Great Library of Alexandria. I slobber ecstatically over the Benefactor's invisible hands and feet, nearly pissing myself on the floor out of sheer gratitude. At that very moment, I heard the hotel servants moving about in my room, so I jumped up to make sure I had locked the bathroom door. A very nice terry-towel bathrobe was hanging on the back of the door, so I slipped into it. I tied up my towel into a towering turban around my head and strode back to the mirror. I felt much more like the pacha ordering his slaves about than the poor stoned wandering scholar I am, waiting for a handout from a Foundation such as the one to which I have, obviously, just sold myself; as they like to say. In my application, I sold them on the idea that it would be of interest for someone with my background to cross the Sahara, taking advantage of commercial transport as far as the village of Tam in Tuareg country. From there, I will strike out back down the old slave trails of the Sahara, which are still being used by the nomads. I will continue right down to the Slave Coast, as it used to be marked on all the maps printed in Europe; because all of Europe was engaged in the slave trade. I intend to find coastal steamers to take me around the big bulge of the continent, stopping along the way at all the old slave markets as far around the hump of Africa as St. Louis in Senegal, north of Dakar. One thing I neglected to tell the Foundation when I applied is that I have left not one foot back in their world, as they think, but a mere fading footprint. This foot I put forward into the Sahara is already firmly implanted in this African world, where my guide so far has been Hamid. I wonder where Hamid is, now?

One Arab hotel servant was on his knees lighting the fire in my drawing room, while another assisted him. Two slightly grumpy young waiters, who looked as if they had been booted out of bed, wheeled in my meal under the direction of a head waiter, while a wine waiter followed him in, nursing the wine, which he set to warm in front of my fire. A fat Arab chambermaid, look-ing like an animated sack of potatoes wrapped in an old lace curtain, waddled around aimlessly, looking for my bags to unpack my clothes. "This is the way I came: no baggage!" I barked this out in my best imitation of Hamid's crude country Arabic. They all looked rather horrified and incredulous, as they speak a quite different Arabic here, but they snapped to attention, all right. You can't treat me like a tourist, is all I was telling them. I settled down to eat my shrimp-salad cocktail and was revolted to find, under the spicy pink sauce, mostly wet lettuce and nameless white fish. I waved without words for my par-tridge and my bottle of Chateau Latour 1952. Finding it corked and gone a bit thin, I waved it away and back to the cellars for another bottle. I thought to myself: Man, oh, man, if I could only show this to Hamid, he would *know* it was all an illusion! After all, he and I were living in a leaky two-room house without inside water in the Medina of Tanja, only last week.

A tall, dead-black Sudanese waiter came in with the coffee, all dressed up like the head eunuch of the late pacha's harem. I had him bring me back the sommelier with a big snifter of *poire* and asked them to turn out the lights as they went. I sank back in my chair to look at the firelight through my colorless *poire* in the belly of the glass. What I saw made my hand tremble, for I was thinking of my journey, of course, and there I was in a bright red movie of fire which was being shown like a miniature TV on the convex side of my glass. I peered into the fire where I saw myself like an ant in a torrent of ants, being whirled along by the wind on a burning leaf like a litter or palanquin all in flames, carried on the shoulders of a streaming throng of naked people, them-selves all in flames, who ran me along through a country on fire, in which trees, grass and the very sky were blazing around me. We rushed through a river of fire, down which we paddled to an ocean of flames, where I ran up the red-hot iron ladders of a fire-boat under whose grated decks burned a seething, white-hot caldron of Whites. In the flaming red wind, we sailed like an arrow from one burning port to the next fiery town on which we swept down to stoke up our ship's boilers with a sizzling stream of white Colonials, who flared up and burned like a gem or the core of an atom exploding. I rubbed my eyes, shivering. It was cold in my chair as the fire died away. A second later, I shot up almost out of my skin, utterly startled by the sudden preternatural racket of wakening birds, all screeching at once in the palm trees outside my window. When I looked out it was morning.

Two days later, when I had bought a rucksack and a little gasoline Primus stove, I said thanks and good-by to my sponsors with my hand over my heart. That is where, along with my U.S. passport, I always carry my money. I caught a very early train out of Algut, up-country to Blida, and that afternoon I rattled through the high mountain passes to Boghari on the rim of the Sahara where the train track ends. There, I caught a bus to Djelfa in the bare metallic mountains of the Ouled Naïl; a tribe of tinkers whose women are prostitutes, loitering around like painted idols, suggestively clinking with lucky gold coins. Long after dark, I changed to the back of a Berliet truck in a rising sandstorm. In the hours after midnight, we passed through Laghouat, where the French painter Fromentin was the first White to spend a summer, more than a hundred years ago, now. He mistook that one idyllic oasis for all of the Sahara, while we barely stopped there at a filling station, under some palms whose ragged heads were whipped down into the driving sand. The yellow headlights of our truck drilled out a sandy tunnel through the roaring streets of the town as we bored our way back out into the thick of the Sahara. The wind scoured the track we followed, tacking across a vast howling plain until, several hours later, we landed in the lee of the long walls of a desert caravanserai. We charged through a banging, broken gate, stampeding the hundred camels of several caravans which had taken shelter in the vast open courtyard. On the far side of this harbor, light streamed out from the tiny windows of one small room, like a cabin built to huddle against the far wall. Someone in there, on the floor, was making tea by the light of a hurricane lamp. Inside, I came across an old Visitors' Book without a cover in which there were signatures and comments dating back into the last century. I added my name: Ulys O. Hanson, III, of Ithaca, N.Y. Moroccans tend to pronounce my name like Hassan, so that is what they all call me back in Tanger: Hassan Merikani. I signed that as best I can in Arabic. I had no comment to make.

• • • •

2

Yes, Jajouka is always itself; a secret garden on top of Owl Hill. Of all the green regions of earth, I know of none more beautiful than Hamid's leaping Little Hills but I had forgotten just how impossible it is in this pastoral place to be alone, ever, for more than a minute or two. To be left alone, strictly, is almost the supreme punishment up in Jajouka, so only the magic act of writing can excuse my eccentricity to my hill-village hosts. Hamid, however, has to know exactly what I am writing and why.

"Well, you might call it my desert diary, Hamid," I tell him. "It's my trip. It's my account of my trek from here to there and back again. That's part of the trouble, you see; you're not supposed to come back the way you went. This desert, you know, can take a lifetime to make it from one end to the other. I feel I only zipped in and zipped out again, like a panic-stricken American. I might as well have been AMERICAN EXPRESS. I only tasted the Sahara, Hamid."

"Who tastes knows," nodded Hamid. What makes him so wise?

"Oh, I got beyond Barbary thanks to your passport of keef but, when once you hear the Sahara, Hamid, when you're actually in it, why, the desert's in you! You know that song the Sahara is singing right now this minute, down there on its long windy flute? *'Oh, you'll cross the Sahara and never come back!'* it sings. But I did, Hamid! I came back and I still haven't seen what I seek: my Black Africa!"

"*Mektoub*," he shrugs. Hamid could hardly care less about anything Black. "It was written," he drones in his pat Muslim way.

"The next time around, I'll write my own ticket!" I hotly reply. "The Sahara still owes me a lot. The next time that I'm down there, I'll take the place over from Ghoul! I'll whip over the desert in my jet and I'll piss on Ghoul's head from thirty thousand feet up!"

"*Inch'Allah!*" Hamid nags after me nervously: "If God wills."

Hamid is, after all, my Baba, my Bab, my little back door into Islam through which the hue of my hide helps me slip in disguise when once I slough off my American cultural color.

"I'm an accidental Occidental, Hamid," I assure him. "I'm an African: same-same, like you. You say so, yourself," I insist, slipping into the loose Arab robes I brought back from the desert. Naturally enough, I have never been able to pull my Occidental mind along inside Islam after me but Hamid knows that and makes all sorts of allowances. After all, it was he who first brought me up here into these gamboling Little Hills where I am both a trespasser and forever at home. I remember, I once asked the caïd up here just how far his authority runs and he swung me around the grand circle of mountain and valley with an expansive gesture of welcoming pride as he stated, quite simply:

"You see that line where it is very very blue?"

The Master Musicians, all dressed in immaculate white woolen jellabas with their hoods up over their turbans, are grazing their flocks on the green and gold mantle of the hills. They are playing their flutes and the crystal-clear current of piping runs in rills down into the lush valleys below, watering and fructifying the crops. Yet, however much I may love their music, the only windy tune I can hear them play is "*Over the hills and far away across the Sahara and back!*" Once found, the words run around in my head with all the maddening reproach of a needle caught in my memory-track. Hot green tears spurt into my eyes and, when I clench them, the desert burns forever on the back of my lowered lids. For one haunted moment, I bathe again in the great Sea of Solitude, for whose barren shores any man who has once not only sighted but surveyed them must sigh forevermore.

"I've got to go back to the Sahara again," I tell Hamid. "There's so much to see and so much to learn. That's why I've got to finish this copy of my Sahara notes and send all these papers off to the people in Switzerland who gave me the money to go on my trip. It's what they call a sort of report: where I went, what I saw. It wasn't my fault I couldn't break through the roadblock at Tam. Tam is a very magnetic, mysterious place. What you see there is one thing and what really goes on is another. You know very well what I mean. I seriously suspect Tam must be the enchanted castle of Ghoul. When the Foundation for Fundamental Findings gets wind of this, they'll send me more money, maybe, to make another trip."

"Thass good!" Hamid states firmly, instead of muttering: "*Inch'Allah*." He firmly approves of my having money when I spend so much of it with him. "Next time, I go too. No man should travel alone. Thass no good."

Hamid, happily, has not yet got a passport and passports are hard to get. So far, he travels only on the magic carpet woven of his imagination and mine. How many times have we sat here sharing his *sebsi*, his keef-pipe, sailing to the States in the ship of Hamid's head. Sure as shooting, that is one trip I am in no hurry to take in cold blood, so I tell Hamid I have no money.

"Thass all right!" he assures me. "You sell me to someone as soon as we get to New York. When you get the money from the bank, I run away and come back. I don't care: you can sell me whenever you like but I'll always come back."

"But you can't do that any more in the States," I weakly insist. "Slavery is dead."

"'*Burn baby burn!*'" quoted Hamid, lighting a *sebsi* of keef. "Thass what the matches say to the box."

The day after that, I went down to Tanja alone and took the ferry across the Straits of Gibraltar to Gib to send off my manuscript from there for security reasons. Right opposite Her Majesty's Post Office on Main Street, I saw in the window of an Indian shop just the very tape recorder I have been wanting all of my life—a UHER! An end to all this painstaking writing and rewriting of words. When the bearded Indian sage in the shop demonstrated to me how well the UHER both records and wipes out the words, my heart went out to the machine and I bought it with what was left out of my Fundamental funds. Now, I am never without my UHER wherever I go. Up in Jajouka, I sling my

UHER over my shoulder like a mountaineer's purse. There is so much wild music running through Hamid's Little Hills that I am as anxious to tape it as a tripper is to slaughter wild flowers. Here, for example, I have a recording I made almost by accident on one of those occasions when Hamid, maudlin with keef, mumbled away as he does about how I am ruining or have already ruined his young life:

3

| Thou |

Thou art the crossroads of my life, Hassan Merikani!

You know what that means in the language we speak. We say about people like you: He can walk in the *souk* of my head, the marketplace all Arabs live in. More than that, you stepped into my head without even knocking or calling out: "*Trek!* Make way!" and you made your home there like my head was your very own house where you walked up and down teaching me school without as much as taking off your big Nazarene shoes. Christian or not, you're an African, Hassan, belonging to us. American passport or not, we know people like you. I may be God's Little Burro or Allah's Ass, like I always say, and I may be a square-headed Berber just down from my own Little Hills, like they call me in Tanja, but I was Hamid the King of the Train before I ever knew you. When I see a prize, I know how to take it. You never do.

I swung into Tanja one day about noon on the back of the train from Kebir and I dropped from the still-moving cars as we glided along by the beach before we got into the station: no money, no ticket; I travel free! I tumbled head over heels six times in the sand and when I got to my feet, there were you. Playing Ping-pong with beachboys in the smallest bikini-slip ever seen on the beach, you were leaping about like a naked *Afreet*, one of King Solomon's magical Blacks. My flesh crawled at the sight of your flesh, the cool hue of your skin. "There goes my *Abid*—my slave!" I swore to myself. "I've bought me a Black." I was a newly ruined man of nearly sixteen who felt he had nothing to lose. How could I know you would cost me so much before we were through?

That midnight, alone, you sat drinking mint tea on the terrace of Fuente's café in the Socco and there, not a full arm's length away from your chair on the other side of the iron grill they took down more than ten years ago now—there hunkered Hamid, ex-King of the Train, hidden under the hood of his ragged jellaba. You slapped at your neck, like my black eye was a tickling fly, because I was trying to peer deep in your ear, drilling to see what you had inside of your head. Now, all these years later, I know. When I'll be dead, Hassan, I still will remember some things that you said. I always remember the first time you turned and your eyes caught in mine—so do you. You jumped up like something had bit you, calling the waiter as you dropped some loose change on the table, and ran up the Street of the Christians, heading for home. I chuckled and ducked through the shortcuts, just watching you dash up that flight of steep steps and into your house, double-bolting the doors without catching your breath. Were you spying on me from out of some little slit of a window high in the wall? Why didn't you turn on a light? I had nothing to do, so I could hang about all that night and all the next day and all the next night until you got over your fright and came out, or until I climbed into your house with you—somehow. I didn't know how.

I hung about easy down in the steep street below, under the arches and deep in the shadows, well out of sight. I slouched in an alley or I prowled in a lane, watching who toiled up the steep street of stairs or who drifted down to see Aissha the Whore in her neat little cupboard under the steps. A sailor crawled out on all fours with his buttons undone and his guide, who was waiting outside, collected commission from Aissha, who brazenly jangled all her gold bracelets right up to her shoulder to pay him his cut. Jimmy the Guide steered the sailor down the steps by the mosque and away out of sight. Then, the Barber Drunk with God, who used to have his barber chair in the middle of his one little room right under your house, where he dyed his own beard bright henna-red, shaved his own head and the heads of his customers, and rolled fancy turbans for his patrons on Fridays, strolled out of the mosque chanting night-prayers. He sang a long holy verse on one quavering tone as he slowly moved up from one broad step to the next of your street until, standing right under your window, he suddenly stopped, climbed into his little shop and he slept. That fat Soussi neighborhood grocer, who stayed open all night, slumped over his counter asleep on his vegetables with his head lolling out in the street. For an hour or so a chorus of cocks crowed on the flat roofs of all the houses in town but nobody passed. Then, at last, your new next-door neighbor and my old friend from the train, Si Mohamed, came staggering down from where a pirate-taxi had dropped him in Amrah, dead with sleep because it was the middle of the night, and he was carrying a big roll of straw-matting to go all around the inside walls of his little house.

"Have you become a snail or are you some new kind of turtle, Si Mohamed?" I asked him politely as I bent down low under his load to look into his eyes. I knew he must have been smoking a lot. People who smoke are always out doing crazy things like that in the middle of night.

"Oh, so it's you!" grunted Si Mohamed. "Here, take the key to my house and open the door for me will you, Hamid, there's a good lad!"

Mektoub! It was written! Inside that one minute, I was inside the house next to yours, like a bee in the very next cell. Already, I knew exactly how I was going to get into your house. Si Mohamed set down his load and started making the tea. I passed him a pipe of our great grass from the Little Hills and we passed an hour or so before pink summer dawn, talking about the people we both knew in smuggling who worked the train. Si Mohamed used to run chickens and contraband meat over the border from Kebir into Tanja, so we had all the same friends. I told him the tale of how I had just lost all of my smuggling capital down in Rabat. He could see I had been really cleaned out: he knew the girl. While he was pouring a fresh pot of tea, I said: "Nice little place you got here. Who's next door?"

Si Mohamed spat on the floor: "A Black Christian! Didja ever hear the likes before in your life! Why, I spoke to the man in the street, the day he moved in on a Friday. Just to look at the man, I thought him a Muslim, of course. I asked if he'd been to the baths, expecting to walk down the steps to the mosque with him, as the muezzin was calling the prayer and, d'you know what he says: I'm a Christian! he says. *Annah Nazrani!* And him Black, think of that! Says he wants to learn Arabic, too! Then, why can't he be a Muslim like everyone else in the world, tell me that? You can hear him moving around in there sometimes and I don't care if he hears *me!*"

I calmed down Si Mohamed and got him back onto the subject of matting, until he made me a fairly good price to fix it up on the wall with wood-stripping screwed into pegs in the plaster. I had two days to do it in, while he made his run to Kebir for his chickens and meat. Not one dirham in advance would he give me, and I half thought of selling his matting to eat when, all of a sudden, a much better idea popped into my head. Si Mohamed went out to borrow the tools because that was part of our contract. He was to get the plaster, wood-stripping and pegs and the screws and, above all, a big heavy hammer to knock holes in the walls for the pegs to hold up the mats. I just sat there and smoked while I thought out my plan.

About seven o'clock in the morning the pounding began, you remember? I knew it was waking you up. Si Mohamed hung around for a while, until he was almost late for the train, just to see me put in my first pegs in the thin wall with fresh plaster and, then, he went away satisfied I knew my job. I did and I do. I took that big old hammer in my two hands and, saying: *Bismillah!* I spat on its head before Si Mohamed was well down the steps. I wet both my hands with more spit that I slicked on its slippery shaft. Hard as that wall was, my hammer was harder! One two three and the wall came tumbling down! There you were like a hole in my picture. Were you really astonished when I came through the wall, right into your room? Really, really? Were you, really? What a *scandale!*

· · · ·

4

It was written, indeed! But does that mean I am supposed to believe on some level that Hamid actually brought me back from my trip, magically? I ought to be downright mad at him if he did it but, instead, I have spent all this time translating, transcribing and, yes, transposing the Hamid I captured on tape. When I read back what is written, I hear how very far it is from Hamid's real speech and I ponder on how much I betray him each time I correct or rewrite. Only this morning, I found myself switching still more of his so-called sentences around, trying to catch at some of the unconsciously rhyming effects he manages to ring from the voluble but wildly incorrect Spanish he still uses with me; although my own bed-and-kitchen Arabic is already good enough to get by. Fact is, the man in the marketplace here in North Africa takes me automatically for a fellow Moroccan as soon as I slip on a striped silk jellaba and slap a red tarboosh on my head. Everyone calls me Brother: "*Hai.*"

Not up on the Boulevard in the New Town of Tanja, though, where I wear my American threads. When I sit out on the terrace of the Café de Paris, every last hustler who ever guided an American gob still slobbers and hovers around but they keep their distance, these days. Not one of them would dare, any longer, to call me American Joe. I guess I owe Hamid that, too. I am Hassan only with him up on his mountain or down below the Socco Chico in the underground keef cafés. Up on this Boulevard-level of town, Alcohol is King. It is not the cool thing to smoke pot in public; at least, not in a pipe. Instead, I take a deep drag on the Casa Sport cigarette I gutted and refilled with great grass I got from Hamid before I pulled my poor self together and struggled up here in the European town for a change of elevation and air. The tangle of traffic, out there in front of me somewhere in the Place de France, looks a bit distant and glassy, I have to admit, but everything is bright, bright, bright! Every last little dancing blob out there is all jazzy-bedazzled with candy-colored light. I adjust my shades with distinction, puffed up with pride at how well the taste of Tanja suits someone like me, and then I carefully drop my eyes to the pen and paper on the table in front of me but my gaze never gets there because I break into a loud laugh. I laugh like a lunatic to think that a year of sea and sand has burned up behind me since I first dropped into Tanja for what I thought might be, at most, a couple of weeks.

Now, I think I have got Hamid safely tied up with his family and flocks on their Pan mountain and here I am back at the Crossroads again. *"Do something!"* I keep telling myself, but what, really, do I *want* to do? If I dared, I would ring my last dime on this marble-topped table and get on my feet and then . . . and then, with bowed head, just shuffle off into the crowd, known to no one, with the wind whistling behind me as I shuffle off into the Sahara again. If I had the nerve, I could launch myself like a leaf on that sea of life, flowing by me out there. If I really wanted to catch up with that tide, I could mutate into just one more mad marabout like the Marvelous Major of Merzouk who was both revered and kicked about by the natives for years until the day the Marines landed, when he threw off his rags and stood there revealed with, tattooed all over his white ass: CIA! *Nay!* Very well, then I will have to become a saint of the so-called absurd, a man without a country, wrapped in a pied cloak sewn of nothing but flags. I've seen some of those cats—Bouhali Brothers—and they really look great—like they really *have* got it made. There they go, their bare feet deep in the dust but their heads, man! their heads touch heaven: *loser take all!* Just the mere thought of that fate makes a shiver run through me. I feel my scalp tingle and tighten on the roof of my skull. My hairs stand on end, one by one; all frizzling out slowly in a fuzzy electric halo that comes down around my ears. My ears are becoming the ears of the fennec who hunts the jerboa; bristly antennae that pick up and tingle with the silky sound of the sand sighing across the Sahara. It crackles like static inside of my head. Grains of sand, more numerous than the stars, are slipping and sliding and I am startled to hear in the roar of traffic on the Place de France, abruptly, the rumbling voice of Ghoul! I could easily blast so much keef night and day I become a *bouhali*; a real-gone crazy, a holy untouchable madman unto whom everything is permitted, nothing is true.

I was thinking along these lines this morning, if you can call that thinking, as I sat at a round marble-topped table on the terrace of the Café de Paris, today about noon. It was hot and I wanted to be alone so I propped this Moroccan leather briefcase I have, full of this manuscript, on the chair beside me, reserving the seat. On the table in front of me, I had my pad of letter-paper over which my pen has been hanging fire, now, for over a month. I hate writing letters but, if I was going to go on, or so I told myself in order to whip my pen-hand into action: "*You better write this.*" This was my letter to the Foundation, from whom I had heard nothing since I sent them a copy of my desert diary; pretty heavily varnished, I have to admit. I want my follow-up letter to be more business-like, maybe. After all, I have to brazen the whole thing out; my failure to cross the Sahara in less than a lifetime; my failure to find myself in Black Africa, floating down the bosom of its broad rivers through the jungle to the sea and, then, to return to the world around its hump. I mean to say to the Foundation: Frankly, I am fresh out of bread. In your service, O mighty Foundation, I have experienced extreme experience and been taken for an Adept along the Way. Extreme experience is, naturally, extremely expensive and so it should be. I have given of my person. I intended to add, rather insolently: "Now, pay me!" I considered enclosing a street photographer's shot of me taken in the thick of the Socco Chico crush and scrawling across it, perhaps: "*Which one is me?*" To a man who has little or nothing to lose, after all, everything is surely permitted when dealing with these powerful abstract entities like Fundamental, for whom, equally surely, after dealing with hordes of applicants like me, nothing is true.

My other less abstract application for re-entry into the Race would be to answer a want-ad I picked out of the Paris edition of the *Herald Trib.* The Independent American School in Algut needs an assistant headmaster. Do they want a Black one? The ad had been running for weeks. It looks mighty like nobody is hard-enough up to take a teaching job in Africa. Besides, nobody wants to hear about Algut, the way things are going there, now. Yet, Algut is nearer the desert than Tanja, I was beginning to tell myself. Of course, I would have to teach a whole year there to get free. "*Are you out of your mind?*" I heard myself asking myself: "*You work? Work, you?*" I talk back so much all the time to that little voice in my head that anyone overhearing me might think I smoked too much keef. Which reminds me, I must have an all-out session with myself and my UHER, one day, just to see if I can make my little voice talk for the tape. I clench my eyes tight for one pico-second, just the time for one all-knowing blink, and I open them again.

• • • •

6

The next thing I knew was the telephone ringing outside the door of my room
in the old run-down Hotel Duende, where I was staying: down in the Socco
Chico, sure enough. As I woke and reached out automatically for my keef and
my pipe, my ear caught the insistent flicking of a dry end of Thay's tape still
whisking around and around on the UHER beside my bed. I rolled over to
switch it off and checked on the battery. It hadn't run down too far, so I couldn't
have been out all that long. I pulled out the bedside lamp and plugged the
UHER in to recharge. My watch had stopped but I could tell more or less what
time it must be by the roar of voices coming up through my shutters from the
little closed square of the Socco below. The telephone went on ringing out in the
hall. In the Duende, they usually let it ring on like that until it rings off by itself.
I was surprised to hear somebody answering it: "*Halloo Yass Halloo!*" It sounded
oddly like Hamid and, when I peered out, so it was: Hamid in an elegant new
white-on-white striped-silk jellaba; short because he is short, the jellaba swung
on the ground. "Yass, the Merikani," he was saying as he handed me over the
phone. I was wondering where he'd got that very expensive jellaba from as, over
his shoulder, I saluted a little group of his cousins the Master Musicians in the
dimly lit hotel hall. They had shucked off their bright yellow leather slippers and
hunkered down against the cold tiled wall with their white woolen hoods up
over their heads. They gave me quite a shock, looking so countrified.

"Hello," I said into the receiver, automatically imitating Hamid: "Yes, hello."

Hamid was hopping up and down in front of me making mad monkey-
faces; wild gestures apparently meant to intimate something about the caller, I
couldn't tell what.

"Yes! Hello, Hassan," said the voice on the phone, so deep I thought for a
flash it was a man's: "You *are* very quick!"

"Glugh!" was all I could answer to that.

"Good, Hassan! Quite right! Now go back to your keef-pipe until twelve
o'clock midnight but don't overdo it. I just phoned to say that Thay won't be
able to make it, tonight, but our plan for the picnic still holds good. I'll pick
you up in my car in the Socco at twelve on the dot."

"Picnic lady!" Hamid was hissing at me as she rang off. Hamid was kissing
my shoulder, hugging my arm as he jumped up and down: "Picnic lady very
good. Very big. Very rich!"

Being the sort of hotel it is, we all went back into my room to blow some
more keef. Master Musicians smoke all the time: they've always got either a flute
or a sebsi of keef in their mouths. We all beamed and embraced each other like
brothers going through all the salaams and salutations like we hadn't seen each

other for a week of Muslim Fridays. Then, they all settled themselves comfortably on the floor while I climbed back into my sagging brass bed with Hamid hopping up alongside me holding a big bag of grass. A pair of pipes shuttled back and forth between us as we went through the ceremonies: I needed some time to get all my buttons done up and work on this plot. Now, that crazy white cat called Thay: him washing out like that right away! That was no good for openers: what did he mean: "*Rub out the word*"? His tale was done, I could see that, and I was glad I had it on tape. And that other voice: that was Milady Mya, was it? Well, that wasn't the first time I'd heard that transatlantic tone. But: "What's all this pack of pied pipers of yours doing down off their mountain?" I asked Hamid point-blank. At the same time, it ran through my head that this grimy group could well be my bodyguard; safety in numbers. And: "Hamid! How the hell do *you* hook up with the Himmers? Tell me that!"

One of the Master Musicians produced a special holiday pipe out of his wicker picnic hamper; a primitive clay water-pipe smoked, as a rule, only during the holy month of Ramadan and at night. Time out for distraction: this particular Master was thrown into paroxysms of gurgling delight at being able to fill his water-pipe from my tap. The mere idea of water leaking out of a wall like that instead of being caught spilling out of rocks or having to be drawn from a well tickled him all to hell. The Masters had all come tumbling down from their village to see me in town and, besides, the big city is full of thrilling adventure, as everyone knows. While Hamid was herding them through the Grand Socco market this afternoon, a lady stepped out of a very big car and hired them to play their Pan pipes at a picnic, tonight, in a cave up the coast. It seemed not at all far-fetched to them that this was a picnic being given for me. "Well, Hamid," I said between pipes, "and what does she look like?"

Hamid rolled his eyes around in his head, making a globular gesture like: "Big!" High praise in Africa and, besides, Hamid's not huge. A lady of leisure about Tanja was once heard to say that Hamid would have been a much taller man if so much of him hadn't been turned up in cock—his famous big brush. Just as I was going to ask him if he'd ever heard of *Imsak*, he bounced off the bed and shot over to the window; having heard, as we all had, a roar like a riot in the Socco Chico below. As Hamid threw back the shutters, the breath of the beast in the crowd came in like a blast of hot air. My first thought was a lynching but I left that lay in Louisiana and, translating myself into Present Time, I said, getting up out of bed: "What is it, Hamid: the Whale?"

My window in the Duende Hotel was like a loge in an old Venetian theater from which I could look straight down onto the paved stage of the Socco Chico, where absurd theater has been going on in dozens of languages, right around the clock every day since forever, perhaps. Visible tale-ends of old-fashioned Arab plots torn alive out of the Thousand Nights and One Night shuttle back and forth under your eyes like bright threads running through a gloomy loom of out-of-work cats slapped into uniform Levis. More up-to-date, highly colored plastic plots tend to pass through after midnight and the bell was tolling, now. There was standing room only down there where a thick throng of extras was boiling about a gigantic old Rolls Royce touring-car which had beached center stage. The crescendo of circus-noise died away like the tide rolling boulders out to sea as a very large lady I took to be the Queen of the Tuareg got out of her car. She stood on the running-board in a hell of a hairdo of beads braided onto her head, clanking her barbaric jewelry and flapping her long desert-blue robes. My first guess was: She's selling something like a magical embrocation of ostrich eggs, for example; so I turned away, saying: "Don't look at it, Hamid; it's on television. Some new kinda 3-D TV!"

Then, I squealed like a stuck Christian pig when Hamid suddenly made a dive past me and scuttled across the room to unplug my UHER from the wall: he is strictly forbidden ever to touch a machine of mine. He pulled out the jack to the charger, checked to see the tape was properly threaded before he packed the UHER expertly into its traveling case, me still protesting, and, slinging the holsterstrap around my neck like a halter, dragged me out of the room, trailed by the Master Musicians. One of them threw my black burnous from the Sahara over my shoulders while we slid down the stairs. As we hit the Socco, a general yelp went up from the crowd when the lady flung up her arms melodramatically, and all the men fell back one sudden step, heels hard on each other's toes. A child wailed out: "*Cinema!*" as Hamid, my handler, hurried me forward like a punchy old prize-fighter being hustled against his better judgment into the ring. I had the impression the lights went up full and, because it seemed to be expected of me, I kissed the lady's hand to a round of applause from the mob. She got back into her car and gave it the gun. Dogs and children ran yapping as old graybeards with turbans waved the young riffraff out of our way when we followed her into the car and drove off to the cheers of fools who knew no more than we did what it was all about.

Now that I remember it, all that she said was "Get in!"

I suppose I didn't dare look at her: anyway, my eyes were glued to her neat square bare blue feet planted on the pedals of the Rolls. As we were spinning so silently up steep Siaghine Street, I ventured to break into the ticking of the clock with some mumbled remark about the car. "Yes," she said, "it's a Rolls I picked up cheap out of an old novel by Lawrence Durrell." What the hell kinda talk is that? I thought to myself and shut up. Our big leather seats were set apart like two thrones in the front of the car but I could smell that the lady had drenched herself in a bottle of Bint El Sudan before leaving her tent. I remarked that all the little knobs on the fittings of the car had fat little closed crowns on them over the letter F. She laughed and confessed that she had bought the old bus at the King Farouk sale in Cairo, years ago now. "It's all solid gold," she admitted, "and the biggest one Rolls ever built. Even the Nizam of Hyderabad . . . you know, the rich one in India . . . never had the horsepower or the head-room that I've got."

We barely skinned through a narrow alley and swirled out around the Grand Socco, nearly taking a strolling policeman with us as we went. We chopped like a great golden hatchet through the secondhand-clothes market where they sort out the bundles of rags from America. My Master Musicians were bunched up in the back of the car like five live white teddy-bears in their rough woolen jellabas. I leaned around to snuff up their good country smell: lanolin from lambs' wool, woodsmoke, spicy Moroccan cooking and keef. I saw Hamid had found a handy little folding "jump seat" in front of the built-in bar and was helping himself to a mixture of drinks. Knowing only too well how he can be with alcohol in him, I reached around to stop him but he batted back my paw, proudly pointing to the crown on his glass, as if that gave him royal permission to drink. Then, he unbuckled his prize-winning chuckle as he gave the back of my hand a wet kiss, saying fondly: "Who is whose guru? Fuck off!" It sounded more like: *Hooz hooz gooroo foo koff!*

"So," said the lady, "you speak Arabic together."

We were shooting through "Suicide Village"; so called by all the rich foreign villa-dwellers on the Old Mountain, who sail through it all the time at top speed. This narrow paved alley swarms like a market all day and all night. We were cutting through traffic like a hot gold butter knife through butter, until that Diving Diana out there on what the English call the "bonnet" of the Rolls, stuck her golden nose right up a camel's ass. Pandemonium broke loose in the street. Moors who know me and know Hamid were squashing their noses against the glass with their hands over their eyes, popping their eyes at me, the lady and the car. The lady gave a blast of her great golden hunting-horns and we swept on, scattering man and beast in our wake. We whipped around the Third Commissariat of Police at Jews' River on two wheels and flashed on out past the Catholic cemetery at Boubana; then, turning sharp right, we flew up the New Mountain Road through the night on this slightly worn magic carpet of hers. There could be no doubt, either, that this was really her car, the way she drove that pile.

My musicians passed me up a slim pipe and, taking the regulation three drags, I spat out the live coal very neatly in a solid-gold ashtray set into what must be called the "instrument panel."

"Do you have to smoke that stuff all the time?" the lady asked.

We whirled past the governor's mansion and Caca Culo castle in the dark and other big estates with their private parks to the right and the left of the road until we came to a spot where she changed gear and we turned off the pavement into a trail down under the trees. I had always intended to explore these big wooded properties running down from the crest of Old Mountain Road to the high cliffs hanging over the Straits of Gibraltar, but I certainly hadn't figured to do it at night. We were bumping down a water-worn lane under lacy acacia trees until the headlights picked up a dark grove of cedar, practically hanging over the cliff. "It's no worse on the car, really," the lady was saying as she ground the back axle over a rock, "than the road from Cairo to Alex."

She flipped on her lights, blinking them twice, and an old crooked Arab fairy-tale crone, with a pointy straw hat like a cone on top of her red-and-white-striped veils and long raggedy cloak, stepped out of a thicket with a lantern in hand, waving us on. "That's Calypso, my caretaker," the lady said. "When I took over this property, I found her already installed in my cave. As if I didn't know the place was magic enough . . . some doddery old English don has been writing to tell me it is . . . actually and historically according to him . . . Calypso's Cave. I thought calypso was a steel band from Barbados until he sent me this book to curry my culture. I can't think how he got my address . . . probably figures I'll invite him out here to explore it but he's got another think coming, I guess. . . . Since we've found you, Hassan . . . and the dollar has . . . has gone . . . well, wobbly . . . I've wiped out my Foundation. The Fundamental has been found. No! . . . let *them* carry the baskets, Hassan. Get out of the car . . . from here on you walk."

The loony old woman with the lantern was leading us down a path around the face of the cliff while Hamid and five little musicians trailed us fearfully in the dark, toting their instruments and the wicker picnic hampers full of food and drink which had been packed in the "boot" of the Rolls. We stumbled around a big shoulder of rock and came into a nice little nook, looking bright Paris-green in the white light of our gasoline lamp. A spring of clear water, ringed with dwarf fern and moss, seeped out of the rock close by the entrance to a big dry cave in which a little fire was dancing away by itself. Below us and so far below that the distance looked dizzy, a highway metaled with moonlight ran twenty miles or more across water to the Rock of Gibraltar swimming away in veils of blue night. The old Arab witch gave a sharp cackle to her half-wild pack of flat-headed yellow dogs, from whom Hamid and the musicians cringed away, reaching for clubs. Madame Mya stood in the mouth of her cave with her back to the firelight, flapping her veils as if she were about to take off as she intoned:

"Ulysses of Ithaca, welcome back home!"

Then, in a voice so different it might have come out of another woman, she said:

"You know, Hassan . . . you and I must be the two most American Americans who ever stepped into this enchanted cave. After all . . . I'm Pocahontas and you're Uncle Tom!"

Wow! Wait a minute, lady! Uncle Tom! That's a hell of a thing to be tagged at this point in the game: where did she pick up on a story like that? But, then, I reflect on how very easy I am to research: Professor Ulys O. Hanson, III, of Ithaca, N.Y. So, after all, I shrug. There may be a little Tom in the best of us, may there not? And, in my own case, casting about in the darkest corner of my mind, I do recall some cousins in Canada, spell their name different, who admit—just admit, mind you—to descent from the runaway slave turned Black preacher Underground conductor and agricultural colonist in Canada with a side show at the Crystal Palace where he was presented to Queen Victoria and was lost. Poor man had nothing but troubles from then on in: trouble with John Brown at his congress before Harpers Ferry, trouble with the Abolitionist Boston bankers and preacher-trustees of his colony, trouble with the white folks down to the end. Poor Tom! How much can he owe to H. B. Stowe and how much does he owe to himself? He billed himself for half a lifetime as The Real Uncle Tom, because he gave her world rights to his not-so-exclusive story in exchange for a nice hot dinner under the kitchen sink. White folks! I was thinking as I turned on my UHER and started recording Mya while she pinched out some pennies for poor old Calypso, who slunk off after her dogs:

7

| She |

She just took her money and went away, didn't she . . . not one word out of her, did you notice? Typical . . . isn't it? That old Berber witch . . . or whatever she is . . . seems to think this is *her* cave and *I'm* paying *her* rent for it. Well, never mind . . . one pays for being an American, I suppose . . . and we *do* screw them in so many other ways . . . all the *time,* don't we? *Calypso's Cave!* You can feel this really *is* Calypso's old cave, can't you? To Homer this was the end of the world where his little wine-dark sea ran away through these straits into nothingness . . . *the Maelstrom . . . America!* That fabulous coastline of southern Spain, strung out over there through the blue, must have looked just about the same . . . except for the lights, I suppose, that frame it . . . and this same big yellow balloon of a moon sailed up there between Gibraltar and Ceuta, the Pillars of Hercules. Funny, isn't it, to think that our dollar sign comes from a snake wound around those two pillars . . . the serpent Baby Hercules strangled in his cradle. That's a really *mad* image for money . . . now, isn't it? What does it *mean*, Hassan . . . or don't you care, really?

What *do* you care about, Hassan-Ulysses . . . only your keef and young dancing boys? Well, don't fret . . . we have more and better of all that down in "Malamut" than even the Old Man of the Mountain ever dreamed a hashish-dream about. Why, all this cool green and blue country north of the Tropic of Cancer is *nothing* compared with what I've got going down south. You know it, yourself . . . the Sahara's pure gold! You've heard of a people called the Foulba, of course . . . the Peuls . . . the most beautiful boys in the world, bar none. You must, *at least*, have seen books of photographs of their ritual beauty contests for which the young men begin preparing at puberty . . . when they're first allowed to wear makeup and start earning their jewelry. Along with huge Floradora Girl ostrich-feather hats and a little leather apron they take off for the contest . . . that's all they *do* wear . . . their jewels. Well, they'll be holding their finals this month . . . and guess where! . . . in the courtyard of *my* castle down there. You see, Cape Noon is their capital rock and on *that* rock *I* built my house: "Mala-mut" . . . where the Tropic of Cancer cuts out across the Atlantic on the map. The Foulba first got there about the time anyone's worm-white ancestors . . . and I'm afraid we've both *got* them Hassan . . . by the time those whites were first grubbing their way up out of the caves, the Foulba had written their own lengthy literature on several hundred long miles of mountain before the Sahara began to dry up all around them. Driving their lyre-horned cattle ahead of them, the Foulba went west . . . and wandered on out of history. When they *did* find the water they were looking for, it stopped them . . . the sea . . . the Atlantic. On the low, level shore they saw my big rock sticking up in that landscape as sudden as Mont Saint Michel on its tidelands. The Foulba say "Malamut's" head touches heaven. Cape Noon, they call: Heaven Rock. "Malamut" is *my* secret garden. "Malamut" and the Foulba, today . . . nearly two million in all of them . . . belong solely to *me,* Hassan: I own not only the Foulba . . . we're *absorbing* new ethnic groups of previously nameless nomads in the southwestern Sahara every day. How many of them could you possibly *have* in a lifetime

Hassan . . . or would you prefer to possess what's left of your old enemies, the Blue Men? I'm telling you, Hassan . . . in Present Time, *I* am the most powerful woman in Africa!

The Word, Hassan! All you have to say is the Word . . . when you know it . . . and *you* can be Emperor of Africa! Emperor Hassan the First! You *do* understand . . . don't you, the move Thay has made . . . was *obliged* to make only today at noon? You *must*, after all, because Thay laid his last words on *you*, my dear . . . not on *me*. That *transfer* of the Saharan Seal to you *could* make *you* the Master of Words when you know what to *do* with it . . . and no one on earth can tell you but *you,* you know. Thay calls it the Roller, rolling out all the words in the world over and over, again and again, since the first Word was spoken. What you hold in your hand is the emerald Beginning and Ending of Words, Hassan . . . as a woman, naturally I *fear* you! As a woman, too, all I can tell you is what *not* to do. . . . That's my nature. *Don't* . . . for example . . . don't press the Seal into wax or putty or anything soft . . . you haven't tried doing that, have you? *Don't* do anything silly and artistic like inking the Seal and running it onto paper. Just *don't,* that's all . . . don't! That's printing, you see . . . rolling out replicas. We'll go into that later. In Present Time, down on Cape Noon, we're fed up with replica Foulbas, you see. They've bred true-blue for so long that they're *all* practically *identically* beautiful! The one perfect specimen multiplied to infinity . . . and why *not?* . . . in some sort of biological barber-shop mirror. Dr. Francis-X. Fard has produced a little prose-poem pamphlet praising the Foulba for being the one people we know in the world who have come up with not *one single* object of culture in all their long history . . . not even a knot, let alone the cord to tie one in . . . not even a *pot!* They boil things by dropping a red-hot rock in a leather sack of water or milk. The Foulba have known exactly how *not* to let them themselves be tied down by *things!* They're innocent . . . beautiful . . . *pure!* Until I laid hands on them, they'd always been as free as the wind. Long, long ago they gave up their writing . . . except just for fun and to teach the young ones . . . they write in the dust where the wind will be sure to erase it. So much for the Word. The one big problem with them is the one you can guess . . . *overweening* vanity! That's how I was able to grab them up cheap . . . the whole lot. When *I* buy, it's *always* in lots . . . things come so much cheaper . . . and the *cheapest* one can get something for in this life, after all, is for *nothing*, don't you think? That's what I like to pay, really . . . nothing at all. You see, I have my *own* little ways of getting what *I* want in life. I have a trick or six I picked up right here in Africa.

This particular, ah, product . . . I owe to Dr. Pio Labesse, an Old African Hand who was . . . well, *really* . . . my second husband and *not* the sixth as the newspapers always say. I'm his widow . . . or *was.* I'm sure Thay has painted you the worst *possible* picture of Pio but, truly, I owe him a lot . . . poor Pio. He had all the lore of North Africa at his fingertips, literally . . . but he lost it. He left it where he is, now . . . in the Past. This one, ah, product . . . is something I've gone into scientifically . . . chemically . . . and refined it out of all recognition, you see, but . . . perhaps, *essentially* . . . it *is* the same thing the original Calypso brewed up when that *other* Ulysses dropped in. What I've done is bring the whole thing up the time-scale to bring it in line with Present Time, so . . . Hassan-Ulysses . . . in *Present Time . . . Look!*

. . . .

15

| You (masc.) |

. . . Of course the sands of Present Time are running out from under our feet. And why not? The Great Conundrum: "What are we here for?" is all that ever held us here in the first place. Fear. The answer to the Riddle of the Ages has actually been out in the street since the First Step in Space. Who runs may read but few people run fast enough. What are we here for? Does the great metaphysical nut revolve around that? Well, I'll crack it for you, right now. What are we here for? *We are here to go!*

So, what are we waiting for, sister soul? Pack up your emeralds, Freeky: you and I have a date out beyond Deadline and we've got it together, as you said very well. This is Gemini, taking off! This is the way we came, you and I; one soul split into two bodies of compatible sexes and this is the way we shall go, taking them with us! Mya Himmer's Ace in Space is Love-All. It still takes a pair to beat old terrestrial Death and roll out replicas all over the universe. Let it be the perfect pair. Who could reproduce accurate replicas better than Pharaonic twins! Come, Cleopatra, all we need is the Emerald and the Emerald is not Egyptian at all but Chinese!

(At this point, Amos let out a terrible shrill wavering yell that turned into a strangled cough, a hysterical laugh and, then, a chuckle. UOH.)

So, laughter is refusal, eh? Well, maybe so. I was just trying to see if I could yodel again the way I did for the captain when he hit me with the high voltage. I find I can't. While he was torturing me, I could hear myself very well: it sounded like a dog taking a long time to die after being hit by a car. On and on the dog trills: won't he ever stop? This dying dog is shocking all the other well-fed dogs in the universe who are barking abruptly and clearing their throats, as much as to say: Why won't he stop? Why won't he die and get done with it? We don't like to hear that. I didn't either and, then, I was horrified to see that the bastard was burning my body but, strangely enough, when I took a good look at him, I saw that Mohamed was as deeply involved in the torture as I. What does he think he is doing? I said to myself. That's what saved me: I was no longer just one person but two. I was you, if you like; perhaps, your sort of Universal YOU.

Well, from that point of view, I was watching an Egyptian priest preparing a mummy into whose fist he slipped the Emerald to send the prone man off on his trip. The mummy was then set spinning, in order to wrap it in an infinite length of magnetized tape on which had been recorded the words, all the words. Current pulsed through the bundle to plate it. The mummy glowed and became perfectly transparent, white-hot. In the green and purple shallows, shimmered a white body which was both you and was me. I thought, at first, that the left-hand side was you and the right-hand me but we kept slipping in and out of each other, changing place.

What a fool that Thay Himmer has been. *"The answer to the existence of a fool is silence."* No one ever told him to play the Emerald onto Black. Mya knows better than that; or she should. But the Himmers are tourists, not to be trusted. There can be no question whatever of taking this whole menagerie into Space. I have a date with the Chinese Dissident Delegate, Mr. Lee. Mr. Lee knows what to do with the Emerald. Thay Himmer foolishly showed it around like a watch fob at a party we gave the China Committee when they came through "Malamut." I caught Mr. Lee taking a print of it on a paper napkin. Back in Pekin, they know how to read. They know, now, what we have. They have the ship but we have the chart. Where are we going? We are going OUT.

The Emerald seal prints in reverse an astral conjuncture, a cosmic crack which opens only once every so many millennia. That is the Way Out through which it is possible to slip in and out of the universe; just as I was slipping in and out of my body under torture, today. This stainless-steel star in which we are sitting, crimped down onto the basalt base, is not, as everyone knows, a psychiatric hospital, at all. But, neither is it a fort! Star Citadel is the base for a rocket and capsule, built in China and delivered by satellite, which can and will be fired from here to Eternity, today or tomorrow. You and I will be fired on a trajectory that knows no return unless the Traveler holds the Emerald as a map in Space and Time to get back.

Now, my pal Mr. Lee knows as well as you and I do that he who leaves an open door behind him, when he goes off on a trip, invites burglars and squatters into his house. When Mr. Lee's hordes of young Chinese technicians with bats' ears and bristly hair standing up all over their heads arrive, any minute now, to fit the capsule into place above us, you must be ready to leave. You won't need any baggage. So that there will be no squatters solidly ensconced in our property when we come back, Mister Lee intends to burn down the Old Homestead of Earth behind us as we take off.

I forgot to tell you that we have to take Lee along. We'll be shipping nobody else. You see, on this sort of flight, one man must steer by the Emerald while his co-pilot keeps an eye on the chart made from a reverse print. It's because of the symmetry, you see. The Universe is spinning and what spins must appear symmetrical whether it is or not. That is the essential illusion but we are symmetrical, ourselves; ambivalent, too. This is a split universe, run between the Image and the Real Thing; one is the mirror-image of the other but the point is to tell which is which. You see that, of course; or, rather, you don't.

Now, Freeky, what you must do is get hold of the Emerald for me, at once. If Mya lays her hands on that Emerald, we've had it: Mya is the one who will be leaving with Mr. Lee. The other great danger is that Black American of theirs. "*I am Black and I am Wise.*" If he knows what to do with his UHER, we could all be rubbed out!

16

| They |

They can all be rubbed out by the *zikr*, of course! *Wow!* The minute I typed those last words to YOU, I knew what had to be done: *Wow! Anything* to get myself out of that trap in Tam. I paid the lady gladly; the Emerald for my UHER, cheap at any price. It was a simple matter, then, to record the *zikr* on a loop of spliced tape; playing endlessly over and over, again and again and again.

I press the old button to give it a whirl; double speed and, then, double that:

Rub out the word . . . Out-word rub Thee . . . The Rub-out word . . . Word out-rub Thee . . . Word rub Thee out . . . Out the Rub-word . . . Rub out the Word . . .

Such is the process.

The word-process in reverse sounds less like blank verse than it does like a garbage-disposal unit built into a kitchen sink. Be as careful about inserting your finger in the running loop of words as you would be about plunging your finger down your own throat. Abrupt word-withdrawal can be a shattering experience. Taken cold-turkey, it can cramp you with chills of panic as the seasick words swirl around in a long ring-a-rosy like a vomit of alphabet soup. The nymph Nausea grabs you by the gullet, throwing you into severe antiorgasmic spasm while Pan, the dumb little brute-god, attacks you along with his goats:

. . . frisking you, fucking you . . . biting you, butting you . . . taking you, leaving you. . . . Gone!

I clench my eyes tight for one pico-second, just the time for one all-knowing blink, and I open them again. They are . . . gone! Gone, leaving me speechless! What a relief to be back again at my own station in life. After all, I and only I; Ulys O. Hanson, III, of Ithaca, N.Y.—or whoever this is that I am—I am the sole captain of this super-stoned subway-system called Patience which burrows under the sands of the Sahara and—man! this subway sails only on keef. *Borbor?* What a bore! What a mothering bore! One thing I can tell you, I have come a long way but I'm back. I am not about to sign any more of that crew on again, ever! I learned my lesson with those characters. I have changed and, I think, progressed.

Could that be the clatter of my coffee cup crashing?

I am about thirty thousand feet high this morning so I have to parachute down from my crown to take a better look at those twin mountains I see down there, looking like loaves of brown bread cast in bronze. They are—if I can believe anything any more—my own feet. From between them, a dark brown *oued* is crawling across the Sahara paved with cement. Higher up, on the marble plateau of the table in front of me, the flash flood of coffee spreads slowly but inexorably across my still unfinished letter to the Fundamental Foundation, blotting it out. I crumple up the soiled page, not forgetting that I still have that other letter to write; my letter of application to the Independent School of Algut. I must remember to ask them if they want their new assistant headmaster to be both a pot-smoker and Black.

Out there in the heat on the Place de France, I can feel the tangle of midday traffic on the Boulevard thickening and tightening around me like a web. When I peer at the scene over the tops of my shades, Tanja appears a bit peaky but I have to admire that every last detail is bright, bright, bright! Dazzled by all the candy-colored little blobs of light frantically jazzing each other out there, I pull down my shades to take a reading on my watch. It is just a few minutes past noon and here I am back on the terrace of the Café de Paris up on the Boulevard, penniless on that very corner Hamid once called the Cape of Good Hope. Slightly shaken to find myself still shipwrecked here, I take out my last white handkerchief to wave it, unconsciously, around like a flag. Forgetting for a moment what I took it out for, I decide not to mop up the coffee with it and break into a lunatic laugh.

I laugh at the very idea of letters. How can mere words get me across half a lifetime in the Sahara and back again in a matter of minutes! The thought of it makes a shiver run through me like someone just walked on my grave. My scalp tingles and tightens like a drumhead over the open roof of my skull. My hairs uncurl stiffly, one by one; all frizzling out in an electronic halo that buzzes around my ears like an alarm. My ears swell and stand up in total erection like the ears of the jerboa when he hears the fennec hunting him down. Tintinnabulating choirs of lullilooing women ululate like a limitless pasture of bluebells, one bluebell to every square mile, ringing out over the Sahara after any short season of rain. A sudden squeal of brakes on the Boulevard in Tanja cuts through the heavy hum of the traffic on the Place de France like the jerboa's dying scream. I nearly jump out of my skin.

I sat there feeling as if I had been turned into stone. Slowly, I swiveled my eyes around like a periscope until I caught the glint off the glass on a big old British car pulled up right in front of me. Trust any White Hunter to spot me as soon as I show the white flag! Slowly and stiffly, I brought the full power of my blackest Black Look to bear on the bold blank face of a white woman, obviously American, despite the desert drag she had on. The cheap blue cotton sari she had pulled over her head made her look dissolute rather than decent; like the defrocked mother superior of some lay order of barefoot working nuns. She hung one mottled-blue arm out of the side of the car nearest me like a slab of bad veal and put her other hand up to shade her eyes from the burning sun as she trailed her big tits back and forth over the steering wheel of her rented Rolls Royce, with its GBZ plates from Gibraltar. In a flash, I dug her essential indifference to all experience and association. That placid stupidity overlaid evident cunning: that soft firmness, her motherly look, was a cover for cruelty. Yet, there she sat projecting all this bundle like a challenge no man could afford to dismiss and, at the moment, she shone for no one but me. Instinctively, I jerked up, stripped naked, lathered myself all over with soap, waved my big cock at her, rinsed myself off, dressed and sat down like a good old boy; a real spade stud. She did not blink. The striped awning flapped over my head as a red-hot gust of the *gaïla,* the noon wind, grabbed at my breath and—who should bounce out of the back of that old British pile but Hamid, my Moroccan mock-guru himself!

I thought sure I had left Hamid safely tied down with his family and flocks on his Pan mountain but trust Hamid to come up with any eerie American couple rolling around Morocco, on the loose in a Rolls Royce. After all, the world is Hamid's parish and all such, ah, "spiritual" chores of this caliber are part of his diocesan duties as a self-imposed "guide." From the back of this rusty old Rolls, a youngish billiard-bald whitey with buck-teeth and bug-eyes, obviously the husband, bobbed his head and grinned out at me; giving me the greedies, too, if you please. I could see at a glance that Hamid had this one firmly fixed on his big hook. Somehow, from even fifteen good feet away, these people embarrassed me: they looked too eager and too shoddily disguised. My first guess was that Hamid had hustled them in a hurry through some "cheap bazaar belong to a friend," where these buffoons come out the other end after great expense, masquerading as ersatz Arabs.

In fact, it turned out that Hamid had found them already dressed like this when he waved them down on the open road, on their way back from their first trip to the Sahara. Hamid was born to be a highwayman rustling Christian captives. All he has to do is to squirt them one look with his watermelon-pip eyes and promise to show them the Rope trick. They loop his lasso around their own necks. When they stumble after him into his Moroccan corral, he paints them in his own colors and rigs them as "Ringers" before he hawks them about in the world. I guessed that the woman took to Hamid's high-handed treatment less well than the husband. She seemed a shade sullen and resentful; the white American look. Hamid bustled up to my table, cunning as a koala bear in his wooly jellaba, coming on strong to me like the spurious pusher of slaves. Hamid always has a bargain but, as they said of a man more after my own hue, Othello: "These Moors are changeable in their wills." So, when you deal in this kinda merchandise on the hoof, you don't shilly-shally around in the marketplace, do you? One single well-chosen word from Hamid, "*Food!*" and he had me on my feet. I was on! I rang down my last dirham on the marble-topped table and the two of us, arm in arm, *à pas de loup,* hungrily stalked our prey in their car.

"Him 'n' Her," as Hamid always called them, were dying to take us to lunch in their cool colonial villa out on the Old Mountain Road, overlooking the Straits of Gibraltar, in the middle of a garden set out with one hundred and sixty varieties of flowering mimosa planted by the brother-in-law of an English lord over a hundred years ago, now, at the end of a delicious ten-minute drive. In Tanja, the past is that close to hand. I am getting all this load from Her, up in front. Back there with Hamid, there is not word one out of Him although I can feel Him practically panting like an Irish setter down the back of my neck. I thought, maybe the language difficulty made for the silence between Him and Hamid but I was wrong. When I got it from Her, as we sailed through "Suicide Village," that they were missionaries from Champagne, Illinois, I felt like peeling right out of the car.

The Hymners, as I decided to call them, had rented a big old house it would take about ten servants to run and there was not one single servant in sight. The Hymners, in fact, kept a pretty seedy house. Piles of old magazines and tracts slithered about underfoot or slid from stacks, high in the halls through which they led us straight to the kitchen. You could see the Hymners liked that room the best. They had modernized it, as she said, with paint, plastics, and appliances. Hymner got down to his chores without saying a word. Like a wizard, he whipped indented metal-foil trays of nameless foodstuffs out of a deep-freeze as big as a bank. Then, like a flash, he slid these through an infra-red ray oven on the wall and slapped them on the kitchen table in front of us piping hot but, before we could get down on all fours to gobble up this great chow, we had to say grace.

That is, Mrs. Hymner—call me Maya; like the Great Mother, she said, coming right out with it—Maya Hymner said grace wrapped in the endless yards of carbon-paper indigo-dipped blue material it takes to make a dress for a dancing girl in the desert. Some of those Guedra girls get so big they have to do their dance sitting down. Maya's gown swathed her like a tent but, when I squinted up my eyes at her, she looked like a giant bluebell to me. She had blue donkey-beads and cowrie shells braided into a sort of wild Saharan hairdo she allowed it had taken three women a week to plait on her head, but she wore no jewelry at all and strictly no makeup; except she was all smudgy-blue around the edges from the indigo dip. Somehow, despite this disguise, Maya managed to look one hundred percent corn-fed, barefoot, big old American girl with enlarged pores and gray skin. I shot this good look at her as she bowed her veiled head in prayer, spilling out a long flowery oriental-type grace over the plastic-topped table. To my astonishment, if ever I can be astonished by Hamid, I heard him gabbling along after her in his best hobbled English. Hymner just stood there agape, wordlessly gazing on Hamid with the liquid look of a novice-master glowing over his latest Adept but there was still no word out of Him. I raised a tall eyebrow as Maya went on pouring out an entire seed catalogue of heavily scented flowers, endless bushel baskets of rare jewel-stones, and piles of precious metals that clinked out of her like a jackpot of more than oriental confusion. At least, I knew where we were at: my mother once had a brush with Bahaï. Lest I be recorded as one of the heedless, when she finished I joined in: *"Amen!"*

All this time, Hamid is piously wig-wagging me to take off my shades. I can see how Hamid might ride right down the line with this Islamic splinter-group but I know it is too late in the day for me. I shake my head sadly at Hamid as I listen to Maya's thick thighs slap-slapping together under her robe as she paddles over to get a bottle of boiled water out of the frig. No stimulants, ever, eh? OK. I adjust my shades with distinction, indicating that I am not about to take them off to look on the likes of this great bargain of his. I can feel that my stiffness excites him. I know my Hamid, after all; what odd commodities have we two not bought and sold? Here he is trying to sell me his Hymners: what is my price? I figure Hamid cannot possibly know what the real deal is about: I don't know, yet, myself. I can see that reconnaissance conversation is not going to be easy. Unless we babble on about Bahaï, it is all going to be: "Have you read that book, whatsitcalled: *The Confessions of Denmark Vesey?*" and guff such as that.

In some ways, Hamid's takeover of the Hymner household was hellishly handy—and I mean it just like that. The Hymners were our meal ticket of the moment, feeding us both on their embalmed American food. Categorically, I refused to move in with them out there on the Old Mountain. I knew better even if Hamid did not. Anyway, he was used to living like a gypsy in seven different houses at once: they could never pin Hamid down the way they could me. I stayed on holed-up in my room at the Hotel Duende, letting Hamid break it to the Hymners just how much I owed in back rent. The going was not all that easy. That old meal ticket had to be punched and punched regular; a lot harder, too, than I had at first been ready to reckon. Happily, the local electricity went on the bum for a few days, during which time the Hymners' endless stacks of nameless frozen foods melted and died in their silent foodsafe. Hamid took over the cooking and it became really worthwhile to drag my ass out there to eat. Their old bus was pretty much always at our beck and call to cart us around wherever we wanted to go: Maya Hymner always heavy behind the wheel of the Rolls, Him always silent in back. Hamid perched back there, too, on the very edge of his seat, straining his ear and his English to make out what she was saying to me; as, with her eyes fixed on the road ahead, she slurred their lurid life-story at me out of the side of her mouth.

This colorless couple from Champagne, Illinois, were living out a drama which they, at least, thought would yet shake the world. Her people were from Canada, originally, and the least said about that the better, I gathered. Was she

"Colored," I wondered? I took a squint at her hair and threw that thought out of my mind. The Hymners "had money." They had once owned a sawmill someplace out West. "Him 'n' Her" had met at the home of some Bahaïs in Illinois: met, married, and settled down in Champagne, as she said. They were both Adepts who hoped to be accepted into the Faith but a couple of things had gone wrong. She told me this when we were back at their villa in Tanja but I swear I could hear the old skeletons rattling in Maya's voice, all the way from the great Middle West. Hymner was grinning and nodding, eager to corroborate every word Maya said. Well, it seems that Maya, at the very instant of conception, when his diamond-headed sperm-adder pierced the delicate membrane of her egg, Maya knew—she just *knew!* She was shy, she said, to tell even Him at first but, eventually, all their circle in Champagne, Illinois, knew, too: Maya was chosen to give birth to the Babe!

Now, not everyone in Champagne swallowed this tale and, when the day came for her to face her, well, her Trouble; why, she found herself absolutely alone. Everyone failed her; especially Him. Hymner, it seems, took advantage of her pregnancy to get himself picked up by an electronic eye in a public toilet, like a Presidential aide at the YMCA. When Maya turned on, tuned in, and heard all about it over the local network, she went into the kitchen of their ultra-modern home and aborted herself with a fork. Two cops in blue brought Him to Her in the hospital and, there on her hospital bed, she forgave Him. She got out and got home before he did. When he got out, she took Him back. But—and that was a hell of a But! he could never become the father of the Babe, now, could he? He had to shake his head: obviously not. So, she sent Him to the hospital to have himself sterilized and the operation so affected Him that he lost all his hair and his voice. Naturally, they had to get out of Champagne overnight and that brought them to Tanja, where else? In Tanja, at least, no one put all your business out in the street; now, did they? He nodded and grinned, content as a capon, confirming all this.

They had now decided, she went on relentlessly, that the Babe should be Black. It was on the tip of my tongue to tell her that would be quite a trick, when I bit the words off with my teeth. So, a spot of my sperm was the price! One diamond-headed sperm-adder of mine was to puncture her egg and plunge on into the Stream of Life; was that it? And did he think he was going to get to watch this? Maya stood there like a sibyl beside the kitchen sink. This child was to be a Mahdi, it was promised: Emperor of Africa. "Togetherness," I thought I heard her say: "You will all assist at the birth." *Great Ghoul!* There was a silence, as pregnant as you wish.

I began to get that old wound-up, wordy feeling and found myself talking too fast and too much. To put them at their ease, if you please! I launched into a largely fictitious tale about my mother, a very big powerful woman she was, too, who had much the same trouble with Ulys O. Hanson, Jr., her husband my father, who had taken off with her best black lace and her add-a-pearl Tecla necklace to go to the Beaux Arts Ball at the old Savoy Ballroom, years ago, and neither hide nor hair has ever been seen of him from that day to this. I could see that the Hymners were profoundly shocked. Panic-stricken, I began to blurt out yet another story; the story, I claimed, of how I had first ever heard about Bahaï. I felt their faces stiffen in apprehension but it was already too late. My technique is to overwhelm one enormity with another, so:

There I am back in Carnegie Hall with my mother, right after the war and still in high school. Up on the stage, Mrs. Roosevelt is sitting side by side with our own Great Educator, Mrs. Mary McLeod Bethune. This duo of dainty dinosaurs is perched on two rickety little old gold chairs pulled up by a skinny-legged gold table on which the girls are munching away at the "Star-Spangled Banner" like sisters until, all of a sudden, Miss Mary lets out a holler like someone just stuck her under the table with a fork. Looking blacker than Granmaw in a pastel-pink potato sack and a hat made of ice-cream cake like Schraffts' melting on top of her meringue of fuzzy white hair, Bethune grabs the mike from the First Lady to bawl at us:

"I want all of you all out there to know that every last one of us here is descended from the Black Kings of Africa!"

Hamid, who had been sitting cross-legged on the floor, biting his nails as he listened intently up to this point, let out a loud snort; got up and left.

Too late! Carnegie Hall is rocked by applause like a mortar barrage. The Hansons, mother and handsome adolescent son, are beaming in the middle of a parterre of one hundred and seventy-seven handsome young Black Kings of Africa from Nigeria; all students at Lincoln University in Pennsylvania. The young kings have been obliged to leave their crowns with the white hat-check girl at the cloakroom, who insists that, made out of gold or not, what you wear on your head is a hat. The kings of Black Africa proudly sweep the streets of New York with their trailing robes gorgeously embroidered in silver and gold. Ergo, not all Black men are slaves or descended from such. Thank you very much! We who have been nothing, can become Black Kings, every one! Mrs. Roosevelt has skillfully fielded the mike and is making her eloquent speech: "Not having had your advantages in adversity . . . ." she seems to be saying.

Mother was a speech therapist so, at that point, she had to give me a big nudge: "She takes Voice!" she whispered delightedly. Eleanor was all too soon over for her and Miss Beryl Brown was announced. I could feel Mother stiffen when Beryl pranced out on stage, wound up in a little strip of leather torn off the skin of Life, like a lady-wrestler with nothing much on but a patch here and a patch there. Miss Brown announced, in a voice Mother could have done something with, that she was about to go into a Magic dance she picked up in Africa on her Fulbright. It was a dance of Initiation but she did not say who was going to get initiated into what. Then, Brown rolled out a big African drum, about as big across as a washtub, and she began to jump up and down on it like a trampoliner. That was all she did but, at every drum-jump—*Boom!* —and she pumped herself up just one more big puff. For a while, it hardly seemed to make all that much difference, she's such a big girl, but, when the drums began pounding into your head, Beryl began blooming and booming and looming so big she could have floated away over Macy's. Before she could explode the proscenium arch with her expanding naked brown-skinned flesh, they eclipsed her just in time with the big golden curtain before she could become what she was about to become, the great matriarchal myth-figure: Mother Maya Herself!

Hamid came back into the room and threw me a look of disgust. I could see that my elaborations had fallen rather flat. I had forgotten to add that, on leaving Carnegie Hall, my mother and I had decided to mark the occasion by venturing into the Russian Tea Room, which we understood was Restricted and, there, Mother had met up with a very nice woman from Larchmont in a mink coat, who told her all about Bahaï and offered her a job as . . . I could feel myself floating away into another one of my stories but I managed to stop. Simulating a sudden attack of brain-fever to the stony-faced Hymners, I rushed back to the Hotel Duende in the clamorous Socco Chico and dashed off that letter to the Independent American School of Algut. By return of mail, they wrote back to say that, what with the dollar and one thing and another, the school was facing hard times, financial difficulties, and blah blah blah. They were dreadfully contrite to carry on like this with a man of my caliber but they simply could not pay for transportation at this point because, what with border controls and currency restrictions and blah, more blah, but it was a deal: I was on.

All I had to do was to go out to the Hymners and hit them up for the bread, I told myself. It was a lot less easily done than said. One of the worst things at their house was that no one could smoke because Maya suffered from asthma and other allergies. Her asthma was aggravated by overweight and her overweight was accentuated daily by Hamid's great cooking, with which he had, finally, hooked her. That girl was a greedy-gut; never stopped eating crunchy peanut-butter snacks between meals. Who ever told her she could play Desdemona? One night, we all dined out of doors by the light of candles in Moorish lanterns, tearing chickens apart with our hands under Hamid's orders, lying around Moroccan-style on cushions and rugs. For a change, there was no Levant-wind blasting through Tanja. The sticky-sweet, night-blooming flowers like *dama de noche*, datura and jasmine, seemed not to bother Maya for once. When the candles guttered out, Hamid and I even dared light up a sebsi of keef, on which we took turns in the dark. The night was lousy with stars and that old pregnant silence again from Him 'n' Her. When Hamid got up and went inside to clean up the kitchen, Maya began to talk.

"Hanson," she said, perverting it into: "Handsome," I thought I heard her; "when you say the Word, the Word will be made Flesh."

"Of course!" I ejaculated, trying to pass it off as a cough. I was on! Coughing in earnest all of a sudden, spluttering and laughing, I got up and stumbled away through the dark garden.

Nothing daunted, Maya was down at the Hotel Duende, bright and early next morning, sitting on the foot of my brass bed. My Moroccan maids out in the hall made like they were scandalized; knocking and laughing, bumping their mops and pails against my door. I opened one blazing eye as I rapidly pulled on my black suit of human skin under the covers before I sat up and let Maya have it hard and straight. I told her I wanted no son of mine to be mooted about as a midget Messiah. I want no son of mine to preach *or* to teach and, besides—Yes, *besides!* I want no son of mine to be even one drop lighter than me. If I make a son, he has got to be *Black, Black, Black*; a real spade, see! Does she figure to raise this child with a white mother and a white father and him fitting into no skin at all? And what if it turns out to be a girl? If she really feels she needs an African for this deal, Hamid is an eager African. Delicately, I indicated something flattering about his painting technique and the size of his brush. As for me, I am only a poor old, retired, spade performer; just shoveling along, dig? Now, would she please be a good girl and go order me a *café au lait* and a *croissant* on the terrace of the café in the Socco Chico below. In the meantime, I would shave my beautiful black puss and be with her in no time flat. I meant that: no time at all. That was it. When I did get down there about half an hour later, she was nowhere in sight.

Within the hour, Hamid came trotting up with a sealed envelope addressed to me. I must have laid it on her, too, about needing that bread. Quite obviously, the letter contained cash, and Hamid, who still cannot read, tried to shove it playfully into my ear; "making it talk."

"Here is the price of the Hymners," I told him. "I have sold you to Her for this. I'm sorry, I know it's not near enough."

Hamid knew what I meant and he wept. I embraced him and told him how broken-up I was to be leaving him but there was just enough bread, there on the bed where I threw it, to take care of the Hotel Duende and buy me a solo ticket to Algut where the term at Independent is starting this week. Hamid was so emotional, he could hardly count his cut of the take through his tears.

"The train is standing in the station, Hamid. This may not be the way I came but this is the way I must go. See; no baggage, Hamid. I must return to the World."

"Here, take all the days of my life!" cried Hamid, much moved. "All I have to give is my brush and I'll do *anything* with it for you. I'll paint this lady from head to toe, if that's what you want. I'll give her my life!"

I do hope Hamid's words are not prophetic, because a very nasty scene took place, just now back in the station, as we pulled out of Tanja under the first autumn downpour. The Hymners did not come down to see me off, naturally, and I have not one dirham left. She even had the nerve to suggest that I sell my UHER and, somehow, between the hotel and the train, the UHER has just gotten lost. Hamid blamed it on her black magic, of course, but he was frantic and made a terrible scene with everyone in the station. My last vision of Hamid was a glimpse from the already moving train. He was practically throwing himself over the barrier, weeping and waving good-by, when, all of a sudden, two tall men who were obviously plainclothes police swooped down on poor Hamid like vultures and bore him aloft, backward over the crowd; astonished and terrified. Hamid was bawling like a calf at the killing until the rumble of the moving train drowned him out and he was drawn away into the mysterious past. What was all that about? What did that mean? Hamid is far too cool a character ever to be busted for keef; what else could he have been up to? Someone's revenge? Beware the fury of a woman scorned and all that but: Would she have taken it out on Hamid? No. I hope not. No. I sat down somewhat gingerly on the brown plastic seat of the train leaving Tanja station at just the right speed. I sat awkwardly because of the sheep's bladder of keef Hamid scored for me as usual, at the very last minute and for a very hurry-up price. I had stuffed what I scored into the Y-front of my jockey-shorts, from which the hard-packed poke of keef had slipped down and bulged like a baseball bat between my thighs. I needed something to steady my nerves, so I was prying into my own zipper like a pickpocket to pull out the precious packet, when a uniformed cop on his beat bumped past my compartment blindly, happily without busting in.

Suddenly, as I stood there swaying in and out of my mind on the last few farewell pipes shared with Hamid, it struck me like a blow between the eyes: I had forgotten to tell Hamid one thing. I had forgotten to tell him why the Hymners had no servants, no servants other than us; no hired servants at all in their house. The Hymners feared local servants might inform on them to the police. In theocratic countries, Bahaï has been considered a heresy tantamount to treason and the penalty for treason is death. Oh, well; are we not all condemned? I wouldn't put it past old Hamid to dodge even Death. However, I do recall what he said:

"Hamid, Consul of Keef, renews this green passport for you in the name of the Old Man of the Mountain, King of Keef. Long live the Assassins! On your Way, you are bound to run into some fellow-Assassins, you know."

"But I'm not an Assassin, at all!" I laughed. "I'm purely a potted professor. I insist."

"We are all of us Assassins," he gravely replied as he gave me the grass.

I find myself sitting back in the train leaving Tanja, gliding around the curve of the beach. I note sourly that they have truncated the beach once again to put in the new port installation and the enlarged railway yard. The necessary new mole has changed the profile of the beach for the worse by deflecting the wind-driven currents to pile up sea-wrack, refuse, and oil slick on the sand. A minute back, we passed a man-made jungle of rusted iron girders, the skeleton of some long-forgotten fun fair, followed by a chain of leprous bathing establishments with *Tea Like Mother Make* scrawled everywhere to attract the vanished British tourist. Jumping up from my seat, I go lurching off down the corridor of my continental coach to the toilet. The cop comes out, still buttoning up. Having satisfied himself that there is nothing contraband lurking in there, he is not likely to come back this way soon.

I stagger into the swaying water-closet, lock myself in, and carefully hang my jacket over the doorknob and the keyhole behind me. Above the immovable frosted-glass window, I turn a flanged air-vent to OPEN, before unzipping my fly. I pull out my business and pick out the body-hot bladder of keef to hug it between my knees while I redress. The old train is picking up speed, *clickety-clix*, as I fish into my passport-pocket to pull out my sebsi in its slim leather case. I fit the two sections together with a handsome brass band at the link. Placing a finger over my tiny flesh-colored clay pipe head, I try the pipe like a trumpet; airtight, good! A masterpiece matchbox the size of a big postage stamp leaps into the overturned bowl of my left hand and I laugh.

I laugh because this whole business is, of course, just a trap well-enough woven of words—or so I must hope—for the meaning, if any, to show through like a lining of silk. What was it the matches used to say before they learned the latest: "*Burn, baby, burn*"? When I bend an ear to listen, the train is already rattling it out: "*Kaulakaulakaulakaulakaulakau . . . .*" I grasp the match firmly and strike it, exploding its head. Before it burst into flame, its head was a heavenly blue. I apply its red hair to the green bush of keef I have packed in my pipe and I suck it all up in one single toke. Exhaling, I breathe: "That's the truth!" blowing it all out the air-vent marked OPEN, from which it trails after the train to plane out over Tanja like a plume. Expertly, I spit the red comet of keef-coal into the open thunderbowl beneath whose open trap I can catch a patch of planet Earth spinning between our magnetic rails. Everything spinning must appear symmetrical: is that what it's all about? I turn back to the frosted window, standing on tiptoe to catch my last glimpse of the blue Leaping Hills through the air-vent; but night has already fallen in cold curtains of rain. I content myself with repeating the saw: "As no two people see the world the same way, all trips from here to there are imaginary; all truth is a tale I am telling myself."

So: there are no blue Little Hills and none of the rest is true, either. I condemn the whole thing. Then, like the governor before the execution, I want to wash my hands but, on this man's train, there is no water forthcoming. No matter what plunger I push: HOT or COLD, nothing flows out of the rocking walls at my once-magical touch. Fortified by a few more pipes, I replace my poke in my pants where it hangs like a blackjack. Pushing my face into the mirror over the basin, I say, I breathe to whoever is in there: "Human problems remain insoluble on purely human terms." Whoever it is I see in there nods in agreement with me. I light up a Player's to cover the keef before I boldly throw open the door to face a mob of Middle East refugees lined up six-deep, all twisting their legs. Then, when I plunge both through them and the swinging glass door in a panic, I see I am right back on that same old circular subway, suddenly; going nowhere again but fast. A handsome old white-bearded Arab loon, all dressed in white, bursts out of a blazing broom-closet, barring my way with an iron-tipped staff.

"You may not pass this way again in a lifetime," he says.

All the people I ever have seen in this lifetime are melded and jelled into some sort of red-hot honeycomb the old cat keeps in his closet. Outraged that we should all find ourselves, still, on this subway under the Great Desert called Life, I explode with all the conviction of a man who has found himself, finally:

"Let me in there again, goddammit!" I cry. "Whether I like it or not, I guess, I'm a Teacher and it's just because all you donkeys are so goddammed dumb that a Teacher has to go over the same old lesson, again and again and again. So, one lifetime isn't enough, eh? Well, give me more! No! More!"

The windows are streaming with gold. I look out to see we are spinning through the Sahara faster than the speed of light, escaping the clutch of the great hairy magnet of the Sun. From behind my back, this little old gink with one eye is asking me:

"Why were you in such a hurry to get here, when the desert gets us all in the end?"

Campoamor
Tanger, Morocco
1965–1968

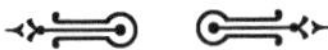

They have all spoken.

As the dervishes desired, I have set down first the voice of one and, then, the voice of the others. In this book, I have not set down my own point of view because I am a man and a man does not know everything. In any case, it is not fitting for him to say everything he knows nor to write everything he says. Of one hundred thousand men, there may be one who knows and, of a hundred thousand things he knows, there may be one he should utter. Of the one hundred thousand things he utters there may be one he should write. If my own opinion had been set down in this book, both friend and foe might learn of it; both the competent and the incompetent might read it.

In other days, the initiate confided their secrets only to those they considered competent; swearing them to the secret. The incompetent, happily, are unable to pierce the thoughts of the initiate who, since the time of Adam, have obtained their knowledge of the essence of things through personal association with those who knew. Therefore, he who seeks the mysteries and the realities must seek out someone who knows, for, from the book alone, nothing emerges.

The Unveiling of Realities,
Kashf Ul-Haqa'iq,
Persia, 13th century

☞ The Naked Lunch Screenplay

The Naked Lunch *screenplay (1972) is one of several versions that Gysin wrote of Burroughs' novel in the early 1970s. This revised draft is part of the Burroughs Collection at Arizona State University Library; different excerpts from other versions appeared previously in* The Third Mind *and* Here to Go. *The intention had been for their friend Antony Balch to direct, with David Bowie or even Mick Jagger in the leading role (the script included songs), but the film never got made.*

Discussing the project in her dissertation, Carol Marie Anderson notes that "the most significant phrases of the novel are sprinkled through the screenplay like clues to a puzzle. . . . Gysin's work is based loosely on the routines of the novel, but his effort is more tightly organized since Inspector Lee acts as the principal character. Unlike the Lee of the novel, he is the focal point around which all the action in the screenplay revolves. . . . Gysin selects themes reflective of his impression of the most important aspects of Burroughs' novel. . . . [He] concentrates on the importance of the word as he shows the value of Inspector Lee's word hoard . . . [and] develops Burroughs' theme of the tyranny of controlling agents and their ultimate demise." These two themes come together in the opening scene of this version, taken from the end of the novel. The same scene opened his 1974 version of the script as well, but with a prelude where Burroughs himself, like an old J. Paul Getty, sits in the baronial splendor of an English country house, coldly watching the tourists who've come to gawk at him.

William Burroughs'
NAKED LUNCH
Screenplay by Brion Gysin

1. EXTERIOR. NEW YORK STREET.

Ambulance into which two white clad attendants
are shoveling a corpse, presumably an O.D.
HAUSER is in a nearby telephone booth. O'BRIEN
is taking care of the onlookers. Ambulance takes
off with a siren.

Sirens.

O'BRIEN: "Stand back folks. . . . Stand back!"

NABOR 1: "They say somebody pushed him."

NABOR 2: "Naw, he was weaving around
unsteady. . . . like he couldn't see
too good."

NABOR 3: "Too much smoke in the eyes, I
guess."

HAUSER: "Hello. . . . Yes. . . . Hello."

VOICE OVER PHONE:
"Narcotics. . . . Who's calling?"

2. INTERIOR. A GIANT TELEPHONE
SWITCHBOARD.

Hundreds of girls are chanting mantras:

VOICES: "Narcotics. . . . Who's calling?"

HAUSER'S VOICE OVER PHONE:
"Hauser and O'Brien reporting.
Gimme the lootenant."

VOICE: "Sorry to keep you waiting. . . .
Here is your con-neck-shun."

3. INTERIOR. NEW YORK NARCOTICS OFFICE.

THE LOOTENANT seen from behind (speaking in
the voice of WILLIAM S. BURROUGHS) is talking
into the phone.

LOOT: "Hauser, I want you and your partner O'Brien to pick up a man
named Lee, William Lee. He's in the
Hotel Lamprey on West 23rd Street.
You know it?"

4. EXTERIOR. NEW YORK STREET.

Telephone booth. HAUSER speaking. O'BRIEN has
now moved up outside the booth and is waiting for
his partner.

HAUSER: "Yeah, I know it. Remember him,
too. Calls hisself a writer."

5. INTERIOR. NARCOTICS OFFICE.

LOOTENANT speaking on telephone in voice of
WILLIAM S. BURROUGHS.

LOOTENANT: "He is. Don't take time to shake
the place down for his stash.
Except. Bring in all books, letters,
manuscripts . . . anything printed
or handwritten. Got that?"

6. EXTERIOR. NEW YORK STREET.

Telephone booth. HAUSER speaking. O'BRIEN
outside.

HAUSER: "Yeah. . . . but what's the angle. . . .
books?"

7. INTERIOR. NARCOTICS OFFICE.

LOOTENANT on phone.

LOOT: "Just do it. And, above all don't forget his briefcase."

8. EXTERIOR. NEW YORK STREET.

Phone booth. HAUSER still listening on phone.
O'BRIEN outside. We see a NAKED FREAK run
down the street past the phone booth shouting.

FREAK: "I got the feeeeear."

HAUSER: "Yeah."

9. INTERIOR. THE BLOODY BATHROOM OF
WILLIAM LEE'S ROOM IN THE HOTEL
LAMPREY.

Looks like some one slaughtered a pig.

Sounds of furious typing from inside the room.

Camera pulls back from bloody mess to find it is
seen through the mirror on the back of the
bathroom door which opens outward (for our purposes) into the entrance hall to the room.

Louder typing sounds.

Still unseen by us the camera advances down the
hall section of the room towards William Lee as
typing sounds get louder.

William Lee's room in complete disorder. There is a
great deal of paper about, manuscripts, etc. To the
left by the bed the camera passes over exotic
luggage from Mexico and the rumpled bed, whose
bloody sheets have been burned by cigarettes.

Lee's briefcase lies on the bed with a revolver
sliding out of it.

There is a tray of food on the bed. Beyond the
bed, WILLIAM LEE is sitting with his back to the
camera, wearing a skinny singlet and a hat, otherwise naked. WILLIAM LEE is writing *NAKED
LUNCH*. He reads what he types.

LEE: (Voice over) "I can feel the heat
closing in. . . feel them out there
making their moves. . . setting up
their devil-doll stool pigeons. . .
crooning over my spoon and
dropper. . . ."

10. INTERIOR. WILLIAM LEE'S ROOM IN
ANOTHER LIGHT.

Two shots of HAUSER and O'BRIEN crooning
over William Lee's spoon and dropper.

11. INTERIOR. WILLIAM LEE'S ROOM IN HOTEL
LAMPREY. As in 9.

WILLIAM LEE seated at his desk seen from behind,
pulls paper out of typewriter as he stands up,
exposing his bare arse. WILLIAM LEE is still wearing hat and singlet.

12. INTERIOR. WILLIAM LEE'S BEDROOM IN
THE HOTEL LAMPREY. CAMERA SEES LEE
FROM WINDOW.

We are looking at WILLIAM LEE standing before
his typewriter which is covering his cock. He is
holding the sheet of paper he has just torn from
his typewriter in his hand. LEE speaks directly in
camera—at the audience.

> LEE: "Most survivors do not remember
> the delirium in detail. . . . I do."

LEE turns towards the bed, throwing himself on
the tray of food which pours, spilling all over the
manuscripts. Revolver and "works" (junk, needle,
syringe) slide out of the briefcase and he shoves
them back carelessly.

Picking a worm out of his egg with a fork.

13. EXTERIOR. INDETERMINATE
BACKGROUND.

CLOSE-UP of a worm wriggling like a baby on the
end of a pitchfork.

14. INTERIOR. WILLIAM LEE'S ROOM IN THE
HOTEL LAMPREY.

WILLIAM LEE on bed with worm on the end of
his fork as in 12.

LEE: "Lunch! Naked Lunch! Have one on me!"

He throws fork and worm back onto the sloppy lunch tray, and starts eating other items on the tray, as he reads bits of his own manuscript.

LEE: *"'Running out of veins and out of money.'*

Yeah.

'Last night, I woke up with some one squeezing my hand.'"

15. INTERIOR. WILLIAM LEE'S BEDROOM IN THE HOTEL LAMPREY.

This is the same scene as 14 but must not look like it at the start of the shot which is:

C U WILLIAM LEE'S hands. One hand (camera right) steals across the frame in big close up and squeezes the other (camera left of center). As the one hand squeezes the other the hands fly apart. The night shadow they were in vanishes as we speedily zoom back to find ourselves as at the end of 14, with WILLIAM LEE on the bed, lunch around him.

LEE: *"It was my other hand."*

16. INTERIOR. HALLWAY OF HOTEL LAMPREY.

HAUSER and O'BRIEN are looking for a room.

They pass two doors and settle in front of a third.

LEE'S VOICE OVER:

"Hauser and O'Brien. . . . When they walked in on me that morning, I knew it was my last chance—my *only* chance. But *they* didn't know. How could they? After all, *I* wrote it."

17. INTERIOR. WILLIAM LEE'S ROOM IN THE
HOTEL LAMPREY.

WILLIAM LEE is back again at the typewriter with
his hat on typing furiously.

Camera advances very slowly on him a short
distance.

> LEE'S VOICE OVER:
>> "I was just tying up for my morning
>> shot when they walked in with a
>> pass key. . . . "

18. INTERIOR. HALLWAY OF THE HOTEL
LAMPREY.

 HAUSER is fitting his special pass key into the
lock. (Camera right, O'BRIEN beyond CAMERA
LEFT).

> Typewriter noise, heard through the door, on the
> sound track.

> LEE'S VOICE OVER:
>> *"This is some special key they can use."*

19. INTERIOR. WILLIAM LEE'S ROOM IN THE
HOTEL LAMPREY.

WILLIAM LEE is seen from the window. He is typing. Over his shoulder the camera can see the door
quite clearly. The key is turning over in the lock
and falls to the floor (in slow motion if possible).
LEE reads as he types.

> LEE: "To open the door even when the
> door is locked from the inside."

As the key falls, LEE turns around face freezing as
he puts on his glasses.

O'BRIEN comes in first, arms spread in greeting
but HAUSER has his snub nosed .38 detective special out, covering LEE from under O'BRIEN'S arm.

> O'BRIEN: "Well, well, well, Bill. . . . long time
> no see, eh?"

O'BRIEN circles the bed (moving somewhat behind
LEE from the camera's point of view) and HAUSER
advances pistol drawn.

LEE stands up revealing his bare arse again.

> HAUSER: "Put on your clothes, Lee. We're
> going downtown."

20. INTERIOR. WILLIAM LEE'S ROOM IN THE
HOTEL LAMPREY.

View over HAUSER'S shoulder pointing his
revolver at LEE. O'BRIEN is standing to LEE'S
right. LEE'S eyes flicker over the briefcase on the
bed before him containing his revolver partly hidden, as he spreads his hands in the old junky shrug.

> LEE: "Can I take my bang first, boys?"

O'BRIEN looks towards HAUSER.

> O'BRIEN: "He wants his shot, Hauser.
> Whaddya think?"

O'BRIEN looks back at LEE.

> LEE: "There's plenty here for evidence."

LEE picks up pants and starts to put them on.

21. INTERIOR. WILLIAM LEE'S ROOM IN THE
HOTEL LAMPREY.

M C U. HAUSER. He is looking off screen at LEE.
He is still holding revolver pointed at LEE.

> HAUSER: "Now, you know we can't do that,
> Bill. Unless. . . . "

22. INTERIOR. WILLIAM LEE'S ROOM IN THE
HOTEL LAMPREY.

As 20. HAUSER camera left with back to us pointing revolver at LEE, who now has pants on. LEE

center facing camera. O'BRIEN to right of LEE.
LEE is looking at HAUSER.

> LEE: "Unless what?"

Camera advances slightly onto LEE framing him
and O'BRIEN in two shot during this remark:

> O'BRIEN: "What can you do for *us*, Biiiill?"

> LEE: "I might could set up Marty Steel.

> O'BRIEN: "Maaarty Steel? Can *you* score from
>   *him*?"

> LEE: "Sure I can. I gotta perfect rep.
>   This'd be the first *time* I. . . ."

23. INTERIOR. WILLIAM LEE'S ROOM IN THE
HOTEL LAMPREY.

M C U. HAUSER. Looking off screen forward right
towards LEE. Still menacing LEE with revolver.

> HAUSER: "O.K. Lee. But you'd better deliver
>   the goods."

24. INTERIOR. WILLIAM LEE'S ROOM IN THE
HOTEL LAMPREY.

As start of 22. HAUSER (camera left with revolver),
LEE center looking at HAUSER who has just
sharply interrupted him, O'BRIEN camera right of
LEE.

LEE takes off his broad-brimmed hat, hesitates a
second but then resolutely throws it on the bed to
cover his briefcase.

> LEE: "Oh, I'll deliver the goods, all right.
>   Believe me."

O'BRIEN moves across behind LEE to the window,
where he looks out with his 'When I get my
Pension' look.

25. INTERIOR. WILLIAM LEE'S ROOM IN THE
HOTEL LAMPREY.

LEE'S room seen over O'BRIEN'S shoulder as he
stares out of the window. HAUSER beyond the bed
in the center of the frame. LEE starts to get his
"works" together.

26. EXTERIOR. THE WALL ACROSS THE STREET
FROM WILLIAM LEE'S ROOM'S WINDOW IN
THE HOTEL LAMPREY.

Seen from HAUSER'S viewpoint. A large poster for
TRANSVESTITE AIRLINES

All the way with TVA
fly
TRANSVESTITE AIRLINES.

27. INTERIOR. WILLIAM LEE'S ROOM IN THE
HOTEL LAMPREY.

As 25. HAUSER center with gun guarding LEE who
is still preparing his "shot." O'BRIEN still staring
out of the window. O'BRIEN looks over his shoulder at LEE.

LEE: "Just an old junky, boys . . . a harm-
                    less old shaking wreck of a junky."

Camera moves in a little past O'BRIEN framing
LEE and HAUSER. LEE starts to affix the needle to
the end of the syringe. HAUSER too lets down his
guard because he doesn't want to see that needle.

28. INTERIOR. WILLIAM LEE'S ROOM IN THE
HOTEL LAMPREY.

C U. LEE'S hands filling the syringe from a bottle
which is clearly marked ALCOHOL.

LEE'S VOICE OVER:
                    "If they dig my briefcase now, I'm
                    done."

29. INTERIOR. WILLIAM LEE'S ROOM IN THE
HOTEL LAMPREY.

M S. HAUSER (camera right) is looking away from
LEE who he thinks is now fixing. LEE is finishing
the action of filling his syringe. HAUSER snarls
over his shoulder at LEE. His words come out so
ugly that he is a little surprised himself.

> HAUSER: "You through yet? . . . You'd better
> not try to shit us on Marty."

LEE handles his syringe, twisting the needle
elegantly to make sure it is tight.

> LEE: "Just two seconds more, boys."

LEE raises his arm in a fast movement to begin his
squirting action. This startles HAUSER who zips
back in position to confront LEE fully again in just
the right position to receive the thin jet of alcohol
across his eyes.

30. INTERIOR. WILLIAM LEE'S ROOM IN THE
HOTEL LAMPREY.

M S. Camera is behind LEE'S right shoulder. Lee
squirts a thin jet of alcohol at HAUSER whipping
it across his eyes with a sideways shake of the
syringe. HAUSER lets out a bellow of pain.

> HAUSER: "Aoooooooow!"

HAUSER paws at his eyes as if to tear off an invisible bandage.

31. INTERIOR. WILLIAM LEE'S ROOM IN THE
HOTEL LAMPREY.

TWO SHOT. Camera looks past HAUSER pawing
at his eyes over HAUSER'S left shoulder at LEE who
drops to the floor on one knee and reaches for his
gun in his briefcase under his hat, with his *left*
hand.

A slug from HAUSER'S gun slams into the wall behind LEE. LEE winces from the concussion and then you hear the shot, a split second later.

LEE is shooting from the floor. He snaps two quick shots into HAUSER'S belly.

32. INTERIOR. WILLIAM LEE'S ROOM IN THE HOTEL LAMPREY.

TWO SHOT. Camera looking over LEE'S left shoulder sees HAUSER receive LEE'S two quick shots in his belly where his vest has pulled up, showing an inch or two of white shirt and bare belly. HAUSER grunts in a way you can feel it.

> HAUSER: "Unngghk!"

33. INTERIOR. WILLIAM LEE'S ROOM IN THE HOTEL LAMPREY.

M S. Similar to 25, but with HAUSER dead. Looking over O'BRIEN'S left shoulder as he tries to tear his gun out of his shoulder holster, stiff with panic.

LEE clamps his right hand around his left wrist to steady it for the long pull. His gun has the hammer filed off so he can use it only in double action. LEE shoots.

34. INTERIOR. WILLIAM LEE'S ROOM IN THE HOTEL LAMPREY.

M C U. O'BRIEN from LEE'S viewpoint. O'BRIEN still struggling for his gun, receives LEE'S shot in the middle of his red forehead, about two inches below his silver hairline. O'BRIEN'S eyes go out and he falls (off the chair) onto his face into the camera, brains spilling out behind.

35. INTERIOR. WILLIAM LEE'S ROOM IN THE HOTEL LAMPREY.

M C U. WILLIAM LEE seen from where O'BRIEN has fallen (but not so low). His hands are already reaching for what he needs: His manuscripts first.

He sweeps his manuscripts into his briefcase, then he fits in his box of shells and finally, on top he places his works, wrapped into a handkerchief with the needle sticking through.

LEE sticks his gun in his belt, puts on his hat and then his jacket before he picks up his briefcase and steps over the dead body of HAUSER out of the room. . . .

36. EXTERIOR. NEW YORK STREET.

WILLIAM LEE is in the same telephone booth as in Scene 1. He holds the phone to his ear with a strange smile.

LEE: "Hello."

VOICE OVER PHONE:
 "Narcotics. . . . Who is calling?"

LEE: "I want to speak to O'Brien."

VOICE OVER PHONE:
 "O'Brien? Nobody of that name in this department. Who is calling?"

LEE: "Well, let me speak to Hauser."

VOICE OVER PHONE:
 "Look, Mister, no O'Brien no Hauser in this bureau. Now, what do you want?"

LEE: "Look, this is important. . . . I've got info on a big shipment of H coming in. I want to talk to Hauser or O'Brien. I don't do business with anybody else."

VOICE OVER PHONE:
 "How many times I have to tell you no Hauser no O'Brien in this department. Now, who *are* you?"

LEE: "Hmm. . . . That's what I'd like to know."

LEE hangs up phone and steps out of the phone
booth shouting:

LEE: "Taxii!"

· · · ·

118. INTERIOR. MINISTRY OF MENTAL
HYGIENE AND PROPHYLAXIS.

CARL at an information desk where a Nordic
Nurse sits in crackling white, not a young chick
but built. Knock out sexy nurse in costume by
Courreges: white leather hot pants.

Naked patient rushes through screaming.

Carl holds up his postcard, saying:
REPUBLIC OF FREELAND.

FREAK: "I've got the Feeeeear."

CARL: "Ministry of Mental Hygiene and
            Prophylaxis?"

119. INTERIOR.

NURSE: "Go right in. Doctor is expecting
            you."

CARL: "*Expecting* me?

NURSE very snide, imitates CARL.

NURSE: "Yes, *expecting* you."

120.A. INTERIOR. CLINICALLY WHITE AND
BRIGHT OFFICE OF HERR DOKTOR PROFESSOR
WILHELM LEE.

(played by William Burroughs).

WAGNERIAN Easter Music.

DR. LEE appears slowly out of a glorious blaze of
light, like Christ at Easter. Kaleidoscopic face
changes follow one another rapidly.

CARL: "I've seen this man before. . . . "

Blazing light behind DR. LEE comes down and he
invites CARL to sit down opposite him. CARL sits
down and crosses his legs, takes out a cigarette and
lights it.

120.B. INTERIOR.

DR. LEE is wearing glasses. DR. LEE seems almost
embarrassed. He fidgets and coughs, fumbling with
the papers on his desk, patients' files. He looks over
his glasses at CARL in a parody of the academic
manner.

> DR. LEE: "Hrumph. . . . Your name is Carl
> Peterson, I do believe. . . . "

CARL nods silently.

> (Music comes over the P.A. System very faint)
> *"Knife fighters*
> *embrace*
> *in adrenalin.*
> *Cancer*
> *is at the door*
> *with*
> *a Singing Telegram!"*

DR. LEE glances up abruptly, puts on his glasses
again and stares at CARL, belligerently.

> DR. LEE: "You know, of course, that we are
> trying . . . we are *all* trying. . . .
> Sometimes, of course, we don't suc-
> ceed . . . to adjust the State. . . sim-
> ply a tool. . . to the needs of each
> individual citizen. . . . "

DR. LEE abruptly pushes back his chair, gets up
and comes around behind CARL.

120.C. INTERIOR.

DR. LEE'S voice trails off, thin and tenuous.
DR. LEE puts his left hand to his forehead, fingers
somewhat awkward and stiff. Then, his voice

booms out suddenly, so unexpectedly deep and
loud that CARL jumps, as DR. LEE shouts in his
ear.

DR. LEE:	*"THAT* . . . as we see it . . . is the only function of the State! Our knowledge . . . incomplete, of course . . . for example . . . FOR EXAMPLE. . . . Take the matter of *Sex*ual DEVI*ATION!"*

121. INTERIOR.

DR. LEE rocks back and forth as if with silent
laughter.

CARL feels suddenly uncomfortable and squirms
around on his seat.

DR. LEE:	"Yeeeees. . . . Sexual deeeviation. . . . Hmmm. . . . Now, we . . . WE . . . regard it as a misfortune . . . a sickness. Certainly, nothing to be ah censured or uh sanctioned . . . any more than, say. . . . uh, syphilis. . . . Yes, syphilis! Ssssssyphilis."

CARL looks more and more uncomfortable.

DR. LEE:	*"On* the other hand, you can readily see that *any* illness imposes certain, shall we say, *obligations*, certain *necessities* . . . *social* necessities of a prophy*lactic* nature. . . . You follow me?"
CARL:	"Yeees."
DR. LEE:	"And in order to eradicate them our society must *impose*. . . . .uh. . . . CONTROL is it not?"
CARL:	"Yes?"

DR. LEE chuckles silently, stops and is, suddenly,
motionless.

DR. LEE:	"Now, to get back to this matter of . . . uh . . . ss*ssex*ual deviation. . . . "

122 A. EXTERIOR. PARK.

CARL is running fast across a park.

It looks as though he is fleeing from DR. LEE but
CARL is running to meet JOSELITO.

122.B. EXTERIOR.

CARL vaults the back of a bench and lands beside a
dark boy who is grinning, delighted.

JOSELITO:	"Hi, Carl!"
CARL:	"Hi, Joselito!"

122.C. EXTERIOR.

CARL turns because he is bumped in the back of
the head and then almost in the eye by a U.S.
QUEER, hung with cameras, all clicking.

A flash goes off:

U.S. QUEER:	"Welcome to the lodge, chicken. Just let down your hair to Doctor and you'll feel better."
CARL:	"Fuck off, you Traveling Christmas tree."

Snapping away at CARL with his cameras.

U.S. QUEER:	"Oh, I wouldn't be calling names if I were you, chicken. You're hooked, too! I saw you coming out of Mental Hygiene."

123. INTERIOR. DR. LEE'S OFFICE.

DR. LEE and CARL.

DR. LEE:	"Treatment of these disorders is . . . uh . . . symptomatic."

124. INTERIOR.

      CARL: "Symptomatic?"

125. INTERIOR.

      DR. LEE: "Oh, don't look so frightened,
             young man. Just a little professional
             joke. Symptomatic means that there
             is no treatment, at all."

DR. LEE goes off into a short peal of maniacal
laughter.

126. INTERIOR.

      CARL: "Oh."

127. INTERIOR.

DR. LEE is suddenly serious, professorially
pompous.

      DR. LEE: "Isolation is not necessarily
             indicated. . . . Your condition is no
             more directly contagious than . . .
             say, uh . . . cancer. Ah, Cancer, my
             first love. . . . "

128. INTERIOR.

DR. LEE gets up with his arms held out stiffly in
front of him, as if inviting CARL to dance with
him as he sings the tune which has come into the
room as the door opens and NURSE comes in.

      DR. LEE (sings):
          "Duh duh duh . . . embrace
          in adrenalin, duh duh duh
          Cancer is at the door
          with a
          Singing Telegram."

CARL whirls around to see NURSE standing at the
door with a telegram.

129. INTERIOR.

CARL:	"That's crazy. I don't have cancer!"

130. INTERIOR.

DR. LEE waltzes over and touches CARL on the
shoulder, taking off his glittering glasses to look at
him closer. DR. LEE'S eyes. He is at his most
seductive and hypnotic.

DR. LEE:	"Ah, the young. . . . always in a hurry. . . . No, Carl . . . I may call you Carl . . . you don't know *what* you have . . . yet. Do you?"

131. INTERIOR.

CARL:	"N-no."

132. INTERIOR. DR. LEE'S OFFICE.

DR. LEE is back on his side of the desk. He is
looking through a file.

DR. LEE:	"It says here that you intend to get married and have taken a blood test, as required by the State."

133. INTERIOR.

CARL:	"All my blood tests were negative, weren't they?"

134. INTERIOR.

Reading telegram.

DR. LEE:	"Yes, Caaaarl, yeeees. . . . But."
CARL:	"But what?"
DR. LEE:	"Carl, I may tell you in strictest con . . . fidence, that there *is* some evidence of a hereditary factor . . . social pressure . . . permissive infan- tile environment. . . . Many homo-"

> sexuals. . . . both latent and overt,
> do . . . unfortunately . . . marry."

135. INTERIOR.

CARL'S face is passing from bewilderment to
outrage.

CARL:	"Whaaa?"
DR. LEE:	"Perhaps before it is too late, Caaaarl. . . ."

CARL explodes.

CARL:	"But this whole thing is ridiculous! I've *always* been interested in girls . . . *only* in girls!"
DR. LEE:	"The Kleiberg-Stanislouski test . . . our semen flocculation test. . . ."
CARL:	"What!"
DR. LEE:	"Nurse will take your specimen."
CARL:	*"Nuuuurse?"*

CARL is hustled off by good teamwork between
Doctor and Nurse.

NURSE:	"This way, please."

NURSE crosses office and opens a door into a
white-walled cubicle. CARL gets up and follows
her.

135. INTERIOR.

DR. LEE grinning outside door after door of cubicle has been closed.

. . . . .

244.A. EXTERIOR. GARDEN OF U.S. CONSULATE
IN A FOREIGN LAND.

The Marines are playing, a tongue-tied lisping
TENOR in a Daniel Boone suit is singing. The
VICE CONSUL is at the microphone making a

speech. Crowds of well-dressed EXPATRIATES are being served drinks by swarthy servants in tarbouches. Interzone Society is there.

VICE CONSUL, an elderly man in striped pants and a cutaway coat is reading from a roll of toilet paper which is blown by the wind and tangles his feet. Can-heat tenor is singing.

MISS FINGERBOTTOM sits at his feet taking shorthand.

> TENOR: *"o, thay can you theeeeeee . . . ?"*
>
> Messy medley of Americana.

244.B. REPEAT 115.B.

> CONSUL: "And we categorically deny that *any* male citizen of the Yeeeew Nighted States of Ammuuurika. . . . "
>
> TENOR: *"o, thay do that Thtar thpangle Banner yet wave . . . ?"*
>
> CONSUL: ". . . . that any *male* citizen of the Yeeeew Nighted States . . . whether operated on in Copenhagen or in Casablanca. . . ."
>
> TENOR: *"Oer the land of the Freeeeee . . . ."*

244.C. (REPEAT 115.C. — this part of shot seen for first time here)

MISS FINGERBOTTOM, the Secretary, is at his feet taking all this down in shorthand.

> CONSUL: ". . . No. Cut that out Miss Fingerbottom."

CONSUL goes back to his speech.

> ". . . has ever given birth. . . ."

245. (REPEAT 116). GROUP OF EXPATRIATES AT THE GARDEN PARTY OF THE U.S. CONSULATE.

GERTIE, LOVELY, queer COLONEL.

COL: "I hear your friend William Lee is in confinement at Dr. Benway's Anxiety Institute."

LOV.:   "Has he given birth to his masterpiece yet?"

GERTIE shows the briefcase hidden amongst his newspapers. Manuscripts still bursting out of it.

GERTIE: "My dear, Dr. Benway delivered the document by Caesarian section. Reams of manuscript have been ruthlessly removed, but I'm looking after his briefcase. Lee calls it his Word Hoard."

COL: "I suppose he's all cut up about it."

LOV.:   "Such a lovely fella."

GERT: "The Consulate wants it kept quiet but . . . ."

· · · ·

266.A. INTERIOR. LEE'S ROOM IN THE HOSPITAL.

BENWAY tells his tale. Vaults into LEE'S bed and lies flat on his ass at the other end of it.

BENWAY: ". . . so there I am flat on my ass with no certificate and Violet never had one. Should we turn to another trade? No. Doctoring is in our blood. For a while, we managed to keep our medical habits by performing cut-rate abortions in subway toilets. I even hustled pregnant women in parks. I was positively unethical. Then I met a great guy: Salvador O'Leary Chapultepec, the . . . ."

266.B. INTERIOR.

BENWAY leaps to his feet and salutes a portrait of
SAL over the door.

BENWAY:	"Afterbirth Tycoon, Controller of Interzone, our Savior."

267. INTERIOR.

Points to a formal portrait of SALVADOR, seen in
every room of the Hospital.

268. INTERIOR.

LEE:	"Yeah, I knew him when. How'd he make his?"

BENWAY leaps around acting this out.

BENWAY:	"In slunks . . . unethical meat imported from Abyssinia . . . where he sends us. Filthy place. There I was under a grass hut, operating with one hand . . . beating the rats offa my patient with the other. Bedbugs and scorpions raining down from the ceiling. As Sally said afterwards: It was only to try me."
LEE:	"To try you?"
BENWAY:	"Yes, he needed a man of my mettle to run this Anxiety Institute. Sally set this place up but it's not his baby, basically. The man behind the whole thing . . . if he *is* a man . . . we know only by his initials, AJ."
LEE:	"AJ! You mean AJ, the Last of the Big Time Spenders?"
BENWAY:	"You've heard of him, then?"

269. INTERIOR.

LEE: "Only vaguely. He sent me some money, once . . . to write a uh movie for him. Never seen it. Never seen the movie, I mean. Never."

270. INTERIOR.

BENWAY: "Lots of money?"

271. INTERIOR.

LEE: "Oh, quite a lot . . . or so it seemed to me at the time. Five thousand dollars."

272. INTERIOR.

BENWAY: "Hm . . . five thousand dollars, eh? Yes, that's one way he does it."

273. INTERIOR.

LEE: "Does what?"

274. INTERIOR.

BENWAY: "Controls people: with money. Wanna see how *weeee* do it?"

275. INTERIOR. RECONDITIONING CENTER IN THE ANXIETY INSTITUTE.

BENWAY is showing LEE around something much worse than Warrendale.

276. INTERIOR.

BENWAY wears a stethoscope around his neck and an elaborate eye-mirror around his head. He is in white, short-sleeves, and very hairy arms if possible.

Camera pans round as LEE sees it and moves in on a man with blank eyes.

BENWAY:	"Step a little closer. You won't embarrass anybody."
LEE:	"There's nobody there. No one looks back."
BENWAY:	"IND . . . Irreversible Neural Damage. Overliberated you might say. A drag on the Industry. Now looka this one. . . . She digs Baby Ruths something special. . . . "

277. INTERIOR.

DR. BENWAY is unwrapping a Baby Ruth candy
bar. A nearly naked woman with terrible teeth leaps
up at the mention of Baby Ruth. BENWAY fends
her off.

278. INTERIOR.

BENWAY:	". . . but they're bad for her teeth. We conditioned her by clamping a set of electric drills to her teeth. The Switchboard we call it . . . and every time she makes a mistake, the drills are turned on for twenty seconds. Left her with cavities. Hear that stomach rumble . . . ?"

Rumbling sound on the sound track.

BENWAY steps back and holds up the Baby Ruth
bar. The woman begs like a dog.

BENWAY:	"Just got her begging for it."

BENWAY tosses her the Baby Ruth and she devours
it on the floor.

LEE:	"Wouldn't that disgust you?"
BENWAY:	"Bored with the whole project, me . . . Drag Alley . . . all oughtta be sent to Disposal."

BENWAY snaps his fingers at a young GUARD in
dingy hospital whites. GUARD goes on reading
NAKED LUNCH.

> BENWAY: "Here, see that this one don't get
> out inna streets. She'd be bad for the
> tourist trade."
>
> GUARD: "I don't know from nuttin'. Empty
> your own garbage."
>
> BENWAY: "Wise guy, eh? Got no respect for
> human dignity. . . ."

279. INTERIOR.

Says "The Mental Hour" with great scorn.

> BENWAY: "Now, I'll show you 'The Mental
> Hour,' a program produced by our
> Dr. Berger . . . learned asshole."

280. INTERIOR. DR. BERGER'S MENTAL HOUR.

DR. BERGER looks like an owl with horn-rimmed
glasses. He is taking notes and the light hurts his
eyes. His TECHNICIAN acts like a Sergeant in the
Army. His ART ADVISER acts like a window-
dresser. His SUBJECT is being set up by the TECH-
NICAL SERGEANT.

> TECH: "Now lissen, I'll say it again and I'll
> say it sloooow. '*Yes.*'"

281. INTERIOR.

With difficulty, in a creaky voice.

> SUBJECT: "Ye-es. . . ."

282. INTERIOR.

> TECH: "Go on. And make with the smile
> . . . the *smiiiile.* Say it."

283. INTERIOR.

> SUBJECT: "Ssssmiiiiile."

284. INTERIOR.

TECH: "No! You're supposed to say: '*We like apple pie.*' Say it. . . . "

285. INTERIOR.

TECH: "Go on. '*We like apple pie and we like each other. It's just as simple as that.*' Say it."

286. INTERIOR.

SUBJECT: "It's just as simple as that."

287. INTERIOR.

TECH: "No! It isn't! Say that part about how we like each other."

288. INTERIOR.

SUBJECT: "But we don't."

289. INTERIOR.

TECH: "You want the walk-about switchboard again . . . or the pail?"

290. INTERIOR.

SUBJECT: "N-oooo!"

291. INTERIOR.

TECH: "Well, say it and make it sound simple, *country* simple. Look bovine."

292. INTERIOR.

SUBJECT: "Bovine? What's that? . . . "

293. INTERIOR.

TECH: "Like a cow."

294. INTERIOR.

ART ADVISER takes up a cardboard Cow's head
and puts it on the subject.

SUBJECT: "Moooo! Moooo!"

295. INTERIOR.

DR. BERGER looks up from his notes.

BERGER: "I think he is unsuitable subject. See
he report to Disposal."

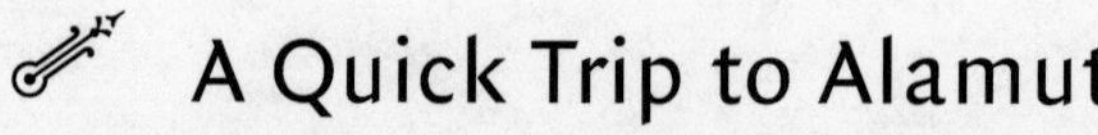

A Quick Trip to Alamut:
The Celebrated Castle of the Hash-Head Assassins

*"A Quick Trip to Alamut" (1973) reflects Gysin's lifelong interest in the
history and legend of Hassan i Sabbah. He was finally able to visit Alamut
in 1973, accompanied by his friend Lawrence Lacina (a photo of Gysin
at the ruins of the fortress, taken by Lacina, graces the frontispiece of
*Here to Go, *the book of interviews with Terry Wilson). The piece was
originally written for* Rolling Stone *but was rejected by the magazine;
Gysin thought this was probably due to his going on about flirtations
with boys.*

Can you score at American Express? At Thomas Cook & Sons? At Hertz? Yes,
you can in Teheran, Iran . . . what we used to call Persia.

"Oh, Brion, you *can't* be going to begin your article like that! It would be
awful of you. Besides, it might be terribly compromising for poor Shams whom
we both liked so much, I thought. I hated his driver Mohammad, of course, but
I think Shams is a really nice guy."

So do I. I agree on one hand but on the other it can't do Shams any harm to
let the world know he can pull just about anything you like out of a hat in Iran
and at the same time I really want to throw a block into his mad plans for getting minibusloads of American Maws up there with blue rinse in their hair and
their bifocals on chains around their ropey old necks. Anyhow, I don't think
they'd survive it. But I agree he is great. Who else could have gotten the two of
us up to Alamut, dressed like we were and with skimpy pimps' pumps on our
poor tender feet from the city?

"Oh, it won't be the blue-rinse ladies up in Alamut. It'll be those muscular
Germans with varicose veins in their knotty legs and their gray woolen socks in
their sandals or hob-nailed boots, all armed with alpenstock and rucksacks on
their backs full of crampons and pitons and long ropes for climbing."

No, it is the British James Bond & Co Ltd crew, they have always been the
biggest fans of the Old Man of the Mountain in his secret castle of Alamut, ever
since the Crusaders sent home intelligence reports about Hassan i Sabbah, Grand
Master of the hash-head Hashishins, the fanatical Muslim sect who practiced
power politics by wielding the knife in the fine art of political murder. Hence
our word, Assassin. Marco Polo picked up the word on his way through to
China. He reported that the Old Man chose only stout-hearted likely lads for
his Fida'i-in, his adepts whose utter devotion to him and his practices became

a fearsome legend from the court of Cathay in the Far East to the court of Charlemagne in the Far West of the known world. Kings were killed on their thrones, a prominent prime minister was felled as he took a stroll through his own private park. Captured Assassins all told the same story. They confessed under torture that the Old Man of the Mountain had trained them and rewarded them with drugs. Adepts were given a potion which put them to sleep, and when they awoke they found themselves in a heavenly garden where fountains were running with honey and wine of which they drank their fill before they fell on passionate maids with flashing eyes and flowing hair who played upon the dulcimer. When the Adept awoke from his dream of Paradise, he was assured by the Old Man himself that come what may he could score for that same stuff forever . . . after he accomplished his mission. The potion was said to be prepared from the hemp plant, cannabis. All the young heads of the world, all the budding James Bonds of the turn of the first Millennium, flocked to his banner.

By the year 1090, the Alamut Academy was the world's finest finishing school for secret agents. The way it worked was elegant, simple. You announce you are starting a commune to beat the Millennium, the next thousand years, in some spot as bare as the hills of Nevada. You make it hard to get in and you announce that once you are in . . . really IN . . . you can never get out again. You won't even want to. The young are so needy of something, they beat their way to your retreat but only the pick of them ever even gets inside your gate where you make them sit on their hard hungry young asses and wait . . . . wait . . . wait. When they're really ripe, you take four to ten of them together inside where you feed them and turn them on. You do this in your kennel, which you tell them is your chapel, your Chapel of Extreme Experience, lowest grade. Food, music, and sex served by chicks and you've got it made. You've got yourself a faithful free worker, a Fida'i, a devoted Dogface. A Dogface must do all the dirty work and you give him plenty of it. If he survives, he may be turned on again a little higher, and allowed to begin his Basic Training, after which he becomes a Rafiq or Private First Class who may move on up to become a Dai. Dais are Sergeants all the way to the top three officers, Dai-al-Kirbal, who answer only to the Sheik-al-Jabal or Master of Masters, the Grand Old Man himself. Obedience to the Old Man is absolute.

Right from the start, the Assassins exerted an influence out of all proportion to their number. Hassan i Sabbah could point a long bony finger and probe with a knife into the very heart of realpolitik wherever he sent his Fida'i-in. His instructions to them were said to have been: *"Nothing is forbidden. Everything is permitted."* Lodges both secret and open branched out through the whole Arab world, all receiving orders from the Old Man in Alamut. A great deal of very special knowledge centered there and not all of it was destroyed in the eventual fall of that capital castle. To this day, however, it remains very difficult to learn much about the initiation of the higher echelons, for whom the simple promise of hashish would not be enough to make impatient of this world and oblivious of the personal consequences of their acts. Exactly how they were "sent" is another matter about which one can only surmise that: *"You can't let that secret out . . . too dangerous."* Anyone who knew would be in practice for himself. Or is he already?

Hassan i Sabbah died at the ripe age of eighty-four in the year 1124, leaving a tightly knit network of castles manned by fanatical adepts whose power spread over another one hundred and thirty-two years, until 1256, when all of them were swept away by the locust-like hordes of the Mongols. Hulagu, grandson of Genghis Khan, unleashed wave after wave and then flying swarms of his hornets up against the imposing pinnacle on which Alamut was built, until at last he could climb into the Eagle's Nest over the mountainous slopes of dead bodies of his own soldiers. The Assassins were slaughtered to the last man and pitched into the valley fully fifteen hundred feet below, and the stones of the castle were hurled over after them. What remains of the castles today needs to be searched for. Hulagu's historian, a Persian named Juvayni, wrote: "Of the Old Man of the Mountain and his stock, no trace was left and he and his became but a tale upon men's lips and a legend in the great world." Yes, and the legend lives on all these years later but what about his stock? Oh, surprise! The Aga Khan of today is the present head of the Sect of Seven, the Ismailis, and he owes his succession to that power and glory thanks to a line which runs right through the long bony fingers of Hassan i Sabbah. But that is a whole other story. Or is it?

Alamut loomed large in my life from the time I first read *The Travels of Marco Polo* in my childhood. I read every version I could find, until I felt I had been there. The legend loomed larger when I grew up and turned on, beginning to have doubts about Inflexible Authority and the nature of the Garden. I read absurdly abstract German theses on Hassan i Sabbah and the mystique of murder. I read French books full of pseudo-romantic rubbish about Hassan's honeyed trap for simple-minded soldiers, making it sound like a pre–World War II Parisian brothel or a branch office of Baudelaire's Artificial Paradise. I read brilliant British travel books by adventure-seeking spinsters, but perhaps the most penetrating book on the real meaning of the mysteries which served the Master in his deadly purpose is a volume in French, signed Betty Bouthoul. The book in itself is a mystery and as such I gave it to my good friend William

Burroughs, a short time after he had published *Naked Lunch*, before 1960. I explained that I had met the author, a portrait painter in Parisian social circles. She was oddly vague about why she wrote the book or what were her sources of research. Her husband is Maitre Gaston Bouthoul, the lawyer for many of the most famous living painters, and he is, at the same time, perhaps the only practicing adept of a very odd discipline indeed . . . the philosophy of war: *polemology*. Who else has there ever been in this branch: Clausewitz? Moltke?

Burroughs and I were living in those days in the famously infamous old Beat Hotel on the edge of the Latin Quarter on the Left Bank in Paris. We pored over the book, passing it back and forth. We read and reread it. The crux of the matter, of course, is: How did he do it? And, beyond that: What is the nature of power? Bouthoul teases the reader enough to make you feel that there must be an answer and in the answer lies the key to Control on this planet. Big stuff. Poor Tim Leary had not yet said: "The revolution is over and we have won," but everyone around the Beat Hotel thought that when we put acid in the water supply, that would do it. Burroughs denounced the Garden of Delights as a pernicious weapon of Control, like junk, but we still harkened back to the echo from Alamut, asking ourselves: *How* did he do it?

What was Alamut really like and was there a Garden? Burroughs and I promised each other that one day we would go there to see for ourselves. In the meantime, Burroughs sprinkled his writings with references . . . even unto the outrageous identification of me with the Master: "See, see the Silent Writing of Brion Gysin, Hassan i Sabbah!" I always felt that Burroughs himself was much more like the Old Man of the Mountain. After all, I have never killed anyone in my life, not even an animal. Burroughs really digs knives and guns: he is forever writing loving details of the specifications of some obsolete repeating revolver . . . *"and, Splat! a bright red patch of blood splashes across his shirtfront above his belt buckle."* Before I met Burroughs, my beau ideal was a library without comic books but I enjoy and approve his glosses on them, immensely.

When I found myself in Iran this summer, almost by accident, I went to Alamut. Oddly, almost everything I picked up in Teheran had something about the Assassins, the local English language daily, plus *This Week in Teheran* and the illustrated *Iran Tribune*, as well as the guidebooks put out by Nagel and Fodor. Most of the information was contradictory, and Persian printers' pied type made nonsense out of the rest of it, but that seemed to figure. Fodor said firmly that the trip should not be attempted by tourists. Nagel suggested that if properly outfitted for an expedition, four or five days might be enough, provided one took a pack-train of mules, well equipped, and with a thoroughly reliable guide from the city of Qasvin, one hundred and fifty kilometers to the northwest of Teheran. I was planning to set out for Qasvin when my eye caught a sign in the street, saying: *Thomas Cook & Sons*. It flashed on me at once that Cook's tours would get me there, unlikely as it sounded to my companion, Lawrence, who was not all that interested anyway, because he had his mind set on something else, like meeting some nice friend with a house in the cool mountains and a swimming pool.

I was right: Cook's could do it. I met the v.p. of the Iranian outfit that runs all three: American Express, Cook's, and Hertz. Mr. Mehrzad Shams greeted me with a dazzling smile when I explained my mission: "Alamut? Why of course. Yes! When do you want to go? Maybe you can go along with the British TV team which is following the track of Marco Polo across Asia. They may have room for you but, if not, I have a young friend who might be willing to take you in his own jeep. He knows the route well. It is the worst road in Iran and maybe the world. One stretch of it took us eleven hours to get through when we went up there last winter, but there has been a bulldozer over that bit since then. You'll make it. You might do it in even one day. . . . Make it a real American 'quickie.' . . . Do you want to?"

Noooo! I want to spend at least one night up in Alamut, in the castle itself, I cried. I *must* . . . I've simply *got* to get to Alamut! I don't know why else I came to Iran. I don't even know why we came to Iran, in the first place. We meant to go to Kabul until the day of the coup and then we found that our charter flight was at least twenty hours long, with a stopover in Moscow and, in any case, at the last minute they switched dates on us so we couldn't go anyway but they wouldn't give us our money back so we changed to Iran at the last minute. It was my idea to fly straight to Isfahan to see all those blue-domed mosques and we hated it. Those bulbous blue domes look like blow-ups of Fabergé Easter eggs left over from the World's Fair of 1625 or something. So we went on to Shiraz and then took a long bus ride across the desert that was supposed to be only twelve non-airconditioned hours long and turned out to be as long as a lifetime. Kerman was OK. We met a family of Persian carpet weavers in their own mud house, and the man's old mother was making a pipe of O in the garden, so we swapped tales with her and her cronies. She was an adorably wicked old thing, like a lot of old junkies in any clime anywhere. She heated the bowl of her Persian pipe, looking like an oboe with a china egg in it, and then she applied the pellet of almost translucent golden colored O to it with her fine old fingers, just above the pinhole of the aperture, which she reamed out with her iron pin attached to a pair of little iron tongs. She plucked a red coal from the fire in a brasero and held it up to the pinhole in her pipe through which she blew a blast which reddened the charcoal. When it was red enough, she put the O on her pipe to it and sucked in a great blast that went *straight-down* into the bottom of her old bellows. She held it as long as she could and let it out in a thin stream of sweet smoke which she blew in the face of her little grand-daughter. She said that at thirty the doctor had told her to smoke for her eyes, and she held a government card as an addict. She needed her eyes to make rugs so she smoked thirty pipes a day. "And fly around like a bat all night," I cracked. She cackled like a banshee when that was translated to her. She had darting little blue eyes like pale chips of lapis lazuli set deep in her head. Granny O, we called her.

Shams smiled a truly Persian smile and said: "Maybe you'll find another Granny O up in Alamut."

At this point, I dropped Burroughs' name but Shams shook his head. I mentioned *Naked Lunch*, of which we had found copies for sale in the airport of Isfahan . . . probably both bootlegged and pirated. I thought someone on the British TV team might have heard of Burroughs or of me, even. One of them was said to be the son of a London illustrator who had done a portrait of Burroughs. I didn't think it worthwhile to add that William had hated it. Anyway, nothing ever came of that project, so I went back to the Hotel America, where the air-conditioner had gone off again or was blowing hot air into the room and Lawrence had gone to a hammam. I hung out in the dingy lobby where the smell of fresh paint gave me asthma but I picked up Bill. Bill is a candidly insane and utterly mad man-mountain from the pasta pastures of New Jersey, looking like a young professional wrestler with long hair and a truly tremendous torso bulging out of a tank-top above a pair of torn dungaree mini-shorts like Daisy Mae wears around Dogpatch. All this balanced on striped silver and blue platform shoes with high heels which brought his bulky five foot nine up to more than six feet. He had all his fingernails painted in different bright colors of nailpolish and each one had a tiny decal of a flower posed lovingly in the middle of it.

Bill had been stranded for five and a half weeks in the Hotel America, waiting for money. *"John Keats died in Rome, waiting for money from home,"* I quote from my uncollected works. "One thing you can always be sure of: bread never comes through if you need it." From here on I go into a long song like the Ancient Mariner coming on strong with his Wedding Guest, about how I once was hung up a whole summer in Rome on the Spanish Steps by the window where Keats died, around the corner from American Express, and all the time that bread of mine was there, you understand, shoved away in some other file like Agricultural Loans & Investments, and I'm there every day going crazy and Rome such an oven so even the trade on the steps emigrate out to the beach at Ostia where I can't even follow them because I'm waiting for my bread, see.

I restrain myself from adding anything crude like: You'll do almost any old thing for bread if ya hafta, huh?

Bill goes into *his* song and dance, all about "grabbin' chicks," as he calls it, a-plenty in swinging New Jersey but tough titty in Teheran or so I gather. I get the message but Lawrence cools him out later by telling how he had been raped by a guard in the National Museum that morning: "So I gave in, what else could I do?"

Since he is not a natural Adept, I see no particular profit in enrolling Bill as one of my Fida'i-in. Lawrence is still not sure he wants to go and thinks he would rather buy a Persian rug with his money. Ah, yes, the money. How much is all this going to cost? I don't know. In my insane insistence to Shams that I simply HAD to get up to Alamut, I heard myself saying: "I don't care what it costs!" It just goes to show how little I've learned in a lifetime. I tried to retract that unbusinesslike statement, but Shams simply smiled like a Persian prince and invited me to a party to meet the boy, he said, who would be driving the jeep. He had one of the oldest family houses up in the hills above Teheran overlooking the city. Why not bring along my all-night bag and sleep in a guest house in the garden? That way we could get an early start before the heat of the day and no need to drive back through the city. Lawrence wanted to come when he heard there was going to be a party. He was still not sure about Alamut, but he packed his little shoulder bag and we waited for Shams to pick us up after office hours.

Teheran is built on the steep slope of the foothills of mountains higher than the Colorados. Between the broad streets and the broken sidewalks, wild water rushes down open culverts through the business section, down to the south station and beyond into an inhabited marsh of slum dwellings. It is said in Iran, that only the Shahbanou Farah Diba has ever been down there. Teheran traffic is said not to be the worst in the world, but that is a statement for the press, made only by visiting heads of state from the East, where, indeed, things may be worse. Westerners crudely declare that it is the most chaotic and dangerous they have ever seen anywhere. One thing about it, it moves. There are no traffic jams unless there has been a thirty-two-car collision. Through rivers of carbon monoxide made from gas cheaper than in Texas, endless streams of cars leap through red lights and green like sex-maddened salmon in mating season, fighting their way up cascades.

Shams was ramming his jeep through shoals of Iranian-mounted Hillman models made of rusty tin cans, he claimed, and driven by crossing sweepers. There was a touch of class in that last remark and it grew as we climbed into the upper suburbs full of huge houses built by the newly rich who had all been their lives in the bottom of the bazaar, he said, shining shoes when they were small and carrying loads on their backs when they were bigger. Some of them have since climbed all the way up into these desirable dwelling areas where one of the first things they do is cut down all the trees so everyone can see their big houses. These shady hills are where old families used to have their country places for the summer, a day's ride out of town when they were built and only ten to twenty minutes from the office as the highways followed, when Teheran mushroomed into a city, but now there are so many cars on the road that the really rich commute in their helicopters.

"Yes, I'm going to have to get one of those," said Sham's friend, the man in the back seat next to Lawrence. "Right here where we are now on this highway, I used to own twenty-four thousand square meters of real estate. They took eighteen thousand away from me to build this road, leaving me with six thousand meters on which to pay taxes. The trouble is that these six thousand meters are cut off in such a way that I can't even set foot on them without trespassing. They won't let me build an aerial road or dig a tunnel, so I'm thinking of buying a helicopter and building a house here. . . . "

"Of course, you'll have a swimming pool," said Lawrence.

Where we were going, they did . . . a kidney-shaped swimming pool—surrounded by immense weeping willows. The house on the hill was all airy rooms and porticos looking out over what I took for Los Angeles. A huge crash-couch under the trees with cushions for twenty-odd turned-on people and a dark boy in a white coat, setting out food and drinks or rolling a joint for you: the place was attractive. Guests gathered like gorgeous moths, as sleek and well-groomed as if they had just slipped out of a chrysalis that afternoon when they woke from their siestas, all Beautiful People. Lawrence sat next to a man who was opening a tin of caviar with care, explaining that this was Golden Caviar and no one in the West no matter how rich he is has ever seen it, let alone tasted any. "Nor in Iran either," quipped somebody out of the dark, "except for breakfast with the royal family. How the hell did you get any of that?"

"I have a little man who brings it to me. He has breakfast every day with the royal family."

"You mean, the Prime Minister? He's dropping in later."

"This is just the milieu I was looking for," purred Lawrence.

I am ashamed to admit that the golden caviar melted in my mouth without going, pop! like I'm used to, so I guess my taste buds are still back in the delicatessen. I latched onto the bottle of vodka, though, having a burning thirst ever since I hit Teheran. I found myself raising my glass to the dark eyes of a big blond youth with tanned flesh like a sun-ripened musk melon. There is an old Persian saying: "Women for duty, boys for pleasure, but melons for sheer delight." Fucked if he doesn't look like a Fida'i to these old bleary eyes. "Whose trail are *you* on?" he asks me pointblank. I barely notice that he is actively being attacked by a chick like a golden lizard who is wrapping herself around him. "Whose trail? Why, on yours, Baby," I say with my eyes but my lips say: "Hassan i Sabbah." The gorgeous girl twists around in his arms like a basilisk, eyeing me evenly. Even these narrow blue blinkers of mine have to admit it, she is stunning. He is on one elbow hanging over her, his sheer voile shirt open to the navel. Rolling one evil eye back at me to show me the white of it, this glittering reptile nibbles his nipple. He shifts, groping for cigarettes, bending over to take a light off me while she rolls her python's pink tongue around in his bellybutton. I am completely overcome, as is my condition constantly.

Later, with the vodka bottle empty in front of me, I find myself babbling like the conduit of fresh mountain water which is filling the swimming pool. Babble like a brook and throw your bread upon the waters, that is my principle. As the Herr Doktor says: "You learn more about people by talking to them than you can by listening to them." Besides, I'm in a hurry. I've just picked up on something said a minute ago and I wonder if this trip is really on, after all. From living in Muslim countries for more than twenty years, I long ago came to know that nothing really happens until it *has* happened. And, even then, you can't always be sure of it. I have just heard someone asking our host and driver-to-be about our trip tomorrow and he said: "What trip?"

Moamer, as I decided to call him, hated us both on sight for some occult reason. Black-bearded twenty-one-year-old hairy Aryan, he stood as straight and silent but slight as the Medean spear he seemed to be carrying. A dark Persian Pan, he sulked like James Dean but, as things turned out, he drove better. Antagonism excites me when I am drunk, so I decided to give him my glittering eye routine and lay on him my version of the career of Hassan i Sabbah, which runs like this:

My boy Hassan was born in Ray, near present-day Teheran, and studied in Nichapour to the east on the old Silk Route to China where he went to a *medersa*, a boarding school in which he shared a study with two other boys who are equally famous in history. One of them was known as Nizam al Molk when he became Prime Minister of the then immense Persian empire. The other was

Omar Khayam, the poet with the jug of wine, who must have been as seductive a character as we find him to be when we read his *Rubaiyat*. These three got on so well together that they opened their veins and mingled their blood in a schoolboy oath that was supposed to hold good for a lifetime. When Nizam became prime minister, he named Omar Khayam state astronomer because he was good at mathematics. Hassan was not, but when he came to court on the strength of their romantic bond, Nizam gave him the post of minister of finance. While preparing his budget, Hassan sought out the help of Omar, with whom he left overnight all the papers pertinent to his financial report which he was to read to the Shah and the assembled court in the morning. When the time came, Hassan picked up his papers and read them aloud, just as he found them. Everyone gasped and then broke out laughing, louder and louder as Hassan struggled on, talking what seemed to be utter nonsense until the Shah stopped him and sent him away in disgrace.

What had happened was that someone, presumably Omar . . . or was it Nizam? . . . had not only scrambled the pages but cut them in four and carefully pasted them together again. Now, this is the random process of discontinuity with which Burroughs and I have been working since 1960 when I called them the Cut-Ups. Moamer yawned, naturally, but I plunged on with my story when one of the other guests asked: "Then, what happened?"

Hassan i Sabbah went home to Ray in a rage, vowing a terrible vengeance on his old pals for having made a fool of him. He fell ill and did not leave his house for weeks on end. Then, he went walking one night in the dark and empty bazaar, where he was not likely to meet anyone he knew, but as he passed the one stall still open, a lowly cobbler called out to him, offering him a glass of tea. When he sat down with this poor man, the cobbler said quietly: "Welcome, we have been waiting for you. You are that man." Hassan recognized by certain signs that the cobbler was a member of the secret brotherhood of the Ismailians whose network reached all the way across the Near East to Egypt where the supposed descendants of Fatima, daughter of Mohammed the Prophet, called themselves Caliphs of Cairo with the pretention to rule all of Islam. When Hassan realized the possibilities inherent in such a connection, he said: "Yes, I am that man."

The cobbler gave him the Ismaili code, including the thirty-three handshakes and stuff, so Hassan i Sabbah set off to pick up the threads of this organization along the trade routes which led him through Baghdad and Damascus to Cairo where, as soon as he arrived, he announced that he was not just a member but the Head of the Ismailians. When you join a conspiracy, join at the top. (Unexpected applause at this point from the man with the golden caviar. "Right on!" he cried.) Within a matter of months, Hassan i Sabbah had thrown the city of Cairo into a state of revolution. When called in by the Fatimid Caliph, he demanded his son and heir as a hostage and, no sooner had he laid hands on this fourteen-year-old boy than he made off with him in the first boat leaving for Syria. On the way, they were shipwrecked and when they turned up much later in Damascus, the boy he had with him appeared to be only twelve years old but Hassan i Sabbah stoutly insisted that this boy was the heir to the Fatimid pretensions. Within a few years, they had set up housekeeping together in Alamut and the rest of the story. . . .

"The rest of the story," said the man with the golden caviar, "is that he gave his assassins the sacred mushroom. Hash would not be enough to explain the hold he had over them."

"How about O?"

"Yes, perhaps, O and mushrooms he learned about from the Turkestan steppes where their shamans have always used them. Hassan i Sabbah was a shaman."

"How about the homosexual side of shamanism?"

"I'm sure the Assassins knew about that, all right."

In my excitement, I laid a light hand on Moamer's bare arm, barely brushing it but he sat still and stiff, staring down at the spot as if he expected a cancer to grow there like a mushroom. We were not urged to stay the night, after all, but took a flight home in a taxi down through what I kept insisting was L.A. Came the dawn and the reckoning. Despite all the Veganins I took before passing out, I had a horrible hangover, and so did Moamer, when he showed up late saying he'd had only two hours sleep. It did not seem to show in his driving, but I clung to the edge of my seat in the open jeep, shivering. Lawrence had come along at the last minute and was stowed away on the top of the things like bedding that Moamer had brought with him. Moamer accepted two Veganins grudgingly and drove like a madman out along the highway to the northwest between desert and bare red mountains. We stopped at Karadj, a market town of one broad unpaved Main Street of one-story stores and gaudy government buildings, lined with trees growing in irrigation ditches flowing with water. Brightly painted and highly decorated with icons and decals and ball-fringe, big fat trucks balled through the dust in which delirious drivers make U-turns and Y-turns and Z-turns while only an occasional X marks the spot of an accident. Wily driving is a matter of pride with the Persians. Moamer dropped into a store run by a Christian Armenian, where he bought vodka and beer, ham, boloney, hot dogs, and everything which, for good Muslims, is forbidden, not kosher, *haram*.

The air was so hot that you took it into your lungs in short sips, like hot tea. I could hardly breathe. Asthma? I asked myself before bothering Lawrence to get into my bag where I had my Spinhaler and my Moditen. I had taken one Moditen at six, along with two Veganins last night and two more each time I came to again during the night. Also three little old pinkies and then just three more of them later: *Codéthyline Houdé*, free across the counter in France, one tube to a customer since the last scare about *la drogue*. I felt fine, fairly fine: finer than Moamer and that was some consolation. He suddenly whipped the jeep off the road and down into a ditch or was it a side-road? Moamer croaked, like a man coming out of a trance: "Just now, I wake up."

We drove up an avenue of trees which may once have led to a farmhouse, but the bulldozers have taken over everywhere in Iran, what with all that good oil money, and new construction in chaos is seen even out here in the bare countryside. Beyond all this mess, the clean mesa land sails up towards magnificent bare mountains all purple and blue and malachite green with copper, no doubt, rising up to a distant peak covered with "eternal" but dingy brown snow. In all this place not one blade of grass grows in the heat of August, only a few ghostly thistles and thorns along the dirt road on which enough dew forms during the night to support them. Yet immense tracts of this totally arid landscape are cultivated during the rainy season. Where there is year-around water on this land, they get three crops a year of all the cereals like wheat, rye, oats, barley, and alfalfa, which they rotate. All these grains were first domesticated, sown, and reaped here in the dawn of our agricultural history.

On the top of the first high ridge marked on my map in Nagel, we stop. "You see that third range of mountains out there? That green spot is just below Alamut." Through my 10 × 40 Japanese binoculars, I can see nothing because the wind buffets my trembling hands but above our heads an eagle is circling as if welcoming us to Alamut, which means the Eyrie, the Eagle's Nest. Down the other side of this ridge is a *tchaikaneh*, a country tea-house by an oasis in the bend of the road growing around a spring of cold water which comes out of the hillside. Moamer drives up real rugged and leaps from the jeep to put his head under the stream, splashing around for quite a while before we can get a drink. While we are reviving ourselves, the *tchaikaneh*-man comes on shouting and waving his arms about. He is furious because Moamer has run the jeep so far into the red earth moist from the overflow that he has crushed three, no, four blades of grass! Moamer tries to make it a laugh but the man is perfectly serious. The little oasis is precious and fragile, shaded by a ring of pole-straight poplars. The poplar is a Persian tree, first selected and grown along these waterways by the people who gave us the lilac, the apple and pear and the rose and the tulip. The willow and the peach came from China. Hollyhocks are blooming around the door of the little adobe house of the *tchaikaneh*. A willow weeps over the low table on which we eat out of doors.

The *tchaikaneh*-man brought us tea (*tchai,* as in China) and truly great bread that looks more like place-mats of heavy brown paper than pancakes. Any Persian who patents this type of unleavened bread and makes it in the States will put pasty white bread out of business. The rest of the meal in this idyllic spot would not be worth remembering if it were not for the melon, THE melon of a lifetime. THE peach, I ate in Georgia, plucking it off the tree where it hung like a golden lantern. THE tomato, I ate in La Ciotat on the French Riviera and THE potato in Tangier. THE melon was not only eaten here, it was cut with THE knife. The moment I saw it, I knew it was THE knife of my life. Perhaps it is just as well I never got to own it, let alone give it to Burroughs, who might learn to use it on the upthrust. The knife is an old hand-tempered steel blade which curves and folds into a shank made of the horn of an ibex, justlikethat. Closed, it looks like a fish whose eyes are the ends of the bolt on which the blade hinges. Moamer got it on an earlier trip from the *tchaikaneh*-man in exchange for his opium pipe. I said: "I want one just like it."

"There isn't another one. I'll give you this one if you really want it."

I did and I do but I never got it, although I gave Moamer in exchange a knife I had from Burroughs, who loves to give them as presents, knowing it is dangerous.

Lawrence was throwing scraps of ham to a foraging hen with one leg in a splint. "If the woman who owns that hen sees her eating ham, then the woman won't eat her . . . not kosher, *haram,*" I said.

"Why, then," said Lawrence, "she'll lay *haram* and eggs."

While we ate, another jeep drove up. "An event to be remembered in the countryside," murmured Moamer, "the meeting on this road of two jeeps."

A dark and plump, slightly dapper city man in a white shirt got out of the jeep with a black case, which he gave to his driver, who handed him a splendid bunch of grapes and drove off. The man bowed slightly to us as he washed his grapes in the fountain and offered them all to us. We refused politely, insisting he keep some for himself. They were the pick of the vineyard, as good as the *stafidi* in Corinth. Moamer bristled when the man drew up a stool and ordered a tea from the *tchaikaneh*-man. He would eat none of our ham but when I rolled a joint, he accepted it solemnly and pulled on it so long that he had to be asked to hand it to Lawrence, who was lying there with his tongue out. Moamer said the man was the visiting male nurse, and when I asked what people around there died of mostly, was properly answered: "Death," said Moamer. "There is no hospital and no transportation except his jeep once a month. He's full of shit. He doesn't care for these people."

"Get that Persian princess," Lawrence hissed, "still jiving on that jazz."

The poor man looked like he spoke English, but he may well not have understood that. We left him there by the fountain, looking wistfully down at his own reflection in the pool with one leg twisted around the other and his arms coiled around him so that one hand under his chin looked like a dove he was fondling. There was something absurdly touching about this post-Hellenic pose. No need to wonder what he was thinking: the big city and sex, these two weirdos from Paris, the lot.

The road down the far side of the ridge to the Shahrud river was the first on which Moamer had to make two and three Y-turns every time we came to a hairpin bend with a hair-raising, breath-taking drop of what looked like anything from five hundred feet down . . . down . . . and down to those silver strands of water at the bottom. And, instead of iron nerves, I had a rusty old hangover deep in my soul. Lawrence was being tossed around in the back like a great Arab lady taking a trip in a howdah, but he rallied to pass us a couple of cans of cold beer from the icebox. Out of sheer bravado, we tossed the empty cans into the landscape, thereby polluting the atmosphere. When Moamer got down to the banks of the Shahrud, he nosed the jeep straight out over the banks of a gully so it reared up like a pony and dropped on its four wheels, running smoothly down into the riverbed, just like he knew all the time it would. Only the poor passenger may lose his teeth or collapse with an attack of asthma.

Years back in the old Beat Hotel, I painted a series of pictures I called *Bathing in the Holy Waters of Alamut.* Thinking these were those, I stripped off to swim. The current is only a couple of feet deep, but strong enough to sweep you away for a dangerous joyride down rapids. But the sun was getting low and Moamer said: "You haven't seen the bad road yet." We crossed a military bridge and started zig-zagging and Y-turning up what Lawrence called Mescaline Mountain, because of the weird faces we saw in the rocks. At the top, we penetrated a real spooky tunnel with a winding path through rockfalls from the roof. This boon to weary travelers was put through by Reza Shah who, Moamer said, "took an interest in Alamut." We took a deep breath when we came out the other side, for there we were, looking twenty miles or more up the Valley of the Assassins. To the left, Lion Mountain, Shir Kuh rises to something like twelve thousand feet with waterfalls flashing off its bare red flanks, down into the river, which runs where it wills through a stone bed almost a half a mile wide, twining ribbons of wild water. A huge tawny rock about three stories high stands by the road down below like a sentinel. Far up the valley are two green patches on plateaus at the bottom of mighty ravines, each denoting a village. If the first one is the Chams Kilaya I find on my map in Nagel, then one of the mightiest Assassins' castle of them all, Maimoun Diz, hangs on a pinnacle some two thousand feet above it. Impossible to identify with certainty even through my 10 × 40 binoculars. With more time one might get a glimpse of it, but it takes real mountaineers to get up there, they say.

Our equipment was pitiful. On my feet, I was wearing a pair of pimps' pumps sewn up for me by the Chelsea Cobblers in London. They were so old and worn that they were comfortable for walking but useless for climbing. They slipped out from under me even on the sidewalks of Teheran. Worse than that, my left foot is totally unreliable since I lost a part of it in a motorbike accident a few years ago. Sure-footed Lawrence was shod with some nifty high heels from Paris, on which he tripped about like a goat. Moamer was wearing some Iranian rope-soled numbers with which he ran through rough mountain streams like a gazelle. We had no idea how little food we had with us, for all that had been left to Moamer. When we came to some houses and he had to ask his way, we wondered if we would ever get there by nightfall. We didn't.

When we came to a bridge, we did not take it but ran on up the riverbank for nearly a mile before we turned into the swift-flowing water and simply churned upstream through the middle. Water and rocks were flying around us but the jeep did not fail and we made it. Fifty yards upstream, we turned and roared up the bank, coming out into a bucolic countryside of green fields and hedges. The hedges, if studied by a paleobotanist, could give one an idea of the age of the road dating back to the Assassins, surely. The rocky track between hedgerows was made for donkeys and mules and not cars. Water tends to rush down it in streams, carving ruts into torrents. Every so often an open irrigation ditch cuts calmly across it, and the jeep rocks and roars through it, nearly jolting Lawrence out of his palanquin. Moamer runs the ruts like they were roller-coasters until we got stuck, and some peasants, on their way home with their cattle, managed to help us get out again as the sun set swiftly at seven.

Up, up and up and, long after dark, we roared up into the almost perpendicular village of Gazour Khan, immediately under Alamut. There was nothing exciting to do in the village that night until we came, you could see that. Sober-faced children and adults stood around stolidly staring at us. They were all wearing rubber shoes cast in a mould to look like they had laces. All the men wear dreary white shirts and dark trousers. Women wear short pleated skirts over their navy-blue pyjama pants and the same shoes as the men. And that is an order! Nearly fifty years ago, now, Reza Shah, father of the present one, issued an order that no one was to wear anything but Western dress and a Pahlavi peaked cap instead of a turban. As a result, perhaps, everyone acts like a lobotomy case in this country, like they had been amputated of their anima. In any Moroccan village, the same villagers would be smiling and swarming all over you. Some kids do follow us up to the spot where we camp for the night, and I notice that the one nearest to me is a dwarf in his twenties. His father is suffering from something in his leg and all I can give him are a few Veganins for the pain. I look in vain for my pinkies, my codeine, which cures colds and the belly-ache, mends broken limbs, and will cover the first installments of even cancer.

We make camp and Alamut is up there, high overhead in the dark. No question of getting up there and spending the night in the castle as Shams and Moamer had done on a previous trip. I am furious. Moamer opens my bottle of vodka and swigs at it, losing the screwcap so that the whole bottle is wasted, later. Then he pulls out his inflatable mattress, pumps it up, sets the better sleeping-bag on it and snuggles down inside without saying goodnight. There are only two beers left to wash down our sandwiches of ham and boloney rolled in pancakes of bread. To cut the melon, I ask for the knife, OUR knife, and Moamer mumbles he has lost it. There is nothing to do but pack it in, so Lawrence gets the remaining sleeping-bag and I roll up in some wet blankets under the stars, which we stare at through the binoculars until we are tired of it.

"Just imagine a three-day-long free-fall through the Milky Way?" suggests Lawrence.

I suddenly find I can't breathe, at the mere thought of it. I fumble around in the dark for my Spinhaler and capsules of Intal. Sitting up, I see several lanterns bobbing around in the dark below us in the most alarming fashion. It looks like a meeting. I nudge Lawrence who sits up gasping: "Jeezus, the vigilantes!" Eventually, two pairs of legs carrying lanterns pass by in the dark on the far side of the chattering brook beside which we have camped. Perhaps they are afraid of us, they are talking so loudly. Later, a few more of them climb past through the night with hoes on their shoulders. Lawrence is surprised to see they are women. "At this hour!" he exclaims. They are the nightshift of water-workers, redirecting their irrigation ditches down to their fields below. We lie there staring up at the 3-D Milky Way some more until I say: "I refuse to believe those are other worlds up there. It is all mere decoration."

Sleep eludes me. The stream two feet away from me is chattering louder since we turned out our lamp. I can hear voices babbling in the brook. Then I hear distant music and drumming. Are those shepherds and shepherdesses calling out to their flocks in the night or is that the water? I hear martial music like armies with silver trumpets and the wild skirling wail of the Mongol pipes, ancestral voices prophesying war. Suddenly, it is Lawrence beside me, laughing. "Sorry to sound so personal but I've just been seeing our arrival in the eyes of the villagers. There you were wearing nothing, apparently, but your pink Indian shirt, unwinding a long pair of white legs covered with mud which you covered with black velvet pants."

"Tomorrow, I want to look good for my meeting with Hassan i Sabbah. I'm going to wear my gold shirt I was wearing in Cannes when Jodorowsky came in to his press conference wearing the same one."

"You remember that English family that was massacred in the South of France where they were camping?"

"And that German hippie in Turkey the other day."

"And what about Easy Rider?"

"Yeah, why don't you roll a last joint with some O in it."

"I'm going to put on my sleep-mask to keep out the stars and start my countdown exercises."

My countdowns are simple enough, something I picked up from the book by Monroe, *Journeys out of the Body*. Burroughs went into *Mind Dynamics*, or whatever they call themselves now, and says they have slightly different techniques, but I've had some real hot-shot successes with my version of this one. My trouble is that I either don't dream or don't remember my dreams on waking. Censor trouble, I suspect. For years, I've claimed that Burroughs diverts my dreams. Be that as it may, I shut my eyes under my sleep mask or leave them wide open as I count down from twenty to zero, making an effort to visualize each number as I go for a spot in space where I say with an attempt at Inflexible Authority: "I fully intend to go out there to meet So-and-So and, when I get back, I'll remember all about it." Sometimes, I have taken quite a hectoring tone. Just as often, or more often than not, nothing happens. This night, of course, I demand to meet Hassan i Sabbah.

The Old Man and I are walking along a high reef of rock looking out over his island, his very last electronically guarded island, presumably in the Azores. It is late in the day and an ominous lead-colored light floods level across the limited landscape under a low lid of clouds, casting long shadows ahead of us as we climb. Impossible to remember what we were talking about because a trio of his agents, his faithful Fida'i-in, suddenly materializes uncomfortably close behind us, supposedly reporting in to the Old Man. I bristle instinctively but he merely takes a real sloppy salute like he is wiping his mouth with a soiled napkin. I glare at these guys. I know they are supposed to be high-mountain Basque herdsmen, back from Vizcaya on home leave but their eyes look a lot too slanty to me. Something gone wrong in

Transmission. I have no time to say this because the landscape erupts behind me. When I whirl around, I can see that our fort on the far side of the island is burning, having fallen under rocket fire. I glare at the Old Man. This is the result of his absent-minded oversight. He forgot to throw in some switch and now all is lost. He looks like a disenchanted Prospero, as played by William S. Burroughs. I glance down at my hands, as instructed by Don Juan, and they are hairy. Am I Caliban? What is the Old Man going to do now? He simply fans out his fine old fingers and raises his shoulders in the old junky shrug. In his deep-set blue eyes, I catch a cold glint of what is it? the knife-edge of laughter perhaps? Or is this old Granny O that I have here in front of me? "That's the life, son," she drawls, "Son cosas de la vida."

In the first light of day, I lie back in my blankets and look up at Alamut through my binoculars. It is higher by far than I thought it would be. "Impossible!" I murmur. The word wakes Lawrence who wants to look, too. "Has someone restored it?" What he refers to are big patches of yellow and red brickwork looking almost brand new, plastered right on the side of the high rocky parapet. The only explanation for these is that the Mongols could not get to them. But how did anyone ever put them there in the first place? Forests of poplar poles must have been tied into scaffolding to cover the cliff-face. Peter Willey, who has written the most recent books about them, says: "The Assassins were at least as capable as the Crusaders—who were responsible for their drugs and murder image—in their brilliant construction of castles, their use of natural land and water resources, their adaptability to political circumstances and their appreciation of the arts. Their system of fortifications was well ahead of its time. Theirs was a very advanced strategic concept of defense in depth which we did not develop again until well into the 20th century."

Because we dawdled, the sun was well up in the sky by the time we got started. By daylight, we could see that our babbling brook was actually a quick-running cascade, tumbling down through an irrigation ditch bordered by the narrow path up which the night-workers with lanterns had come to regulate their sluices. On the far side of that, yawned a precipitous canyon from which the water had been diverted to serve the village directly below the green platform on which we had spent the night. Looking almost straight up into the light, we could see that Lion Mountain is all striped by such colossal canyons with sharp hogsback ridges between them. Alamut rock thrust up between a network of these ancient erosions that make it stand out from the rest of the mountainside like a natural fortress on which only eagles would think of building a nest.

Providentially, a man with a mule came along and carried me up the first lap, until we got to the spot where even a sure-footed mule could not go any further. Less sure-footed by far, I slipped off his back to look down the hellish deep pit that still another stream has cut around the back of the castle rock. "Don't fall in!" cried Moamer. I had not thought of it yet, but I did then and I went on thinking or dreaming about it for the next couple of days thereafter. Worse than that, I had an all but irresistible urge to throw myself over. Where this urge may be coming from, I'll think about later. For my very entrails were grabbed and my eyeballs seemed to jump in their sockets as I stared out across this almost bottomless red pit at what looked like an emerald saucer hovering in space, hung between the silver rivulet of the stream so far down below and the sun-tipped summit of Shir Kuh towering like an angry cloud above. For a long moment, I could simply not take in what I was seeing, until I looked at it through my binoculars. Then, I could not believe my eyes when I saw it. That far cliff was still in deep shadow and my 10 × 40 glasses are so strong that to see through them clearly demands that one rest them on something solid. My hands trembled and sweat poured down into my eyes. I had the dry heaves, mountain sickness from the thin air at this altitude, and I was gasping with asthma. The bright dancing image I caught, jiggled around like a drop of water on a redhot stove. When my hand was steadied, what I saw was still running like a reflection seen in a windowpane streaming with rain. What is it, what can it be? I kept asking myself. I decide it is Paradise, Paradise garden as seen in a raindrop. So, there really *was* a garden, I sighed.

Why, there still *is* a garden, I panted as I climbed on up after Moamer and Lawrence and a small mountain boy who had attached himself to us. I gave him my binoculars to carry and the copy of *Naked Lunch* bought in the airport in Isfahan. I needed my hands free, for my feet were too big for the goat-path across the vast curtain of loose rubble which hangs from right under the castle, down and down and on down without a shrub or a blade of grass to cling onto should one make one single mis-step. And there was still worse to come for, at one point, I heard a cold voice say inside me: "You can't make it." I dared not look down but I twisted around to glance again at the garden and saw that the first rays of the sun had just struck it. All the dew on the poplar trees and green terrace of grass, greener than any seen this side of Heaven, was turned in an instant to vapor. A cloud like one's breath on a mirror burned off this tiny plateau, like a miniature garden on a tea tray hung out over the gulf where Alph the sacred river ran through caverns measureless to man down to a boundless sea. I could not go back, so I scrambled on up to Alamut, gasping like a fish out of water.

At the top of the scree, the solid rock at the peak has been cut through from one side to the other by a tunnel which I would not like to have to stand up in when the wind is blowing. I threw myself on its floor, feeling around for my Spinhaler only to find that I had forgotten it in the pocket of my other shirt. That gave me time to think a few thoughts about my asthma, for it is a fairly new acquisition of mine these last four or five years, instead of the classic asthma which the victims suffer since childhood. In my childhood my mother had the asthma, not me. At three and four years of age, I used to like to listen to her chest when she had a crisis of bronchitis. "Brown kittens," I called it. Later, she had to get rid of a chow dog she dearly loved because its fur gave her asthma. So, when doing research through some really insane books on modern psychiatry, I came across this far-fetched analysis, I made a note of it:

"An asthma attack is brought about by separation anxiety and means that the patient is trying to inhale his mother, so that he can keep her safely inside his chest in order to feel permanently protected. At times, he has fantasies that she is already within him and this brings about a struggle between his ego and the respiratory apparatus 'containing' her."

Wow, does it ever! And who is this inside me, pray, who is trying to push me over? I simply can't look out the front end of this tunnel because the flat roofs of the village are fifteen hundred feet down there beneath my feet and the soles of my shoes are so badly worn that they slip and slide under me even on the paved streets of Teheran, I keep reminding myself. Have I climbed all the way up here to have a wrestling match with the ghost of my mother, whose asthma I suffer from only since she died, far away and alone and in misery? Or is this the Old Man himself, who is said to have delighted in throwing strong men over? When the Frankish so-called King of Jerusalem came here to parlay with him, Hassan i Sabbah is said to have simply snapped his long bony fingers at a sentinel posted right up here where I am clinging right now and the boy jumped, snapping to attention in full flight as he flashed past the astonished eyes of the Norman usurper. Burroughs loves this example of Inflexible Authority, and I used it myself in *The Process*. I had better be careful.

A severely plain shepherdess of about fourteen, dressed in their national travesty of Western clothes, suddenly appears with three goats behind her and offers me a handful of broken shards of pottery she has culled from the landslide of ruins of this castle destroyed by the Mongols just seven hundred and twenty-three years ago. "Snow came late to the Alborz mountains and the valley of Alamut that winter of 1256," the historian, Juvayni, records. "Men of a hundred years of age could not remember such a mild winter. It made things easier for the Mongol invader. Hulagu's hordes assaulted the castle with mangonels and the ears of its defenders with wild pipes screaming constantly for three days and nights until the nerves of the besieged cracked and crumbled like the walls of Jericho. At Hulagu's orders, the last Grand Master of the Assassins, Rokneddin the Parricide, was thrown over the same cliff which had provided such sport for his predecessor, Hassan i Sabbah."

Who am I, Rokneddin? Never.

Moamer and Lawrence and the goat-footed mountain boy of about ten came back at that point to say they had climbed further up, and Moamer had even followed the local lad out around the edge of the cliff and down into a sort of cistern cut out of the rock. He claimed that he had been so scared shit-less that it had been hard to get back again. There were the remains of paintings on plaster, he said, defaced by centuries of graffiti. I have no desire to see this, ever. I had very little desire to climb further up, either, so I lit up a joint and just sat there transfixed in the niche of some ancient Fida'i sentinel, staring stoned across at the hanging Garden of Delights as it floated out over the dark red abyss and into the sunlight like a miniature Paradise planet carved out of jade and flashing with emeralds. "Yakh Chal," the boy said, pointing to it. Moamer laughed. "He says it is called the Ice Box or the Frigidaire, probably because the sun strikes it so late in the day. Yakh means ice and Chal is a ditch or a hole. Hence, the Icebox." It looks fairly close, but the boy says it takes a whole day to get there and a day to get back.

The round keep of the castle is the largest heap of stones still standing on Alamut, and the goat-path to the upper terraces winds around it. No point in looking down around there, either. The view from the top is like a blow in the brain, overwhelmingly unsettling. Covered with snow and ice as it is in the wintertime, windswept and battered by storms, it must be even more terrifying. Keeping my eyes on my feet to be sure what they were doing, I came with gratitude into what Shams called the court of the castle somewhat grandly. It looks more like a room about ten by sixteen feet which has collapsed and the floor fallen in, filling up a foundation cut into the rock. It holds water or seems to, for a few spiky sedges were sticking up among the fallen hand-hewn blocks of what looked to be limestone. A corner of wall still stands and I had Lawrence take a picture of me in front of it. "For Rolling Stone Enterprises, click!" he cried, clattering away after the mountain boy on his high heels from Paris. When I was sure of what I was holding onto, I craned out with my binoculars and got a really close view of the brickwork. Even the Mongols could not pry it off the cliff face, and it looks as if the bright red and bright yellow bricks had been laid yesterday. When the Mongols were trashing the castle, curtain walls over empty expanses between projecting rocks were easier to kick out completely, but traces of masonry remain on either side of these gaps and one is still crossed by an arch over a hole or horrible chute, through which one could slide so easy and glide right down onto the flat roof of the village, except for that deep canyon between us.

Looking around at what remains up there, one is bound to conclude that most of the figures anyone advances about the Assassins are fanciful. First of all, the space is small, no matter what towers and turrets were built on it. For a long time, it was thought that Alamut was the only castle belonging to the sect, but several more have been discovered as recently as 1972, and now it is recognized that they had fortified at least three valleys in depth and their strongholds reached out to Syria in one direction and unto the marches of Afghanistan in the other. The capital castle of Alamut may well have been an all but impregnable stronghold, held by but a handful of picked men around the Grand Master, who ruled through the power of his mind as well as by his long knife. The long knife, after all, was wielded by one single man at a time. No need of vast hungry armies to pamper.

The final downfall of the Assassins is said to have been brought about by someone named Tousi, who had been kidnapped and held in Alamut. By the time Tousi was ransomed, he had learned the weaknesses of the last Grand Master, Rokneddin, who was said to have killed his own father. Tousi gave the plan of the castle to the Mongols on the condition that he would inherit the library of Alamut, which has been said by some historians to have comprised the extravagant number of two hundred thousand volumes. Even this number of modern books would need a huge space to be stored and consulted. Ancient handwritten manuscript on parchment would be even bulkier. Nowhere in the ruins as one sees them today would there be place for such a collection. Perhaps what these writers referred to was the power in these books, for the Assassins inspired many other secret societies in Asia and in Europe who adopted their techniques of iron discipline and their philosophy that the end justifies the means. In Europe, their methods of initiation, their method of appointing officers, their emblems and their insignia and other trappings were imitated by such groups as the Knight Templars, the Hospitallers and the Society of Jesus, the Jesuits founded by Ignatius Loyola. Today, Opus Dei in Spain is said to owe much to someone's studies of the Ismailis. Are there others?

Fire: Words by Day— Images by Night

"Fire: Words by Day—Images by Night" (1975) was first published in the Gysin issue of Udo Breger's journal Soft Need *(no. 17). The piece provides a fascinating glimpse of Gysin's concerns at a crucial moment, after he had survived several operations for cancer, including a colostomy. The North African desert settings of his first novel,* The Process, *merge with his reflections on death and the afterlife that would later dominate his second novel,* The Last Museum, *framed by the narrator in his hospital bed struggling with the cruel ironies of his fate. Intercut with these points is a series of more or less autobiographical episodes, often dealing with sex and death; some, like the tale of the colonel at Brighton, were taken up again later in his small book of childhood memoirs and also in his final novel.*

Words by Day   Images by Night

Here he lies where he swore he never would be. "Live it out with an open hole in my gut and a plastic sack of shit on my lap for the rest of my days? Not me!"

So he cried then, but here he lies now in this stinking hospital cot with his rectum removed. Enough. Now he knows that he is not a man, as the Arabs would say, not a man of one word. No. If he had been he would not be lying here with his asshole sewn up like a duck, like a stuffed duck, and all his own filth pouring unchecked from a permanent hole in his colon. Not he. He would be back out there in the infinite Sahara with them and, with any luck, dead. But, alas, he was not the slave of his word, so: here he lays himself open to what possible purpose between life and death, while he writhes away melodramatically in agony, shame and despair? All but unable to live. Afraid and unwilling to die. Poor He.

That night I am suddenly, dazzlingly out in the Sahara again on a trail I know well. The perfect path. It is hardly more than the faintest of tracks, leading from nowhere to nowhere, not marked on any map. The passage of men with camels and wheels has left a wandering trace across the black reg. This glassy bedrock of basalt is scoured and polished with golden sand blown by the hot wind which whistles and howls down from the low-lying dunes to each side. Here I am where I want to be. I know and I love this place. I have been here before and it fills me with inexpressible joy to be back. Naked and alone in all this blinding glitter of sand and sun, I am utterly unafraid. No baggage. This is the way I came and this is the way I must return. I could burst with the joy of it. As instructed, I hold out my hands in front of me to inspect them, to make sure I am here. I am. I look down at my entire body, running my hands over my unscarred belly, my cock and my ass, poking my right middle finger right up my rectum, clutching it tight with the ring of my sphinctre to make sure. I am whole. The unthinkable operation has been a bad hospital dream. I give a great shout that echoes out over this unutterably beautiful desert.

The bright curtain of sand falters and falls at my feet. Far ahead and perhaps at a crossroads but at a distance I cannot judge, there is a tiny domed Arab construction, a white-washed *koubba* which could be the tomb of a distinguished traveler or even that of a small and forgotten desert saint. I remember it well, a half-ruined structure of sun-baked bricks with an elegant egg-shaped dome. I must get there again, but when I take one single stride towards it the golden curtain of sand rises in front of me. I am in total darkness. I am awake.

Here he lies in his bed, weeping like a woman: except that these women who surround him day and night are nurses who do not weep even in the scary and sorrowful face of death. All around him in the ward, cancerous old women die in the early morning, totally exhausted by their long nights of grimly determined struggle, die with a little gasp of disbelief. Old men die in the evening shouting their lungs out, terrified of the cold and the dark. Do not go gentle into that dark night, Pops. What are you fighting for? There is nothing to fight. Life and Death are a draft between two open doors marked: In & Out. Your own arrival did not open them nor will your departure close them if you leave tonight.

I wake up screeching like a bat in an empty room, attached to an iron bed under bright lights. I know at once where I am. I am in the Yellow Wing, the dread of all expendable agents up for termination of contract with extreme prejudice for talking too much. I am in agony. The agency has purposely fumbled an atomic experiment made upon me. I am in agony, agony. U.S. Army Intelligence has castrated me, made me a eunuch and snatched my entire asshole right out from under me. What they have in store for me here is much worse than death. Having ruined my body forever, they now want the rest of me. They have shot me up with an overdose of their soul-destroying hallucinogen to work on my nerve fluid, their new secret drug, BZ.

They ripped out my rectum and cut off my coccyx at the end of my spine, to really get in there and scoop me out like a rotten old cantaloupe, tearing and twisting all the yards of my guts so that shit comes uncontrollably pouring out of a permanent hole in my side as big as an old silver dollar. My stoma. Look, here is my artificial anus gurgling like an obscene baby mouth that spews blood, mucous, and a long soft snake of shit into a plastic sack that sticks onto me with a ring of karaya gum. Seen through my plastic bag when it is clean, my stoma looks like a shiny wet rosebud of tender intestinal flesh with a puckered border of stitches oozing blood around the edges of its petals. In this operation my navel has been pulled far over to my right side and they have given me a new belly-button with a plastic tube sticking up out of it. Because I am not the man I was, they have given me a new name on my chart: Neugeboren. Mr. Newborn. I know a German joke when I hear one. Or is that the name of the man dying in the room next to mine?

Out, out! I must get the hell out of here. I throw my wasted legs over the side of my bed and fall to the floor with a yell like one of those old men. I have torn a needle as thick as my little finger out of the vein in my right arm which was attached by a plastic tube to a drip of whole blood, a bright red glass jar of blood taped to the bedstead. In agony, agony, I pull out the catheter stuck deep into what is left of my cock. Then I yank the tube out of my belly and fall flat on the floor across which I slither in the blood and shit gushing out of me. As I try to get up on my hands and knees, I see a thick yellow gas flowing down the walls of my prison, welling up all around me. I have been hermetically sealed into this room. Pulling myself up by one leg of the bed, I see that one wall is made of ground glass, I don't know how thick. I must break it. I know I am on the seventh floor of this building but I must smash that glass and throw myself out. People have fallen further than that and survived. I don't care. One way or the other. I want out. The metal chair in the bathroom will do it. But when I crawl into the bathroom and pull myself up by the washbasin to the level of the mirror what I see is so strange that I faint, perhaps. As I fall I pull a cord which sets off an alarm and in comes my night nurse, black Sister Geneva, to wrestle me back into bed. It takes her forever. Back in the bed, it takes her another eternity to poke the fingerthick tubes back into my veins and my body. In the process, both she and I are covered from head to foot in my blood and my shit. Suddenly I realize it. This is love. This is true love and I laugh.

"Why do you laugh?"
"Woman, you call me down if I cry and you call me down if I laugh."
"Are you laughing at me?"
"No, it is I who am inane. I can't cry any more so I laugh at myself. Why should I be laughing at you, girl? You are the very first woman in my life that I've ever had a crush on and now it's too late, so I laugh."
"You're so vain."

"She is black and she is beautiful. She has hands like silk but a tongue like a thorn and even her mind crackles with starch! All artists are vain, baby, and that's the very first time in my life that I hear myself calling me that, an artist!"

"Why, are you ashamed of it?"

"Maybe. An American lady artist I knew a long time ago went to Egypt with 'artiste' on her passport and the Egyptian cops pulled her in as an unlicensed whore."

"Is that what you are?"

"No. I am a man, a mere man, no matter what roles I have played in no matter whose bed. Now that I am not a man any more, I'd be better off dead."

"You're ungrateful."

"Yeah, that's what Sister Felicity says. Practice makes perfect. I'll make it next time."

"Life and Death are only one breath apart."

"If I could believe that I'd leave you tonight."

"You can't, I won't let you. Besides, no one ever died yet from just holding his breath."

"That's all you know, Sister Morphine. Just wheel on the drug trolley, will you. I've got a date."

That next night, I am out on my trail again, nearer this time to the *koubba*. Much nearer. I can almost reach out to touch its ruined doorstep as I collapse. It must have rained around here since I last came this way and they say it may not rain more than once in a lifetime in this exquisitely perfect desert. Was it that long ago? The saltpetre crust of the whitewash has broken in places where the rainwater ran down blood red from the soft bricks which someone unknown piled up to erect this empty monument in the middle of this empty universe. I glance down at my hands as instructed and see that they are running with blood. Perhaps some passing assassins have slaughtered someone here or sacrificed a camel to splatter these crumbling mud walls with blood. No time to tell because blackness falls like a blow on the nape of my neck and I am back in my blood-stained bed again. In the darkness. Awake. English rain is pouring down the glass wall of my hospital ward. The downpour has utterly melted and wiped out my little *koubba,* reducing its elegant egg-shaped dome and thick walls to a heap of rubble, like an evil magician's cruel trick. And I laugh.

"What are you laughing at now?"

"I was just thinking that William S. Burroughs could probably commit suicide by holding his breath, if he wanted to."

"Oh, you and your fancy friends, poo! I'm in charge here and I can't, I won't let you go."

"What were you telling me about the Sisters of Mercy you worked for, what they do for the terminal cases?"

"Oh, the good sisters, the nuns! They dole out the elixir of morphine like cough syrup or they leave a full bottle of tincture of heroin by the patient's bed."

"Mother of Morphine: Tincture of Horse! Even Burroughs never mentioned such marvels to me. Why can't I have some, an overdose?"

"You told Professor yourself not to give you any more opiates, didn't you? It's marked on your chart."

"I don't want to leave here with a habit. I just want to go. I just want to go quietly so, why can't I have a Sister of Mercy come in here and take care of me right with a nice little overdose? After all, I was brought up a Catholic."

"The good sisters might say you were being punished for your sins."

"What sins? Sexual sins against old Mother Nature, namely: Mrs. X. God? God is terrible and She is Black!"

"And you claim you are a black man, yourself, a black man in a white man's skin."

"Wow! Have I been telling you that in my delirium? I must be telling you everything, everything. Yes, I've often said that and thought it was true."

"But both your parents were white."

"Sure, I was slipped into the wrong colored packaging and delivered to the wrong address. I was a mistake in the mail. Just look at all this lousy oatmealy skin. Not enough melanin. I've lived the best years of my life in Morocco and it can't take the sun. When I'm with Africans, I forget that I'm white. But they can't forget it. I stick out like a sore thumb. From miles away across the deserts or mountains, I look like a colonial cop or a mercenary. What side am I on?"

"Roll over here and I'll show you."

"Sister Morphine, are you trying to tell me that I am a martyr to Love? That I've been impaled like this because I loved my fellow men not wisely but too well, in fact, inordinately? It may be so but I wouldn't want to believe that of old Madame X., not even of Her!"

"You be careful of Her."

"Oh, I know, She has sent me Sister Geneva to straighten me out but it's too late. It's too late for me, now. I've taken my pain pills for tonight and it's back to the desert for free!"

Sure enough, this is the third night and I am actually inside the *koubba*. The space is extremely restricted, about six by six feet and the interior is half-filled with drifted sand. Forgetting my basic instructions, I look down at my feet which are shod in a pair of those handsome yellow and red leather desert boots they make by hand out of gazelle skin in the oasis of El Golea. I am wearing a voluminous blue desert garment dyed with indigo, as big as a bedspread with a hole for my head in the middle, flapping around my bare body in the *gaila,* the hot desert wind. I wear nothing else. I scuff at the sand with the toe of my boot, unearthing the corner of a fine woven mat of the kind they make all over Africa where there are reeds growing by rivers, even those fossil rivers which flow underground. I bend down to pull at a corner of the mat, half expecting it to come away in my hand but, to my surprise, this reed mat is of fairly recent manufacture, still in good shape. When I stand up, I notice a big hole in the wall to my right through which I can walk, followed by Garmeeta, to my surprise. I didn't know she was here. She is not wearing her starched white nurse's uniform but the same sort of indigo blue garment that I am. Hers is cut and draped differently with big silver brooches holding the loose folds of it together on her shoulders, showing her big black breasts. She stands so close to me that I can smell and identify the curious African perfume in her hair: "Bint El Sudan." Her hair is done up so elaborately that it must have taken several women a week to work on her kinky curls with a hot iron like worked horsehair woven with cowrie shells. It looks like a curious sort of hollow crown. "Garmeeta of the Garamantians," I say to myself without emotion. "Why does she have to be here?"

Outside in the Sahara in the shade of the crumbling *koubba,* some curious tribe of small squat people comes suddenly rushing over the dune to sit down in a row. There are six or eight of these curious dwarfs whom I take to be the survivors of the original inhabitants of these sands before they dried up. They pay no attention to us while they set out their merchandise on the ground as itinerant Arabs do in a *souk.* What they have to sell, apparently, are loaves of something wrapped in heavy gray plastic. I read the word FORT on them and I jump to the conclusion that these must be loaves of plastic explosive stolen from some faraway military installation. I turn to look at Garmeeta when she touches my arm. She is shaking her head to tell me: "Don't have anything to do with these people. Pretend they're not there." These little people are wiped out by her words. When I look back they are fading out with demoniacal grimaces, shaking their fists. A great blast of sand sweeps down from the dune and envelops us all. I almost smother as I swirl through a sort of siphon. I am awake.

"Were you asleep or were you hallucinating?"

"You make them both sound like crimes. What are you trying to do to me, woman: take my dreams away from me, too? You were in this last one, as a matter of fact."

"I know."

"How do you know?"

"You were calling my name."

"Geneva?"

"No. I told you I hated that name."

"Oh, did you? And when?"

"Just now, when you asked me."

"What did I ask you?"

"My real name. I told you my real Island name is Garmeeta."

"Voodoo? Rastafarian?"

"Something like that. So what's in a name?"

"Everything. The world is as we name it. Nothing more, nothing less. So, your real name is Garmeeta. Do you know who the Garamantians were?"

"Yes."

"You have to be kidding me. Who?"

"The charioteers who left the first track on the desert with chariots. Didn't Herodotus write about them?"

"You know too much for a nurse."

"Why shouldn't I? Because I am black?"

Snow, beautiful snow, as blue as cocaine. Or is it sand? Sometimes at night in the desert under the full moon, all the dunes seem to turn into blue snow cold enough to freeze your bare feet in the silky sands. But he is too small to be walking alone at night and he is traveling very fast. He brushes the cold snow from his own icy nose and tastes it, numbing his tongue and his gums. He wipes his chapped lips with the back of his ice-covered mitt. He is lying on his back in the bottom of a big box, a fast horse-drawn sled which speeds along like the stars streaming away overhead beyond the lacy, snow-covered trees. He is covered with rank-smelling buffalo robes and gigantic grown-ups are looming above him. They are swigging down bottles of bootleg liquor against the cold weather and singing at the top of their lungs: *He Swore That He Loved Her But Oh How He Lied!* They are sailing over the hard snow through the crackling night with the colored curtains of the Northern Lights swinging overhead. They are on their way to a wild winter wedding in the wilderness where they are waiting for him: Uncle Bill, his Mother, and Uncle Phil. The horses are steaming with sweat. Great plumes of steam stream out of their nostrils when the sled stops in a clearing high above a frozen river. Everything is pure white except the snow underfoot when he is lifted down, gasping at the smell of bootleg whisky on their breath. The lovely snow has been trampled and stained bright yellow with horseshit and horsepiss in the light of a swinging lamp. A huge bonfire in the middle of the clearing has blackened the snow. In its flickering light, birch trees are dancing, birch trees from whose bark the Red Indians made their canoes. There are no more birch-bark canoes. The Indians have departed and we have come.

Swaddled in muskrat furs and unable to walk, he is picked up and shown to all the shiny red faces flushed by the whisky and the fire. He hears a half-hearted cheer from them as he is carried into a cabin, a log cabin where he is set down on a bunk covered with an old stained Hudson Bay blanket with red and white stripes. A rifle and a huge cartridge belt bulging with bullets hangs over his head. "Whose kid is that?" asks someone unknown and is told that he is the bride's child by her first husband, Missing In Action in the last war overseas. She comes in on Uncle Bill's arm, her head on his shoulder. You can see that they love each other, whatever that means. Uncle Bill catches wild animals like the silver fox and small boys in his traps. One day last winter, he walked into one. That is why they cut off his toes and he cannot walk. They go out and everyone goes with them. Uncle Phil comes in and he looks different. Uncle Phil built this log cabin to live in with Uncle Bill. Uncle Phil is very sad. When Uncle Bill and his Mother walk in the woods together without him, what they do, what they do! People are cheering and stomping around in the dirty snow outside the cabin, howling with alcohol and shooting off guns. Uncle Phil bends over and kisses him as he picks the rifle off the nail over his head, takes one shell out of the heavy cartridge belt and shucks it into the gun, well greased. For a moment, the gun wavers around wildly in every direction, even pointing at his head. Gravely, he tells Uncle Phil that you're not supposed to do that. Uncle Phil is as sorry as a grownup person can be, which isn't much, and he goes out behind the log cabin where no one can see him. There is a lot of drunken cheering and wild gunfire going on outside in the firelight but one single shot penetrates through the rest of the noise and they stop. Outside, someone crazy starts shouting that Uncle Phil has put the gun in his mouth and shot off the top of his head. Someone else picks him up and they speed away under the stars. He is sleepy but he says something smart to hide his sorrow and terror. What is it? A grownup says: "That tongue of yours will get you into trouble all of your life." Something hits him hard in the mouth and he wakes.

"I picked up a black boy under the arcades of Regent Street at Piccadilly and he swore that, for money, he would show me what it was all about. He had been whipping Englishmen for years, tying them up. He had bound them face down on their beds, tied them up in their kitchens and hoisted them to the ceiling on their clothes-drying racks, beaten them to a pulp before or after fucking them in the ass and the mouth. Now, why in the hell would they want him to do such things to them and pay for it, too? I had to find out. In an old suede jacket and Levis, I made the rounds of the baths and the leather bars but no one, for either love or money, would even talk to me, let alone show me what it was all about. If you have to ask, they all told me, you don't need to know. Like a fool, I kept repeating that I was interested in pain. Apparently, the subconscious doesn't know how to take a joke. Now I know.

"Tell me, nurse, do you think I really did all this to myself? If I did, why did I do it? Who is this I who would do this to me? What enemy voice got in here with me and properly impaled me on my own I? Is all this a joke, a cruel joke of the most exquisite malevolence? Look at what happened to my old Sufi friend, Professor Shah, who stepped out of his doorway in Tangier and was crushed by a runaway truck before he could manage to mumble his mantra and I don't even know one! On the back of the truck was written Orange Crush. *What kind of Joker is that and who is mine?*

"The only desirable death is the Lust Todt. *I've named it for our German friends: the Lust Death. Not the appallingly boring old* Liebestodt *with some screaming soprano caterwauling over a corpse. No, the Real Thing. Death dealt in the moment when two men are one. Death dealt by one's other self. You know, I think that's what I've done to myself but this method's too slow. I've got to rewrite it along the lines of what happened to two old schoolmates of mine.*

"Look at what happened to Oliver, he had all the luck. At eighteen, I handed him over the editorship of our school magazine and then life opened a long parenthesis between us. Picture him all these years later, ghostwriting the Autobiography of the Queen for her in his luxurious London digs. Wrapped in nothing but a loose Persian robe, he is writing with a peacock plume. His valiant valet, as the newspapers called him, is at work in the kitchen when he realizes that they need a really sharp knife for the roast. Doorbell rings and in come two likely lads from the Meat Rack under the Arcade. Oliver pours them two Bloody Marys and sends one of these young Irishmen out for a carving knife. The remaining Mick whips out a length of clothesline and ties poor old Oliver up for the last time of many. Fucking him in the ass with his dirty big uncircumcised cock, this leprechaun marks time until the knife comes back from the sharpening. Which it does. So, poor old Ollie comes for the last time on the rug as they cut his throat. Death in Orgasm! Mm, what luck!"

"You'd like that?"

"Scary, eh? Now, look at this little item in tonight's paper. It's only a very small headline but it jumped out at me from across the ward. Catholic Priest Found Bound in Bathtub. *Somehow, I don't know how, I knew at once who it was and I hadn't thought about him ever in all these years. He was my redheaded hero of school days but I never spoke to him again when he decided to become a priest. Did I guess even then that he too would get his* Lust Todt? *I can't say I did.* The nuns in whose convent he had lunch every day found him fully clothed. *Hm, that's what the nuns say. They would.* A young man seen climbing out of the bathroom skylight was caught as he jumped from the roof. *Lucky Tony, is all I can say, and poor young man. Leave me now, girl, I want to depart to where I am."*

He goes, not to the desert as he intended but, of all places, to Brighton, and he is only four. The Colonel is taking him for a walk out on the wooden pier to see the live Golliwogs. His own Golliwog is under his arm, a black satin doll of royal African elegance, just his own sozie and whom he loves more than dear life. Golliwog has a splendid Afro wig of fine Persian lamb fur, bright shoe-button eyes and a smile a mile wide. He wears a double-breasted scarlet satin waistcoat with solid gold buttons, a swallowtail coat and long gingham pants in a black and white check. When you pull down his pants, Mr. G. has a twist of black taffeta for a cock the size, or a bit more than the size of his own. The Colonel keeps a live weasel buttoned up in *his* pants.

Eldridge Cleaver lets it all hang out. Mr. Big Brown Bear, he comes in behind some old friends from Katmandu: Ira, Jerry, and Anne who met him at a poetry reading where he was pushing his pants. Cleavers, he calls them. He goes around the corner into the bathroom with a little suitcase he is carrying and, a few minutes later, he comes back wearing the first pair of Cleavers. It is to gasp. High-waisted matador skin-tight two-tone brown and beige bell-bottoms on Cleaver's frame is already something but this well-proportioned cock-piece with his own horse cock stuffed firmly inside it is too much for the little boy who learned from the Colonel. The penny drops as he reaches out to grab. Eldridge, utterly unruffled, has already launched into his sexual politics spiel about penis pride and society, what to do about automatic erections in public, being body language and Yours Very Sincerely written in the most sincere language of them all. Ira keeps yelping: "The spear of Longinus, the Spear of Destiny! Constantine had it, Charlemagne had it, the Hohenstauffens and Hitler had it. Can't you see that it's the same thing!" Cleaver is cool. He disappears for a minute and comes back in a black velvet model with a black velvet cock-piece. Now you see it and now you don't. Eldridge is batting back eager questions about copyright and percentages and agents' fees and marketing and the whole textile industry being involved. He is going to make millions of dollars and bring about a world-wide sexual revolution leading to Liberty, what else? The Colonel, who has been sitting quietly in a corner as he diddles the little boy on his knees, gives a terrible snort, lets the little boy slide off his knees onto the hard hospital floor, and stamps out of the room stiffly, in a rage.

The Colonel is an Old Family Friend, complete with carnation in his lapel and a narrow smile made of many false teeth carved out of ivory for him by a Chinese dentist in Kuwait. For forty years, the Colonel was a Secret Agent on the Persian Gulf. He knew all those hot dusty desert countries long before they found oil or had, even, well-defined borders marked on the map. It was his job to keep them like that. Playing off one Arab sheikhdom against another was a perilous game, more like parcheesi with its snakes and ladders than like chess, but he had one great advantage: he liked what the sheikhs liked, hunting with falcons and very young boys. For him, a boy over thirteen years of age was already an old man. He was a real chicken hawk. Sometimes, this got him into great favor at court and sometimes, even there in the Gulf, that got him thrown into a deep dungeon, usually over a case of sexual jealousy and jealousy can be a cruel jailer. The Foreign Office, knowing what risks he ran, had him fitted out with a cyanide capsule in a hollow tooth, in case he was tortured and forced to let down the side. He never did. So, when he retired from the Service, he came home to England to settle down by the seaside at Brighton where the chickens, the working-class chickens run wild and nice little lads of good family, still under thirteen, can be plucked as they run around in the shallows at low tide with a pail and a prawn-catching net. He netted a lot. He promised trusting mothers to take their little boys out on the long wooden pier where the blackface comedians in red-and-white-striped blazers and straw boaters strummed their banjos in a base imitation of American blacks.

This little boy hates them at sight, a whole lot. This little boy cries, stamps his feet on the boardwalk, screams with rage when he sees these outrageous white men with shoeblack on their faces right up to their piggy pink eyes. The Colonel bends down, snapping at Mr. Golliwog with his bright yellow teeth. This little boy is so surprised that he shuts up. The Colonel gives him a first penny and then a second one as he steers the little boy and his Golliwog into a cabin, shutting the door. The first penny is to get your fortune told, later, and the second penny is not to tell as the Colonel takes down his pants. The first penny goes into Golliwog's waistcoat pocket but the second penny gets lost. As the Colonel grabs the little boy's paw to put it on his penis, the penny drops. The penny not to tell drops between the floorboards and is lost in the sea far below. When he is finished, the Colonel grabs back his first penny, furious because the second penny has been lost. Outside the cabin, there is a glass case with the upper half of an old Gypsy woman inside of it. When you put a penny in her slot, her head wobbles and her eyes roll around in her head as her stiff waxy hand deals out a card, a handwritten card with your fortune. His card reads: *You will be happy all your long life with lots and lots of children but no wife!* This little boy dances up and down as his fortune is read to him. This little boy wants his fortune card to take home with him but the Colonel coldly refuses. The fortune, like the penny, belongs to him. This little boy hugs his Golliwog, frowning. This little boy tells his mother all about it when he gets home.

When the Colonel hears from the little boy's mother, he reaches into the back of his mouth and unscrews his tooth. The capsule of cyanide falls out into the palm of his hand. He holds it up to the light. It is full, of course. So, he pops it into his mouth and crunches it like an after-dinner mint. He falls back in his bed, writhing in agony. He goes on like this for a long time, all night. In the morning, his charwoman lets herself in with her key and finds him with a mouthful of bloody feathers from having eaten his pillow and bitten his wrists until they bled. Here he is lying in a pool of black and bright yellow bile laced with blood but he is still partly conscious. She runs out to call the Pakistani doctor who lives down the street. The Pakistani doctor sniffs the bitter almond smell of the cyanide and starts asking questions like: Where did you get it? The Colonel keeps a stiff upper lip, never admits that he was ever in any Foreign Service. Don't know what you're talking about, never heard of any such thing in my life. The Colonel keeps a stiff upper lip until he recovers, only to find that he can no longer have an orgasm, let alone get it up.

The little boy's mother does not press her complaint, but the Colonel feels that life is not life without sex, positively not worth living unless he can get it up. So, he pops up to London to see a chap he knows at the F.O. This chap and a few more whom the Colonel importunes all answer that cyanide capsules can be issued only to active agents in the field. They can offer no explanation as to why his first capsule did not work. Back in Brighton, the Pakistani doctor plays hard to get but, finally, comes up with a capsule of cyanide, fresh. His price is high, but. The Colonel has to hand over his every last penny. It almost kills him to do so but even this second capsule does not. Here he goes through it again, all the agony, the orgasms of agony, again and again and again but still he does not die.

The little boy never hears what happens to him, finally. He is too busy learning to read and write.

How to get out of this pain? How to get dead? How could he have chosen to hang onto this half-butchered live meat still hanging on the surgeon's stainless steel hook? When his nurse rolls him over to change his foul-smelling dressing, the humiliation of it and the shame can make him twist up his face like a baby and weep. Where is his stiff upper lip? They have crucified him to this bedstead, introduced into the intimacy of his veins these constant drips of serum and whole blood. In an aside to Geneva his nurse, he says he hopes the blood comes from Jamaica, black blood. But why couldn't they just let him lie there and hemorrhage, let him die in the fine old Roman fashion with his friends around him? As it is, his visiting friends come crowding up to his bedside to shout at him because he has grown deaf. They all tell him how lucky he is to have pulled through these operations. You'll outlive us all they keep telling him, with your new plastic parts. One thing you will never have to go through again is the humiliation of having to take a shit. Get well, you look good. Other only semi-visible visitors swim up beside his bedstead but, like the Greek ghosts in Homer, they cannot speak. They drop in unannounced from all over, from Paris and Tangier, New York and New Delhi, Katmandu and Tibet. They can stay for only the few flickering seconds he manages to keep them fixed in the corner of his eye without really looking at them directly. As soon as he does, they disappear without a sign.

Ever hear of Eileen J. Garrett, Garmeeta? She was the witchiest woman in the world in her day. Garrett, Garmeeta? It sounds like your tribe. Ever since I was a little boy, all the loony ladies have always loved me at sight. They used to say to my mother: "You've got an Old Soul here, my dear, do you know it?" I hated that. Servant girls used to sing to me: *Little Curly Headed Darling With His Mummy's Eyes.* They sang that to make me yell and scream and stomp around the nursery in paroxysms of rage. I wanted to see the lovely bright world out there through my very own Eyes. Years later, Eileen J. Garrett said about me and my good friend Touche: "Ah, you young men, you are both Old Souls but you've a long way to go." To catch up with her, she meant, and it was true. She was up to such tricks! One night she invited us up to her penthouse apartment, twenty-three stories above the White Turkey Restaurant on Madison Avenue opposite the Morgan Library, to see Maurice Sandoz produce the Stigmata, no less. It turned out that he did not want to do it for us. He had promised the Pope he would not produce the Stigmata again, even though he was a Protestant and a Surrealist to boot. Eileen wheedled him into it with her blarney. She was great. Touche used to call her the Fiddler Crab because she always came dancing and darting in at you sidewise with all her psychic antennae snapping at you as she gave you the insidious old elbow, cradling her huge old tits in her arms as she advanced. In Killarney green satin she was a sight.

The room we were in was all uncurtained plate glass looking out onto the upper floors of the Chrysler Building whose windows were blazing with light. The walls of her penthouse were entirely lined with mirrors half-hidden by luxuriant green plants growing up to the ceiling. Eileen talked to her plants: "Come, come my little greenies, grow for Mother!" she cooed as she swept around the room stroking them. Sandoz sat silent in an armchair with carved wooden arms. Eileen popped more champagne. When Sandoz went into meditation with his eyes shut, a red rash appeared on his forehead. Then his sweat ran down red from his hairline. Eileen, smacking her lips with satisfaction over her glass of champagne, whispered to Touche: "The Crown of Thorns, look!" The next stigmata to appear were two deep red spots on the backs of his hands. Touche put down his glass and went tiptoeing over to touch them, put his finger into the wounds like Doubting Thomas. Sandoz snapped out of it, shaking his head with a strangled cry. As he gripped the wooden arms of his chair, his knuckles turned white and a long blob of something really weird sort of slurped down out of the little finger on his right hand. "O, look Mister Sandoz!" Eileen exclaimed, "ectoplasm as I live and breathe!" His chin dropped in horror as he opened his eyes to look down at the stuff and then, with a really tremendous internal effort, he seemed to suck it back up into his finger again. Touche helped the poor man to the bathroom when he asked for it. He locked himself in there and was silent for so long that Touche came back to consult with me. Should we tap, should we rap, should we break the door down? We went back to ask Eileen and what did we see on the living-room floor? Nothing but this huge great big Kelly green satin ass. Eileen was down on her hands and knees, combing through the pile of the rug with her long red fingernails all around the armchair. She cocked a wise old beady eye at us and tipped us a wink. "There are more tricks in this trade than you could shake a shilaleagh at!"

Through the long, the relentless hospital day which begins before dawn, from one round of painkiller pills to the next he wallows around like a gigantic soluble whale in an infinite ocean of agony. Diving, dying, dissolving into these elemental waters sweeping along at top speed, he has no defenses at all. Every last molecule of his expanded being is matched by and married to a unit of pain. If all that is pain, then he is the tint, the dye, the very color of it. When without warning what was color is suddenly sound, he leans back out of himself for a split second to laugh, to listen and laugh. Out there and in here are—ringing out through the Universe are banked choirs of crazy ecstatic voices screaming along in exquisite suffering, agony. Or is it praise?

On the fourth night, I am about ten feet from the *koubba* when a big Blue Man, the biggest desert dweller I have ever seen comes bounding out at me, roaring like St. John's burning lion out of the Apocalypse or the Muslim archangel Ghabril announcing the End of Time. I have a hot rush of feeling for him. I never saw anyone like him before but I trust him. I love him. How can he be a Mauritanian nobleman? His face is bright orange and his eyes are like diamonds, bright blue. His face is square and a bit flat like a big cat but he is clean-shaven. A very dashing indigo turban is tied around his head in a particular fashion to tell where he comes from in the Muslim world but it could be the Gobi desert for all I know. He knows me all right as he rushes up to embrace me, to warn me, to tell me something for which words are worthless, superfluous, unnecessary. A furnace roars out of his mouth on the hot wind which whips up his billowing blue robes. An electric halo of fire crackles around the flapping stuff. He is outlined in tongues of stylized flames like those wrapped around Celestial Messengers on a Tibetan thangka. As his robes lift, I catch a glimpse of his tough attendants hanging back in his shadow. They are certainly Arabs but small, thin and dark. He is in a terrible hurry to tell me something important in one solid information bloc. He holds up the five fingers of his right hand streaming with gold. I understand at once, perfectly. With his left hand, he throws out a quick curtain of fire across the dune down which the little merchants came tumbling. My heart leaps up with the flame. I have found what I wanted: the right way to die. The best thing I can do, ever, is walk into that flame. But I can't. There is no time. The shades are rapidly falling, falling because all this has taken place in less time than it takes to bat an eyelash. Now and now and now, ever so slowly, the eyelid is coming down. Across the chasm of this wink, he calls wordlessly:

"*Come back tomorrow, the fifth night, and you can walk into the fire!*"

When they interrogate him on Communication, he says he is against it. When they bring in the Universe, he replies that it is undoubtedly a fascinating construct but it must inevitably have a few flaws and he fully intends to streak out through one of them into Nowhere. Right out. His favorite place, what a laugh, like his desert, that unlivable space. Instead, he is entombed with two German soldiers who have been buried alive for two years in a mine shaft which opens under his feet at a dinner party on the Old Mountain for the ex-secretary of the ex-Foreign Secretary, or a garden party given by Christopher in Chelsea for the Rolling Stones. The mine shaft turns into a sordid cafeteria for Lesbian Singles ferociously wolfing down Danish pastries. He is horrified to see that some of these are in the shape of his hands. "You are a lot dumber than you look, even," one of the Lesbians says with a snort. Deborah is there in the garden being photographed by Tony in one of her beautiful hats. He has a long letter from Tony in his pocket but no hands to get at it, all about Dhiravamsa and the Vipassana Path. When all of a sudden, the little dwarfs from the desert come swarming through the green English hedge, setting their goods out for sale on the lawn. Carefully, he bends down to look at their wares. He sees at once that he made a mistake when he read what was written on their gray plastic packages. Because the first letters read: FORT, he jumped to the conclusion that this was explosives stolen from army stores. What he reads now is: FORTAL, the name of the painkilling drug he relies on to get back to where he really is—outside the koubba, *ready to walk into the flame.*

"Stop hallucinating! I told the doctor and he has cut off your FORTAL. Stop!"
There was no fifth night. By then he had lost the ability to write. He was unable to scribble that last sentence which would have read:
"So this is what happens to . . . ."

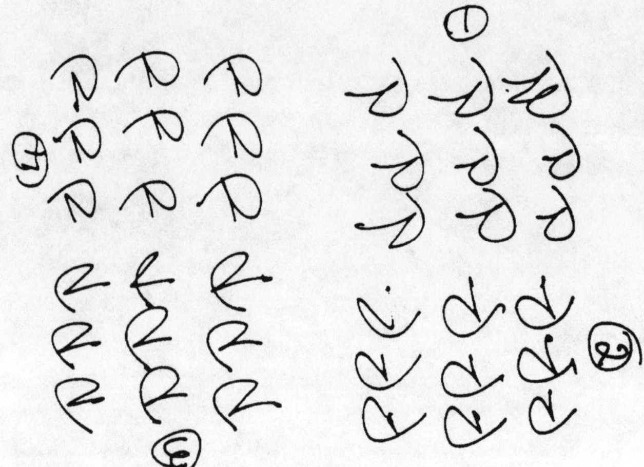

L'intention de ces signes
est de faire pivoter
sur elle-même
la page - l'espace pictural
ainsi :

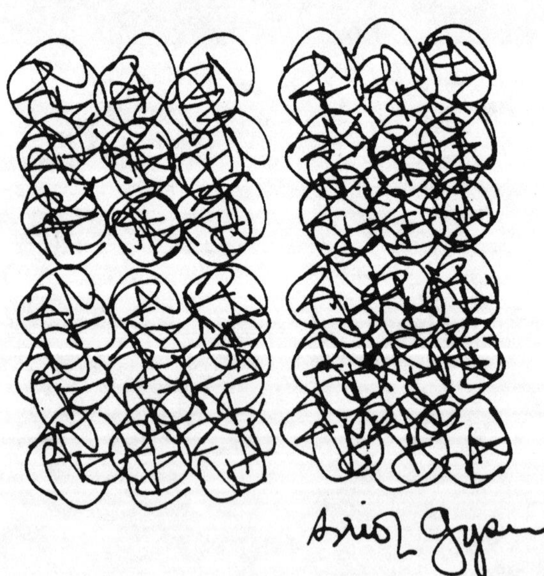

"Untitled," from the journal *Luna Park*, 1976. Ink on paper, 8 1/2 × 11 5/8
inches. Original in collection of Marc Dachy.

Psacré Psilocybin and Magic Mushrooms

"Psacré Psilocybin and Magic Mushrooms" (1977), originally written in French for Art Press International, *chronicles some of Gysin's encounters with hallucinogenic drugs and their place in different cultures. This was the only piece he devoted specifically to his drug experiences.*

I was six years old that summer and I was reading *Alice in Wonderland* to my nanny. She especially loved the story of Alice and the mushrooms. It made her laugh a lot. She was fourteen years old and named Rose Wild because she was a Redskin. She didn't know how to read or write. I tried in vain to teach her to read but she wanted none of it. About mushrooms she knew everything.

They're spirits that come from the moon, my grandmother taught me. When you eat some you can dance with them, you can go to the moon with them if you like. From each of the four corners around their umbrella you eat a little bit, a tiny bit, and then you drink hot tea. After a while you see everything. They're magic mushrooms. My grandmother knows where to find them, how to make them come out of the ground with words. You want some?

That happened in Banff in the Rocky Mountains in 1922. The day of the big national holiday, the whole Wild family, everyone who was left of the tribe, donned their finest attire, all their feathers and beads and skins and, riding their pintos, their small stocky horses with multi-colored coats, they descended the mountain from their reservation with women and children, without fanfare, solemnly, and without any gesture or smile for the white tourists who applauded them on their ghostly and almost silent passage. The short procession went down the only lane in the village of summer visitors, slowly and with distant gaze, passed the small stone bridge and climbed up toward the big tourist hotel, an immense pseudo-medieval chateau clinging to the mountain, its peaks eternally covered with snow. These poor Redskins were paid to entertain the tourists at cocktail time. They must have been thirsty but all alcoholic drinks were and still are strictly forbidden to the Indians. They knew only hallucinogenic mushrooms and peyote but never spoke about it to the whites, never.

| The Message from Divinity Avenue |

The mad summer of 1961, I was broke in Paris, alone or nearly in the famous fleabag Beat Hotel, rue Gît le Coeur, in the middle of August and without a cent to get back to Tangier where I'd been living since 1950. Burroughs and Ginsberg and Corso & Co. had decamped there, abandoning me in my sordid room, and I owed months and months of rent to the saintly Madame Rachou, who kept the hotel. I spent so many days without eating that I lay about on my bed from weakness, unable to muster the courage to go down to the bistro and see if I had any mail.

I no longer expected anything from anyone, but one fine morning someone brought up an imposing envelope for me struck with the seal of Harvard University over the address of an institute on Divinity Avenue. That was already promising. They were inviting me very formally to participate in a group experiment with psilocybin, an extract from the mushrooms known as magic mushrooms. This research was apparently sponsored by Harvard under the direction of Dr. Timothy Leary. I knew quite well who he was.

Earlier, all expenses paid, William Burroughs had been invited to participate in a colloquium on this new drug organized by the institute directed by Drs. Leary and Alpert—the one who later became the "guru," Baba Ram Das. Their intention was to get Burroughs to testify as to the value of their experiments with this "inoffensive and beneficent" drug—an experiment they conducted at the greatest risk and quite carelessly on prisoners in penal institutions as well as on waitresses, taxi drivers, and whoever they crossed paths with day or night, perhaps especially at night. Burroughs was properly horrified, and when it was his turn to speak, he said so right out.

A short while after, I received a tiny package by mail, so tiny that they had to attach a tag with my name and address on it. Inside was a minuscule pharmaceutical bottle with the name of the manufacturer: Sandoz, Switzerland, with a branch in New Jersey. They included neither directions nor dosage. There were twenty-four pills, tiny as pink grains of sand.

A friend passing through, famished for chemical experiences, absolutely wanted to try some and we each took three, but after having eaten well for once. Pity. The effect was rather pleasant but minimal. A bit later, we each swallowed three more pills and then we slept. . . . Waking was very fresh and pleasant, very. The effect floated around us the whole blessed day until we drank just a bit of alcohol, resulting in total confusion. We agreed, the passing friend and I, to wait a few more days before starting over with the pills that remained.

Meanwhile, a second little bottle arrived by mail for Burroughs, who had asked me to forward his mail. I remembered quite well that he had publicly sworn to never take any more—never! They put me through hell, he declared to me, they chased me through the white-hot streets of Minraud bronze! They tortured me terribly! I don't want to hear anything more about mushrooms.

Well. I decided to gather myself for several days in order to purify myself like the Redskins do and then I would take the entire bottle. Those twenty-four little pills of I didn't know how many micrograms would be my chance to find the great dance of the magic mushrooms. But, contrary to the Indians, I was not going to pray. I was going to work. To that end, I prepared my materials for painting: etching needles and brushes, a miniature box of Windsor & Newton watercolors, my lacquer-based color inks from Sennelier and a hundred 5 × 8 bristol board cards. All that was spread out on my big worktable, which took up more than a third of my sordid hotel room. Another third was taken up by my bed, stuck between two enormous armoires with mirrors forming a sort of alcove in which I could lurk as Henri Michaux did, according to what he wrote in *Miserable Miracle.*

But the great journey in a bed never did much for me. In extreme conditions, I like to wander, seek out adventure and make it happen rather than endure it like a mollusk. When in 1954 in Tangier I took mescaline for the first time, I had a very astute guide who advised me: Arrange things so that you'll be sheltered from any worry. Protect yourself against any attack from outside. Avoid any untimely interference in your life that day. Inform all your friends that you are invisible for them as though you had gone on a journey, which is true. Spend your day and night in the best possible conditions. Listen to the loveliest music. Go walking in a beautiful garden. Pass some time with animals. Visit a museum. You'll see the retouchings, the restorations, and you'll recognize the fakes as though you were examining them with an x-ray. Listen to more good music. Make love if you can.

| A Gorilla Named Congo |

It was true, more than true! In a garden he had me choose a beautiful white trumpet of datura whose greenish tint toward the base of the cup denoted that that flower had just bloomed and was still full of its rocketing strength. When I plucked it, it emitted a cry! Yes, a cry beyond or below the threshold of sound, a sob that broke my heart. I appreciate plants quite differently since then. Immediately all around me I saw the entire garden alive. Everything, everything, all the flowers and plants and even each blade of grass was turning toward the setting sun by small sudden clicks. Everything was alive like me on this earth, everything was breathing.

At the entrance to that fabulous garden on the outskirts of Tangier, the tall dead husk of a eucalyptus still stood, in whose bare branches lived, rather poorly, a chained gorilla from the Congo. His Belgian masters had passed a very long chain about his waist that he could not break and in his tree they had hung a big truck tire where he could swing, the only joy left to him except the ferocious joy of scaring visitors. His chain was long enough to let him descend to the foot of the tree screaming with rage when he felt like it. The hold of his chain was hardly reassuring when he feigned an attack, a forceful descent and escape.

That day I approached him with firm step calling: "Congo! Congo!" He pretended not to hear me, no more than the wind. He was admiring his big black satin gloves. He studied his nails with care. I threw peanuts to him that he let fall, indifferent as the rain. I tapped hard on the dead trunk of his tree, I drummed my hands on it. He frowned, admitting that I was annoying him. He gazed out to the distant forest above my head acting totally indifferent but the crease of his mouth and the flare of his nostrils betrayed him. I kept insisting. With the help of a branch, I touched, I pulled a little on his chain. By then he was boiling with rage, ferociously showing his fangs. This obliged him to look at me with a rattle in his throat that died on his lips when he sized me up. His jaw fell to his immense chest. His shrewd little eyes filled with terror, grew wide. He was trembling. As though he had just received a kick in the stomach, his big body deflated. I saw the yellowish white of his upturned eyes when he lost hold of his branch and fell. He fell like a sack at my feet. K.O. The force of my gaze as an illuminated man had struck him down.

Not in the Beat Hotel, nor in the Place Saint-Michel, nor at the Jardin des Plantes, nor at the concert where I heard Arthur Rubinstein and where I had, I'm convinced, a strange "flash" with him, nor in my bed, did I meet a gorilla from the virgin forest this time. For more than three days and two nights, the psilocybin had complete hold over me and I did not sleep. I was out of commission except for three great flurries of artistic activity that shook me like hurricanes. Galaxies of mushrooms danced around my worktable leaving their traces upon my little cards. Spouts of mushrooms flowed from my fingers sketching mycologic forms over my bristol boards in three orgasmic ejaculations.

I made use of this experience as well in several passages of my novel *The Process*, translated into French as *Désert Dévorant*, Flammarion 1975.

Paris, 14 March 77
(translated from the French by Jason Weiss)

✎ Not by Me

"Not by Me" (1977), published in the journal Creatis, *treats the development of Gysin's artistic methods—primarily visual but also literary—and how they eventually led him to photography. At the time of writing this piece, he had been incorporating photography into his many experiments using painter's rollers, to produce the series of visual works called* The Last Museum *(also the name of his novel a decade later). These works, bearing a sort of syntax similar to that of contact sheets, were based on the Centre Pompidou both in the images employed and in their repetitive patterns: Gysin had moved into an apartment directly across from the museum when it was first being constructed and remained there for the last decade of his life.*

Crossing the Sahara during the winter of 1951–52 with a veiled Touareg noble for guide, I took his picture. I mean, really took it, literally robbing him of his innocent vision of the real world when I revealed its mere image on paper to him. He had never seen a photo until I gave him his. He accepted it gravely as he would any gift, touching it to his heart, his forehead and his lips before slipping it under his flowing blue robes as his medieval code of courtesy demanded, without examining it.

"No, no!" I laughed, "go ahead, look at it. It's a picture of you and your camel."

"Oh?" he said, pulling it out again as gingerly as if it were a summons from the camel-tax collector. Expressing his warrior's disdain for all such inky-fingered penpushers, he added: "I do not read."

"That's not a letter. That's a picture, a portrait, an image of you. Don't you see your camel in there and you, too?"

"No," he admitted, peering out over his blue face-veil and straight across the photograph, flat as the desert on the palm of his hand held up at eye-level: "No. I can see no camel coming."

"Not like that! Here, hold it upright and you'll see for yourself."

"Ah, yes," he murmured politely, "may the blessings of Allah be upon you and all your family." Then he added, dryly: "You are my friend and if you say that is a camel, I can believe you."

"You're looking at it upside down. Look at it this way. Now, can't you see it's a photo of you?"

"Ahooooo!" he gasped, letting the veil slip off his face, revealing his visage, his features for the first time since I knew him. "That's my camel! That's me!"

Since then I hear he has moved into the lobby of the new package-tourist hotel in the oasis and learned a few words of English: "Take photo! Take photo! One dollar," says he.

Could I be an antiphotographer? Well, you see. . . . I remember the fury of that band of Greek peasant girls who came rushing out at me under the Lion Gate of Mycenae in 1935, screeching: "No pictures! No pictures!" as if they all thought they were Jackie O. "We know the dirty things you do with your camera," they snarled. "You turn us upside down, stand us on our heads so you can see under our petticoats when they fall down."

"When they fall up, you mean," I shouted back. "Get the hell outta my picture. I'm not a fucking fashion photographer!"

Evidently, they had been allowed a peek at the reverse image under the black veil of some ambulant photographer who took pictures while-U-wait with his wooden box camera on a tripod and a pail of water to wash his prints. Today, those girls' sons and grandsons are sending back Polaroids of their foreign-born children from whatever cold country they have to go work abroad in these days.

"No," I said to myself firmly, "you are a poet, a painter. Photography cannot be a hobby for you. Never take a picture unless you can sell it."

That took me years. I came back to photography in a very roundabout way.

During World War II I was taught some Japanese by master calligraphers of several styles: *kaisho*, *gyosho*, *sosho*, *tensho* and *reisho*, as well as by some aesthetes who practised both *nijimi* and *kasuri*. All these *kanji* characters hang on the page . . . the picture-space if you cannot read the meaning . . . like trailing vines hung with the fruits of a knowledge I did not have time to cull. Instead of going to Japan, after the war, I went to Morocco, where I lived for some twenty-three years. Now, Arab calligraphy also runs from right to left but instead of dangling it races across the picture-space, the page, like an army with lances, pennants flying. So, to turn writing with a brush into painting, I wrote . . . . I scribbled one script on top of the other, thus controlling . . . policing the picture-space with a kabbalistic square . . . while inadvertently producing a grid. I did not "create" this grid. It created Itself. There it is, pinning down all pictorial space in all directions and, whoever has done it, It was not painted by Me.

Awed, like the celebrated old Chinese painter whose inkstained beard looked like his paintbrush, I bowed three times in front of the Great Collector and disappeared into my picture. Back to the desert for Me.

Grids and permutations appear everywhere in nature and art and were, quite obviously, not invented by me. My Permutated Poems (recorded and broadcast, BBC 1960), when written or printed or processed by computer, are

word-grids produced by the process, not by Me. The permutation of any potent five-word phrase (in English, at least, and Chinese) gives you a cogent
poem of five times four times three times two times one lines, a poem of 120
lines with a built-in music of its own. Perfectly simple. When I first heard it, I
flipped. Running across the Divine Tautology, I AM THAT I AM, in Huxley's
book on mescaline, it looked suspiciously crooked to me . . . asymmetrical . . .
wrong. So, to remedy what Jehovah is said to have said, I began shifting the
words about for what I felt were purely pictorial purposes. After all . . . what is
sacred? Like photographs, words are mere images, clichés of matter. Whazza-
matter . . . why not?

Leaving that big fat THAT in the middle, I switched around the final I AM
and . . . Wow! IT asks a question! So self-assured only a second ago . . . a mere
pico-second ago and now IT is asking a question. Looka that! I AM THAT . . .
AM I? Its 120 possible permutations ring through my ears like the links of a silver chain spinning through space. The Divine Tautology comes apart in my
head and I fall out for a second or two, at least. I like to think I heard what Sir
Isaac Newton claims he heard when the apple of Gravity hit him on the head,
the Musick of the Spheres, he said. Now, if you call that *satori* . . . or a camel
crossing the Sahara, I can believe you. You are my friend, are you not?

When Ian Sommerville put this and other poems like "Junk Is No Good
Baby" and "Kick That Habit Man" through the computer, the printouts looked
like word-grids rolled out by a roller. Intrigued, I cast about for some way to put
this dimension into my painting and in Rome 1960, a house-decoration paint-
roller presented itself. This roller was already commercially cast in a cellular pattern which I altered, merely adapting it to print out a permutative grid which I
could roll on out towards infinity, pushing aside the classic constrictions of conventional pictorial space. Today, every painter of airport-size canvases is after
something like this, intending to take over museum space. Such was not my am-
bition. Happily, my own new units of space were providentially the size of contact photos, very small. Again, the choice was imposed by the readymade roller,
not by Me.

While preparing the illustrations for our book *The Third Mind*, put together
with William Burroughs between 1960 and 1965 and, thanks to Gérard-Georges
Lemaire, first published in French translation by Flammarion (Paris, 1976) and
now published by Viking (New York, 1978) . . . I let single contact photos drop
onto my roller grids, into which they slid as if made for each other. They were.
For the first time in thirty years I felt this gave me the right, since I could sell
them, to take photos in series to fit my grids. But, chosen for the images they

carry, contact strips in the picture automatically create an architecture of their own. For example, when collaged onto and into a black-and-white grid, vertical strips of a black nude on a white bed become a voyeur's nightscape of shabby Paris hotels: see "Portrait of Francis" (1963).

Ten years later, when I first saw the project for the Centre Georges Pompidou in 1973 it gave me one of those old goosepimple flashes of déjà vu. It looked so like my first roller drawings in color, "Plans" (Rome, 1961), that I abandoned my self-effacing spurious Zen pose long enough to exclaim:

"This is the Last Museum, what else? And who designed it but Me!"

Art is the tail of a comet. The comet is Light. Light travels at the speed of 186,000 miles per second in every direction. Of course, I can think much quicker than that . . . right outside the galaxy and back in less than a nano-second . . . but sometimes I don't. I am slow. It took me years to realize that the spool of film in my camera is a roller. Perfectly simple. All I must do to organize the thirty-six possible images into a single picture is to plan my exposures when I roll my whole film over my subject. And my subject has chosen itself. Putting on my 200mm lens with trembling fingers, I jump inside the black box of my camera and count: six times six is thirty-six. No more paint, no more glue! Thanks to Mr Eastman, I am painting with light.

Light like a diamond, the construction brand new, paint still glistening wet: I never did anything more exciting in my life.

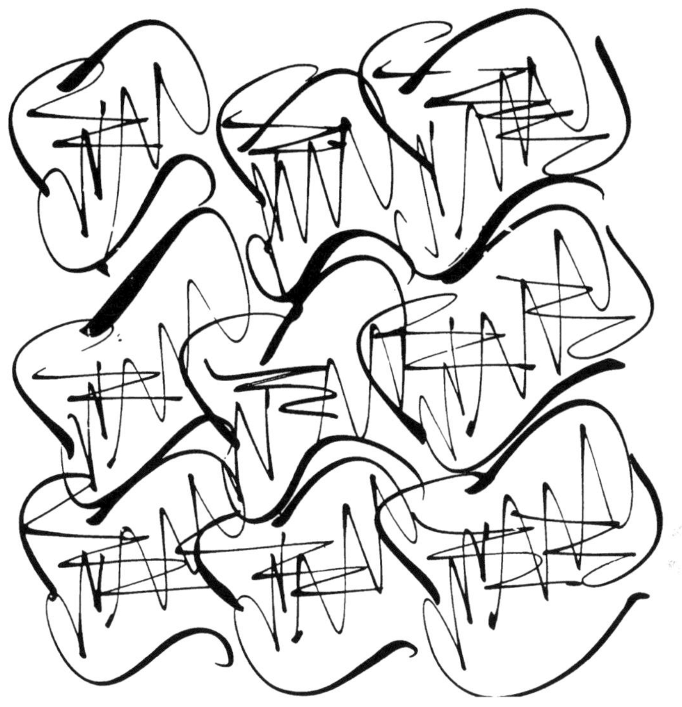

Project for a long calligraphic poem, from the journal *Soft Need*, 1977

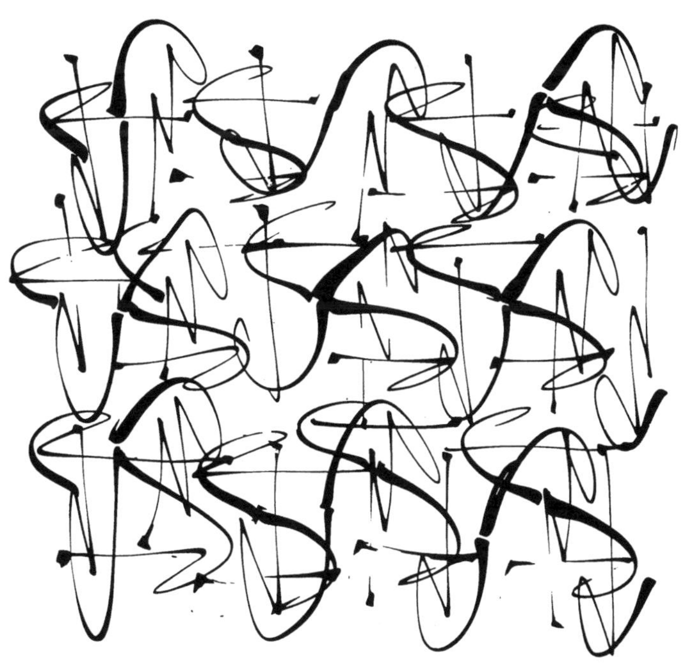

Songs

"Songs" reflects another of the activities Gysin engaged in intermittently throughout his life: writing song lyrics. During his first two years in New York, in the early 1940s, he worked as assistant to costume designer Irene Sharaff on seven Broadway musicals (including By Jupiter, Lady in the Dark, Banjo Eyes*); at that time he was also a close friend of songwriter John Latouche, who wrote for a number of Broadway shows (*Cabin in the Sky *and, with Duke Ellington,* Twilight Alley*). Later that decade, Gysin wrote a musical based on his biography of Josiah Henson, which was never produced; only the lyrics for* Nowhere Street *(1949) survive from that project, set to music long after by saxophonist Steve Lacy (1979). Gysin described the setting for the song when I interviewed him with Lacy in 1981: "There's a separation with his great love, he's decided to make it north, and she's left in a kind of deserted town like Cincinnati, a suburb of Cincinnati in 1850. She comes on stage and the leaves are falling and lights are coming on in the houses and going off in others. Mysterious—a kind of haunted house sort of thing, and frogs croaking."*

Lacy eventually wrote the music for nearly twenty songs by Gysin, all sung by Irène Aebi—including a ballet, Stuff, *that used many of the lyrics written for the script of* Naked Lunch. *Gysin and Lacy sometimes performed their work as a duo at poetry festivals and other venues. One of their earliest collaborations (1976) was "Somebody Special," written in 1972.*

From that same year, "Clementeena Soopastar" was originally part of the Naked Lunch *script; Gysin later performed it himself on the solo record* Orgy Boys, *which hints that he may well have been an old song-and-dance man at heart.*

The spellbinding "Dreams" (1975), a permutation lyric, was written for music that had come to Lacy in a dream and was their first song together, only a couple of years after their initial meeting.

"Gay Paree Bop" (1980) was written for Lacy's band before a big tour of the United States.

"Sham Pain" (1982) and "Stop Smoking" (1984) were set to music by guitarist Ramuntcho Matta, which they also recorded with other work together. In the early to mid-1980s, Gysin performed with Matta's new-wave band at art galleries, concert halls, festivals, and openings; describing himself as the oldest living rock star, Gysin seemed quite rejuvenated when he was up on stage.

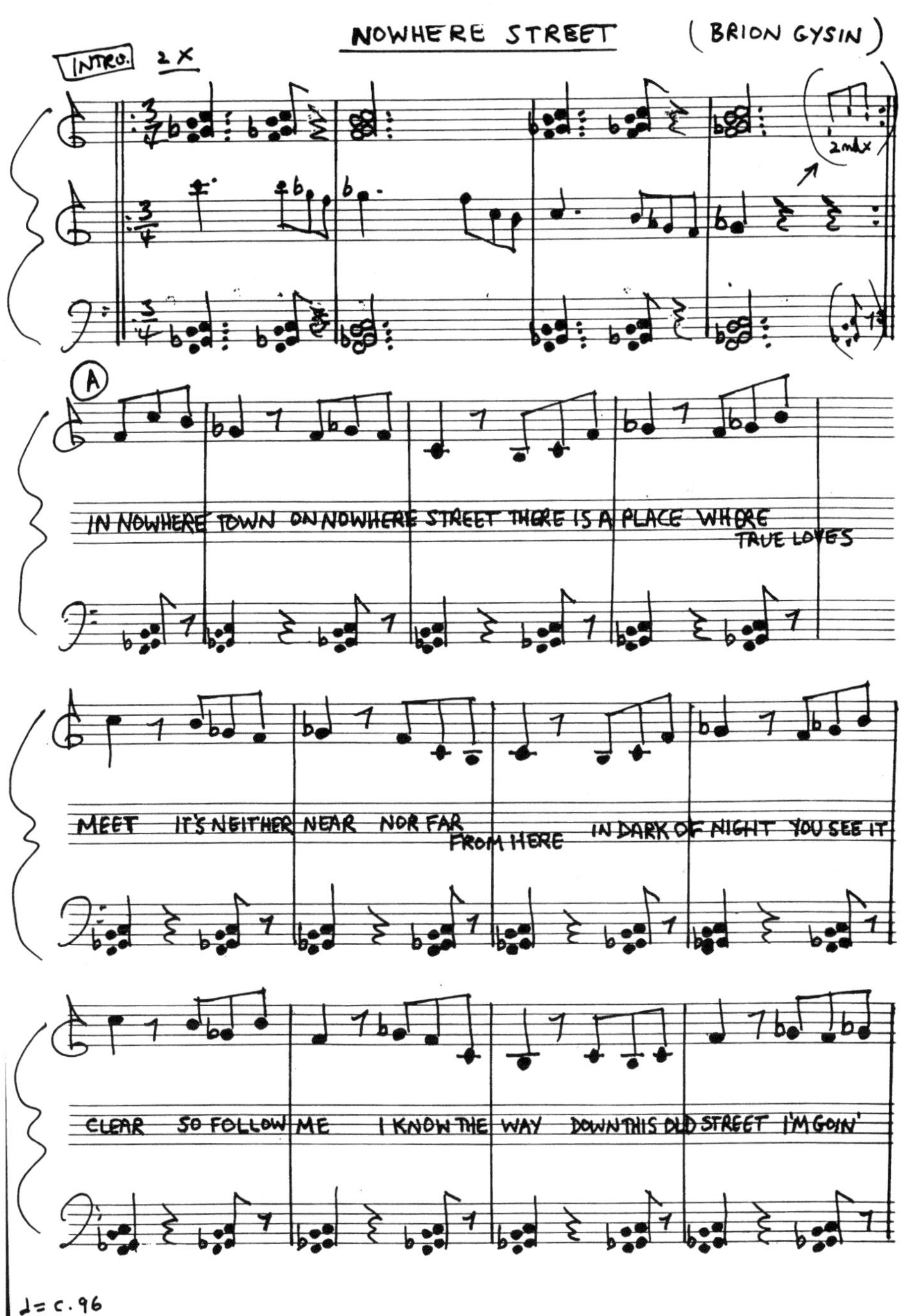
NOWHERE STREET   (BRION GYSIN)
INTRO. 2 X
2 mdx
A
IN NOWHERE TOWN ON NOWHERE STREET THERE IS A PLACE WHERE
TRUE LOVES
MEET   IT'S NEITHER NEAR   NOR FAR
FROM HERE   IN DARK OF NIGHT YOU SEE IT
CLEAR   SO FOLLOW ME   I KNOW THE WAY   DOWN THIS OLD STREET I'M GOIN'

♩ = c. 96

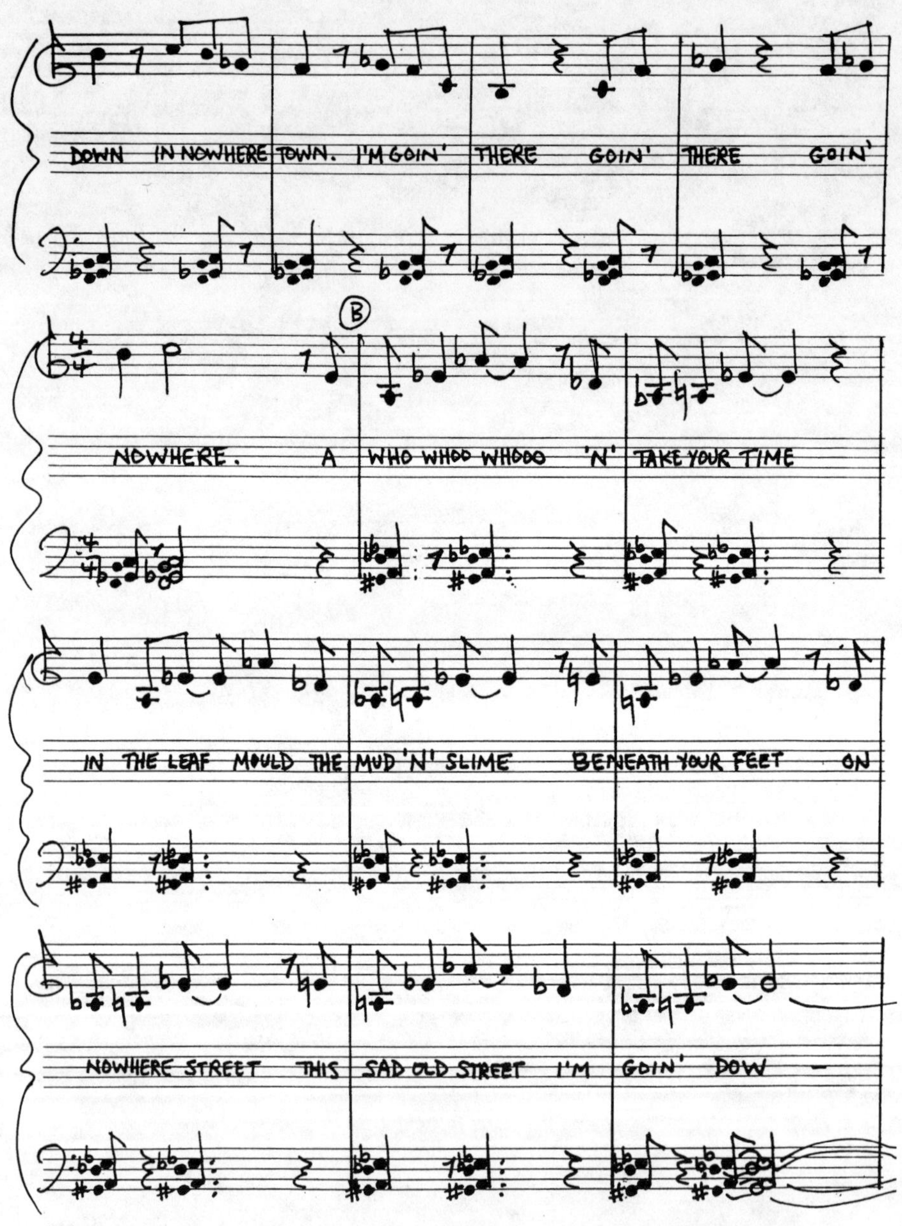
DOWN IN NOWHERE TOWN. I'M GOIN' THERE GOIN' THERE GOIN'
NOWHERE. A WHO WHOO WHOOO 'N' TAKE YOUR TIME
IN THE LEAF MOULD THE MUD 'N' SLIME BENEATH YOUR FEET ON
NOWHERE STREET THIS SAD OLD STREET I'M GOIN' DOW —

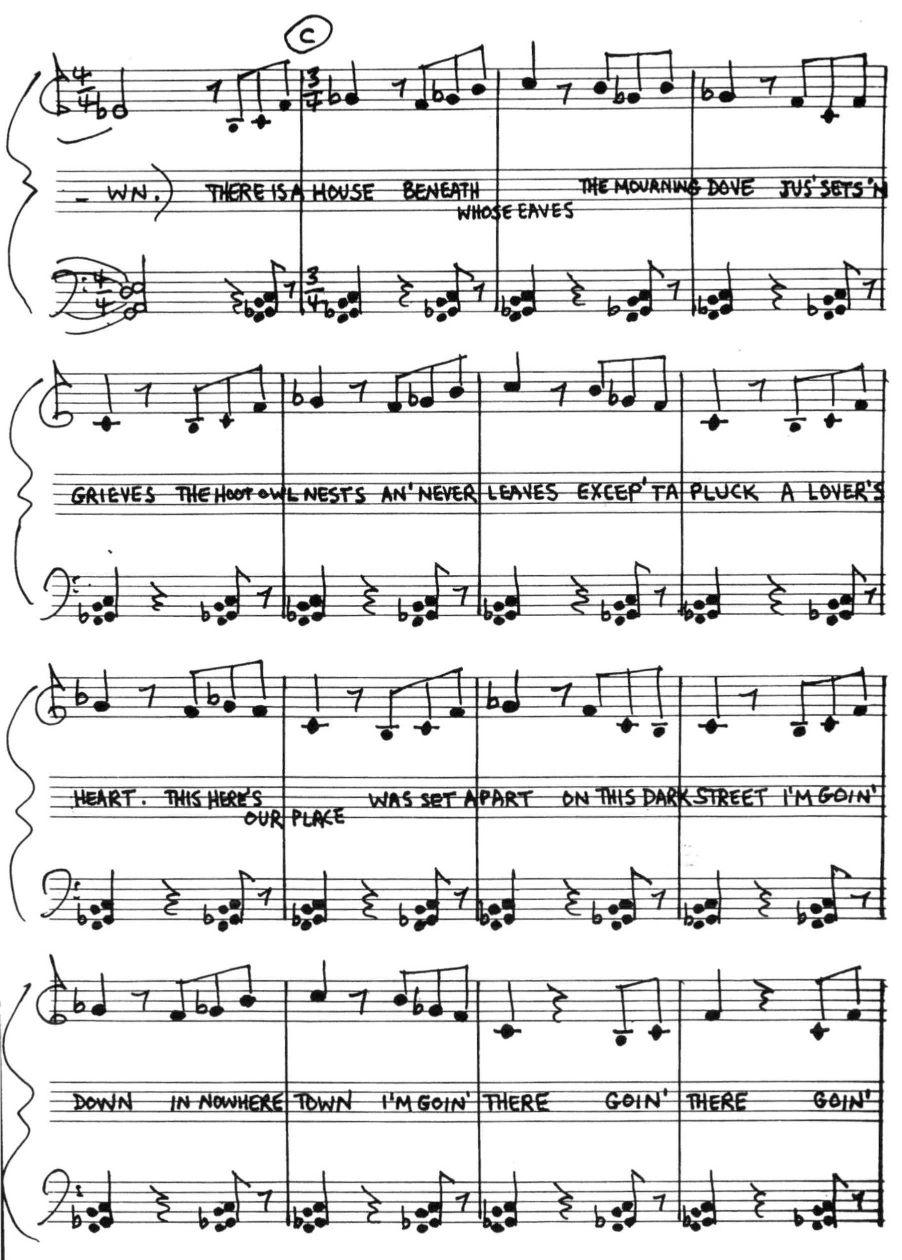

WN.) THERE IS A HOUSE BENEATH WHOSE EAVES THE MOURNING DOVE JUS' SETS 'N
GRIEVES THE HOOT OWL NESTS AN' NEVER LEAVES EXCEP' TA PLUCK A LOVER'S
HEART. THIS HERE'S OUR PLACE WAS SET APART ON THIS DARK STREET I'M GOIN'
DOWN IN NOWHERE TOWN I'M GOIN' THERE GOIN' THERE GOIN'

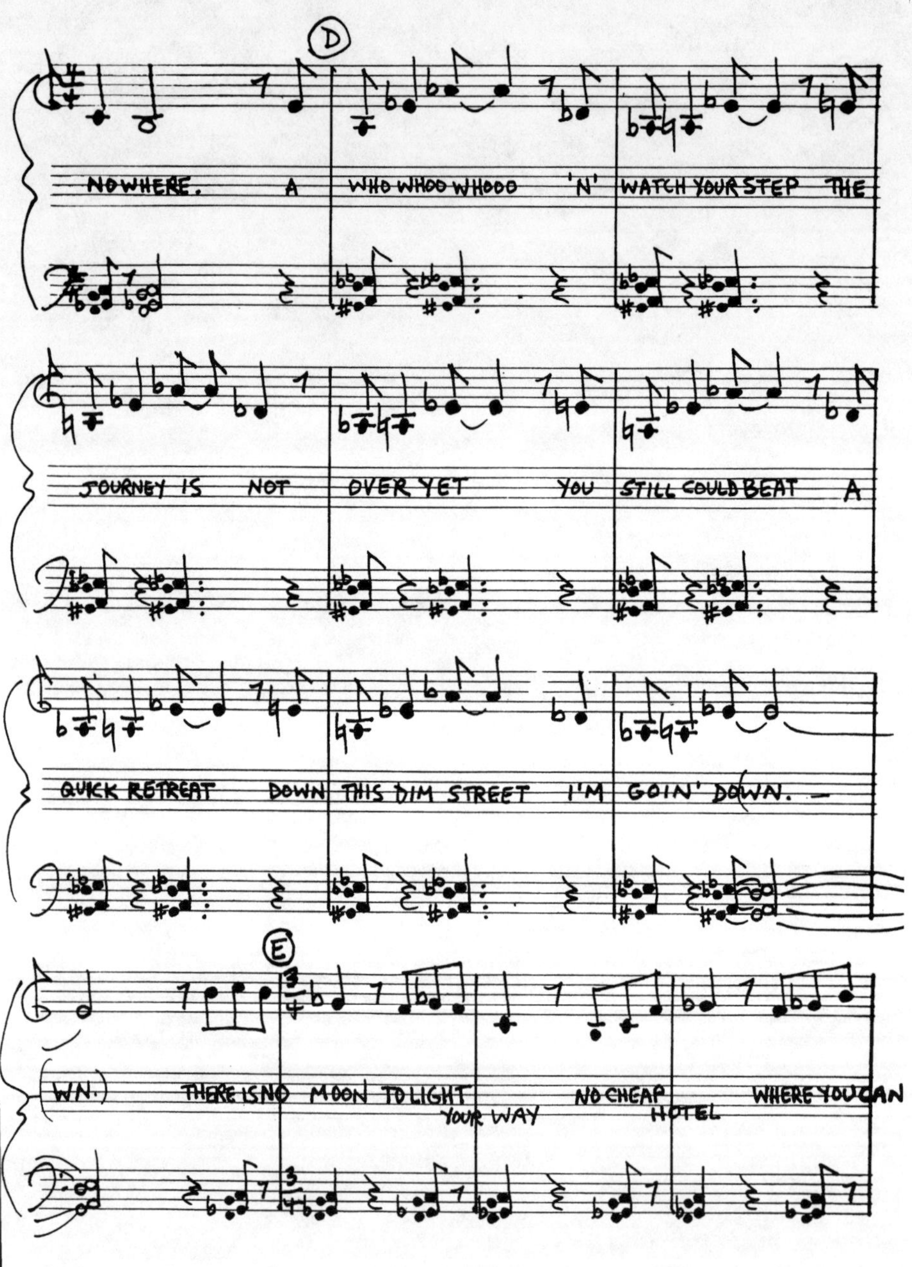
D
NOWHERE.   A   WHO WHOO WHOOO   'N'   WATCH YOUR STEP   THE
JOURNEY IS   NOT   OVER YET   YOU   STILL COULD BEAT   A
QUICK RETREAT   DOWN THIS DIM STREET   I'M GOIN' DOWN.
E
WN.)   THERE IS NO   MOON TO LIGHT   YOUR WAY   NO CHEAP   HOTEL   WHERE YOU CAN

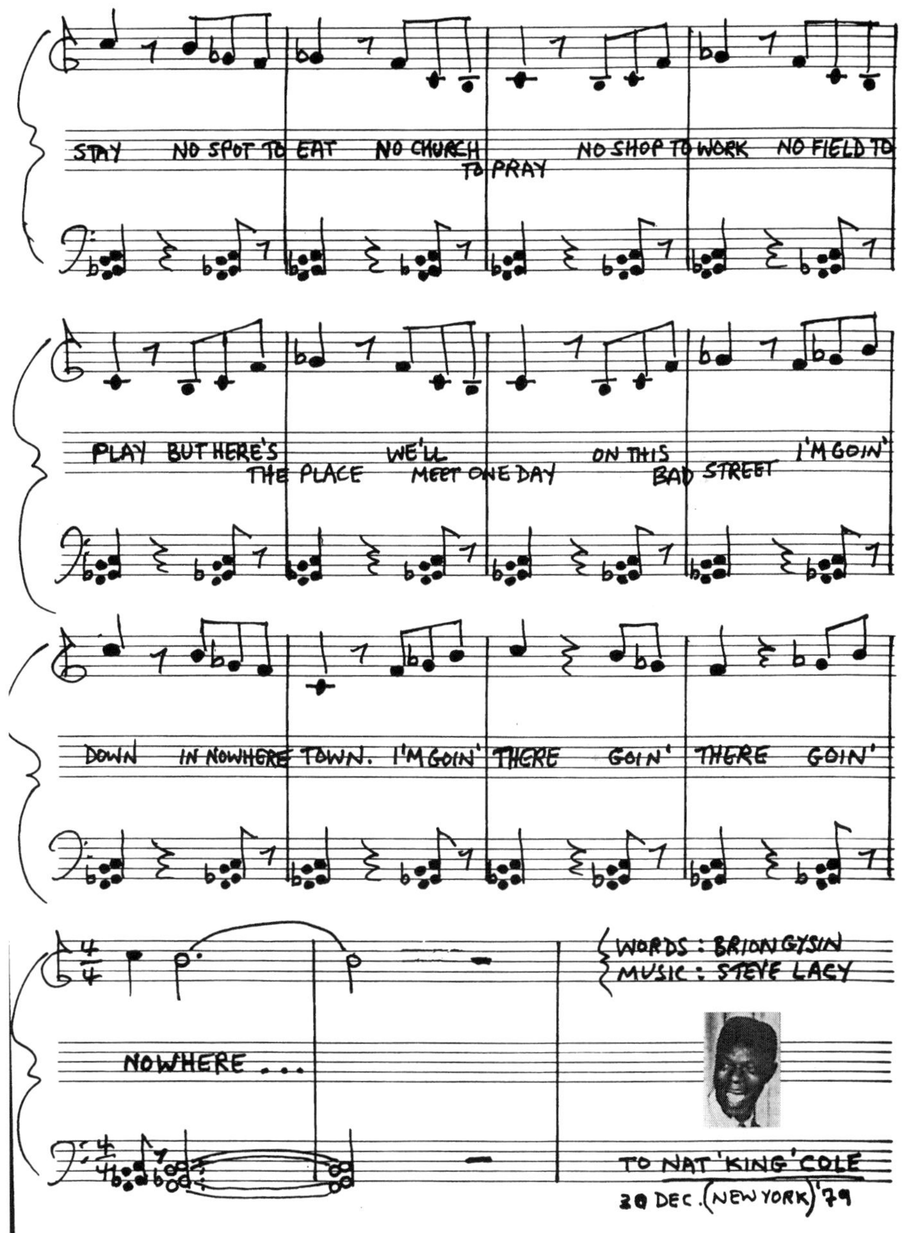
STAY   NO SPOT TO EAT   NO CHURCH   TO PRAY   NO SHOP TO WORK   NO FIELD TO
PLAY   BUT HERE'S   THE PLACE   WE'LL   MEET ONE DAY   ON THIS   BAD STREET   I'M GOIN'
DOWN   IN NOWHERE TOWN.   I'M GOIN' THERE   GOIN' THERE   GOIN'
NOWHERE . . .
WORDS : BRION GYSIN
MUSIC : STEVE LACY
TO NAT 'KING' COLE
30 DEC. (NEW YORK) '79

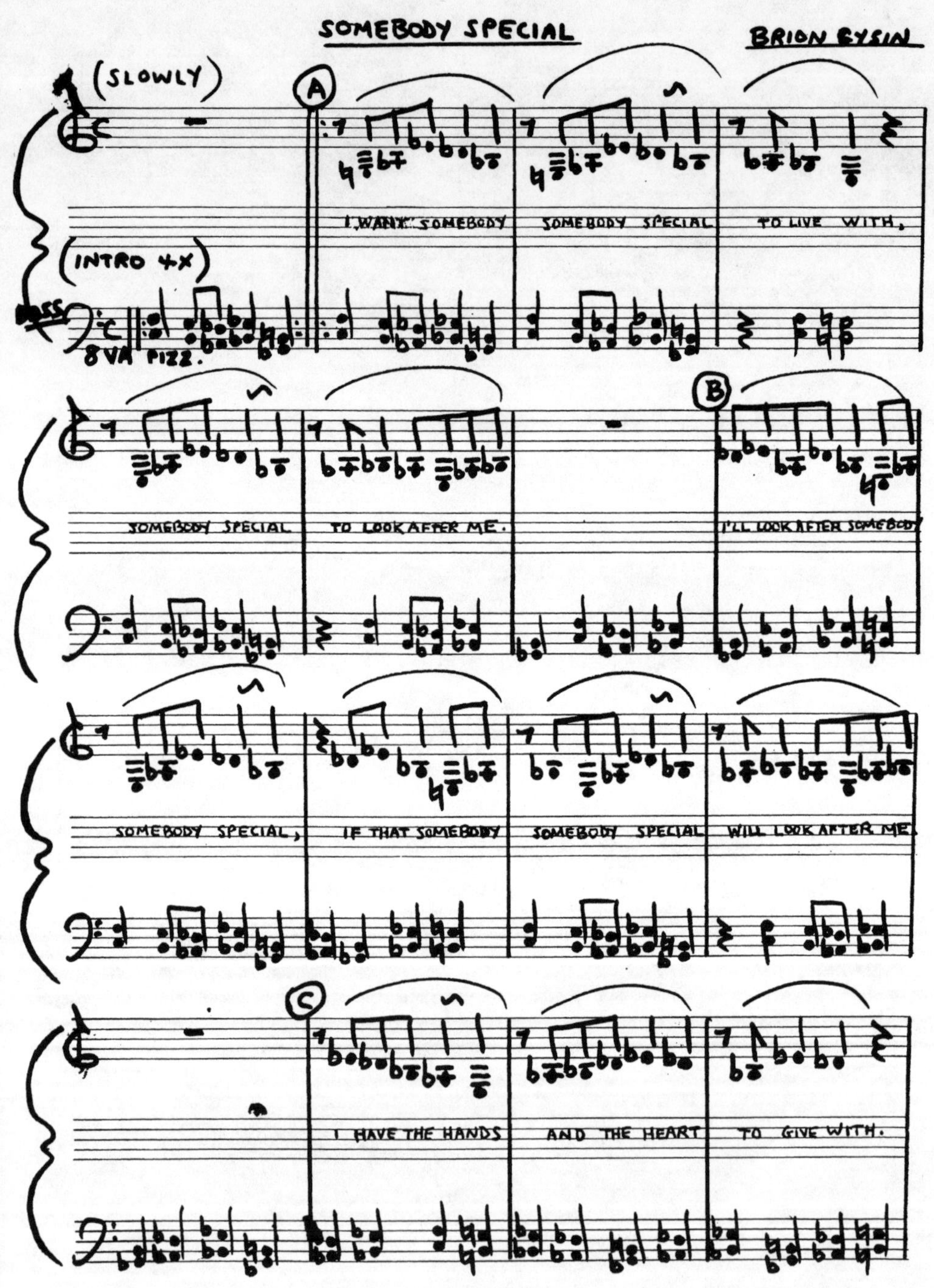
SOMEBODY SPECIAL
BRION GYSIN
(SLOWLY)
(INTRO 4X)
BASS
8 VA PIZZ.
I WANT SOMEBODY
SOMEBODY SPECIAL
TO LIVE WITH,
SOMEBODY SPECIAL
TO LOOK AFTER ME.
I'LL LOOK AFTER SOMEBODY
SOMEBODY SPECIAL,
IF THAT SOMEBODY
SOMEBODY SPECIAL
WILL LOOK AFTER ME.
I HAVE THE HANDS
AND THE HEART
TO GIVE WITH.

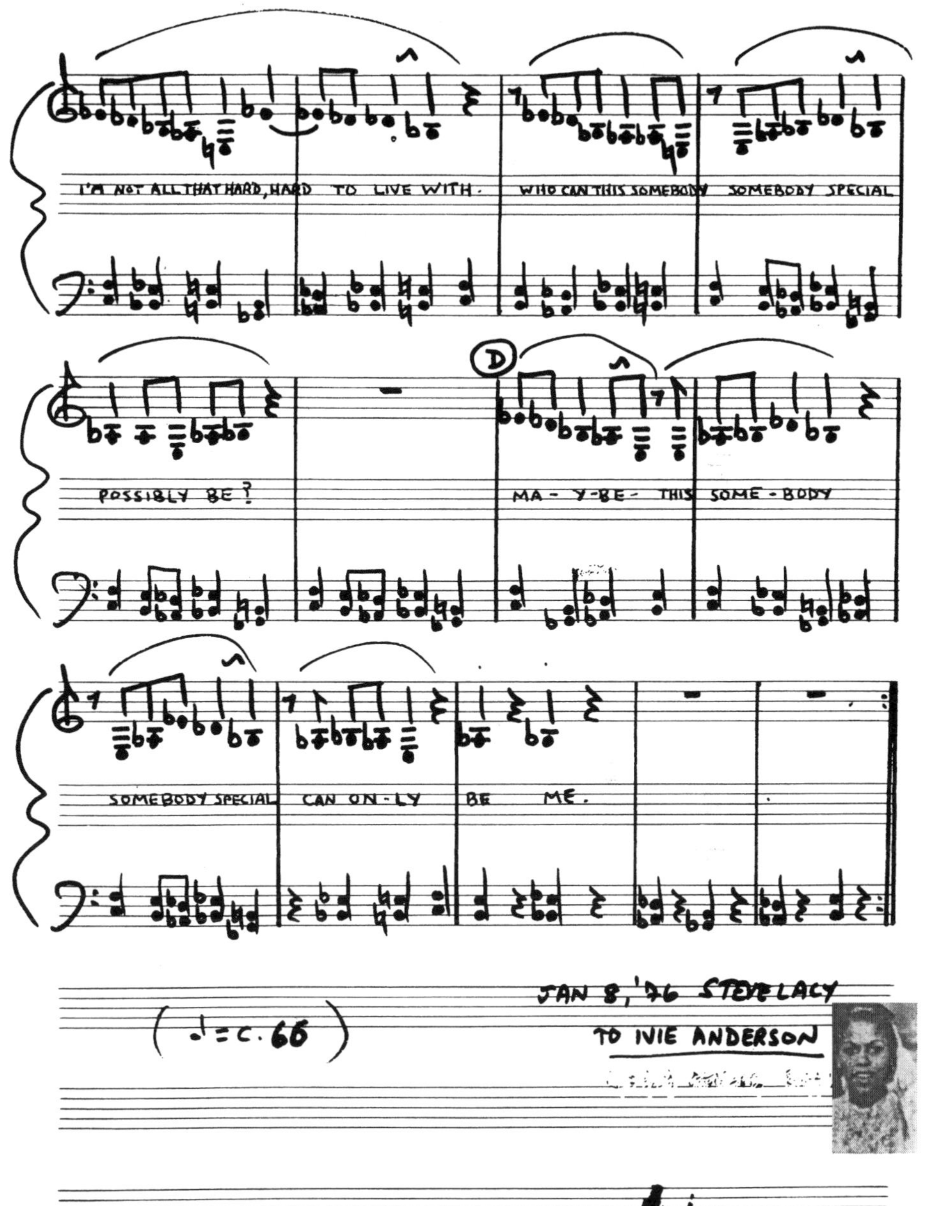
I'M NOT ALL THAT HARD, HARD TO LIVE WITH.
WHO CAN THIS SOMEBODY SOMEBODY SPECIAL
POSSIBLY BE?
MA - Y - BE - THIS SOME - BODY
SOMEBODY SPECIAL CAN ON - LY BE ME.
(♩ = C. 66)
JAN 8, '76 STEVE LACY
TO IVIE ANDERSON

Clementeena Soopastar

Clementeena Sooperstar
couldn't tune
her own guitar,
couldn't come in
on the bar,
couldn't sing
a note.

Yet people came
from near and far
came by 'copter
came by car
to hear her
clear her
throat
ha ha ha
wavering
ha ha ha
quavering
ha ha ha
wobbling
ha ha ha
gobbling
ha ha ha
SLAVERING
ha ha ha
all the way
ha ha ha
every day
ha ha ha
all the way
along
to the
BANK!

Clementeeeeena!
ya should-a
seen-a!
Reeeeeally
rank!
Ya should-a
heard-a
worse'n murd-a
her lyrics
stank!
You c'd do
bett-a
should'na
let-ta
go laughin'
ha ha
go zappin'
ha ha
all the way
ha ha ha
every day
ha ha ha
all the way
down
to the
BANK!

Clementeeeeena!
nobody feeeeena
who c'n blame-a
who c'n shame-a
her records are
ALL
on the charts!
Clementeeeeena
nobody keeeeena
to worm her way
into
your hearts.
Really knows it
never blows it
She's got you
and you
and you only
to thank
ha ha ha
as she goes zapping
ha ha
laughing
ha ha
sashayin'
along
to the BANK!
BANK! BANK!

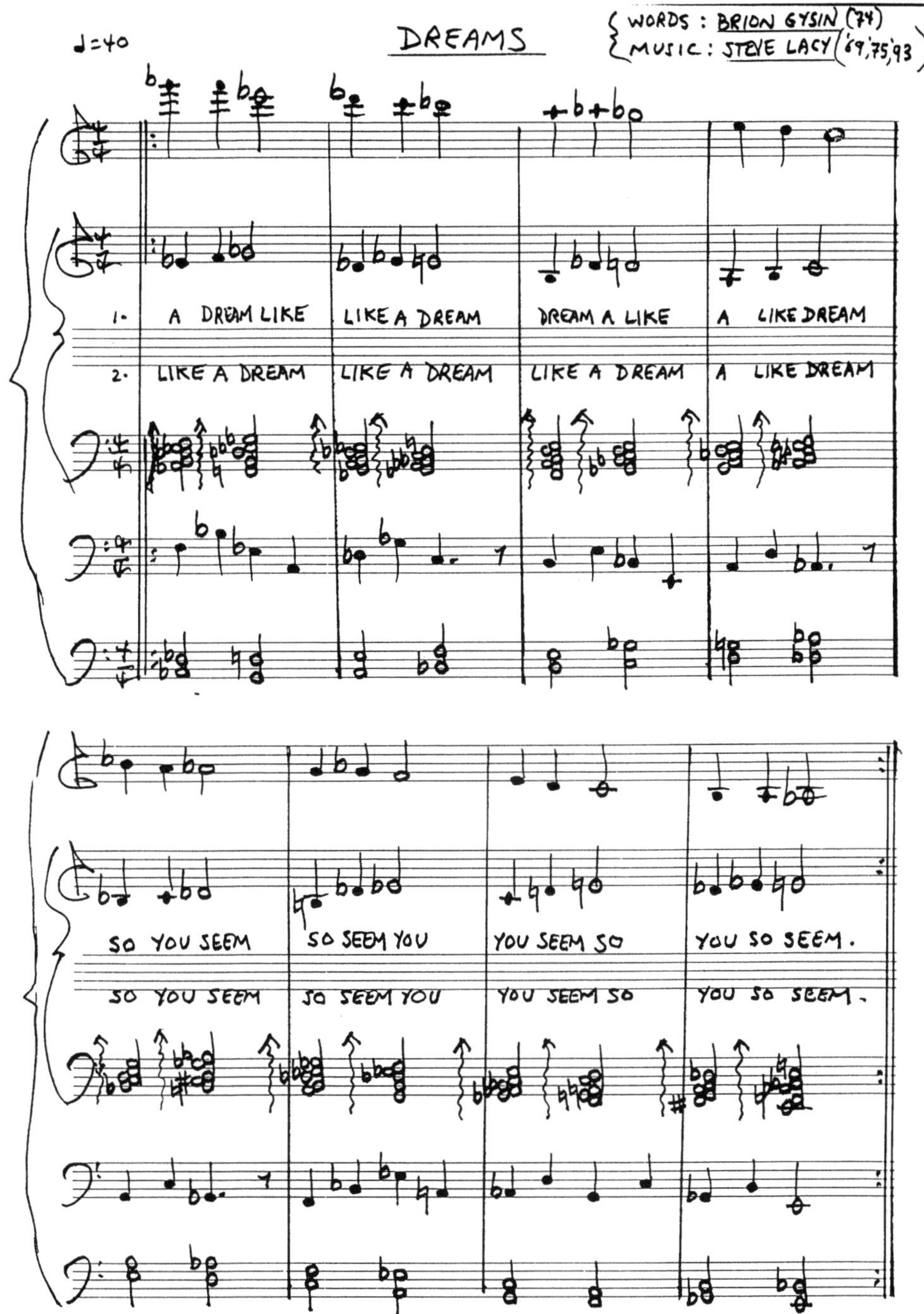
DREAMS
WORDS : BRION GYSIN ('74)
MUSIC : STEVE LACY ('69, '75, '93)
♩=40
1. A DREAM LIKE | LIKE A DREAM | DREAM A LIKE | A LIKE DREAM
2. LIKE A DREAM | LIKE A DREAM | LIKE A DREAM | A LIKE DREAM
SO YOU SEEM | SO SEEM YOU | YOU SEEM SO | YOU SO SEEM.
SO YOU SEEM | SO SEEM YOU | YOU SEEM SO | YOU SO SEEM.

Gay Paree Bop

Hey Gay Paree Bop!
Taka looka me pop
footloose 'n' free pop
singin' onna rooftop
rooftop? rooftop?
Rooftopsa Gay Paree Pop!

Who tell it cool
take me for a fool
notta liksa me pop
Hey Gay Paree Bop!

Bop alonga me pop
only you 'n' me pop
far as you can see pop
rockin' inna treetop
treetop? treetop?
Treetopsa Gay Paree Pop!

Who tell it hot?
Me? Thanksa lot
notta liksa me pop
Hey Gay Paree Pop!

Bop alonga me pop
hittin' onna highspot
drinkin' lotsa wine
feelin' veeeery fine
an' freeeee pop!
Free in Gay Paree Bop!

Who tell it free?
Notta liksa me pop
hey ya gotta pay
pay it alla way . . .
From here to Gay Paree Bop!

Sham Pain

Champagne! Champagne! Champagne!
We know all about you
we know what ya do
Complain! Complain! Complain!
Ya insane! Insane-insane-insane!
Wad a bore—wad a bore
we do this before
we gotta go through it again?
And again and again and again?
Ya gimme a pain!
Complain-complain-complain
I remembah ya well
you an' ya game . . . ya own li'l game
ya face is familiar—familiar as hell
an' I seem ta recall
we had some kinda ball
but . . . fa tha life of me darlin'
I can't see ta remembah ya name
ya long noble name
now, ain't that a shame!
Ya think ya so grand
we go strike up tha band
but let's not
have no toast in
champagne
champagne-champagne-champagne
pour it away downa drain!
Wat a pain! Wat's ya name?
Ya long windy name
caviar, toast an' champagne?
Thass a drag! A real drag!
I ain't inta ya bag
but thank alla same.
We don't need it no more
take it back ta tha store

Complain! Complain! Complain!
Wad I say all along
is ya come on too strong!
Like ya feel ya got some kinda claim
ya insane! Insane-insane-insane!
Wha'd I do wuz so wrong?
An' why am I allus ta blame?
We do this before
we gotta go through it again?
An' again an' again an' again?
Ya gimme a pain!
Champagne-Champagne-Champagne
we don' wannit no more
take it back ta tha store
Complain! Complain! Complain!
This is ruff! Enuff is enuff!
Who needs all this stuff?
Like I said before
I make love. You make war
ya act like ya onna campaign!
Ya wanna mix pleasure an' pain?
Wad a bore—wad a bore—wad a bore
we gotta do this some more?
I know ya so well
Wad tha hell! Wad tha hell!
It's back inna battle again!
Wad a bore—wadda bore—wadda bore!
Take it back ta tha store
we don' dig it no more
Complain! Complain! Complain!
Champagne-Champagne-Champagne
ya gimme a pain!
You an ya fifteen syllable name
a pay yay yay yay yay yay yay yay
yaaaaaaiiiiiiiiiiiiiiiiiiiiin!

Stop Smokin'

Stop smokin'
stop smokin'
aha ha ha ha!
Coff coff
stop smokin'
smokin'
aha ha ha ha!
Ya jokin'
ya jokin'
ya gotta be
jokin'
coff coff aha
quit smokin'?
Ya gotta
jus' gotta
be jokin'
whoever
quit smokin'?
Ya never
quit smokin'
not ever
quit smokin'
aha ha ha ha
quit?
This is it
ya jokin' jokin'
coff coff ya ha ha

I'm croakin'!
Ya had it
you an' ya habit
itisn't the coff
coff coff
'at carries ya off
it's the coffin
they carry ya off in.
Nicotine
's mean
real mean.
It's a curse
coff coff coff
but coal tar
is worse
far worse
it's rough
it's stinkin'
it's tough
ruff ruff!
'cuz ya can't
get enuff
ruff ruff ruff!
Of course
ya can saddle
ya hoss
coff coff

or ya hearse
an' ride off
coff coff coff
inta Marlboro county!
I'd walk a mile
smile smile
for a camel
not a coff
coff coff coff
in a carload!
Yaha ha ha ha
in a carload
uv coffins
Go ahead
smoke ya dope
coff coff
you gotta hope
cuz ya had it
bunny rabbit!
An' it ain't
the coff
'at carries ya off
it'sa coffin
they carry ya off in

Stop smokin'
I ain't jokin'

☞ Hamri's Hands

*"Hamri's Hands" (1981) was written as the preface for a cookbook by
Hamri, the painter, tale spinner, and legendary cook from Morocco, who
was also related to the Master Musicians of Jajouka. Paul Bowles introduced Gysin to Hamri in 1950 and they became fast friends.*

Hamri is a most remarkable man. How he came to be a great cook and how
he came to be a great painter reads like fiction. In fact, it *is* fiction. In my novel
The Process, now long out of print even in paperback, there is a fairly (or un-
fairly) full-length portrait of someone very like Hamri, everso lightly disguised
as Hamid. But the whole truth of the matter was beyond my powers, naturally,
being a tale as complex as the weaving of a very fine flying carpet, worthy of
the *Thousand & One Nights.* That, by the way, was the name of the restaurant
we opened together, back in those faraway golden days when Tangier was International Tangier, a freewheeling city-state where anything went. And it did,
it went. So did our restaurant, of course. And so did we, each his own way.

How we opened the restaurant in the first place had less to do with food
than with music, oddly enough. And magic, too, now that I come to think of
it. Everything to do with Hamri does. The music was made by his maternal
uncles and cousins, the Master Musicians of Jajouka. I first heard a mere
snatch of their piping in 1950 at the midsummer *moussem* of Sidi Kacem, in a
sacred grove on the Atlantic coast a few miles south of Tangier. I turned to
Paul Bowles who had taken me there and said: "I want to hear that music every
day of my life!" The very first time you hear your very own music, it grabs you
by the ears. You are ready to dance to that tune for the rest of your life. I still
am. My only tune was "Over the Hills and Faraway." And that is just where I
found them, of course, in the blue-green foothills of the Rif. When I told the
Master Musicians what I had said, "*Glis ma rasek!*" they laughed. "Sit. Sit. This
house is your house. Sit the rest of your life."

It was my turn to laugh. There was the matter of money, even up in those
magic mountains. "Why don't you go back down to Tangier," they went on
smoothly, "and take a tiny café as big as two straw mats. Hamri will do the
cooking. We will make the music and we'll divide up the daily take, every
night." Back down in town, we told a fashionable Moroccan friend about it,
for a laugh. The Wily Prince, as we called him, did not laugh. "I have just the
place for you," he said. "Some intimate friends of mine have a wing of their
palace they would be glad to rent to someone like you." So there we were, set-

ting up in a palace with a group of the Master Musicians in residence and their music ran through our marble halls like the very air we breathed, day and night. It was heaven. It was, also, hell.

In my considered opinion, to run a great restaurant—and that is what we had from every point of view but the price—you really have to be born in a casserole and brought up behind the cash desk on the broad lap of a genuine French Madame who keeps all the accounts in her head and her beady eye on every last ball of twine. Then, you need a whole slew of brothers and sisters and in-laws you can crack the whip over. Ill-paid, ill-housed, ill-fed off scraps, never thanked nor given a holiday ever, they must fear and obey you, worship the very ground you walk over them on. Like Argus, you must have a hundred eyes to make sure they never steal even a lump of sugar. You just may manage to break even like that. To prosper and become really rich, you must have the grand manner. You must be able to present bills so breathtakingly big that the customer loses his voice as he turns out his pockets. For years to come, he will inflate your reputation and his own by boasting about how much he paid. We learned the hard way from Texas tycoons who found our bill for a birthday bash with a cannabis cake too cheap: "We didn't come here for a bargain. You've spoiled all our fun."

Hamri and I were not really cut out for restaurant-keeping. It was almost with a sigh of relief that we folded and went back to our painting.

Hamri went on cooking, of course, as well as painting. Not me. That may have been one of the reasons we never got around to putting together the great Hamri cookbook we planned from the start. In the meantime, other so-called Moroccan cookbooks have tried to pillage some of Hamri's kitchen lore. So, Beware of Base Imitations! Without Hamri's own hand to it, nothing is genuine. Through the years, he has gone on refining his cuisine to a point where he cannot bring himself to do more than barely taste food cooked by hands other than his own. His own hands are golden. *Manitas de Oro*! He laughs about it but you can taste his thumb, his magic thumb in every dish.

So, here at long last is the book: How to do it Yourself. Well, you can always try. But, if Hamri can put his cooking hand in this book as well as he can in his own cuisine. . . . Why, let's eat this book! Are all these delicious dishes he is talking about printed on paper-thin pastry or pastry-thin paper?

Mmmm . . . good! *Bon appétit*. Good luck!

Paris

4 Aug 81

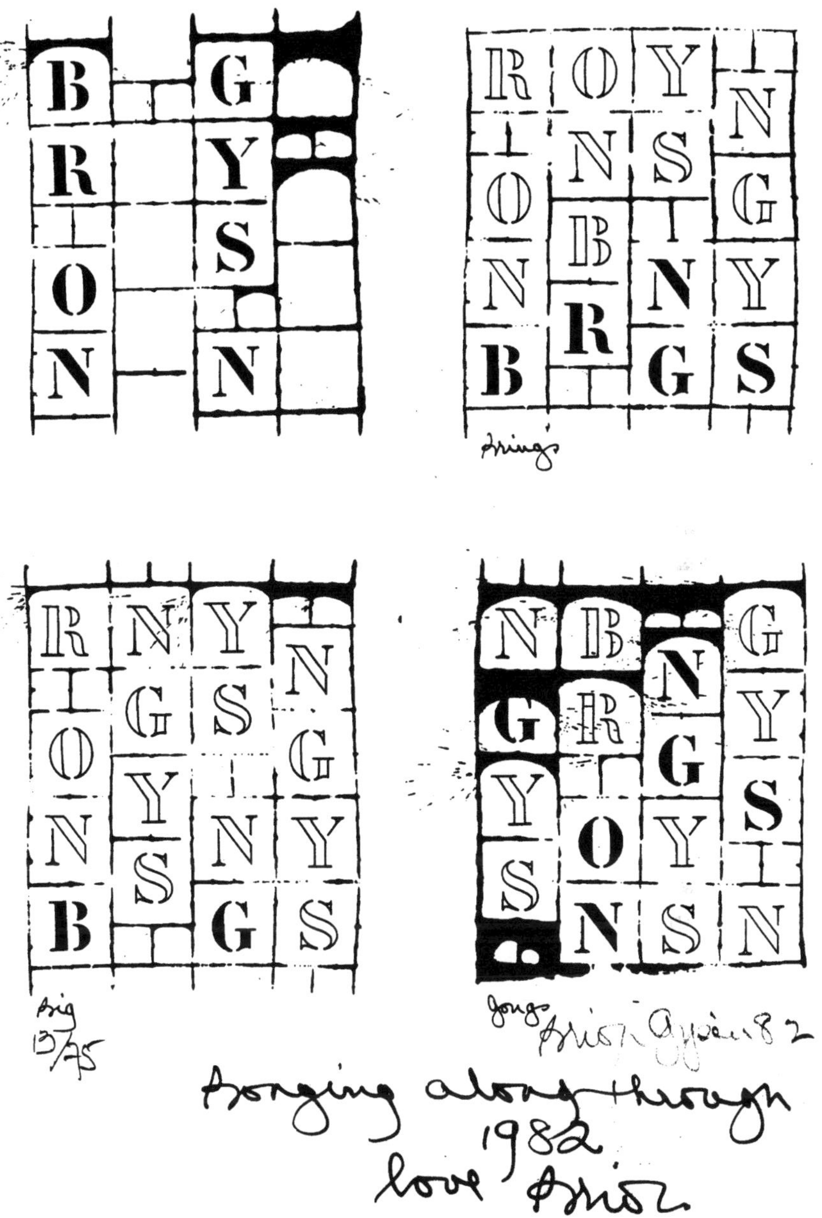

New Year card, 1982. Ink on paper, 8 1/4 × 11 5/8 inches. From no. 13 of 75 photocopies, signed and mailed by Gysin. In collection of Jason Weiss.

Snapshots from the Family Album

"Snapshots from the Family Album" (1982) was never published in English, other than as this excerpt, which appeared in Here to Go. *Gysin used to refer to it as his "baby book," which covered mostly his early youth and adolescence. The French translation,* Légendes de Brion Gysin, *a book of some sixty pages, came out in 1983 and was accompanied by various photos in his possession that dated back to before his own birth up through his arrival in Tangier in 1950.*

Yes, I am. I am Here. I remember. No one can separate Me from Mamie, the doll lovingly misnamed for the lost Belgian nursemaid, Amie. The world has just recently been invented and it revolves around Me. Me is my real name, no matter what they call Me. My daily voyages of discovery, out claiming all these newfound lands as mine, prove to Me that everything belongs to Me, everything, everywhere. Puddles are ponds, washtubs the ocean. The sky is my ceiling, a walk in the backyard is a dazzling adventure. You can see just how vast the green world was in the summer of 1917. And how new! Lovely sunshine, falling nowhere else. We are in Deseronto, Ontario, Canada.

In this lush jungle back of Granny's house, the dangerous thicket of reeds behind Me is taller than Me and as difficult to get through as the high picket fence it resembles, there in the back-go-round. Purple flag lilies, iris, bloom in the damp ground. Flowers fascinate Me. No bee has yet stung Me. A bright glade of goldenrod as tall as a forest of trees can hide Me from Mummy. She cannot smell them. The flowers give her asthma. Are we not, perhaps, on our way to the privy to make Business? The privy is that first wooden shed with only that one tiny window to let out the flies. All these years later, the stench is still in my nostrils. To do Grunts, as we call it, my china potty is better for Me. My nappies can still wet themselves and so can my cot. A mystery. Hard to tell who does this to Me. Daddy's Little Soldier stands up to urinate. That's what we call it, not pipi. No baby talk for Me. Say your night prayers to find Daddy. Whoever He may be.

Hurry on back past the woodshed and under the clotheslines to the back porch covered with prickly wild cucumber vine. The screen door on a spring can pinch fingers or send Me flying into the kitchen where Granny is making a gingerbread man with cherry red eyes just for Me. Granpa is hiding upstairs with a book. Granny calls Granpa "Poorwill." There is also a bird called Poorwill. Granny sleeps in the same bed with him. Mamie and Mummy sleep in the same bed with Me. Mummy has brown kittens (bronchitis) in her chest. The sun wakes Me. Her kittens are purring and all the birds in the wide world out there are singing for Me. My Early Morning Breakfast has been laid out for Me by the Fairies. Mummy has warned Me to be quiet as a mouse or the Fairies will stop bringing it to Me. Eating out of my Hi-diddle-diddle Dish with my silver pusher and thumb-spoon, drinking out of my somewhat battered silver christening mug, gives Me time to plan yet another glorious day.

. . . .

Marjory Hartigan kissing me in England, May 1920. On the back of this snapshot, in Granny's spiky hand: *Caught again at Brighton, Eng.* Clever old Granny got it wrong, though. This tender assault is taking place in London's Kensington Gardens, near the statue of Peter Pan. "Do you believe in fairies?" I am reluctant because of the whooping cough. Sailing from New York in January I gave it to all the other children at my fourth birthday party aboard the old *Mauretania.* Dame Nellie Melba gave me the party and drew picture stories for me on a big envelope. That morning, I had heard her "exercising her organ" as she called it, with her cabin door open. An inhumanly beautiful sound. "Mummy, Mummy!" I cried, "listen to the nightingale!" Melba overhears me and comes flowing out of her cabin, overwhelming me, carrying me all over the ship to tell everyone on board, from the Captain to the cooks who made peach melba for my party that "out of the mouths of babes," this was the most utterly thrilling, the most staggering compliment of her long career.

Melba made me a star. She held me up in the lounge and people clapped. She held me up on the Captain's bridge and the crew cheered. The Captain himself showed me over his ship. He put earphones on my head to listen to the icebergs that sank the *Titanic.* In the crackling wireless room, "Mister Sparks" sent messages from me to Granny back in Deseronto and on ahead to London to announce my impending arrival to Grandfather Gysin, signed: Master Brion. Later, I blew out all four candles on my cake while Melba sang "Happy Birthday" to Me. Feeling gracious, I allowed them to put me to bed.

I woke up screaming. Screaming for Mamie. Screaming for Mummy. Screaming for anyone because I needed attention. When it came, it came as a shattering surprise. A drunken steward poked his brutal head in the door of my cabin and snarled: "Shaddup ya lil shit! Shaddap or I'll knock ya lil block off, ya hear me?" That left me as breathless as if he really had chopped off my head. Life had unbuttoned Me. The very idea that a steward, *anyone* dared speak like that to Me! The world was not what it pretended to be, after all. My universe needed revising before I dropped off to sleep. I woke up another man.

I woke up at sunrise in England, loving the world. Nanny had knotted blossoming chestnut boughs to my shoulders, so I could fly with the fairies all night. Early Morning Breakfast was there with melba toast cut like sailboats and birds. My social life was adequate. I was not invited to castles but I did know a few eligible little girls. A Field Marshal's granddaughter invited me to an Easter egg hunt, in their charming old house and garden at Banbury Cross, to ride a fine horse. There were some little Honorables present who spoke and acted as if they never had to make Grunts.

. . . .

I cover the waterfront of Littlehampton with my prawn-catching net sloped over my shoulder like Daddy's rifle, cogitating on my first poem: *"Sailors, ships and smell of tar . . . ,"* still burning in my nostrils only sixty years later. Stuck for a second line, I meditate on sailors. While we were having tea on the lawn at Grandfather's house, four nearly naked men carrying ladders came to repair the damage done to his house when a wartime Zeppelin was brought down in flames on Streatham Common, across the road. These magnificently manly men have blue and red drawings all over them. One man has a Chinese dragon wound around his arm. Flags and anchors. Hearts and flowers. A whole peacock fanning its tail all over his back. In the War, they were Sailors. Sailors are Jolly Jack Tars. They smell good.

"When my ship puts out to sea . . . ." We are sailing to America, soon to see Aunt Kit in Kansas City, Mo. Sailors are nicer than stewards. Nobody knows and nobody cares what a sailor wears. Sailors don't have to be tidy when they sit down to tea. *"When my ship puts out to sea . . . ."* Mummy has to be my amanuensis. I can read but I can't write yet. *"I can't sail it very far . . . ."* Mummy must have been my first editor, too: *"Because I must come home for tea."*

A rude woman on the beach, seeing me teeter on a diving board drawn up on the rocky shingle, has the impertinence to call out to Mummy: "Madam, your little girl is going to hurt herself."

Tinkerbell, the Peter Pan fairy, dances on the ceiling of the hotel dining room when a handsome young waiter plays with the sunlight on a silver fork.

In our own cabin on this inferior boat from Southampton to New York, we find an old woman in our upper bunk, drinking her heart medicine out of a bottle with three stars. When she tosses her potty out of the porthole onto the head of the pilot, according to Mummy, they throw her overboard. Otherwise nothing to report on this boring Atlantic passage on a second-class boat.

Kansas City has a real live mermaid in a theater, Annette Kellerman. A naked man who locks himself up in chains, can jump into the same tank of water and come out, Houdini. A little lady in huge feathers of flame: Loie Fuller.

I am sitting on a board across the arms of a barber chair, having my curls cut off. In the mirror, I can see around the curtains into the Turkish bath. Naked men in there, sailors, are chasing each other, playing at leapfrog and piggyback.

Aunt Kit grows a mysterious fruit called papaws on a vine over the sun porch of her California Spanish-style stucco bungalow on a triangular lot.

A slice of American pie in Kansas City, Mo. in 1920.

. . . .

In 1932, back to my English public school, Downside, in the depths of the Depression, across Canada by cattle train and the Atlantic by cattle boat. The Headmaster's egregious chauffeur Tom picks me up at Southampton.

"Late again, sir. You'll catch it." I laughed. It was weird to be called sir again. I dropped off to sleep as we wound our way through the countryside I got to know so well, Hardy's Wessex. Three times a week, we used to go pub crawling through its narrow stone-walled lanes covered with ivy, from one old inn to the other, reeling back to Downside dead drunk. Nearer school, we had haunts in the ancient hedges by the Roman road, leafy tunnels and refuges from the rain, hollowed out by shepherds centuries ago. Since then, generations of Downside boys have lain in them with a chum, smoking forbidden cigarettes, enjoying each other's company, enjoying each other—forbidden fruits.

Downside was, is, beautiful. A little world of its own, monastery and school since the Middle Ages. With Henry VIII and his landgrab of the monasteries, the Reformation expelled them to Douai in Flanders. They came back under James II and fled again when he did, to return when George IV was much under the thumb of Catholic Mrs. Fitzherbert, his mistress. The dates, if not the details, are incorporated into the Gregorian arms of the Downside abbey and school. Do they still appear in a bold black seal on the dead white glaze of the thick Wilton china we ate off in the Refectory? The four Houses of the school: Caverel, Barlow, Roberts, and Smythe, are named after English Catholic martyrs, rich benefactors, titled people, all well-connected. The Benedictines have been called the great Country Gentlemen of the Church.

The Monastery and its Abbey loom over the school, fairly mysterious and apart. Up long echoing stone-vaulted corridors, musky with the smell of men and incense, schoolboys can visit monks who are relatives or close friends of the family or even monks on whom they have developed a schoolboy crush. Such monks may give special instruction, others come down to take daily classes. One or two sleep in the school buildings and take on scholarship boys for extra tutoring in preparation for Oxford. The Headmaster is always a monk.

"The Sack," as we called him, was a fairly alarming figure: more than six feet of black Benedictine sacking, out of which emerged a tiny chinless head with a great beak like a nose. His voice carried for miles in great squawks. He slushed his words in a way so easy to imitate that it was our constant delight. He reigned over many generations of raw backsides beaten into hamburger by his birch and his malacca cane. Middle-aged men, who still bore his stripes across the ass, sent their sons back to Downside for more. Age had mellowed him by the time I came along. As the Daimler swept into the quad and drew up by the bell tower, there he was waiting for me in the middle of the night. He so nearly filled the Gothic doorway that he stood in a nimbus of light. Tom the chauffeur muttered a mock *God help us all!* The Sack threw a long shadow across all our lives. He never beat Me. More's the pity, perhaps. Might have learned something useful like those noisy leather joys in which the English, the Germans, and now even the Americans so delight.

An Encomium for Allen Ginsberg

*"An Encomium for Allen Ginsberg" (1984) was, apparently, the only text
Gysin ever wrote about another writer. Though never really close friends
with Ginsberg, and sometimes skeptical of the poet's public persona, he
nonetheless gives credit to Ginsberg and even the Beats, especially for their
activism and influence. This piece was written for the festschrift* Best
Minds: a tribute to Allen Ginsberg, *ed. Bill Morgan and Bob Rosenthal
(New York: Lospecchio Press, 1986).*

Historically, it would be hard to find a more political poet than Allen Ginsberg. Leafing through the *Penguin Companion to Classical & Byzantine, Oriental & African Literature,* one finds only the old Roman satirists who might be
considered political. Greek Old Comedy and Aristophanes were satirical, but
they were playwrights. The devious Byzantines were busy getting their tongues
cut out and being blinded for religious reasons, for heresy and not for their
poesy. Pre-Islamic Arab poets were rather like African griots who ran off at the
mouth with two different kinds of publicity. Sometimes you paid them to
start, and other times to stop, or the poet took to flight. Poets often had trouble with heads of state like Fidel Castro who has imprisoned poets for twenty
years. Allen was lucky to be expelled from Cuba.

Allen had a spot of bother in other places like Czechoslovakia, where he was
crowned King of the May one day and run out of the country the next. And
India, where Madame Gandhi learned of his Hip Hindu poets he had sown on
her parched soil only after he had left for Japan and eventually Canada, where
he descended on my mother in Vancouver. His visit made her into the lady
with a salon for Pacific poets who has been posthumously beatified by the local
avant-garde movement known as the Western Front. Thus do poets dispense
their beatitude. Allen has always had plenty of beatitude to bat around and in
the Inscrutable East he picked up pointers on how to wield pacific powers over
the multitudes.

He gave a dazzling demonstration of this art at the Italian poetry fest we
called Beatniks on the Beach. Shaping up more like a rowdy rock festival, it took
place in front of a jerrybuilt stage on the sands of Castelporziano near Ostia, the
ancient port of Imperial Rome through which Cleopatra sailed up the Tiber on
her barge trailing all the perfumes of Arabia. The Communist mayor of modern
Rome had invited both American and Russian poets to participate: Ginsberg
and Corso and Burroughs to cut Yevtushenko and a couple of stalwart Party

Poets with their KGB bodyguards. Night fell as we took off for this wild stretch of sand just before you get to the Roman Bareass Beach, where about five thousand very sunburnt young people were dancing naked around bonfires, reeking of shish kebab, sunoil, and cannabis. The stars were out.

Even before the first pushy poets latched onto the mike and wouldn't let go, it began to look like a riot was brewing. Catcalls were followed by fistfuls of sand whipping across the stage followed by bottles. Allen leapt to his feet and with outstretched arms began intoning an interminable *OMmmmmmm!* We all picked it up and the audience soon settled back into it too, grinning up in evident appreciation. The evening was saved. Nobody else but Allen could have done it.

Allen has taken on a lot more vicious mobs than that and bigger ones. He is our first naked poet in the thousands of years since antiquity. Howling *Gay Lib!* he took on the Moral Majority. He took on the CIA for dealing in tons of Junk from the Golden Triangle. He took on the Imperial Presidency and the IRS and the War and the Bomb and nuclear energy. Poetry versus Plutonium. We'll see who wins that one but Allen is still in there fighting and he has friends, whole generations of them. His voice will be heard for a long time to come. The Beats are not just one more literary luncheon society but the first ever to have influence on a planetary scale. Allen built up the Beats by seeing to it that their work got published, and he took the news on the road to Katmandu and Katmandon't. Nothing deterred him.

One cannot deny that Allen Ginsberg has changed the world at least somewhat. Since him no one should settle for anything less from a poet.

Paris, July 10, 1984

Calligraffiti of Fire

"Calligraffiti of Fire" (1985) was written on the occasion of Gysin's last major work as a painter, a sequence of ten canvases conceived in the style of a makemono *or Japanese folding book, which collectively bore the title. The text was printed in the catalogue when the paintings were shown at the Galerie Samy Kinge in Paris, in March 1986. For years, above all due to a lack of adequate space, Gysin had been relatively inactive as a visual artist. Thanks to James Kennedy–McCann, whose Akademia Foundation sponsored him in his final years, Gysin was able to rent a studio and achieve this work, which drew together a number of his ongoing methods and concerns. He liked to say that it took him seventy years to create these paintings, which he executed in seven days. The title itself points to both the past and the future: the calligraphic thrust in much of his painting, ever since his studies of Japanese and Arabic calligraphies in the 1940s and 1950s, and also his interest in the younger graffiti artists, notably Keith Haring and George Condo, who were fans and friends of his. The paintings remained in Kennedy-McCann's private collection through the rest of the decade and resurfaced only in the early 1990s when a Dutch bank took possession of them. The work was not seen in public again until the summer of 1998, at the Edmonton Art Gallery in Canada, in the largest retrospective of Gysin's career as a visual artist,* Brion Gysin: I Am That I Am, *organized by John Geiger, José Férez Kuri, and Bruce Grenville.*

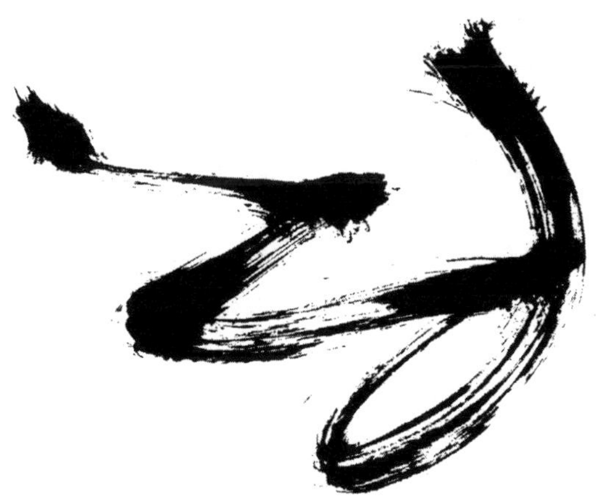

Brion Gysin's "personal sign," used throughout his calligraphic work

My picture is to be read from right to left across ten canvases. We are in the oriental picture space.

My picture reads from right to left like a Japanese folding book, a *make-mono.* There is a celebrated *makemono* in the Boston Museum of Fine Arts representing fire racing through the endless bamboo and rice paper pavilions of an imperial palace.

I pored over this great masterpiece in the 1940s when I was studying Japanese in the army.

After the war, Japanese art shops opened in New York, where I bought a blank *makemono.* I played with it like a silent accordion for years before daring to make even a single sign on it. I was still looking for my sign, a sign of my own derived from the cursive Japanese *so-shō,* called "grass writing." I looked deep into plant forms and found what I wanted in the soy sprout whose explosive power can overturn monuments.

But Japanese calligraphy dangles like vines falling out of the picture space. It was not until I got to Morocco in 1950 that I became really aware of Arab calligraphy, which rushes across the picture space from right to left like an army with banners. When I wrote my own sign repeatedly linking it across the picture space, I discovered dense Moroccan crowds dancing across my pictures. For me, they danced to the music of Jajouka, the hill village of the Master Musicians who still celebrated the Rites of Pan under Muslim disguise. Their magical music held me spellbound in Morocco for what is still a third of my lifetime, from 1950 to 1973.

There at last I dared take out and unfold my *makemono* to make my first Big Picture with stone-ground Japanese ink and British watercolors. Entitled *A Trip from Here to There, a Journey to Jajouka,* it is about a meter long. The New York MOMA catalogue has a note on how to handle a *makemono* according to the Japanese view of the picture space.

Alfred Barr bought this from me for the museum while we were staying with Peggy Guggenheim during the All-American Venice Biennale of 1962. My work can be seen at the Museum of Modern Art in New York on application.

Back in New York in 1964–65, I found a smaller blank *makemono* on which I worked with bright Japanese oil pastels.

When the Akademia Foundation approached me in 1985 with their "Fire" project, I showed them this *makemono* entitled *Summer Fires 1965,* made to be "read" in ten movements. I had always wanted to paint a big picture across ten canvases, hence: *Calligraffiti of Fire.*

The Sculpted Line

*"The Sculpted Line" (1985) was written as the preface to the catalogue for
the show* Keith Haring *in Bordeaux.*

What an event it was for me, the first time I saw Keith Haring draw on a
wall.

Here in Paris, coming through an ancient alley next door to my own view
on the Monster Museum of Beaubourg, the Centre Pompidou, Keith whipped
out a Magic Marker to sign a wall for me, for us. He put it into the last clear
space in the midst of the wild tangle of the local French graffiti which has
sprung up so recently here in emulation of New York. You cannot sign the
Paris metro the way they still sign the subway. Only Keith has been invited to
cover a paper set up for him in the metro and local collectors collected it pretty
quick.

As I stopped to watch Keith repeat his copyright Baby, my jaw dropped.
Why? Because the way he did it was so different from what I expected to see
him do. The line he produced was not a drawn line but something quite else.

Lines can be drawn or pulled or written or scribbled or scrawled or, now-
days, be sprayed out of a can. Keith Haring's line is something else. It looks a
bit like an engraved line or a sculpted line but it is not either of them. It is a
carved line, like the one the man made when he first used it to cut what he
wanted out of the air in the back of the cave. It has been deduced from evidence that the man cut his own copyright Bison in the total dark way back
there. How was that again? How could he? Well, he could because he could feel
his new line, feel it in the dark because he carved it. No telling, of course, exactly how he did it nor will I tell you exactly why I consider Haring's line to be
a carved one, carved rather than drawn. But it is or, at least, so I think.

Paris
October 1985

The Last Museum

The Last Museum *(1986), Gysin's final novel, was written and rewritten many times, starting in 1968 when Gysin received an advance to write a novel based on the Beat Hotel (which initially incorporated the events of 1968 in Paris as well). The first chapter, from a version titled* Beat Museum-Bardo Hotel, *was published in the Gysin issue of* Soft Need *(1977); the second chapter appeared as a separate chapbook from Inkblot Press (1982); versions and out-takes from the final draft of the book were published in a rare artbook edition of two hundred copies with fifty-two drawings by Keith Haring, under the title* Fault Lines, *which include the two drawings reproduced here (another Haring drawing also served as the published novel's cover).*

"The Door," adapted in 1984, was taken from the opening pages of the novel; Gysin performed this text with Ramuntcho Matta's band at The Casino in Paris, among other places. The two brief introductions offered here were written in 1982 and 1986: the first, to accompany an excerpt from the first chapter that I tried unsuccessfully to get published; the second, as his text for the book jacket, which was never used.

In his introduction, Burroughs described the novel as: "a guidebook, a map for navigating the area between Death and Rebirth, or for rising above the dreary repetitious cycle. . . . Brion Gysin has written a modern Book of the Dead, for those souls who could never be content with any Western Lands. . . . Here, souls are flying apart from the center in specialized shards, all going separate ways, packing bags full of memorabilia. . . . In the Land of the Dead all pretense is swept aside. Attics yield up their dusty secrets. . . . This cannot be prettified, and Brion Gysin's vision spares neither himself nor the reader."

Nor does it spare many of his friends or acquaintances, for that matter. Even more than The Process, *this final novel revisits many points in Gysin's own life as a sort of "fractured autobiography," in Robert Palmer's phrase.* The Last Museum *may also be considered a last vision, the author's sly farewell to all that he gathered up in his rather fantastic, if always uncertain, life. Yet here too, it reflects the logical extension of a familiar impulse. As Palmer remarked in his foreword to the 1987 reprint of the earlier novel, "Getting Out—out of [the] prison [of words], out of the body, and ultimately out of this world entirely and into space—was for Brion the Great Work. The purpose of his art . . . was Liberation."*

The structure of this novel, set in the near future, draws on the history of the Beat Hotel—in Paris of the late 1950s and early 1960s—crossed with

The Tibetan Book of the Dead, *also known as the* Bardo Thodol. *The after-death Bardo plane consists of seven zones of one week each, here corresponding to the protagonist's ascent through the hotel, at one floor of illusion per week. However, the novel ends at the fourth floor, with some knowledge of what lies ahead upstairs. In working on the book over the years, Gysin kept extensive scrapbooks where his ideas accumulated added texture; in 1978 he even went around by car to the California places mentioned in the narrative, where the protagonist has built his Museum of Museums. As in his earlier novel, the protagonist,* PG *the Sixth, is a composite of Gysin himself* (BG) *and an imagined descendant of J. Paul Getty. Moreover, as a number of characters tend to merge into others, there are also aspects of Ian Sommerville in the protagonist, who, like the protagonist, died in an automobile accident (in 1976) and to whom the novel was at one time dedicated.*

A couple of final notes. First, Gysin makes constant use of his own themes and phrases ("Kick that habit, man," "I am that I am"), particularly the recurring description of flicker and the experiences of the Dreamachine. These are woven in among many comic references in the novel as well as the inclusion of friends (not only Burroughs—who is even mixed up with Baudelaire in the second chapter, where Le Festin Nu, *the French title of* Naked Lunch, *is confused with* Les Fleurs du Mal—*but also Burroughs characters such as Violet the baboon). Second, just as Gysin was a renowned raconteur, and much as in* The Process, *this novel is especially noteworthy for its oral quality, the voices written such that they can be heard.*

The Door

In the Rue Gît le Coeur
on the Left Bank of Paris
in the Latin Quarter
near the Place St. Michel

There is—or there was
this rundown, fleabitten
"Maison Meublée" 13ème order
the hotel without even a name . . .

Until, because of the Beatniks
like Burroughs, Ginsberg & Corso
who lived there in the flying Fifties
and the psychedelic Sixties,

it got to be called
the old Beat Hotel.

When I got there this last time
this very last time
it was round about midnight
and cold as the grave.

The street door was closed tight
and there wasn't a light to be seen
but I thought I smelt grass—*Mmm*!
and heard sneaky Moroccan music . . .

So I knocked: Duk Duk Duk!
like the Ayrabs do
"Hé, la porte!" I cried: "Ouvrez la porte!
Fissa . . . Fissa!" I added
in my best colonial Arabic:
"*F'ta el bab!* Open the door!"

"*Eshkoon?*" breathed the door
"*Eshkoon,* yourself!" I snapped back
"Who said that, who's that?
Or was it the wind?"

"*Eshkoon?*" creaked the door again:
"*Ouesh asm'ek?*
Who are you? What's your name?"

"I don't hav'to tell *you* my name!" I cry
"Open up! I own this hotel and
I gave it its name . . . its new name.

I dubbed this old dump the Bardo Hotel
because of its 49 rooms on 7 floors
like the 49 days and nights after death
in the *Tibetan Book of the Dead*."

"Tibetans don't run this hotel no more,"
groaned the door. "I know that," I said,
"As I told you just now
I bought this historic monument
for my Museum of Museums in Malibu.
I'm having it moved out to California tonight
and you . . . Door . . . are going along with it!" I said.

"Not me!" squealed the door. "Not me! Pas moi!
I don' wanna have no truck with no Tibetans
I won't!
I am the Door and the Posts of the Door
in the Ancient *Egyptian* Book of the Dead.

No mortal can pass through my portal
until he gives me his name
his *real* name."

"Well, if you're so smart, then
tell me my name
I'm not sure I have a real name
a real secret *real* name."

"All the big Beatniks, your famous pals
Burroughs and Ginsberg and Corso
knew their real names," sneered the door.
"That's why their names are up there
on the plaque on the wall
inscribed in gold letters of marble
paid for by the Ministère de la
Culture and the Ville de Paris . . .
You read French?"

"None of your business," I snarl
"Of course I read French. Open up . . .
Door!"

"Not without your real name.
If you can read French you can see
that all the bonafide Beatniks
with names . . . real names
have their own rooms in here,
as the plaque says: Forever!"

"Forever?" I cried.
"Forever and a day," swore the door.

"Well," I swore back,
"That day is coming tonight!
Lemme in there . . . I'm calling the Coast
This whole show is due out there at dawn
in sunny southern California
I'm having it set down square on the
San Andreas Faultline . . .
You know all about that, don't you?"

"Of course I do," admitted the door,
"Everyone does.
When the Great Earthquake comes
the whole state of California
is going to slide into the Pacific.
Say! You wouldn't do that to us,
would you?
Wipe out all your old buddies?"
It sobbed.

"Yes," I said firmly, "I would!"

Hotel Bardo

/   Chapter 1   /

In the year 2000+plus, little PG the Sixth has all the money in the world, or thinks he has, since he has created the Museum of Museums which runs from his Ancestor the Founder's Museum in Malibu to Death Valley. Into this area surrounded by the Great Wall of China he has gathered all the treasures of the world and set them out on the San Andreas Faultline for future disposal.

His most private hobby is the Beat world and the Beat Hotel in Paris circa 1960, in the time of his ancestors, PG the Second and PG the Third, the Dear Ear, both friends of the Beats.

After his "accident" he finds himself in the old hotel which is for him the Bardo. He begins in Room One.

The Bardo has seven rooms on each floor of seven, forty-nine days and nights.

The Last Museum: Back Jacket Copy

Long after the Beatniks themselves had suffered a sea-change, their rundown old hotel in Paris, known as the Beat Hotel, became a "collectible."

Rich little PG Six, who inherited the Last Museum out in California, felt bound to carry the whole thing off to set it down on the San Andreas Faultline along with all the other treasures of the world which his forbears lined up for the day when southern Cal cracks off and slides into eternal oblivion.

When he got to the hotel and had to pass through its mortal portal, he found the seven rooms on each of the seven floors to be as full of monsters as the Tibetan Bardo in their Book of the Dead.

Is there sex after death? Here he finds every hilariously perverse answer to that burning question.

☞ The Last Museum

Chapter One

For I have been a boy and a girl and a bush
and a bird and a dumb sea fish . . . .
—Diogenes Laertius, VIII, 77

| Ground Floor, Week One, Room One |

Rap! Rap! Rap!
Knock! Knock! Knock!

"Let me in, it's cold as the grave out here!" I can hear myself crying as I pound on the narrow street door of the old Beat Hotel on the Left Bank of Paris in the Latin Quarter. "It's cold as the grave and I'm out here all alone in the dark. Lemme in! Lemme *yinnnnn!*"

"Gnyaaa!" yawns the door without budging an inch. "Go 'way!"

"Who said that?"

"Me," groans the door. "An' you, who are *you*? Whazya name?"

"I don't have to give you my name," I snap back. "I own this rotten old flea-bitten French rooming-house. I bought it up lock, stock and bistro. Open up!"

"Whazya name?" grates the door again. "Nobody gets in without he gives me his name, his real true secret name. Whaz yours?"

"Secret name? I wish I had one. I'm the richest little boy in the world and I don't like to give out my name. My name makes things cost double, at least."

"It's gonna cost ya the world to pass through *my* portal, sonny boy. So, gimme ya name. Cough up."

"Well, the newspapers call me Little PG or Young PG Six."

"I don' give a shit what the newspapers call ya," groans the door. "What we want is your real true secret name. Everyone has one. If you don't know yours, that's just . . . plain . . . dumb."

"Fuck you!" I yell, giving the door one swift kick.

"Ouch!" it yelps. "Violence won't get you nowheres in a hurry."

"I'm gonna have you torn off your rusty old hinges tomorrow!" I shout. "I bought this historic monument, the old Beat Hotel, to have it moved out to my Museum of Museums in Malibu where I've collected all the other great historic monuments in the world. Scattered over the big part of southern California I own, I've got the Sphinx and the Pyramids, the Acropolis and Versailles and the Louvre and all that pinned down along the San Andreas Faultline. You know about the Faultline?"

"Sure," squeals the door, "everybody does. When the great earthquake come, as it must, the whole state of California is goin' to slide off under the Pacific Ocean."

"Only half the state," I insist. "And not one day too soon!"

"Ya gotta be jokin'."

"I am not. This renowned rat-trap, the old Beat Hotel, is going to be set down next to the Agora of Athens which I have made into the shopping mall of a small town in Apollo County, California called Palmdale, Palmdale-on-the-Bulge, the first to go."

"You don't *mean* that," moans the door.

"I do. My magical movers, a reputable Swiss firm called Interdean International Movers, can do anything I tell them to do. They brought over the Great Wall of China for me to set down along the line of the Los Angeles aqueduct, out across the Mojave Desert past the Diamond Mountains to Death Valley."

"That figures," admits the door rather churlishly, "but your Interdead Irrational Movers can't move you in here tonight unless you come up with your name and not just your number, Little PG Six."

"I'm exhausted," I whine. "What I need is a good hot bath."

"Yeah," sniffs the door, "you sure do. Phew! You're ripe."

"If you mean I smell bad . . ."

"You do. All dead people do but I like it. I'm kinky that way. 'S only normal."

"I had an accident back there," I admit, "but I'm just as alive as you are and I'm not going to take any more of your shit!"

"Shut up and stop screaming, willya. Nex' thing we know ya'all be wakin' the dead an' scarin' the naybors. So, can it! Lemme tellya, I'm freakin' out too, I'm that lonely. Let's put it this way: I wanna piece an' you wanna peace an' I wanna you only. Ya follow me?"

"No, I don't but it does sound familiar. What kind of proposition is this, anyway? I don't understand you."

"I don' unnerstan' myself, sometimes. That make ya feel better?"

"Is that an Ancient Egyptian accent you're trying to put on?"

"Yeah," chuckles the door, "howja guess? I am the Door and the Posts of the Door of the Ancient Egyptian Book of the Dead."

"Have you been drinking or smoking or shooting or sniffing something?"

"Juss takin' what comes along natural, like you, f'rinstance. 'Cept, how could I know that the richest l'il old boy in the world would come along tonight wantin' ta get inta me?"

"You're making a big thing of this. All I want is a quiet night's sleep before they take out the hotel. I don't like the turn this conversation seems to be taking, sexually. I can't follow you, don't want to."

"I'm a soft touch. Whyncha touch me. Juss cuddle up. Y'all see I'm hot stuff. Out here all night all alone, I get kinda horny. In my day, I seen lotsa young boys, booful young boys like you, take out their cocks an' piss on me. Thass wha' I really like . . . Golden Showers. Whyncha try?"

"I haven't needed to take a piss since my accident."

"Juss take it out anyway. Maybe that'll help ya remember ya name. You want this hotel for your Museum of Museums because of that bunch of Beatniks who lived here, doncha?"

"Yes."

"Well, they all knowed their real names. Thass why their names are up there in the street on the wall above your head, inscribed in gold letters on marble paid for by the Ministère de la Culture and La Ville de Paris."

I took a step back into the street to look up and, at that moment, the heavy iron shutter on the bistro began to roll up very slowly, like the iron fire curtain in a theater before each performance.

What it revealed was a scene I knew from old photographs taken back in the twentieth century before I was born, at least this last time. Of course it looked strangely familiar but rather dreamlike. Through the steamy etched glass window and door, through the lace curtains and the spindly aspidistra plants, I could see the grubby little old bistro like the set for a faded French black-and-white movie made when my ancestor PG One was alive. The name *J. B. Rachou* was painted on the glass door in the calligraphic hand of an old-fashioned master sign painter. I recognized little blue-haired Madame Rachou, herself, inside there jumping up and down like a bellringer as she put her whole weight on the pulley which raised the heavy iron shutter in short jerks. She looked like some sort of toy on a spring, and for the first time since my accident I laughed heartily as I put my hand on the door to open it as soon as she had raised the shutter sufficiently.

On stepping inside, when I put my foot on the crazy-tiled floor, I felt a slight wave of vertigo, as if I might fall into the pattern. I felt not quite sure where the level of the floor was. This gave Madame Rachou time to skip behind her celebrated zinc-topped bar and jump on to an overturned wooden wine crate. It gave her the elevation she needed to dominate her whole domain, not only the three marble-topped tables with slim cast-iron legs but the whole hotel, all forty-nine rooms on the seven floors of it. She could do this with the aid of her Light Control Panel. Facing the bar, next to a door with a glass panel through which she could control the narrow hall and the door I had been talking to, was a panel of electric switches. Under each of these was a small enamel plaque with the number of the corresponding room. Above each of these was a tiny flashlight bulb which lit up as soon as the light was turned on in that room. Furthermore, she could look through the door into her dusty dining room which had a window giving on to the stairs and see at least the legs of anyone coming in or out. Behind her zinc counter, her short arms crossed over her pale blue dustcoat with a round smocked collar such as French working-class people wore every day except Sunday through the last century, she looked like a proper little tyrant if a kindly one.

"*Bonsoir*," she greeted me, "we were expecting you."

"I wasn't even expecting to be here, myself," I mumbled sheepishly.

"I'm afraid you'll have to wait a while for your room. That young lady got here just ahead of you. You recognize her, of course, she was in the same accident with you. She was hitchhiking."

A gigantic American chick with a backpack and a bedroll and God knows what all else piled around her seemed to have materialized at one of the café tables. I knew I had seen her someplace before but I said, "No, I don't think so."

One of the bulbs on the Light Control Panel began to glow and burst into nova before it fused and went out.

"That will be Room Eight for you, Ma'mzelle. It is being vacated. You," she went on, turning to me, "you will have to go into Room One."

"I didn't know I had to go into any room," I objected. "You know who I am, don't you?"

"Of course I do," she snapped, somewhat vexed. "You will have to go through all the rooms, one after the other, except for Rooms Two to Seven on this ground floor which have already been torn out by your rather over-zealous Swiss movers. Even Room One should not be available. They wanted to take it out too but they had trouble trying to get the plaster ceiling down in one piece."

"Because of the painting of the nude woman," I nodded. "I know all about that. I gave orders for them to take great care about that painting. My curator of French painting considers it a masterpiece."

"Masterpiece, hmph," snorted Madame Rachou. "I don't think it's decent. An insult to womanhood. If I had known someone was painting that on my ceiling, I would have put them out of the hotel."

"I've only seen photographs," I admitted, "but some of my curators did find her a bit pornographic. They dubbed her The Open-Gate Girl. By the way, that reminds me, I should call my museum to tell them I'm here. Do you mind if I use the phone a minute? You can put it on my account. I've got to get through to the Coast."

"That line is for local calls only," she said a bit sharply. "They know you are here."

"How could they? I didn't tell anybody I was coming over to check out the old Beat Hotel. I didn't know I was coming, myself."

"This isn't the old Beat Hotel," she said, looking at me severely over the top of her steel-rimmed spectacles. "This is the Bardo, the Bardo Hotel. You will spend your first week here on the ground floor in Room One. Take the key off the hook on that board by the door and cross the corridor. You will find yourself facing the door to Room One."

Little used as I am to taking orders from anyone, I found myself doing as I was told. The hall was dark and dirty. As I passed it, I gave the front door a swift kick in its backside.

"Smart ass!" it snarled, "You'll never get out of here alive."

A big bed with a dirty sheet draped over it filled up most of Room One. Another dirty sheet hung over the window which gave directly on to the street. Room One must have been a small shop at one time because one wall was lined with empty shelves. I threw myself on the bed and looked straight up at the famous Open-Gate Girl with her tits hanging down like ripe cantaloupes and her thighs spread wide apart. Her exposed vulva glistened like seafood. I was horrified to see that my pants were open and I was getting an erection. I remembered what my guru back in California had always warned me, that in the Bardo one must avoid welcoming wombs and the temptation into the first dreary rebirth that comes along.

I sprang out of bed to pull back the sheet over the window because I heard chanting out in the street and there was the whole band of the antique Beatniks with their heads shaven like Tibetan monks wearing next to nothing at all. They have nothing much on but the skimpy off-the-shoulder orange robes of Buddhist brethren and it is snowing. Their noses are blue with the cold, icicles dangling. Their bare heads are shaved blue and they are handling long ivory rosaries of skull-shaped prayer beads, long as skipping ropes. Ginsberg and Orlovski and even Giorno can just about get by in this drag but on Burroughs wearing his very American hat and glasses it looks simply embarrassing. Kerouac looks kinda cute and so do some of the anonymous acolytes and hangers-on who are earnestly passing around a community copy of the Bardo Thodol, the Tibetan Book of the Dead, handwritten on dried banana leaves and, in the act of doing so, destroying it. This gives me great satisfaction. That's the way I like to see them go. There is the very last copy of the Bardo Thodol which I bought from the very last Dalai Lama for a huge sum of money and it is dissolving into dust between their greedy fingers. I am delighted. This is just what I hoped would happen to it. I fall back on the big bed with my cock still sticking straight up, pointing into the twat of the Open-Gate Girl.

"I'm Suzi," she smiles as she settles herself down on my cock with a very feminine flurry. "I'm Number One Girl at the Sphinx," she gurgles as she works it into her. "I take care of the Specials, like you, you dear old thing you!"

"The Spinx?" I murmur.

"Yes, the Sphinx. The Sphinx is the Number One House in the world, in the Universe! And I'm Top Girl in the Sphinx, after Madame, of course. I'm the most expensive whore in the world. Madame sent me. Sends me to you. I can do everything for everybody. Age sex creed color etcetera mean nothing to me but more money and more love, of course. I love Love. And money is nice too. It's that simple. Love is lovely. I love everything and more than anything, I love monsters like you, you know. People with a little too little of this or that or none at all or simply much too much of some other little thing like two fully developed cocks hanging down between their legs, or a hunchback, or something."

"Ouch!" I cry, horrified, "get the hell offa me, willya. Ya breakin' my balls and I never even heard of a man with two cocks."

"I take care of the curious, the crippled and the careworn," she insists. "One crack out of my wise whips can bring down a government, ruin a country, start wars, change maps, wipe out the entire population of a continent if I wanted to . . . but I don't. I want only one thing and you know what that one thing is, don't you? You do, you do! It's you you YOU!"

"And I want you to stop humping me! You're hurting me."

"You silly old thing," she coos in my ear, "why don't you let yourself go, darling . . . hmmmm?"

"Because I'm already gone, I guess," I manage to mutter.

"Oh, come on! You can be utterly frank with me. Tell me everything, every last little thing. All your plans hopes fears ambitions and secret desires. There's nothing I don't know about men, nothing I haven't already been through with them, time and again. I've had millions and millions of men crawling at my feet throughout all of history. There's nothing we haven't seen at the Sphinx. We've had flagellations and crucifixions going on day and night for years, forever. We deal in bondage servage slavery humiliation mortification suffering torture disfigurement detention retention, you name it! We've got sacred prostitutes, consecrated nuns dressed up to here in starch on the front but behind their bare asses are hanging out for you to pinch or to stroke kiss caress suck penetrate and paddle but not to whip because a good whipping can put a girl out of commission for days if you break the skin. The Syndicate won't stand for it. Madame has to be very strict. We all wear six-inch high heels and a money belt, nothing else during working hours. You come in off the street along the entrance hall through three sets of swinging doors that buzz as you pass them and there is Madame to greet you from behind the Cash Desk with her curls piled high on her head like a heap of gold coins. You buy your plastic chips with the Sphinx stamped on them from her and they are good for girls girls girls! A Gurl makes her own price with a customer who pays her in the chips she turns in to Madame at the end of her shift and gets credit for them at the Syndicate Store. No cash changes hands but you can get anything you want in the Syndicate Store, anything in the whole wide world. That's how I was able to commission this image of me I live on in, the Open-Gate Gurl, direct from the artist who painted it without even knowing what he was doing, of course."

"I guess that goes for most of them," I manage to mumble from under her muff which she has thrust in my face like a hairy wet mop.

"Yep, that poor painter's dead. Got cancer of the rectum and committed suicide. Say, just give me your tongue a bit, willya!"

"'S lucky for me I don't have to breathe any more but I won't give you head."

"Wow! Wonderful! That's it, you've done it," she cries, "now you're talking. You're doin' swell, just keep that up."

She is humping me like a sex-maddened sea cow I saw once as I sailed past on my yacht while she was jerking herself off on a buoy in the Catalina Channel. Over Suzi's shoulder I catch a glimpse of a whole gaggle of school kids, shading their eyes as they press their little wet noses against the plate-glass window which gives on to Shit-in-the-Bed Street.

"Hey, there's some kids out there watching us. Lemme outta here, willya!"

"I'm coming! I'm coming!" she cries.

"But those kids out there! They got nuns in hot pants out there behind them. And cops. And someone who looks like my mother! Oh, wow!"

"That's our public," she pants. "Oh, I'm so excited, darling. I'm so glad for you. This puts you back in the picture."

"Just let me pull the curtain a sec."

"No, no, no! They have every legal right to watch. It's good for minors to attend the whole show and see all the Special Sexhibits. It's Museum policy, approved by the state laws of California."

"What do you know about Museum policy and what's this Paris scene got to do with California?"

"Stoopid! Don't you even know where you are now? You're in the Museum and you gotta be glad of it. Men and boys will line up from here to eternity just to be laying where you are right now, babe!"

"You mean that as a transitive or as an intransitive verb, doll?"

"I wooden know, I owny work here."

"Say, the whole room seems to be vibrating. It feels like an earthquake. Can you hear that rumbling sound?"

"Don't you just love it! That's only silly old Vesuvius, dearie, grumbling away as usual because we're having such a good good time in here. Aren't we? Don't pay it no mind. Sometimes at this time of day there's a quick rain of fire but it's only a shower and it clears out the crowd, tourists and holiday-makers. What's nasty are pumice stones as big as your head. They're so light they don't hurt much but they do pile up in the street something awful like pumpkins. You and I don't hafta worry about those silly old poison gases, do we, since we got no more need of breathing, anyway. The worst that can happen to us is that we get buried in that fine volcanic dust that hardens like plaster of Paris and we get sealed up in here, like in Pompeii or Herculaneum where the Villa de Lirium was once supposed to have been, if you can believe the word of your ancestor the Founder's architects and advisers. You see how the image can rise again and come back around again for a retread, you follow me?"

"Yes, I do and only too well. It's the very thing I want to make a break with, forever. Enough is enough! Let's have no more retreads, no more images of images of images. It's all done with mirrors. We want the real thing now and nothing but."

"If you're so smart then, what is it, the Real Thing, according to you?"

"Enlightenment. Let there be Light."

"Lava, liquid lava burning bright, that's the one thing we really do have to worry about."

"Hellfire?"

"And brimstone."

"Wow!"

"Yep, that's the lot. Let's get going again, shall we?"

"I can't get it up because of all those people staring in here."

"OK, honey, forget it, but let's split before the ceiling comes down. I've got my Rocket on the roof. We can go for a spin in the country."

Her Rocket on the roof is an out-of-date model and I don't much like the looks of it but I have to admit Suzi does know how to drive it. As soon as she ignites it and throws in the gears, you know that this pile is really hers, the way she handles it. We are flying low over Normandy, apparently, barely skimming over farms and tiled rooftops. Cows and even cathedrals loom up alarmingly only to sweep away under our exhaust. According to her control panel, we are traveling at twice the speed of light. She has one hand and elbow on the steering and the other deep in my crotch where nothing is happening, naturally.

"Where are we going?"

"This is my afternoon off," she says. "I asked Madame if I could take you to meet an old pal of mine who is nine years old going on ninety. A real little Buddha. But, then, everyone is having little Buddhas these days, aren't they? I don't want to boast but my little Buddha is something special. You'll see. Like you, my son's an Old Soul, of course. My son! Oh I know you two'll make out, get it on together. It's a real break for an Old Soul to score for a beautiful young body, you dig."

At that point she was looking deep into my shallow blue eyes and just missed the spire of what looked like Chartres Cathedral.

"Suzi!" I yelp, "you better watch out or we'll have another accident."

"Accident?" she screams into the wind of the world. "I never had an accident yet. You're the one had the accident, Buster."

"Don't look at me like that. Look where we're going."

"This old contraption of mine knows its own way out here, knows its own way to the FUNNY FARM. You see, I just leave it on automatic. This old soft machine of mine, we've been over this trail together so many times, I can't tell you. My own little Buddha has been up here with the Tibetans ever since he was going on four. What happened was, I had passed out at home once on some bad stuff somebody gave me and when I came to he was gone. Just like that. No note to mamma. No nothing. Just picked up his skateboard and sailed away by himself up the highway and I didn't see him again for nearly nine months. Time enough to have had another one, you'll say, but since I was working at the Sphinx night and day I had my Fallopian tubes pinched off. I was beside myself with worry, you can imagine, barely able to get through the night-shift on the old workbench. Madame was very kind. She put me into Room One where I take on the Specials like you, my dear. I was into Tantric Kundalini and Tai Chi and Rajneesh and all those sorta sexual disciplines, so I could take care of it. I really dig working in One. Instead of being out on the parlor floor with the rest of the girls, I can meditate between clients. It's got so's I can use my meditation in my business. A shift goes by like a song and I draw down more money. Men are so silly. Lots of French businessmen and even Cabinet ministers always want to play Cock-a-doodle-doo or, as they call it in French, Co-co-ri-co! Can you imagine, they wanna play Rooster! I have a rubber cork with red white and blue cock feathers stuck into it which I ram up their asses after tying their hands behind their backs so they can go flapping around with an erection while I play the broody hen. It's all so very French, isn't it?"

"Suzeee! watch out where you're going! You just ran over a whole flock of chickens."

"That musta bin the farmyard of the old château, I guess, so we're gettin' there. The old château is at the end of this long avenue of trees. Don't mind that noise this contraption makes, we're not fallin' apart. That's just my air-brakes. Ooops! That almost did it."

As we sweep down the avenue of bare trees, I shut my eyes against the glare of the low winter sun hanging like a big billion-watt bulb setting between the evenly spaced trunks. They were planted at exactly the right distance apart and we are traveling at exactly the right speed for them to produce flicker in the alpha band, at between eight and thirteen interruptions of light per second. Well-remembered galaxies begin to spin through my interior space, flashing in all their unearthly colors. I am delighted, naturally. It means that my EEG has not flattened out yet and the old brain is still working.

"Just wish you'd shut up a minute."

She is babbling on about her business as women will, boasting that she is the only whore in the whole wide world who knows how to provoke ultimate orgasm in the male by some fancy figure of love only she knows how to perform properly, called Napoleon on the Ramparts. "Here we are. We have arrived," she says. "So there! Aren't I clever!"

And here is Burroon, William Siegfried Burroon, as I have suddenly decided to call him. I know him instinctively because I would never have recognized him from his pictures in my archive or his old movies Uklut and I used to have at home. And here I am home again. Whatever just happened? And how? It is almost too much for me. William is standing out on the broad front steps of our old château in the rain. His silver-rimmed glasses are glinting out from beneath the huge hood of a woolly Moroccan jellaba beneath which his pale and impassive old junky face looks like two ivory profiles stuck together. I stand there stock-still for a long minute. I don't know what it is but something really radical is happening inside of me. As soon as he speaks, I know what it is:

"You're looking good, Ion," he says, "in the, uh, circumstances."

He mistakes me for his young friend Ion Sommerville.

Now I know all about Ion Sommerville. I've studied up on him and his short life so I want to check at once to see if I have by some goofy mistake in transfer become poor Ion. Sommerville crashed his car, killing himself on the way back from the country post-office where he had just received a copy of a scurrilous personal attack on him by an ex-friend in Amsterdam. This article has a graphic description of his penis, its shape and size, so I flip down the codpiece of my space suit to check on it. No doubt about it, the cock in there is my own. Any man would know his own penis anywhere, now wouldn't he? After all!

Buroon is welcoming me into the old château, making it sound like this is his place more than mine. I laugh, knowing these old tricks of his and turn back on the driveway to see what has happened to Suz'. And there she is doing prostrations, full Tibetan prostrations, flopping around in a big mud puddle in front of a small red-headed boy of about nine, in the orange-red robes of a Tibetan monk. He is not making the least move to help her up. He just stands there with an angelic smile on his shining face and he is standing in the foot of a rainbow. As she embraces his bare feet the rainbow seems to cleanse her too. She needs it.

"That's my little tulku," Buroon purrs in my ear as he lays a wooden arm over my shoulder. "I'm teaching him the basic tricks, like how to deal with women. You gotta terrorize women, thass all. That talkative mother of his is a perfect pest, a real pain in the ass. C'mon inside."

"That's a truly beautiful little manchild," I say. "And, may I ask, just what else are you teaching him?"

"Actually, I'm supposed to be teaching him English but in fact he is teaching me how to spell. You know what a sloppy speller I am. The only trouble with his English is he speaks it with that excruciating singsong East Indian accent. Otherwise, he knows more English grammar than I do. Knows the difference between a transitive and an intransitive verb, for example. More'n I do. Say, you feeling tired? Wanna go lay down for a while?"

"What I said was: what *else* are you teaching him, William? I know *you*."

"Tut tut, young man, let's have no more of that kind of talk. I'd like you to remember you're in a monastery."

"A monastery? It looks just like the old homestead to me, the place my great-great-grandfather Longfinger brought back stone by numbered stone from Normandy and set up on our spread out in Montana."

"Maybe it is. I dunno, me. Thought it was a movie set."

"It always did look like a movie set."

"Maya, Maya! Doesn't everything? All is illusion. Everything is illusion except the chow, eh? But the chow here is terrible. Either it's putrid wild boar for dinner with the evil old Comte de Vile who owns this dump or else it's rice rice rice with the lamas. What I wouldn't give for a good bowl of chilli at Horn & Hardharts! Or a T-bone steak even better!"

"This is my private study in here."

"Room Twenty-three, eh?"

"No, not really. We don't have numbers here, normally. I just chalked up 23 on the door, meaning: 23 Skiddoo! You'll see, the lamas have signs up all over the place, like: *Lamas' Dining Room* . . . and, *Lamas' Library.* On the front stairs it says: *Lamas' Staircase.* I have to go up the back way."

"What happens when you get up there?"

"It says: *Lamas' Bedrooms No Admittance at any Time under any Pretext.*"

"But you get admitted?"

"I know what they're doing in there. For a long time I hoped they were at least fucking each other in the ass, down on all fours in a ring on the rug. But now I know better. They're just sitting in the lotus position in front of the television like anybody else."

"Why do they have all those signs up?"

"To keep out the sneaky old Comte de Vile who is supposed to be handing the place over to them lock stock and barrel. On the one hand he really wants to give it to them to save his soul but on the other hand he just can't bring himself to sign the papers. The lamas got some kinda psychic headlock on him but he's still kicking. Time is on their side and they know it. The Comte thinks they're in deep meditation in there and maybe they are. Who knows what you're really doing when you sit watching television all day and night? You don't even know yourself half the time."

"Do you watch television, William?"

"Oh, I slide in there sometimes to sit with the lamas but you can't smoke. His Holiness suffers from asthma and that's that."

"But isn't that a bit odd for someone like him to be suffering from asthma? I always thought asthma was psychosomatic."

"When you've breathed the rarefied atmosphere he has breathed, my boy, it may not be at all surprising that the smog down here below on this level gives him asthma. When you come from the high altitudes he has known, you can easily be short of breath down here."

"Now that I come to think of it, I don't know what's happened to my own asthma. It's gone, just like that."

"And so," Buroon observes gravely, "so has your breath."

"Yes, but I seem to be getting on with my second wind for a while."

"For a while."

"Tell me, how did you end up here, Bill, you of all people? Have you become a Believer? Do you really and truly go along with this Tibetan trip? Tell me."

"Well, no, I wouldn't say that, not entirely. But, as I always said, you do have to take a broad general view of things. You see, my books weren't selling all that well and I was sick and tired of that lecture tour circuit. Never getting any writing done. All the time hopping in and out of airplanes. One damned faculty tea after the other with the faculty wives. Ugh! I like staying in all those good hotels for a while but that soon wore off. The whole thing was a drag and for not all that much money once IRS got its teeth in it. They're still on my ass for back taxes. They won't let you catch up. How can you? The more money you make, the more bread they want from you. It's a losing game. And then came this call. When I realized the lamas had set up a Buddhist monastery in the Normandy château your great-grandfather Senator Longfinger had brought over to the States stone by stone from France before World War One, how could I refuse? It was an offer I could *not* refuse, you understand me?"

"Oh, only too well!" I titter. "William, you really amaze me."

"The lamas invited me here for a Retreat and I retreated, thass all. What more can I say? I get along fine here. I like the lamas and the lamas like me. What more can one ask for?"

"I'm glad you feel at home here."

"Right away, I had a flash with His Holiness. We stay in touch whether I see him or not. We stay in a state of constant communication, night and day. I'm in clover."

"In *my* clover," I insisted.

"In *our* clover, old man. Take it easy. You'll like it here, during the stay you been booked for."

"In what used to be my own house!"

"Nobody can hold on to his own house forever. Besides, you always used to say youda burnt this place down behind you if you coulda. Why didncha?"

"Oh, I expect I can still learn something from the old homestead, even at this late date . . . even in my age and at my condition, as Madame used to say. English prepositions gave her a lot of trouble but I don't suppose they worry you, do they?"

"Ion, my boy, you have to take a broad general . . . ."

"That's enough out of you, Billyboy. It looks like you are giving your wholehearted approbation to this Tibetan trip, are you?"

"At some point in life, one can do worse than attach himself to something big rich powerful ancient holy *and* smart."

"But that sounds like the Catholics!"

"They're not all that ancient and the Church of Rome ain't all that smart."

"Despite what you've always pretended, you're for Control!"

"Can't you just see the Dalai Lama in the White House?"

"Don't be absurd, William. You're . . . you're irresponsible!"

"Why not? What've I got to lose? For the moment, I got it made. The lamas have a sensory deprivation tank in the wine-cellars in which I can immerse myself for as long as I like with my little Tulku. The two of us just sorta, ah, slop in and outta each other for hours. I mean psychically. And is it ever tasty! You really must score for a young body while you're here, Ion. It brings back the memories."

"I'm not all that interested in any mouldy old memories."

"Well, if you can say that and mean it, my boy, you've come a mighty long way, let me tell ya!"

"I don't want memories. I want the real thing."

"Uh, I don't rightly know just how much more of that you can have."

"Well, what *can* I have? What else does this old dump have to offer? Tell me."

"Oh, the Comte de Vile has his own shooting gallery in the basement and one of the finest collections of handguns in the world to practice with."

"I know all that. I first learned to fire my pistol on that range in the cellar when I was a kid of eleven. I'd just learned how to do it. Me and Luke my Indian lover just my own age used to lie flat on our backs on an old mattress and shoot our wads at the twat of Suzi the Open-Gate Girl on the ceiling. We used to keep score. Without touching yourself with your hands, you had to ejaculate with enough force to spatter her thighs. Only two points if you hit her knees or her tits. Three or four points depending how low you hit on her belly. Five points for wetting her pubic hair. Six full points for a bull's-eye anywhere around the clock. Player disqualified for touching his cock with his hands or blowing down over the flat of his belly."

Buroon laughs, briefly. "I thought you didn't want any old memories."

"Do I get to see Luke again? How long can I stay?"

"Not for long, I'm afraid. But make yourself at, uh, home, of course. I gotta cut out for a minute to see what His Holiness can do for you about a new outfit."

"I could do with some clothes."

"It's not just threads you need, boy, it's a body. I'll have to ask around, find what's available."

"Oh, just any old thing will do to time me . . . I mean, to tide me over."

"That was a very revealing slip, young Ion. Rash statements like that have a way of coming true, only too often. What we want for you is something eminently suitable, something perhaps better than your last deal, if possible."

"Last time around wasn't all that bad. I got a square deal, I guess . . . after a fashion. One thing I learned for sure on that trip is that *any* body at all is better than *no* body at all. That's why people are so scared of dying, isn't it?"

Buroon just stares back at me stonily, eyeglasses flashing warning signals. Well, as I know William, I have no clear idea just what these signals mean. The hood of Buroon's Moroccan jellaba drops back of itself. He is wearing a little skullcap from Marrakesh with Arab letters woven into it around a ring of green bicycles. His ears seem to be quivering. He lights up from inside like an electric hotplate getting ready to fuse.

"We are terribly sorry, Old Soul," says a singsong voice out of Buroon's mouth speaking with a very marked Anglo-Indian chi-chi accent, "but we seem to have nothing available for the moment in the way of suitable accommodation for you, owing to the, ah, reconstruction work which the Museum is doing in the

Bardo. You have seen the state of Room One. Rooms Two Three Four Five Six and Seven on the ground floor have been dismantled and shipped to Palmdale in California. You can perhaps profit from this, ah, anomaly in our arrangements by taking instruction. Someone on the other side is ready to give it to you. Look into the mirror on the door of the wardrobe."

Turning to the mirror, I drop my sheet to see how the old bod has come through post mortem. To my surprise, I am about nine years old and I have a hard-on. Buroon's little tulku is in there smiling as he offers me a saffron robe. I can see it is the orange dressing-gown I once got for Christmas and never much liked.

"Luke!" I cry, slipping into it. It is icy cold out there on the old sleeping porch and snow is drifting in under the blue-and-white striped canvas.

"Oh, PG," the other little boy laughs, "that's your mother's name for me. You remember my real true name, don't you: Uklut?"

"Yes, of course, that's your own real secret Indian name, isn't it? Since I've been away at boarding school I almost forgot."

"Never mind. Shall we begin the instruction?"

"Oh, I'm tired of instruction. What kind of instruction you got?"

"You should remember. After all, you were the one who showed me. For that body you got there to last through the holidays, it must be anointed all over with sperm."

"Not in my hair! I won't get my hair wet and, besides, neither one of us can come yet."

Uklut laughs. "Just you wait!"

Thus doth he attain into the Station of Intimate Friendship (Khullah), in that he is permeated with the love of his Beloved, mingled with his Blood and his Flesh, both within and without, whence the necessity of wetting through and through (Takhlīl) the hair.

Takhlīl, Takhul (intimate penetration) and Khalil (legitimate pal).

"You really do love that little Indian boy, don't you," I can hear my mother saying as she pulls my bare arms and legs off the familiar naked brown body I wrap them around every night, "but I really do think that you and Luke should be wearing pyjamas."

"**B**ut you went right on doing it, didn't you? Doing everything."

"Not Takhul, that came later. He was my Khalil, though, always."

"So, what did you *do* at that age?" Suzi insists.

"We moved out on to the sleeping porch in winter, in summer we slept in his wigwam but there was always his family about. You know, Suzi, sometimes you sound like my mother."

"That's what I mean. What were you *doing* together? Who started, ah, 'doing things' or how did you call it?"

"We called it that, 'Doing things.' I started it. After all, I'd had my first sex, if you can call it that, when I was four."

"When you were *four?* How *about* that! Who with?"

"With a British colonial colonel in Brighton. Someone I met through my mother."

"In Brighton, England? And how did that happen? With a colonel! What were you doing there with a colonel?"

"Oh, that's all too complicated to go into, babe. Anyway, it doesn't count since it all happened before my mother had both of us circumcised."

"Circumcised? Who, you and the colonel?"

"No, stoopid, me and Uklut. I had an accident in the woods that winter I was eight, no, nine. I stepped into a trap. Out in the winter woods with Uklut, we fell on a trapline laid by some stranger, some interloper on the Longfinger reserve. That's how I got this funny left foot, like Oedipus. Our family doctor did a good job on it or I wouldn't be able to walk. Uklut hurt his hands getting the trap off my foot and he had to be operated on, too, in our kitchen. Nearly lost his hands, both hands."

"In the kitchen?"

"In our huge family kitchen as dark as a cave full of steam and hung all over with white sheets, I remember it well, at seven o'clock on that winter morning when the doctor could get there on a horse-drawn sled through the snow. I was OK, more or less, but not poor Uklut. The night before, my Daddy gave me his last shot of heroin, at least he said it was his last. There wasn't enough for Uklut. Buckets of sweat were pouring off him all night but he never cried. I did, a lot. When the doctor came, he gave us all shots."

"Daddy included?"

"Mummy too. How did you guess? She's the one pulled the castration number on us."

"Castration? You've got to be kidding."

"Well, circumcision. She's the one told the doctor to circumcise us both under the anaesthetic while he was fixing the rest. When we woke up, we both thought she'd had it cut off. We both woke up screaming because we were stuck together with dried blood and my mother was there, pulling us apart, saying, 'I thought I told Luke's mother not to put the two of you in the same bed any more after your operations!' Thanks a lot."

"Wow!"

"She said she had us both operated on because we were touching ourselves."

"And each other."

"Ah, yes."

"And were you?"

"Of course we were and why not? You should see Italian mothers encourage their kids to pull at their puds. Helps 'em grow up, a whole lot."

"And your mother, you never forgave her?"

"I didn't say that."

"What did you say, there under your breath?"

"Maybe I mumbled something about blaming the doctor because of the heroin but my father gave us both more after that."

"Your father? What happened to him?"

"Oh, he OD'd eventually and, later, my mother ran off with the man who laid that trap."

"Who was he?"

"Oh, a veteran of one of those wars where they all came back junkies. He had a pension and he holed up in our woods. He was crazy, crazy like a fox. When they found him, he told my mother he was Lady Chatterley's trapper and that got to her, I guess. He entrapped her. It didn't work out, even at that."

"Yeah, I'm glad I'm a girl but any girl's life is a trap, you can believe me. Look at our own relationship, such as it is. It isn't working out either," said Suzi.

"I'm sorry about that, babe, but the heroin leaves me a little bit lame in the third leg, sometimes."

"Is that why you haven't made love to me properly? Why did you bring me back here to this room in this sordid hotel? Don't you know who I am? I'm Special Suzi, doesn't that mean anything to you or don't you like girls, at all?"

"Hi, Suzi. Excuse me, but I think I'm going to take another shot to fix that."

"Junk is no good, baby. Why don't you stop!"

"Why don't you stop talkin', babe, while I cook me this shot."

"Kick that habit, man!"

"I'm kickin' it, I'm kickin' it! Juss you watch. Hope this doesn't upset ya, all this blood. I think I got a good vein left in my foot if I can only find it. This left foot of mine sure looks like an old fibrous root, don't it? I understand Lord Byron would never let anyone see his club foot. He took opium. Helped him a lot."

"It's not helping you."

"No, but this is better than O. It's Horse. At least, I hope it is. I scored for it last night down in the toilet of the Select where I picked you up."

"I hear there's been some funny stuff floating around the Select recently. Hope you didn't pick up on some of that. They're talking about hot-shots and such stuff. You better be careful."

"It's too late to be careful. This stuff has been stamped on pretty heavy but it's good stuff."

"Why did you bring me back here if you like that stuff better than me?"

"Open your legs, honey, open them wide. No, wider than that. You see, you look just like the Open-Gate Girl on my ceiling. Look up, look up! Yeah, go on looking up, baby, while I line up this shot."

A flash went off in my head just as soon as I put that needle in my vein. When I open my eyes, here is the good Doctor B hovering over me. We are back in the big kitchen of our old Normandy château in Montana. It is hung with sheets and full of steam just like it was when I came to from my operation. Buroon looks like Lady Chatterley's husband's doctor, right after World War One in the early twenties. He is speaking to me very severely, like a movie star.

"Young man, you have been very lucky to come back here. You weren't supposed to do that with the very first body His Holiness rustled up for you. How many spare human frames you think we got? Nobody told you to go slithering back to Room One again with Suzi. Partly because of the trouble you brought on yourself by having those other rooms on the ground floor torn out and sent off to California, you'll find yourself back here in the old nursery. You can sleep on the sleeping porch if you want to but there's to be no climbing out on to the roof to kill bats with a coal shovel, like last time. You hear me?"

"Where's Uklut?"

"Uklut is busy doing something for me, for a change. You'll see him later. I suggest you go upstairs and lay down for a while. Get some rest. Time-travel takes it out of you. You know your way around the house. Don't go up the front stairs marked *Lamas Only*, that's for the monks. Take these back stairs through the kitchen. Pick yourself up a clean sheet on the way through. If His Holiness has anything to convey to you, I'll, uh, communicate with you. Take a Long Sleep. Pleasant dreams."

. . . .

When I come around again, here is Buroon again, hovering over me. He looked more than ever like a nineteenth-century country doctor at the deathbed. "Ion, Ion!" he keeps calling me. I know very well I am *not* Ion Sommerville.

"I am not, I am not," I go on repeating under my breath. "I am not."

"There," he says, "that's just it, exactly. Your first week here has run out and that makes a couple more young male bodies you've gone through in the short time you've been out here with us in the old château. Whatever are we going to do with you? What next?"

"Yeah," I manage to murmur, "what next?"

"I'm afraid you're not going to like it but the fact is His Holiness has no more boy bodies to hand. I'm terribly sorry, but I'm afraid you'll have to double up with Iona."

"I'm a week here?" I mumble. "I'm weak."

"Yes, you should have spent the first seven days in the Bardo, but since, thanks to you, young man, all the rooms on the ground floor have been torn out and sent off to California with the exception of Room One, His Holiness has been kind enough to allow you to stay on out here until the time comes when you must move on upstairs one flight to Room Eight. The time has now come. You'll find Room Eight at the head of the stairs to your left. Since your own museum people rather maliciously reserved it for you in advance, you'll find it already very fully occupied by a female entity called Fiona."

"Her name was Iona a minute ago."

"Iona, Fiona, what does it matter? Your museum people meant to give her your job."

"My job? I don't have a job! My life has been my job."

"That's just it. That's why you'll have to share the space with her."

"How big is this space, is there room there for both of us?"

"Of course not. You'll have to get into Fiona."

"And become a real girl?"

"Well, I don't know about that. You'll have to see. Room Eight has an iron-barred window on the staircase. She'll be in there, expecting you. If things don't work out . . . and I don't say they will because there's no real reason why they should . . . don't blame me, my dear. Blame yourself."

Chapter Two

| Floor Two, Week Two, Rooms 8 to 14 |

. . . "Say, my feet are getting wet! Either we're shipping water or this skiff has sprung a leak. Shereefa, would you give us a little light here with your Zippo? There, you see, there's six inches of water in here. We've got to bail her out. Who's got something to bail us out with? Maybe one of Fiona's boots. Take off your boots, Fiona. Ooops! Be careful, Fiona, we've just shipped a whole lot more water. Look, Madame Barchou, look look look! This water has letters in it. It's thick with letters like alphabet soup."

"*C'est la Chie,*" Madame Barchou replies, calmly turning her miner's lamp on the bottom of the boat, first, and then sweeping the surrounding waters with it. "*C'est comme ça.* It's been polluted like that ever since the beginning of printing. Pollution. Word pollution. Logorrhoea. You see, the publishing houses are further upstream on the shady side of our street and when they can't sell a book, why, they pulp it and pour it back into the Chie."

"What a waste."

"Oh, it's only the words that are wasted and washed away down the drains. The pulped paper is salvaged and bleached of the inky words which are wrung out when this . . . this porridge is pressed out and rolled into reams of paper again to be reprinted with words. So it goes on. Nothing is lost but the worthless words which pour through here on their way to the river beneath Antonia's windows and then on down to the sea, I suppose," she finished dreamily. "The Sea!"

"*Nuestras vidas son ríos, que van a dar en la mar!*" sings Poochie deliciously.

"So don't tell me words are worthless!" cried the duchess. "I've used lots of words in a lifetime and I know what they're worth. Of course, there are all *sorts* of words, aren't there, and some are worth more than others. Some people's word may be worthless and words may be worth more at one time than at another but look down there, look! The waters of the Chie are phosphorescent with the exquisite deliquescence of decaying words . . ."

"I do."

"What do you mean, Ms Waterbee?"

"I mean that every time I said I do at the altar or in front of the judge or at the registrar's office, it meant a whole lot more bread for me. I've been married a lot."

"Oh yes, but that isn't what I was talking about, I . . ."

"Sidi Sherkh al-Alawi," Shereefa pronounced flatly, "say: *El Ahl Dyal Kiz!* . . . !" she went on in Arabic.

"I don't understand a word of Arabic, what does that mean?"

"He say: *The Soul of Words is in the Ink.*"

"That sounds pretty profound. Just let me think about it for a minute . . ."

"No Ink, no Letter. No Letter, no Word. No Word, no Book."

"I'll go along with that. It sound perfectly reasonable. Not all that profound, perhaps. You see, Shereefa, what we're talking about is bad books."

"There is no bad books," Shereefa insisted stoutly. "The Books is sacred!"

"Oh, of course, Shereefa, *THE Book* is sacred but we are talking about books the publisher can't get rid of. They can't sell them or even remainder them in the bookstalls down by the Seine. They can't give them away. Nobody wants them even as a gift. They can't burn them. That is forbidden. It is absolutely forbidden to burn books. They used to burn books and their publishers along with them like poor Etienne Dolet over there in the Place Maubert. He was not only burned at the stake in the 1500s but even his bronze statue was knocked down by the Nazis here in the 1940s to burn him a second time, melted him down to make cannons. That sort of thing got a very bad name, so they boil them."

"Thay fwhat? Boil publishers?"

"No, they boil books, boil them in vats with a bleacher in the water to leach out the words, the ink."

"Is better?" asked Shereefa, utterly shocked. "Boil them? That hurts."

"Look," said Madame Rachou with a little laugh, "just look into this inky black water by the light of my lamp. It looks perfectly black out there, doesn't it, black as ink? But here in my hand when I cup some up . . . not that I'd drink it, *parbleu!* . . . but you can see that the color is pure illusion and so are the letters unless they have been anointed with ink."

"No," states la Bathory flatly, "not true. I just picked up a very bad word in Hungarian, look!"

"Well, nobody here but you reads Hungarian, my dear. Are you sure it isn't just a piece of pied type? All the words in the world must be flowing through here. Hush! If you'd all just stop talking for a minute, perhaps we could make out what they are saying as they babble, bubble . . . mutter, mumble . . . murmuring old slogans, old saws . . . all human memory . . . a palimpsest. . . ."

"*L'immense et compliqué palimpseste de la mémoire,*" murmurs Madame Rachou. "M'sieu Baudelaire said that. He used to drop into my bistro for a glass of wormwood with Gérard de Nerval, as he called himself, and that nice little M'sieu Latouche: he was so witty we all laughed, even M'sieu Baudelaire. He didn't laugh much. He lived with his mother. She and her second husband, le Général Aupic, lived just up the street and across the square. He had to go home to lunch alone with her every single day in the week and he was often drunk by then. He was morbid and surly when he was drunk. I liked him a lot. He always looked to me like someone who'd been a long time in jail. He had that look. He kept a permanent room in the hotel to do his writing in."

"*Les Fleurs du Mal?*"

"No, *Le Festin Nu.* The police came here and took away all the copies to pulp them and pour them into the Chie right under our street, under our feet and under his nose. He used to sit there in my bistro morosely preparing his absinthe, letting the water drip drop by drop through a lump of sugar, turning it cloudy as one of his black moods would settle down on him and he would turn nasty, poor man. He always said the water was washing away his words and like that nice young English tubercular poet he admired so much who died in Rome, his name was writ in water, *le pauvre*."

"But no!" cried the duchess. "His words are immortal. I'm sure even Fiona here knows them: *Lesbos, où les baisers sont comme les cascades!*"

I merely hung my head and went on bailing out the boat. I'd never even heard of this Baudelaire but the word Lesbos made me prick up my ears. I thought I knew what they were talking about and it made me blush.

Freddy laughed. "Well, if you can still blush, Fiona, that's a good sign. Your heart's still in the right place. His best poems are about love between women and I know them all by heart. We learned them in French class with the nuns at the Convent of the Sacred Heart. That was a long time ago. The nightingales were singing there. That's where I got my start. My, aren't we taking a hell of a long time getting nowhere, hmm? You know what I mean. When do we get to Antonia's landing? What's holding us up, hmm?"

· · · ·

Chapter Three

| Floor Three, Week Three, Room Fifteen |

"This isn't a room, it's a cage," I growl at Madame Rachou when she pops her fuzzy blue head into Room Fifteen. "With those iron bars on the window, it's a prison cell. It's as cold as the grave and there's almost no light in here. I can't live like this."

"No, of course not," she smiles over-sweetly, "you're dead. But don't blame me, my dear, blame yourself."

"I seem to have heard that line before," I admit glumly. "Someone smart is always telling me that."

"Yes, I guess," she sighs. "But after all it was you who ordered your world-movers to take out the old hotel to fit it into your mighty museum of memory. Since they tore out the three floors below us here, everything has been all askew in the Bardo. I've had to move up here myself and abandon the bistro. There will be no more entries or exits. Everything I could salvage from the past down below is stacked up here around you, all the loose ends of history, all those loose leaves of manuscript abandoned here by all sorts of writers, like the Beats for example."

"I know. That's why I've just decided to call my Museum of Museums the Beat Museum. Since my head-on collision with the Ma Movement in California, that sounds better to me than MOM."

"Well, make the most of it. You'll just have to manage in here for a week."

"A week?" I exclaim. "There's no bed. Nothing but all these unnumbered pages of typescript pouring out of this old broken black suitcase."

"You can sleep on top of those things of Fiona's," says Madame as she starts to ooze out of the room.

"Fiona's?" I yelp. "Whose Fiona?"

"Yours," she comes back, "the Curator of your Glory that was Greece Department."

"Assistant Curator, and I fired her. If she shows up here, I'll kill her all over again."

"Silly," she says, "you can't kill the dead. Besides she says she has your power of attornity. Power of eternity, I mean. You'll still have to deal with her and here she is now," cackles Madame Rachou as she slams the door hard enough to crack the full-length mirror on the back of it, and in the mirror there is Fiona, only a reflection of her, deaf, dumb and blind I hope.

As I stare at her, frozen in horror, she turns into the antique cult statue of Ma which we have in the MOM at Malibu in the Villa de Lirium built for my great ancestor, PG One. He, of course, did not belong to Her or I would not be here but I feel Ma has been after me since I can remember. MA MA MA!

Ma is the Mother goddess, Kybele the Castrator with a broken nose on her powerful bull dyke mug. Wearing a mural crown like the towers and walls of an ancient city, she sits there enthroned with her fleshy thighs spread wide and stained black with the bloody sacrifice of their manhood which her male adepts must cut off and toss up on to her lap. RAH RAH RAH! MA MA MA!

When the Ma Movement grew so strong in California that they invaded my museum to celebrate their bloody rites, I made every effort to chase them. I ordered the Basilica of Kybele in the interior patio of the Villa to be walled up. To my astonishment, this alienated the majority of my own staff. All the women and most of the men, too, turned out to be members of Ma. In the end, it was they who chased me. RAH RAH RAH! MA MA MA! YOU CAN BEAT THE MOM BUT YOU CAN'T BEAT MA!

The sound of their chanting and the snaky music to which they drove themselves into a sacred frenzy drove me to take refuge in the last sacred male sanctuary which I had placed out on the Mojave in El Mirage Lake. I brought over the tiny Greek island of Delos and set it down in this dry lake where I had it protected by a moat flooded with blue tinctured male urine to keep off the Ma people. Only uncastrated adolescent boys and men were allowed on the holy island which the ancient Greeks held to be the birthplace of the blond sun god Apollo. This was to be my last refuge in a world driven mad by Ma. I was on my way out there when the accident happened.

Who has not seen members of the Ma Movement snaking down Sunset Boulevard in the late afternoon when Ra is drowning out in the Pacific to the West as the last-minute shoppers go schlepping along to the Bigboy Supermarkets? Who has not shaken their filthy begging paws from off the sleeve of his sharkskin suit? Who has not angrily refused to drop even a thin dime into the clanking collection-boxes of these expert "dingers," these newly ordained metragyrtes with heads shaven like monks except for their long toplock of hair? This lock is for Ma to yank them to Her bosom, pitiful specimens that they are in their baggy yellow dhotis sagging between their self-shaven loins like transextites wearing soiled babies' nappies above their smelly yellow Day-glo running shoes. Who has not brushed off these pestiferous painted postulants as persistent as horseflies? Who has not slammed a screen door in their clownish faces plastered with oriental makeup? Who has not grabbed for his own cock and balls as soon as he hears the mad bloodbeat of their hypnotic trance music coming down Rodeo Drive? Far away in your safe-house in Brentwood you can still hear the distant silver tinkle of their finger cymbals and the insane gnat-whine of their flutes which go dancing along in your inner ear long after the music has stopped. What man in his right mind has ever broken his stride to listen for even one nanosecond to the pernicious doctrine they preach as they run down the street after you batting their false eyelashes like vampire bats? Yet who has not seen the sensational crowds they gather on the corner of Hollywood and Vine or in Times Square or Trafalgar Square, the Place Saint-Michel on the Left Bank in the Latin Quarter of Paris, or just about anywhere else? How about that? Haven't you ever felt a twinge of sick curiosity about Ma yourself?

To set my face against Ma has cost me my Museum of Museums and my life, everything but this narrow room in the old Bardo Hotel, yet as long as my magical island of Delos still glimmers out there on the golden desert haze of memory, I will not fall into the wombtrap of Ma the Castrator nor be born again except as the sun god, Apollo Himself.

When I paw through this shoal of paper on which I float, my eye is caught by a scrap of newsprint. It amuses me to remember or think I remember that I once cut this out of a paper myself:

You and I are not who we claim to be. We are not who we were only yesterday nor are we who we will be tomorrow. Our bodies are by no means static. No living thing can be at rest. A different person looks back at you each morning from the mirror. We produce a whole new skin surface each week. The entire lining of the mouth is washed down and digested with every meal. Each blink of an eye flushes hundreds of cells down the tearducts. All in all, we lose a soup plate full of cells every day and this loss has to be made good.

I re-read this several times and each time I laugh. Who can be at rest, ever? Who looks back at you from the mirror? Have I eaten the entire lining of my mouth as a sadistic nurse in the Horsepistol, what I called Horror Hospital, told me an AIDS victim had done, eating away his own lips in a night of agony? And how is this loss to be made good at this late date?

The next thing I pick up is a couple of pages torn out of a glossy gay magazine with an amusing line drawing by Keith Haring. The text is about a bullfighter who comes a dark splotch of come on his pale silk panties . . . when he sees the bull with a bloodshot eye lolling his scum-covered tongue at him like a lover in a leather bar. (See illustration.)

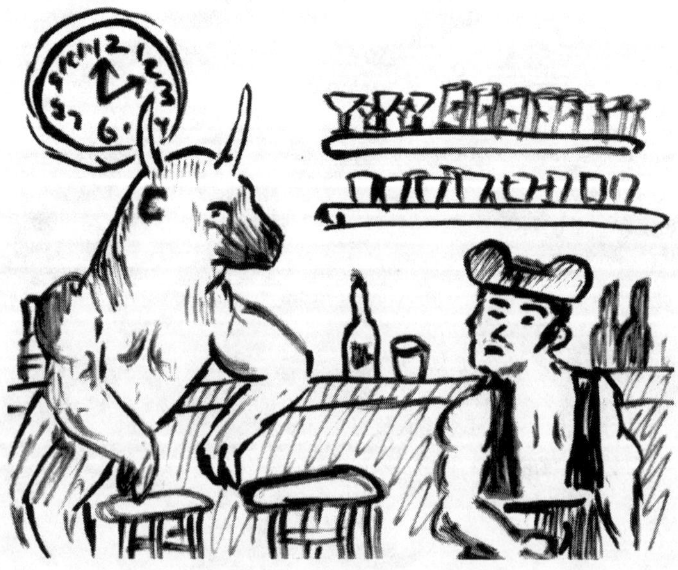

"Untitled," by Keith Haring, from the book *Fault Lines* © The Estate of Keith Haring.

He knows that the bull has eyes to really get him by ramming the razor-sharp horn that he happens to favor right up his rectum. *Olé!* He knows he is Deadly Diego the Diestro and the bull knows it too. In response, his own big hard smelly uncircumcised cock throbs through its knot of varicose veins. Both he and the bull stand there panting for the moment of Truth with the Little Death of orgasm for one and the final spasm out there in the sandy arena for the other. The whole arena is holding its breath while these two, man and beast, measure each other. Man vs. Beast. Since the Ace of Spades is up, you play it.

What you do is, you slowly pluck your *espada*, your ace up the sleeve, out of the red rag wrapping it. Don't bat an eyelash between you and your bull's eye. Stay on target. Sighting your right eye straight down your blue blade directly into the small depression over his left collarbone, you lean into your sword with the whole weight of your body behind it. Ideally, the bull should lean into it, too, taking it directly into his heart, *recibiendo.* The thrust should take you through the living coral of his lungs into the palpitating cavern of his truly magnificent body as big as a truck, right down into the flaring pump of his scarlet heart. That's all there is to it. What are you waiting for? Your blade should slip into him up to the hilt. Before he can raise his horns to toss you into the bleachers, he drops dead. You have taken his life from him harmoniously, amorously. Loving you and you only at that moment of truth, the colossal crowd surrounding you bursts into cheers.

Your personal pay-off is an orgasm, the Little Death right out there in the arena, the bull's-eye of all eyes. You ejaculate into your skintight pink sexy silk kneepanties and ten thousand throats scream up into hysteria as they see the dark patch spread into the bull's blood smeared across your crotch. Chicuelo Segundo was a great expert at this. Big bumbling bull stumbles and crumbles to his baggy knees, drunk on his own blood, coughing up a king's ransom in rubies. As he blows out his last great bubble of blood it bursts and spreads out like a ragged red flag on the sand where it blackens instantly as he falls at your feet. For a solemn second or two, you gaze down on death with bowed head. Then you lift your chin proudly raising both arms slowly in a magnificent theatrical gesture you practiced for hours in front of your full-length mirror back in your local hotel. You take off your hat to your public, turning gracefully in a full circle on your slippered heel, inviting more and more applause from the public piled up on the tiers of the ring surrounding you. Cheering you to the skies, they break out a pentecostal host of white handkerchiefs like clouds of doves taking off when the cannon is fired at noon in front of the fucking old Seville cathedral. Today is your day. You are its hero. Your triumphal tour around the ring is carpeted with carnations. Strong silent Spanish men smile a tight smile as they sail their expensive Cordoban flat hats at you like frisbees. Their women go mad as maenads at full moon time.

That is one way it can go. The other way is awful. When your bad day comes, you lunge in to lean on your sword and it hits bone. The steel buckles under you. A bullfighter's *espada* has been known to bend like a bow as it skids over bone and flips into the air like a spring. In Cordoba once, this *torero*'s sword flew through the air like a glittering arrow while everyone was gawking up at it. His *novia*, his promised one, was there in the best box with her long greasy black hair over her arms and her arms full of flowers, his heavily embroidered cape draped over the rim of the ring in front of her. Was the sun in her eyes as she gawked up open-mouthed like the rest of them? The slim blade came whistling down out of the dazzling sky and straight down her throat, passing right through her. Her lover's *espada* pinned her to the wooden seat she was sitting on, right through her asshole.

Trouble is, at that moment the crowd's red-hot rivet of attention is fixed on her and no one is paying any attention to you. No one but the bull, that is. The bull has just impaled you, too, right up the rectum with the horn that he favors, and tossed you as high as a basketball scoreboard. What goes up must come down and you land on his other horn after turning a full somersault in the bright air. Now he can swing you around a couple of times before flinging you with all the force of his bullneck against the wooden *barrera* or he can twirl you around a couple of times like a friendly fistfucker might do to you one Saturday night in The Mineshaft or The Tubs on Christopher Street in New York. You can thank your lucky stars that the bull's horns have been "shaved," as they call it, filed down. The surgeons who are waiting for you in the wings will have less trouble with nasty old infectious splinters of bone when they get you laid out on the operating table.

> *Then the Lord of Death will place round thy neck a rope and drag thee along. He will cut off thy head, tear out thy heart, pull out thine intestines . . .* (Oh! Ouch! That hurts!) *. . . lick up thy brain, drink thy blood, eat thy bones, etc., but thou wilt be incapable of dying. Even when thy body is hacked to pieces, it will revive again . . .* (Oh no! Not again! C'mon, lemme outta here!) *. . . and again and again.* (Oh! Oh! Oh!) *The repeated hacking will cause intense pain and unbearable torture.* (Oh! Noooo!)
>
> *Bardo Thodol*, The Tibetan Book of the Dead

Next thing you know, you wake up screaming. You are alone in a bone-bare room under a glaring white light, *The* Clear White Light! Leather and chains buckle you down on an icy cold chromium bedstead. You know where you are, of course. You might as well go along with it. You are in the Ultimate Cancer Ward at the far end of the Yellow Wing. Your veins have been pulled out of your arms like garden worms and attached to gravity drips of fresh blood hanging from stainless steel gallows on each side of the bed. Your arteries ache. You know what you are here for. Yes, you do. Your big mouth, that's what's done it. You have been talking too much, from away back, blabbing your secrets and theirs away to your other self, that feminine one. Naturally, She blabbed. She told them all, so now your contract is going to be terminated with extreme prejudice. And why not? The Agency is taking care of people like you, everywhere. They have just snatched your old asshole out from under you and now they want the rest. It is their due. Sucker, pay up!

Violet, that blue-assed baboon dressed up as a nurse, made you sign for the operation, remember? Then she shot you up with BZ, their new drug they call soul-destroying, as if you had one. The two great antique Greek surgeons in pale green chitons and masked, Professor Kokalos (Dr Bones) and Professor Haemos (Dr Blood), ripped out your rectum with the aid of an electric apple-corer and sawed off the end of your coccyx, that little knuckled tailbone at the end of your spine, in order to get in there and scoop you out like a rotten old cantaloupe. With one rubber-gloved fist up your ex-asshole and the other plunging down through a nine-inch incision from your sternum to your shaved pubis, they gleefully shook hands with each other in the depths of your belly . . . (Dr Livingstone, I presume) . . . darker than darkest Africa. *Les petites mains de la haute couture, les biaiseuses de chez Paquin* were called in to stitch you up again, all but your stoma which will never heal because it is round, round as a Maria Theresa silver thaler. This is your anus-praeter, your brand new artificial anus. Get to love it as fast as you can. There it is down there on the left side of your gut, gurgling away like an obscene baby mouth drooling a long snake of blood, mucus and shit into a transparent plastic bag attached to the skin of your stomach by a sticky ring of karaya gum. Look on it rather as a shiny wet red tea-rose of tender intestinal tissue with its puckered border of stitches oozing tears of blood like dewdrop rubies around the edge of its petals. In order to achieve this expensive artistic effect, they have moved your original mothering navel, the bellybutton you were born with that last time, they have moved it over four inches to the right, your tight right hand. At the middle point of the suture, they inserted deep into your central chankra a new umbilical cord of plastic tubing to drain off your new navel.

You have been reborn. You will find your new name on the board in the matron's office, when you can get there and read it. If you can read.

• • • •

Chapter Four

/ Floor Four, Week Four, Room 22 /

. . . Then I heard my door slam shut so hard that I laughed. My good doctor left in one hell of a huff. In my book, that could mean only one thing: he's madly in love with me, poor old washed-up me, held here in total restraint. I laughed out loud for the first time since I found myself here in Tomb Twenty-two of the Bardo. It is absurd. He has fallen in love with me when what he meant to happen was that I would fall in love with him. So, I thought to myself, death is just as ridiculous as life, is it. I laughed until I almost choked.

Sinking back into my rotten old memories of love, I found myself once again in that Paris I discovered or was thrust into when I showed up at my great-cousin Antonia's historic town house on the Seine, Number One Paris, the oldest private residence in the city, she always claimed. I was fresh out of my expensive English public school, outfitted on credit by the school tailor with six lounge suits and two dinner jackets but no tails and not a penny to my troublesome name which was, according to the newspapers, the Richest Little Boy in the World. Who would believe that I had only fifteen dollars a month? Cousin Antonia Longfinger did because she knew all about the Longfinger Legacy and our mutual ancestor's infamous will by which I could be utterly disinherited because my mother sent me to this Catholic school and then OD'd on us. Antonia took me in and gave me a superb bachelor flat on her top floor, high under her many-gabled roof with a flowering terrace overlooking the Seine and Notre Dame right across from us. Her handsome housekeeper was a Scots gentlewoman in reduced circumstances who adored me. At the age of eighteen, I made the most of it. Lady Fiona used to have the kitchen send me up delicious meals with more than enough caviar and champagne to have my own guests whenever I wanted. I gave little parties for any young people I could find in this strange household of old women.

Antonia entertained lavishly, mainly women. She had her own Day in the week when she received hordes of people, mainly women. Her day was Friday, no, Friday was Clifford Barney's Day when she, too, received mainly women. All the Great Ladies of Paris had their days of the week when they held their salons but Cousin Antonia's Day was the most exclusive because she was the Vicar General of the Lesbians. She received the faithful of her peculiar parish in a very impressively lofty Gothic great hall which had been the chapel of Joan of Arc, the Maid of Orleans, herself, in person. Antonia presided over these receptions like the Mother Superior of a very fashionable convent. Pilgrims were permitted once a year, tourists never. Only the chosen few were ever invited to stay on for the party after the party to participate in the very private ceremonies which took place there, no men ever admitted. All the highest ranking Gurls in the world passed through Antonia's hands, from royal queens-in-exile off Balkan thrones to reigning and retired queens from Hollywood. The house was so huge and so hospitable that a number of adepts moved in to become her permanent court.

I rarely went out of the house except when I had to because of this queer-looking character who followed me through the streets of Paris wherever I went. Night and day, he lurked in this sinister alley called Chienlit Street which ran up from the river past the front door of Antonia's house. As soon as I ever stepped out into this street, he would loom up out of the shadows to follow me to the Sorbonne for instance. I had to go there to take a course in "La Civilisation Française" and get my student book signed by a professor in order to draw my miserable stipend of fifteen dollars a month. This sinister shadow would sneak after me even through the echoing marble halls of the Sorbonne until I ducked into the full flood of chattering French students in which I would lose him or think I had. No such luck. There he would be hanging in some dark doorway or hiding behind a lamp post to skid out and slither after me until he had me practically running all the way home. I told our house-keeper Fiona about this and she offered to beat him up for me. She was that big and tough, she could have.

"I know the one you mean," she laughed. "Tall, dark and thin as a rake, isn't he? Well under thirty but sort of stooped over, no? He's a Greek who lives in that little fleabag hotel without a name up our alley. He's been trying to get Antonia to invite him for ages. We all call him Mr Grease."

He cornered me, finally, in Sylvia Beach's bookshop, Shakespeare and Co. There was nothing Sylvia could do but introduce us. He forced her hand. He was good at it. The Greeks know no shame. I turned to leave but he followed me out, inviting me for a drink on the terrace of a nearby café. When the time came to pay, he said he had no money. He had ordered himself an expensive whisky and a pack of imported cigarettes. I had to pay for them, too. Back in Athens, he claimed, his family was rich, very rich, but because of some trouble he had with the new regime down there, trouble over some political poems he had published, he was an exile in Paris. Owing to the bothersome currency restriction imposed by his enemies, no one could send him any money from Greece. His mother would if she could but his father was furious with him. When he suggested we dine in a Greek restaurant in the Latin Quarter where he would introduce me to Greek food and retsina wine, I guessed I would have to pay for that too. I said, thanks very much but no thanks. I was wising up. Where did I dine? It wasn't quite true but I said I always dined with my cousin Antonia. I was not about to invite him into the house even when he followed me right up to the door. To get shut of him, I practically slammed the heavy door in his face but at once he began knocking loudly. When I poked my head out, he said he was hungry. I slipped him five francs in a fury.

On Antonia's very next Day, there he was in the house, having attached himself to Sylvia and her real heavy French girlfriend Adrienne to invite himself in along with them. Birdlike Sylvia Beach was in charge of those English language writers in Paris like James Joyce and Hemingway, while lumbering Adrienne Monnier, who had a French language bookshop across the same street, was in charge of the French writers of note like Gide and Cocteau. Those were two more you really had to watch out for. And creepy little old Marcel Jouhandeau— oh Wow! Wandering hands. But the Greek had them beat. Within the week, there he was all the time up in my private quarters on the top floor, eating and drinking every night along with me and my few young friends. They all hated him on sight. I guess I got drunk. The next thing I knew, he had gotten so drunk he passed out on my bed where I found him snoring next morning when I woke up on the floor. Remember the story about the Arab who let his camel put just its nose under the edge of his tent? He woke up next morning to find himself out in the Sahara while his camel snored on beside him, comfortably wrapped up in his canvas. I simply could not get rid of this man. When they finally threw him out of his nameless hotel up our side street, he moved in on me permanently. And Antonia never even knew. He was wise enough to keep out of her way. The house was big enough. He intercepted my mail, read my letters, poked into my private papers, tried to worm every last Family secret out of me, psychoanalyzed every last thing I said or did. He never let up on me. Sometimes he amused me. He knew or had known practically everybody and he was as full of maliciously spicy gossip as any good Greek. I was all ears, of course. He went out of his way to titillate me with tall tales about all the great ladies who gathered in Antonia's house on her Days and especially about those who stayed on for her secret sessions in Joan of Arc's chapel. We could hear them stomping around raising raucous hell down there under us.

"You know," mused my Greek, "I do believe your bathroom in there is directly above the high altar. Don't you just long to get a peek at what they're up to down there? I'll bet we could. If we could crawl in under that false floor of your bathroom where the plumbers get in, maybe we could drill a hole through the ceiling and look down on them directly. I dare you."

We could and we did. It was all pretty crazy. I don't really like to look back on it even now, all these years later. I was disgusted and scared. But there was an outrageously funny side to it, too, that made me want to laugh hysterically when I first caught sight of the mad mêlée going on down there below in the chapel. A lot of those lovely ladies on the far side of their menopause were horsing around with their girlfriends dressed up as cowboys, shrieking, "*Hi-Ho Silver!*" at the top of their lungs, while an old Roy Rogers record was bawling out "Home on the Range." Clad in studded leather chaps with ten-gallon hats clapped on their fair heads, they were stomping around in their cowboy boots, jumping on each other's backs playing horsey. A couple of couples would run full tilt at each other until all four of these gay old girls were rolling around on the floor splitting their britches with laughter. Then Cousin Antonia appeared and what seemed to have begun as a wild game became something much more serious, more deadly. She waved her arms about and threw back her head to let out an earpiercing yodel. It didn't sound the least like her. All her adepts fell into a chorus line, baying like banshees or bloodhounds giving voice after their quarry, a man, Orpheus the Poet who had spied on their mysteries. My blood ran cold and turned into water. A bonedeep chill ran all through me because, in those days, I thought of myself as a poet.

Stifling in the tight spot we had wedged ourselves into, I thought it was all part of the nightmare when I felt the hot breath of this Greek in my ear as he hissed, "I'm going to tell your cousin Antonia we did this unless you do what I say, let me do what I want to you, right here and now, do you hear me?"

He was fumbling with the buttons on the fly of my English tailored trousers and I had to admit that my young cock was as hard as a rod, excited into a state of almost painful erection by the weirdly erotic scene down below. The ladies were letting down more than their hair as he poked his penis between my bare feet while he sucked me off avidly, deepthroating me. It was the first time anyone ever did this to me and I really didn't dig it that much. It sort of disgusted me. But what was a poor boy to do?

What I did was to look around the house for a girl or woman. There was one fairly young hanger-on around the house whom I found slightly seductive, the more I thought about it. She was a dark White Russian ex-princess named Natasha, naturally, who seemed unattached. I learned later that she was fairly recently divorced from a Rumanian diplomat who had caught her *in flagrante delicto* with a girlfriend. Down one of the mysterious dark corridors of the vast house hung with tapestries, I waylaid her. Pulling the dusty old arras around us, I grabbed her and kissed her. To my surprise, she went off like a fire alarm, smearing her red lipstick all over my face, shocking me into an instant erection as I fought for my breath with her tongue in my tonsils. At the same time, she would not let me lay hands on her sex but caught my hot mitts with her claws to press them against her big breasts, instructing my fingers how to roll her nipples between them, "making bread" like a blind kitten does to its mother. She pants and she moans, twisting her knees together like a little girl who wants to make pipi, squeezing her thighs until she begins to come like a rainbow, biting into my milky young neck while running her fingernails up and down the nobs on my spine until I tingle all over like a tomcat. But I still don't have my cock out. As soon as it's over for her, she goes for my face with her nails, snarling like a tiger or tigress, I guess I should say. Flinging me off her, she slaps my face twice with a forehand and a backhand and goes storming away down the dark passage without looking back once, furiously combing the sparks out of her long black hair.

"What the hell was all that about?" I asked my Greek when he discovered her marks on me. "Didn't she like me or what?"

"That standup whore!" he raged, mad with jealousy. "Her Rumanian husband divorced her because she would never let him get into her. She would never let him penetrate her with his penis. She must have a very tough hymen because she's been selling her virginity to a lot of rich old lesbian ladies like your cousin Antonia who gave her the famous *Coup du Colonel* and it didn't even work on her."

"The *Coup du Colonel*, what's that?" I asked eagerly.

My Greek was always full of lurid details about the revolting things he preached to me under the banners of Freud and Marx and Trotsky. At that tender age, I was transfixed and goggle-eyed. He was forever planning and plotting and preaching and poetizing, too, in the coupled names of snotty young Rimbaud, that was me, and his rotten old lover Verlaine. The Greek hung around my young life like the Old Man of the Sea, taking on different slimy shapes and sizes at any old hour of the day or night. He still had no money but he kept on inviting me to stay in his parents' palace in Athens that summer. All I had to do was to get enough money out of Antonia for us to sail off together to Greece. In Greece, he would pay me back double so I could send one half back to pay off Antonia and live off the rest all that summer. Getting money, cash money out of Antonia was not all that easy. No matter how little you asked for, she would give you a little less than half that amount, pleading poverty. I know just how she felt when you ask me for money. We left for Greece in extremely reduced circumstances as deck passengers on a boat from Marseilles.

Before we took off, I had my first woman, thanks to him too. He introduced her as a childhood friend from nursery days in Athens when they had played house together. They played doctor and nurse a bit later. Then they played postman at parties and petted. By the age of thirteen, she was his girl. She was hot stuff. Even before she grew tits, he said with a leer, she had "quite a reputation." When she showed up in Paris, he brought her around to one of Antonia's Days. On sight, Antonia hated her. Heleni Argolaki was the Greek shipping heiress aged twenty-one, just exactly two years and six months and two days older than I was. In Real Time, perhaps, she had at least a couple of centuries on me. Although she was married, the newspapers still called her The Richest Little Girl in the World.

"Why," she laughed, when we met under the frosty gaze of Cousin Antonia and her assembled Ladies, "we were *made* for each other! We must celebrate this at once if not sooner. My husband would just love this but fortunately he's gone back to Athens with his nurse and the baby."

"Love me, *Agapemou!*" was the first Greek word she taught me in the taxi as she very nearly slammed the car door on the hand of Mr Grease, our Greek, our mutual Greek who was trying to scramble in after me. "Hotel Regina!" she snapped to the driver. Whatever she said was like that, an order.

When we got out of the taxi in front of the gilded equestrian statue of Joan of Arc in full armor, she said, "That's why I love the Hotel Regina." I was still wondering what she might mean by that as she propelled me through the revolving doors of this staid old hotel in the shadow of the Louvre. So, that's why she didn't stay at the Ritz like anyone civilized. The uniformed flunkeys within bowed low and no wonder. She looked like the *Vogue* magazine picture of several too many millions of dollars on stiletto heels. Topped by a towering surrealist hat like a lobster pot with a live lobster in it and tricked out by Schiaparelli, she was painted and varnished like a Byzantine ikon reeking of something called Shocking. It gave me an asthma attack, *instanter.* I very nearly collapsed in the hotel elevator. The sniggering bellboy seemed to think I was panting after her and maybe she did too from the look on her. I was practically down on all fours as I followed her down along the upholstered halls of the hotel to her seemingly endless suite of rooms.

"That's your bathroom in there," she advised me. "There's a blue dressing-gown hanging up there. I'm going to slip into something more comfortable. You'll find me in here."

When I did find her in there, I didn't recognize her. She may not have recognized me either, as I stood there with nothing on but my stinky argyll socks and

my only slightly soiled boxer shorts, gawking at her and breathing with difficulty. We stood there for a long endless look, like strangers. Out from under that
aggressive hat and down off those threatening stiletto heels, her face wiped clear
of her theatrical makeup, she had lost the shell of sophistication it all gave her.
Down on her own bare brown feet, with her shiny black hair falling down over
her bare breasts with dark nipples, she looked like some little Greek peasant girl
from the islands being offered for sale to the Turks. Or maybe, just maybe, antique Andromeda chained to her rock. When she jumped head-first into the
huge French double bed, she flashed me the full moon of the first woman's
bare ass I had ever seen. I noticed the soles of her feet were dirty. My asthma
suddenly let go of my lungs as it can at times, abruptly. With a wild war-
whoop, I jumped after her into the hay.

I performed quite well, I think, several times in a row before she began to
show me a few new ways, new ways to me at least, new ways to do it. As time
went on, what began to worry me was the extent of her own satisfaction. Was
she enjoying this, really? Maybe I wasn't doing so good since the first few times
around she was mum, with never a word or a moan out of her. Was this all
right? I tried harder. Each assault was taking more out of me and took longer
until, finally, she began to murmur and then to say and then to yell and then
to scream, "No! No! NOOOOOOOOOOOO!" What the hell was the matter, did-
n't she like it? Or what? Women began by being a mystery to me and throughout a long life have remained so. So much the better. I understand I am not
alone in this. It doesn't really worry me all that much but sometimes I do wonder. What *did* I do wrong? Then or ever?

The next time I saw her was a couple of months later that hellishly hot summer in Athens, in the bar of the Megali Brettania, the old Grande Bretagne
Hotel. She was dressed all in black, chic Paris black, painted like an idol and
covered with jewels, sitting small in a huge tapestried chair like a throne, surrounded by a pack of fawning Greek courtiers, not another woman in sight.
For her and for me, there was no one else in sight but us two, I think, as I
strode across the shining marble floor to her. I just said hello but did not take
her hand or bend over to kiss her. She looked up brightly and said, "Go get
your gear together and be back here in an hour. My captain has just phoned
from Piraeus to say we must sail before sunset." All the surrounding Greeks
held their breath, you could hear it. You could hear things clicking together in
their ivory skulls like a break in a pool game. All their ideas about Heleni and
her millions were adjusting themselves almost audibly. Not one more word
need be said. They knew all about us. Yes, just from her words and her tone of

voice, they knew all about us or they thought they did. They did not know about me, though, except what they read in the newspapers. If there was one more word to be said, it would have to be said by me, so I said it.

"No," I said. "No, I can't. I am sorry."

And I was terribly, desperately, sickeningly sorry. I had just come from the doctor who told me my Wasserman blood test was positive, I had syphilis. In those long-ago days, penicillin was still a whole World War Two away ahead of us. Syphilis was then a matter for suicide. Years, many years of painful treatment were not sure to wipe the last trace of it out of your bloodstream or save you from a long long lingering death-in-life. The worst! The Bible says you can pass it on to your children *"even unto the third and fourth generation"*!

Poor Helenaki, she thought she had a bad enough secret for me but I had an even worse one for her.

Her husband was divorcing her because she was pregnant. Apparently, he had every reason to believe this child was not his. She said it was mine. How could she know, really *know* this? How could *I* know? I had every reason not to want to believe her. I started counting on my fingers. Incubation means counting. How long does it take for syphilis to incubate? How long does it take for a baby? Count the days, count the weeks, count the months, count the moons and the suns and the nights that led up to this. How long does it take to forget a story like this? I hope to have forgotten it before I wake up in the morning.

What day is this, Adam? How long, oh how long have I been in the Bardo? Life was just one long sequence of questions: is death going to be, too? I wonder.

"**D**on't you have any health insurance, Blue Cross, Medicare, Social Security, anything like that?" Dr Adam is expostulating all over me. "There *is* the matter of my fee, you know!"

"You've got to be joking," I mumble. "At this late date? I couldn't afford it. I haven't got any money, cash money, never did. Everything's all tied up in securities, properties, my Museum. Can't touch it. Nobody can."

"All you rich kids, you super-rich kids, give me a swift pain in the prostate. You're all the same, every last one of you. Ask you for money and what do you get? Excuses. The best one can hope for is a bum cheque, a little bouncy cheque, a sheaf of chic autumn leaves. I happen to know you never paid your old school tailor. And me?" Adam splutters all over me, "And me? You know how much I always got for an hour of analytical therapy? You know how much it costs to run a place like the Bardo?"

"Not much. It shouldn't cost much. Accommodation as shabby as this should cost nothing. The Tibetans or whoever it is ought to pay us to stay here.

Instead of which, we all have to pay the earth to get into this dump, the whole earth! The whole earth and everything in it. Where does all that wealth go? To Tibet? Do the Tibetans issue our Visas, our Exit and Entry Permits, collect the rent? There's something wrong here, something very wrong. After all, I own this place. It's all mine, in my name. I own the Bardo Hotel, I invented it. These Tibetans are my tenants, after all. They bore me, bore me to death, quite literally. I don't trust them, never did. I put the Egyptians on the front door, the street door, to keep a close tab on their comings and their goings. Cheats and liars, all religions ought to be taxed out of existence. It was understood in our contract that they were to keep Madame Ra on forever."

"You mean Madame Rachou, don't you?"

"I know what I mean. I feel I'm being swindled. Things are not going as I had planned them anywhere. I can't quite see how all this is going to end. Can you?"

"Well, sort of. I've taken a degree in that too, in Necromancy, as a mattra fack, came from the same or, more correctly, through the same mail order source in California as my others. All equally valuable. Everything, anything, that's what we're here for. I'm your doctor, only your doctor, not your fortune-teller, and that's what you're asking. How can I tell when or where it is all going to end? I'm not writing this, you are. I'm here only because you are."

"What I want is something like a statistical study I can understand."

"Too late, too late! Madame Ra Chou has taken her account book with her, her hotel register and all the identity papers deposited with her before they flew her to Palmdale or Los Angeles airport or wherever. Nowadays, Madame Ra sets in the West as Ra does, in the West where the Sun dies every night in the Pacific. You should know all that, you're a Westerner, yourself, aren't you?"

"As I was saying before I was so rudely interrupted, I'm an American and I want to see some facts and figures."

"Big Nurse doesn't release her figures. She sticks to the rules. A Room a Day. A Floor a Week. Forty-nine Rooms in the Hotel. Rooms must be vacated daily. You see the privileges you get with your money, even here. What's left of the Hotel Bardo is revolving around you."

"And as it should, as it ought, as it must, it has to. This is MY hotel. As you say, I am writing it or, rather, I am writing it if you say so. Me, I don't buy that for one second, one single second. Why would I write myself into a situation this miserable?"

"Complain complain complain! Oh, dearie me, what a kuf*fuffle!* You have only your self to blame and you know it. Apart from the privileges showered, positively showered over you, my dear, everything is going on schedule."

"But those upper floors up there, is it worth it? What goes on up there? When you do make it up there, is it worth it? Why am I being kept in the dark down here on the Fourth Floor of my own hotel and no one can tell me exactly what's going on upstairs? Surely Mickey must know, and Violet."

"Neither one of them's talking, not even in AMSLAN."

"When I first took on the place, they told tales of a blithe spirit singing away up there on the very top floor, in the attics, singing up there like a lark, a lark with a little lead in its wings but a lark all the same, Gregorio Corsorio. He had a whole chorus of blonde Scandinavian girls with crowns of burning candles on their heads who lined the spiral spinal staircase in perpetual adoration singing an endless chorus like a litany, *'Grrreggggoooooorio! Gregggorrrriyoooo Corsaorrrriyooooo!'* I thought that so charming that I bought the place sight unseen and unheard, on mere hearsay. You may say I behaved stupidly, quixotically, oxitacally, outrageously, I don't care, really. I am that I am, and that's all there is to it."

"If there's one thing I hate it's birds. Pigeons, larks, anything with hot dusty dry feathers, vermin of the air, shitting all over the place, ugh! As for the birdsong you're talking about, Mickey blew out the sound system long ago, playing his own *Greatest Hits* so loud he burnt his huge amps and couldn't replace them, not here. Before that happy day, people were always complaining to Madame Rachou about the awful noise but she had a soft spot for him like she did for all young ones who had been in jail. Big Nurse isn't like that at all."

"I thought you said you couldn't jail a monkey. When was Mickey Monkey in jail?"

"Not Mickey, Gregorio grew up in jail, so he claims. That's what made him such a good poet. All poets ought to be jailed."

"I don't want to take up any more of your time, doctor. I've always thought of myself as a poet."

"Before I go, there's this matter of my fee . . ." he begins again.

"Fuck you and your fee!" I explode. "I want out of here. Give me a shot, a hotshot of something. I'm wasting my time here with you. I wanna go, you hear?"

• • • •

Aboard the *Dionysus* there was champagne on deck and there was our ineffable water rat, Mr Grease, flirting outrageously with the sailors. I stumbled on board blind with fury at the idea we both had to go to his doctor, his "skin specialist," as they were called politely. I grabbed the champagne to get drunk as quick as I could, nursing the idea of hitting him over the head with the bottle and dropping him into the harbor. The buffet table, set out with paper-thin cucumber sandwiches, was decorated with vine leaves which he wove into a fillet and passed to Heleni to crown me Dionysus. Snarling, I tore it off my head and threw it into the filthy garbage floating on the oily port waters as I staggered toward the gangplank which was narrow. I caught a glimpse of her bosun, Heleni's boatswain, as he ran his lascivious hot black Greek eyes over my too tight white summer pants, brazenly. When he licked his greasy lips, I charged at him like a ram. A sailor caught me, respectfully, as though to help me, but he helped me far too insistently, I thought, letting his horny hand slide far too far down the small of my back. Like the young Dionysus in those far-off days, my forms were fluent and remarkably rounded. None of these grinning Gricks needed *Dent's Smaller Classical Dictionary*, London 1910, to read: "*The form of his body is manly but approaches the female form by its softness and roundness. In works of art he appears as a youthful god. His expression is languid and his attitude is easy like that of a man who is absorbed in sweet thought or is slightly intoxicated.*" Only the last word applied. I was so drunk I very nearly fell into the harbor. "*Youthful, beautiful but effeminate god of wine,*" indeed! I wanted to kill myself.

I ran pellmell down the quay, cutting blindly through the throngs of hysterical Greeks loaded with luggage, pushing and pulling and screaming as if they had just escaped from the Turkish massacres in Asia Minor. My own Greek came running after me, screaming.

When he caught me, we fought. I flailed at him blindly but he wouldn't fight back, letting men in the crowd pull me off him. "I'm not going one more step with you anywhere ever!" I cried. "Not even to the doctor's. I can't stand any more of those hotshots of Salvarsan in my veins and the cheeks of my ass are sore, swollen hard as a board with bismuth. I'm going away somewhere. I need a holiday. A long holiday from you, you shit."

In a nearby low-down café heavy with the odor of hashish, he gave me some of the money he owed me, owed me and Antonia, and he wrote me the name Thamyra in Greek. This was a blind peasant poetess who lived in the mountains on the island of Naxos. She had been in Athens that previous winter giving recitals of her poetry to elegant audiences in Athenian salons. She was well-known on her island. All I had to do was to ask for her. With no luggage at all, he put me on the night boat leaving for the unstilled Cyclades. I would have a rough passage, outside the harbor the meltemi was blowing. As I went aboard, he pointed out that this ship called the *Theseus* belonged to the Argolaki Line. I had to stop him from telling the ship's purser on board that I was a friend of the family and therefore had nothing to pay.

The little inter-island steamer was as filthy as all Greek ships are, its open decks packed with peasants in black who seemed to be going to a mass funeral somewhere. Someone told me they were pilgrims bound for the holy island of Tinos where they have a miraculous Virgin. There were tight family groups around children bawling for food. Great golden loaves were broken and passed from hand to hand to be eaten with dead-white goat cheese and wrinkled black olives to be washed down with retsina, their bitter white wine. A few fathers became tipsy and violent quarrels broke out and as suddenly subsided. Those who had secured the best places defended them against all comers as they huddled close to the steam pipes or sought a windbreak before we got out into the open sea.

Just then a rusty old woman in black hobbled down the quay screaming as she dragged a great big shaggy copper-coated goat behind her. Moaning that she was a poor old woman and nobody ever waited for her, she drove the tawny beast up the gangplank just as it lifted and threw them both flat on the deck at my feet. The goat jerked free of her, bucked and clattered out a warning tattoo with his cloven hooves as he got his bearings. I stood between him and the companionway. He cocked his bronze horns and shot me a chilling glance of recognition out of one malevolent golden eye. I feinted as he flashed by me with one flying leap down into the thick of the deck passengers below.

Pandemonium, literally, broke out down there. Brave men grabbed at the big ram, but he worked like a boxer with horns and they fell back in comic surprise, trampling those behind them. Whole families set to drubbing each other with baskets and bundles exploding while children sat wailing, smeared with food. The orange goat bounded everywhere. He was a whole flock of goats and he swept the deck. Only a mother and child were left stranded under the cold searchlights which suddenly came on, turning it into theater. The sight of these actors made me sag over the rail with a lurch of sick curiosity. This drab woman the color of ancient dust was being yanked and dragged around by her husky little boy as he lunged after the goat, roaring and bellowing. Mother and child were coupled by a yard or more of chain riveted around her waist and his. She could just restrain him but it was a real struggle. He might have been eight or ten and big for his age but still a child. He was a child except for his huge, his monstrous head. His lowering great head was set on a powerfully arched neck, silky with tight black hair that grew down like a pelt over his naked shoulders. He bellowed until foam flew from his muzzle. He had the head of a young bull. His mother, a peasant Pasiphae, strained at the tether that bound her to her baby Minotaur.

The heat in my cabin was intolerable. As soon as our ship shuddered under weigh, I plunged into nightmares. I was shut in a coffin with a slamming lid. One golden eye with a vertical pupil swam through the crack an inch from my own eye. The goat! I dragged my body back to life with a superhuman effort like Lazarus. My cabin door was slamming back and forth with the pitch of our ship. I staggered to my feet, my head pounding with fever, to hear the clatter of the goat's hooves out on deck—or was it the engines? I couldn't breathe. Air, I must have air!

Piled up even in front of my door, the pilgrims slept wrapped up in their sheets like mummies. Under the harsh decklights, it looked like a scene in a plague hospital. Ah, the great disaster, I thought resignedly, they were trying to escape the eruption and now they have all been overtaken and are dead. The damp night air was a palpable blanket, a shroud through which one could hardly breathe. I fumbled around until I found the brass catch to my cabin door and fell back into dark chthonic underground mythological dreams.

The clanking of a donkey-engine woke me about midnight when I looked out to see we had put into the brilliantly lit little port of Syra. The sleepers had vanished. We were drawn up close alongside the quay like a stage boat run in on the set for an operetta. I could almost reach out to touch the flat walls of houses painted rosy coral and pale lemon-yellow under pink tiled roofs. I dropped a coin to the scuttling waiter below on the terrace of a busy restaurant full of elegant summer people in starched white who ate seafood at tables set out on the cobbled quay right under our bow. The lame lurching wail of a Greek tango ran on like a forgotten tap. The town clock in a tower hammered out midnight on its cracked bell. Before the waiter could bring me a bowl of iced Corinthian seedless grapes, a choir of massed voices swelled down a narrow street from which the pilgrims wound out waving green branches and carrying garlands of ivy. They swept blindly through the diners and up the gangplank on to our ship. The waiter stood to attention with my grapes and crossed himself with a napkin.

The pilgrims chanted lustily as they hung our ship with green. Our masts stood like stripped trees whose branches lay piled about their feet. Vines coiled like cordage: ivy twined through the rigging. Our lifebuoys became laurel wreaths. Our whole ship burgeoned into a floating island bursting with leaves. Our sailors took up the chant and leaped about wildly, casting off green ropes. Our next port was the holy island of Tinos to which the poor pilgrims were bound. Tinos is rock-barren: they had gathered this verdure to freshen her shrine. I slept through their debarkation, still deep in the green smell of broken branches, to wake only with sunstruck Naxos straight ahead. There was

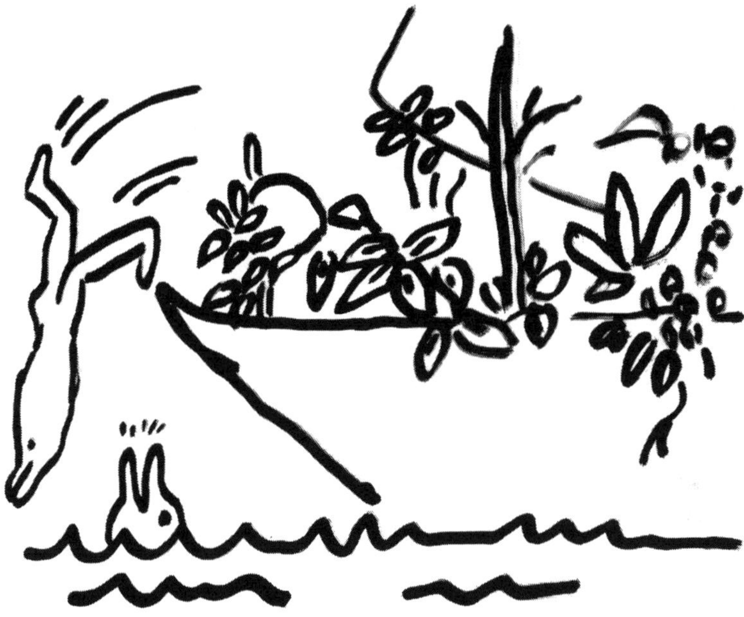

"Untitled," by Keith Haring, from the book *Fault Lines* © The Estate of Keith Haring.

not a single sailor on deck but a school of friendly dolphins sporting in our glassy furrow piloted us into port. Leaning far over the prow, I was more than tempted to throw myself overboard after them but at that sacred moment a quite good-looking Greek cabin steward came up behind me to put his hot hand on my ass, my sore ass! I hauled off and hit him one.

I thought afterward that a contagious kiss from me would have been much more like divine punishment from a sick young demigod on the run for his life, his more than life, his immortality.

Doors are slamming and slamming all over the Bardo. People are leaving and more people are coming up the stairs. All hell is breaking loose out there. When and where have I heard this noise before? Adam just burst into my room again blubbering, completely hysterical as only an old anti-psychiatrist can be. There was so much noise, so much screaming and yelling of oriental ladies tearing their veils off and tearing the lining out of their throats that I could not hear a word he was saying.

"Shut up!" I snapped. "I could kill you! You know what you've just done to me, don't you? You've just yanked me back here into restraint, back from the best time of my life when I very nearly became the god Dionysus. I was beginning, just beginning to sense the godhead coming down on me like a mantle, like an incandescent helmet as hot as a hairdrier when you barged in here. What the hell is all that row going on out there?"

. . . .

A light like a billion-watt bulb floated up through the bars on my window. The Great White Light! the Ineffable Light the Tibetans are always talking about. I was transfixed, of course. I felt I could see it, naturally, because it ran straight up my optic nerve and through the disintegrating mass of my freshly reawakened brain right down into my hypothalamus. My narrow cell began to revolve like an old 78 rpm turntable and the bars of my window on the spiral stairs to spin past at between eight and thirteen flickers a second, the alpha rhythm of my soft old brainbox. An overwhelming flood of intensely bright abstract patterns in supernatural colors exploded somewhere behind my blind eyes where multi-dimensional kaleidoscopes whirled through endless space. Dazzling lights of unearthly brilliance and color were developing in magnitude and complexity at great speed. Infinite acres of geometric wallpaper and rubbishy canvases by painters like Vasarely spread all around me. I was the pivot in the center of developing worlds, giant galaxies hurtling through my own interior space at the speed of light. It all means that my EEG has not flattened out yet and the old brain is still working. I laugh uncontrollably.

Long experience of Gysin's Dreamachine in my Museum's Chapel of Extreme Experience had taught me what to expect. I had long ago learned to read these computer images to the point where they turn into dreamlike sequences like holograph movies. I knew I could expect to see the symbols of all the great world religions float free from this background noise to pass slowly and majestically across my field of vision. The Cross in all its variations flashed as brightly for me as it had for Saul on his way to Damascus racing down an avenue of trees on the buckboard of his chariot as the sun set behind the tree trunks, producing flicker at his alpha rate. So he fell off his chariot and came to as Saint Paul, more's the pity for all of us. As I said before, all these religions ought to be taxed out of existence. Then the swastikas spinning clockwise and counter were followed by a magnificently jeweled Tibetan *dorje,* raised like a club or a sceptre. The all-seeing eye of Isis floated by, eyeing me knowingly, succeeded by other eyes flashing fire. The crescent moon of Islam or the BVM and the blue hand of Fatima gave way to the symbols of forgotten religions or, who knows, those of other planets. I waited expectantly.

It was not an unmitigated delight to find Heleni Argolaki standing in front of me. She was looking good, as they say, looking like Helen of Troy or the Love Goddess or any one of those ladies. If I hadn't known the look in her eye so well, I might've thought she was glad to see me. The supreme charm of Venus was said to be her fascinating strabism. Her eyes were ever so slightly cocked so that you could never be sure exactly where she was looking. This gave her an unearthly air, an unearthly stare, so they said. Only a goddess of beauty could afford what would have been considered a fault in any ordinary girl. Helenaki achieved her effect differently. Her eyes were the color or the colors of all the seas her ships sailed worldwide in all weathers. They could be smiling or stormy but what made them unlike all others I've ever seen was a break in the iris of her left eye which made it look, as I once told her, like a keyhole. She was furious.

Long before I could escape from Greece myself, Heleni had sailed away and gone to Lausanne to have her baby in the clinic where all good rich Greeks are born to give them Swiss nationality. If I had thought about it all, I would have suggested the States for the boy to become President like all those other bastards. I may even have said so to Cousin Antonia when I got back to Paris to tell her the whole story. She looked very grave and said, "I suppose you *should,* but I don't think you *ought* to marry her."

"Because of my illness, you mean?"

"No, my dear, because of your money. I'm going to send you to Washington to see my lawyers and your lawyers. Do you even know who they are? No, I thought not, nor did your mother. You have no idea of the complexity of the structures, the legal structure of my holdings and what will be yours if you handle it properly, five generations of money, big money."

"Six, in my case. But what you say is perfectly true. All I know about it is what I read in the newspapers, what I know from my own name and number. What should I do?"

"Go see my lawyer. She'll tell you all you need to know about the dangerous network of wills and their codicils imposed upon us by our ancestors, yours and mine, and their money. One thing I can tell you is that you must not, NOT marry before you are twenty-five or you'll find yourself a pauper without a penny. All your fortune hangs on the last will and testament of a ferociously Protestant old lady you may never have heard of. Ask my lawyer, she'll tell you."

I very nearly asked her if that went for her too. Was that why she had never married? I thought better of this and took her advice, following it almost to the letter. She advised me to go to Switzerland first to see Heleni but not to see the child unless Heleni insisted on it. When I got there she didn't. Maybe the child had already been sent to Greece, I don't really remember. Heleni was still in Switzerland because of some complications she'd had. I thought immediately of my sickness but didn't dare ask her. Antonia had advised me to offer to acknowledge the child legally, giving it dual or even triple nationality since Heleni wanted it to be Greek as well as Swiss. Since I was not Swiss, she merely thanked me gracefully. I did not offer marriage and was embarrassed to say why, over money. Like poor Mickey Monkey, I was already ashamed or at least somewhat ashamed of my money. In any case, I did not have it yet. It took all Antonia's lawyers and mine several years to fight all that through so I could start my collecting. The first thing I ever dickered for was the Acropolis and Heleni had already beaten me to it, offering her millions to have it restored under plastic or something silly. We never saw each other again from that day to this, more's the pity.

In my next analytical session with him, I told Dr Adam all about this, all. He said, "Don't be silly. That Great White Light you saw was the fireball that followed Shereefa's aura as she was wafted upstairs, a part of her Holy Assumption. As for your syphilis, that's what got Mickey talking and singing, a syph throat."

"Don't you mean a strep throat?"

"I mean what I say. Eva and I decided to give him clinical syphilis when we read a paper in a medical journal about the artificial induction of disease in order to produce, ah, unusual results. I may say that this was a highly underground medical journal some years old. Its publication had been suspended by the Medical Order as being quite contrary to the Hypocritic Oath and all that old-fashioned nonsense like the germ theory which Dr Burroon so rightly objects to. It was found to be financed by the Armed Citizens' Group and suspended indefinitely, if you follow me."

"I don't want to."

"If you don't want to follow me into space, I don't blame you. It must be beastly out there. Hope I don't have to go, ever. Anyhoo, the chancres in Mickey's larynx made it possible for him to talk and even to sing, made over his voice-box. I speak as a layman for your benefit. For the first time, he was able to form words, recognizable word-sounds. Until then he'd been barking like a baboon. Only Eva and I could understand him. It simply made his career, of course. You know all about that, so now for the real news. Your son is dead."

"My son! What are you talking about?"

"Yes, your son with Helen Argolaki, he committed suicide. Went up to his mother in their villa in Kiphissia and shot himself. Put a pistol in his mouth and pulled the trigger, spattering her from head to foot with his blood and his brains."

"When did this happen?"

"Very recently. If you hadn't been fucking about with the floors of the Bardo, he might be here by now. You'd get to know him, perhaps."

"Oh, no!"

"Oh, yes! For all I know, he may be in California waiting for you but to meet him you'll have to be born again. If that's what you want, you'll have to leap into the next waiting womb that presents itself."

"That's not what I want, not at all. That's got nothing to do with it. When one of those cultists asked me years ago, way back when, what I wanted, I said and I say: I want out. Out out out, understand?"

"You can't go. They've closed down the airports. Argolaki Airlines are the only ones operating."

"You know the only thing Heleni said to me just now, back there? She said, 'I've thought of you every day of my life all these years.' And I said, 'Why? Have you got visible scars?' I'm that awful. She'd never evacuate me, even if she could."

"She can't. It would take another woman, entirely."

"The very least homage I can offer her is to say that she's the only one, the one and only, the only woman of my life. What more can she ask for?"

"She can ask for and get a whole lot more than that, the way they're settling those suits out there in California. I wish I'd been a lawyer instead of a doctor, sometimes. That's what comes of Unethical Culture."

"But what's this story about my presumptive progeny? He must have been a big boy, a man, a middle-aged man or more. Look how old I am. I feel very guilty, all of a sudden. He must have had a terrible life with her to do that at his age, don't you think. Was he normal?"

"Well, he never married, if that's what you mean."

"I don't. I mean physically. You know what I mean. Heleni wanted him to be a mythological monster like the Minotaur."

"That was your idea, I'm sure, knowing you as I do. People say he was a very beautiful young man, something like young Foutaise, I'm told. Spoiled rotten. Sick, you know. Maybe you missed something there."

"Incest, you mean?"

"Well, that's highly mythological."

"Mythology is one of the worst worn-out old tracks I know. I want to get free of that. I want to get out, as I told you. Why don't you give me a hotshot of some stuff to relieve me of myself, some carbamates for in extremis solutions. You must still have some, you're an old CIA man, aren't you?"

"I'm a medic. Not a murderer."

"Often one and the same thing, no? But you're absolutely right, I'm not a murderee. If I had been I would have been done in long ago by some inept kidnapper, wouldn't I? How do you feel about reincarnation?"

"Yours for a better life! I'm all for it."

"I'm not. Being born once was bad enough."

"When we are born, we start to die. The very beginning begins the end."

"Nonsense. Who said that? First, when are we born? We begin to be born when we are conceived and when we are born nine months later we are not born all of a piece nor are we born separately, not any more than a fish in the sea in a school of fish nor a bird in the sky nor a bee in a hive. Skindiving off Algeria first brought that home to me. A school of fish is a fish. One single fish is a snack. Birds in the sky, ditto. When I was a kid on the Longfinger estate at Lost Lake in northern Montana, I saw the migrations of geese. In North Africa, I saw the arrival and departure of the storks. Follow the leader. If there is no flock, there can be no leader. One fish cannot swim alone in the sea and yet that is what I always wanted to do. To be that one fish, a loner looking for a way out through a crack in the sky, a hole in the universe through which I could get out forever. That's what attracted me so to the San Andreas Faultline when I saw a relief map of our Pacific Coast in the New York Museum of Natural History. It looked so like a sandpile on the seashore that the next wave might cause to crumble and be swept away by a storm like El Niño, the breath of a mythological manchild which wore away the shore right up to the front door of my Museum in Malibu."

"That's too bad."

"No, that is good. That's what I wanted. *I* called up the Tempest. I am, or I was, Duke Prospero. Like any normal child of my sort, I used to grumble that I never asked to be born. As I grew up and educated myself, I thought I might have been better born in the Italian Renaissance. I began to believe that I had been until I read what the Signore Salvati, the Chancellor of Florence, said to Ugolino Caccini in the month of May 1400 on the death of his son. He said: *Even if the soul does not die and the body is reborn, that harmonious combination that made Pietro my son has been destroyed forever.*"

"He did, did he? Intuitive ideas are difficult to modify."

"What do you mean by that?"

"Metempsychosis is an essentially intuitive idea. There are no solid grounds on which one can base such an idea. No proofs. No nothing."

"How about this . . . all this . . . our presence here? I can guess why *I'm* here. I can't imagine why *you* are or why we are seeing each other, if that's what you like to call it. We were never all that intimate. I remember the first time I ever set eyes on you without knowing who you were. Isn't that just a little bit odd that we're always meeting in hospitals?"

"No, after all I'm a doctor."

"Yes, I remember you mumbling that when I came to and found you by my bedside in that hospital run by the Spanish nuns in Tangier. Those nuns believed pain was good for the soul, so no pain-killers. *La vida es pena*, they said to me, very Spanish. We are born to suffer. As she tore that dressing off my raw wound to which it had stuck, it was you who gave a squeak of pain, not me. I was getting used to it. You still had not given me your name when the Greek Ambassadress bustled in with her limping husband whose father had been a poet, a Nobel Prize winner. I don't know why they liked me unless because they carried on a family feud with the Argolaki clan, maybe. She brought her French chef with her to feed me up and His Excellency the Ambassador brought the Egyptian Book of the Dead, I remember. Do you think that's how I got in here?"

"I haven't the faintest idea."

"And you?"

"Oh, one thing just led to the other. I sometimes wonder myself but I don't pore over the problem, you know. Why do you?"

"And then my Moroccan manservant came in to say that one of the more exotic ecstatic orders, the Brotherhood of the Aissaouas, was holding their week-long *moussem* up in the mountains. Every year, he and my other man Salah, the black one, used to pack up our tent and equipment to camp out up there. Besides the extremely peculiar practices of the Brothers, there was quite a licentious nightlife in the greenleaf cafés made out of branches where dancing boys shook money out of their country clients and admirers. There was no question of my going but I knew who you were by then, the notorious antipsychiatrist, so I asked you if it would interest you to see quite a few score adepts fall into the trance dancing. You asked me how much it might cost and if they could change American Express cheques up there."

"I deny that, categorically."

"The title of the Egyptian Book of the Dead is: *The Book of Coming Forth by Day*, at least, that's how it is translated into English. It really runs: RU NU PERT EM HRU. I construe that last word to be like the Arab word *Hrooj* with a soft final letter, which means coming out or going out. So the true title would be: *The Book for Going Out by the Way of Light*, I think. I'm no scholar but I did check it with Breasted. The Clear White Light of Illumination. Don't you think that's what I saw back there?"

"If you like. Are you trying to make me suggest that you are due for a move up to Floor Five? Knowing Her Holiness only as slightly as I do, I can almost guarantee that she must have taken complete control up there. You might not like that."

"I wouldn't. I am hoping to skip it. Besides, she wouldn't want me. I know too much. No, I was projecting a real flit, hoping to skip that stage entirely and land on Floor Six or Floor Seven or even fly right out through the roof. Surely there must be some kind of trapdoor or skylight. How about that?"

"Of course, there could be a dusty attic full of cobwebs and vampire bats, Tibetan entities, but there is said to be no roof anymore, no roof at all despite the rumor that your Cousin Antonia landed on our roof by mistake when she flew back from her monastery in Japan for her very last Annual Party. Cosmic gossip maintains that when she took off in her rocket, her blast-off burned down the roof. Others claim that there never was a roof over our poor heads. The sky's the limit."

"There is no limit. Where there is no Time, there is no limit."

"We're still bound a bit by Time, old man. Things like that body of yours haven't gone completely to pieces, not yet. Who to believe? What is Truth? Like that poor old provincial Roman Governor, Pontius P. Pilot, wasn't it? I wash my hands of the whole matter as a sanitary precaution against idle rumor. And with that said, I must leave you, old chap, move on."

"Cosmic gossip," a voice whispers right into my ear, a voice with a slight foreign accent, "cosmic gossip hath it that you are my fodder."

For one hilarious nanosecond, I thought of snapping back, it was a male voice, that I was not his "fodder" and he couldn't eat me. It reminded me of Cuvier, the famous French nineteenth-century naturalist whose pupils rigged themselves out in old bones one night and crept into his bedroom to scare him to death. "*Hoo hoo hoo! We're going to eat you.*" Professor Cuvier opened one eye and said sharply, "Horns and hooves? As a graminivorous species, you can't." On the other hand, for all I knew, this might well be one of those blood-drinking, bone-grinding Tibetan entities their holy literature is so very fond of: "*licking human brains, drinking blood, wrenching heads from corpses, tearing out hearts: thus will they come, filling the worlds.*" Just in time, I did remember that these were mainly goddesses holding blood-filled skull-bowls: "*Dark-Green Ghasmari drinking blood with majestic relish, the Yellow-White Chandali wrenching a head from a corpse, her right hand holding a heart, her left putting the corpse in her* mouth and eating it, *Dark-Blue Smasha tearing asunder a head from a corpse and eating it.*" This was far from the fibrefree diet the good Dr Adam had promised me and besides, it sounds very anti-feminist. "*The Yellow Bat-Headed Delight-Goddess holding a shaving knife in her hand.*" We all know what she holds that in her hand for, castration, making men into eunuchs. Delight-Goddess, indeed! I could feel my tired old balls retract up into my abdomen in a helluva hurry. How could they ever have made a son for me?

My good judgment advises me: Say nothing. Do nothing. Hold nothing. Just lie there, lie doggo. "*Thy goal is the Unbecome, the Unborn, the Unmade, the Unformed.*" In my circumstances and in my condition, I have found this impossibly difficult.

"I have come to help you." What worrisome words! His sibilant whisper tickles the hairs of my ear unbearably, like a gnat caught in the trap of my ear. I'd give anything to work my little finger in there.

"Help?" I murmur miserably. I mean to say, I don't want any of your fucking help, thank you very much. Go away. Mind your own business. Just leave me alone, willya!

"Yes, yes," he hisses, "you have only to do what I tell you."

I groan. The young are like that, they always seem to think they know better than you do what you want, you old fogey. The young are insufferably bossy.

"I've come to release you from your restraint. Please excuse these cold metal hands. I lost my own playing with firecrackers. These are my stainless steel prostheses. I can handle them pretty well for this kind of work but some things I could do before my accident I can't do anymore, like roll a good joint, for instance. You don't happen to have a stash of hash on you, do you?"

I roll my head around as indignantly as I can in negation. Anyone attending my deathbed or worse should bring his own stuff, his own shit, I am very tempted to tell him. Can't he see what a state I'm in after twenty, twenty-five days dead. Twenty-eight? I am furious.

Can't this apparently well-intentioned young man with stainless steel hands just have pity! I really don't want him to revive me. I am too far gone. Doesn't he realize what happens to an old body? A rotten old body that's falling apart isn't worth saving. All the protein that glued me together has fled. My skin is flaking and peeling off me like parchment. Nothing is left of my muscle but dried sinew, cordage. I've been here too long. My name isn't Lazarus and even he . . . migawd! Just think what poor old Laz' must have looked and smelled like at that fancy funeral party when they pulled him out of his coffin. Muttering burlap, mumbling, "Thank you, Master, thank you." Not me. I don't intend to go to one single more party, ever. I don't want to go back to Capri or Positano or even Capistrano as a swallow. I mean to get out of here and come back again never! Heavenly reunions with one's Loved One? Ugh! There is no one I ever knew in this world I want to see again.

A story like this can have no happy ending.

Or can it?

Bibliography

| Works by Bryon Gysin |

Beat Museum-Bardo Hotel Chapter 2. Oakland, Calif.: Inkblot, 1982.

Brion Gysin Let the Mice In. West Glover, Vt.: Something Else Press, 1973.

The Exterminator. With William S. Burroughs. San Francisco: Auerhahn Press, 1960.

Fault Lines. With Keith Haring. New York: Schellmann, 1986.

Here to Go: Planet R-101. Interviews of Gysin by Terry Wilson with additional texts. San Francisco: Re/Search, 1982; London: Quartet, 1985. Rpt., London, N.Y.: Creation, 2001.

The Last Museum. New York: Grove; London: Faber, 1986.

Légendes de Brion Gysin. Trans. Brice Matthieussent. Montpelier, France: Gris Banal, 1983.

Minutes to Go. With Sinclair Beiles, William S. Burroughs, and Gregory Corso. Paris: Two Cities, 1960.

Morocco Two. Oakland, Calif.: Inkblot, 1984.

The Process. New York: Doubleday, 1969. Rpt, Woodstock, N.Y.: Overlook, 1987.

Stories. Oakland, Calif.: Inkblot, 1984.

The Third Mind. With William S. Burroughs. New York: Viking, 1978.

To Master—A Long Goodnight. New York: Creative Age Press, 1946.

Who Runs May Read. Oakland, Calif.: Inkblot, 2000.

| Secondary Sources |

Ambrose, Joe, Terry Wilson, and Frank Rynne. *Man from Nowhere: Storming the Citadels of Enlightenment with William Burroughs and Brion Gysin.* Dublin: Subliminal, 1992.

Anderson, Carol Marie. "Visions of Reality: Brion Gysin's Evolving Experimentation with Reality." Ph.D. diss., Florida State University, 1987. Ann Arbor: UMI, 1987. 8721829.

Brion Gysin: Calligraphies, Permutations, Cut-ups. Paris: Galerie de France, 1987.

Férez Kuri, José, ed. *Brion Gysin: I Am That I Am.* London: Thames & Hudson, 2002.

Lemaire, Gérard-Georges, ed. *Colloque de Tanger.* 2 vols. Paris: Bourgois, 1976–79.

Re/Search no. 4/5: William S. Burroughs, Brion Gysin and Throbbing Gristle. San Francisco, 1982.

Soft Need no. 17: Brion Gysin Special. Basel and Paris, 1977.

23: Brion Gysin. Montrouge: ICBM/Cactus, 1993.

Discography

OU Records. Ed. Henri Chopin. London. 20/21 (1964). "I Am That I Am," "Pistol Poem."

OU Records. Ed. Henri Chopin. 23/24 (1965). "Junk Is No Good Baby," "No Poets Don't Own Words," "Scissors."

OU Records. Ed. Henri Chopin. 40/41 (1972). "Poems 1960."

The Dial-A-Poem Poets. Ed. John Giorno. New York: Giorno Poetry Systems, 1972. "I Am That I Am."

10+2:12 American Text-Sound Pieces. Ed. Charles Amirkhanian. Berkeley: 1750 Arch Records, 1972. "Come to Free the Words."

Axe. Ed. Guy Schraenen. Anvers. 1 (1974). Gysin record included with journal.

La Poésie Sonore Internationale. Ed. Henri Chopin. Paris: J-M Place, 1974. Book accompanied by two cassettes. "Junk Is No Good Baby."

Poesia Sonora. Ed. Maurizio Nannucci. Milano: CBS/Sugar, 1975. "I Am That I Am."

Dreams. Steve Lacy and quintet. Paris: Saravah, 1975. Lyrics to "Dreams" by Gysin, sung by Irène Aebi.

The Brion Gysin Show. Munich: S-Press, 1978. 33-minute tape of Gysin performing his sound poetry.

The Nova Convention. New York: Giorno Poetry Systems, 1979. "Kick That Habit Man," "Junk Is No Good Baby," "Somebody Special," "Blue Baboon," and conversation with William S. Burroughs, Timothy Leary, Les Levine and Robert Anton Wilson.

Steve Lacy/Brion Gysin. *Songs*. Therwil, Switzerland: Hat Hut Records, 1981. Lacy sextet, with vocals by Aebi and Gysin.

Orgy Boys. Therwil, Switzerland: Hat Hut Records, 1982. All words and voice, Gysin.

Self-Portrait Jumping. Brussels: Made to Measure/Crammed Discs, 1993. Gysin songs, poems and stories, set to music by Ramuntcho Matta, performed by Gysin, Matta, and musicians.

Recordings from 1960-1981. Chicago: Perdition Plastics, 1995.

1001 Nights. Brussels: SubRosa, 1998. Live performance of Jajouka musicians recorded by Gysin in his restaurant in Tangier, mid-1950s; "Jilaloo," performed by Gysin.

The Poem of Poems. Milano: Alga Marghen, 1998. Cut-up poem recorded by Gysin, ca. 1960.

The Pool KIII. Milano: Alga Marghen, 1998. Sounds from a swimming pool, plus musicians; composition by Gysin, recorded by him in the late 1950s or early 1960s. (Recent research suggests that this recording was made by Paul Bowles, though it was found in Gysin's collection.)

Permissions

The following works are copyright © Brion Gysin and the Estate of Brion Gysin and are included in this collection by permission of the Estate of Brion Gysin and other parties where stated.

"Am I the One?" Unpublished; printed by courtesy of Harry Ransom Humanities Research Center, University of Texas at Austin.

"An Encomium for Allen Ginsberg." In *Best Minds: A Tribute to Allen Ginsberg*, ed. Bill Morgan and Bob Rosenthal. New York: Lospecchio Press, 1986.

"Brion Gysin Let the Mice In." In *Brion Gysin Let the Mice In*. West Glover, Vt.: Something Else, 1973.

"Calligraffiti of Fire." In *Calligraffiti of Fire*, catalogue of Gysin's series of paintings. Paris: Samy Kinge, 1986.

"Clementeena Soopastar." In *Orgy Boys*. Therwil, Switzerland: Hat Hut, 1982.

"Cut Me Up * Brion Gysin." In *Minutes to Go*, by Sinclair Beiles, William S. Burroughs, Gregory Corso, and Brion Gysin. Paris: Two Cities, 1960.

"Cut-Ups: A Project For Disastrous Success." *Evergreen Review*, no. 32 (1964).

"Cut-Ups Self-Explained." *Evergreen Review*, no. 32 (1964).

"Dreamachine." *Olympia Magazine*, no. 2 (Paris, 1962).

"Dreams." In *Dreams*, by Steve Lacy. Paris: Saravah, 1975. Set to music by Steve Lacy as sung by Irene Aebi. The handwritten manuscript reproduced in this book is by Steve Lacy. Published version by Sacem, Paris.

"Fire: Words by Day—Images by Night." *Soft Need*, no. 17 (Basel, 1977).

"First Cut-Ups." In *Minutes to Go*, by Sinclair Beiles, William S. Burroughs, Gregory Corso, and Brion Gysin. Paris: Two Cities, 1960.

"Gay Paree Bop." In *Songs*, by Brion Gysin and Steve Lacy. Therwil, Switzerland: Hat Hut, 1981.

"Hamri's Hands." Unpublished.

"I Am That I Am" (1959). In *Brion Gysin Let the Mice In*. West Glover, Vt.: Something Else, 1973.

"I Don't Work You Dig." In *Songs*, by Brion Gysin and Steve Lacy. Therwil, Switzerland: Hat Hut, 1981.

"Janicot." In *Hepta*, catalogue for Françoise Janicot show, Musée Galliera, Paris, 1967.

"Junk Is No Good Baby." In *The Exterminator*, by Wiliam S. Burroughs and Brion Gysin. San Francisco: Auerhahn, 1960.

Keith Haring drawings for *The Last Museum*. In *Fault Lines*, by Brion Gysin and Keith Haring. Munchen, N.Y.: Schellmann, 1986.

"Kick That Habit Man." In *The Exterminator*. San Francisco: Auerhahn, 1960.

The Last Museum. New York: Grove, 1986.

"Minutes to Go." In *Minutes to Go*, by Sinclair Beiles, William S. Burroughs, Gregory Corso, and Brion Gysin. Paris: Two Cities, 1960.

Naked Lunch. Unpublished film script. Printed courtesy of William S. Burroughs Collection, Special Collections, University Libraries, Arizona State University, Tempe.

"No Poets Don't Own Words." In *Orgy Boys*. Therwil, Switzerland: Hat Hut, 1982.

"Not By Me." *Creatis* (Paris, 1977).

"Nowhere Street." In *Songs*, by Brion Gysin and Steve Lacy. Therwil, Switzerland: Hat Hut, 1981. Set to music by Steve Lacy as sung by Irene Aebi. The handwritten manuscript reproduced in this book is by Steve Lacy. Published version by Margun Music, Newton Center, Mass., 1986.

"The Pipes of Pan." *Gnaoua*, no. 1 (Tangier, 1964).

"The Poem of Poems." Unpublished in full form; short excerpt published in *The Third Mind*, by Brion Gysin and William S. Burroughs. New York: Viking, 1978.

"Potiphar's Wife." In *Stories*. Oakland, Calif.: Inkblot, 1984.

The Process. Garden City, N.Y.: Doubleday, 1969.

"Psacré Psilocybin." In French, *Art Press International*, no. 7 (Paris, 1977). English translation unpublished.

"A Quick Trip to Alamut." Unpublished manuscript.

"Recollections of a Lost Seascape." *Town and Country* (July 1947).

"The Sculpted Line." In *Keith Haring*, catalogue for show, Musée d'Art Contemporain, Bordeaux, 1985.

"Sham Pain." *Brion Gysin* (record). Villeurbaine, France: Mosquito, 1984.

Snapshots from the Family Album. In *Here to Go: Planet R-101*, by Brion Gysin and Terry Wilson. San Francisco: Re/Search, 1982. Full text only in the French translation, *Légendes de Brion Gysin*, trans. Brice Matthieussent. Montpellier: Gris Banal, 1983.

"Somebody Special." In *Songs*, by Brion Gysin and Steve Lacy. Therwil, Switzerland: Hat Hut, 1981. Set to music by Steve Lacy as sung by Irene Aebi. The handwritten manuscript reproduced in this book is by Steve Lacy. Published version by Margun Music, Newton Center, Mass., 1986.

"Stop Smoking." *Brion Gysin* (record). Villeurbaine, France: Mosquito, 1984.

"That Secret Look." *View*, nos. 7 and 8 (1941).

"This Is Sam Francis." In *Sam Francis; paintings, 1947–1972*, catalogue. Buffalo, N.Y.: Albright-Knox, 1972.

"Time and Brother Griphen." *Town and Country* (November 1947).

To Master—A Long Goodnight. New York: Creative Age Press, 1946.

"Unpublished Notes on Painting." In *Back in No Time*, catalogue for Brion Gysin show, Guillaume Gallozzi Gallery, New York, 1994.